Glenallen

Glenallen

Mary Ryan

St. Martin's Press
New York

Library of Congress Cataloging-in-Publication Data

Ryan, Mary.
    Glenallen / Mary Ryan.
      p. cm.
    ISBN 0-312-08797-7
    1. Ireland—History—1922- —Fiction.
    2. Women—Ireland—Fiction. I. Title.
    PR6068.Y33G6   1993
    823'.914—dc20   92-43176
                                       CIP

First published in the Republic of Ireland by Attic Press.

First U.S. Edition: March 1993
10 9 8 7 6 5 4 3 2 1

For Johnny

Acknowledgements

I would like to express my grateful thanks to the following for the invaluable help which they gave me in the writing of this book:

Mrs Kitty Cunningham and Mrs Anne Forde who provided me with considerable background material about Nottingham and Galway respectively during the nineteen thirties and forties.

Séan Dior who gave me a wealth of material about the Free French in London and helped with the occasional forays into French.

The Imperial War Museum, London, the British Embassy and the Abbey Theatre Press Office, Dublin for responding with immediate courteous help to my requests for information.

I have been blest with wonderful support from the staff of Attic Press and would like to express my appreciation of their painstaking and encouraging work.

In particular I would like to thank my husband, John Hederman, for his support, suggestions and inspiration which contributed so significantly to the whole of this book.

Dublin, 1991.

'The earth hath bubbles as the water hath and these are of them.'

William Shakespeare (Macbeth)

BOOK 1

Prologue

Yesterday I went back to Glenallen. First was the mountain, Knockshee, watchful as ever, then the heavy gateway, stone pillars. The driveway was manicured, the beeches along one side in luxuriant leaf. At the end of the driveway was the house, now almost overtaken by virginia creeper, but there it was, waiting, inexorably patient, as though it knew I would return. The trees threw shadows across the daisy-sprinkled lawn, to the hedgerow beyond where the wild flowers demarcated the edge of the fields. The ornamental lake was still there, its stone border neat, its surface now covered in water lilies with flat green leaves and delicate blooms.

'So,' I heard Dan mutter, shaking his head a little as he slowed the car to a crawl: 'This is what it looked like!' He had never even seen a photograph; I had destroyed them all. My chest constricted. I could hardly breathe. Behind us in the back seat Michael, blissfully oblivious, his dark head bent, played with the red fire engine I had bought him in Ballyharris, making noises appropriate to fire engines about their business.

I thought of what the receptionist in the hotel had told us the night before; she was young - a summer job - and assuming that we were foreign had welcomed us warmly. She had blue eyes and freckles and belonged to the new and prosperous order.

'I'm Irish,' I said, smiling, and she looked at her registration book, raising her smooth young eyebrows.

'I used to live near here a long time ago,' I said, 'at a place called Glenallen.'

Her eyes widened. 'Glenallen House?'

And then she confided that there was supposed to be a ghost at Glenallen, now, nodding her head to impress the visitors, the ghost of a Mrs Regan who used to live there once. Grief surprised me, grief for the lost potential, grief for our youth. How could you be a 'ghost', Harriet? We should have brought Helene, I thought, and Catherine too - as some sort of equaliser. Even now I needed reinforcements to confront Glenallen and its beauty and menace. For me the years had collapsed and I was young again, vulnerable and full of belief.

I fought this grip of the past. I looked at my son beside me, my grandson in the back seat. This was just an old house, I told myself, and everything that I had known here was long gone.

But where was the beginning?

Chapter 1

I was born at a time when the corncrake came every summer and tourists were rare. My home was at Ballycloghan, County Galway, stony country where the sky is wild with clouds and shifting light. It is a place where you can be drenched in one parish and dry in the next, and sometimes have all four seasons in one day. In those days it seemed to be indifferent to the seasons, caught in its own exclusive dimension of time and space, as though nothing could intrude or change it.

We had one hundred and twenty acres of land, some of it good, some liable to flooding in winter when the Garryogue would burst its banks, some of it reedy and poor. We grew barley, oats, mangolds, kept some stores and reared farm horses, Irish Draught horses with stamina and patient manners. It was the horses which sustained us during the economic war.

My father died in the winter of 1924 when I was five years old and my brother Tom was nine. I always missed my father, although I had never really known him; all I had were vague memories of being on the knee of a big man who smelled of tobacco, and of knowing that when his arm was around me nothing in the world could touch me.

Afterwards, imagining that his spirit was somewhere near, I often asked him, 'Why couldn't you have lived; why couldn't you have waited to die later like other fathers? Didn't you know how hard it would be without you?'

I asked my mother once, angrily, why he hadn't stayed to look after us and she had put down the rolling pin and dashed away the sudden tears with her forearm, whispering, 'A stór, a stór... He didn't want to go.'

He had been a bookish man, although his formal education had been minimal. His books, the occasional precious note in his stiff handwriting still among the pages, were kept in a row of shelves in the parlour and I glutted myself on them during the long summers of my childhood. Charles Dickens was there in umpteen cloth-bound volumes with Victorian illustrations; so was Walter Scott, numerous volumes of poetry and a variety of books and pamphlets on Irish history and the land question. He had been something of a Fenian and quick to seize the opportunity to buy out the farm from the landlord under the scheme set up by the Windham Act of 1903. But of all the books he had, it is *The Dream of Gerontius* that I remember most - not the poem itself, but the terrifying plates.

After my father's death the farm was managed by my mother with the help of Jack Stapleton, the farm labourer who had always worked for us. He had a cottage nearby with a small plot on which he grew onions. He was a widower with one son, Paddy, who was a year or so older than myself.

Tom and I went to the local National school, but Tom left when he was fourteen to work full-time on the farm, at which point he convinced my mother to increase the number of mares from two to four. He had a way with horses, rode them bareback, galloping sometimes around the pasture and yelling like the Indians he had seen in the pictures, while the cattle stood and stared at him, convinced he was mad.

I was proud of my brother. He was strong and tall, with thick brown hair and a handsome face. Like my father he was fond of books, although he had little time to give them - except during the long dark evenings when he would pull up a chair by the range and disappear into *Treasure Island* or *Robinson Crusoe*, blotting out the world and the chatter of myself and Mam. My mother would walk carefully around him to get at the kettle, half laughing at his trance-like state.

He read the *Irish Independent* every day, and after the dinner would open it carefully, lean back in his chair and read bits out to us.

I remember looking at the back of the folded paper while he read, seeing on one occasion the photograph of a big old country house and staring at it with some sort of morbid and inexplicable fascination, a feeling half way between nausea and dread in the pit of my stomach. The great house in our own locality had been destroyed during the Troubles and we children were forbidden to play there, the ruins being dangerous.

Visitors would call in the winter evenings, neighbours who were my mother's life-long friends, and they would sit around swopping yarns and telling ghost stories until I was afraid to leave the lamplight and the company and go up to bed, and would curl against my mother pleading for reprieve.

We had no close relatives; my father had been an only child and my mother's two sisters had died of TB which was rampant in the country at the time. But she had a maternal uncle - Matthew O'Mahoney who kept a grocery and hardware

11

shop in Galway, an old bachelor who never came to visit.

'As mean as ditchwater' my mother said of him, 'And him with neither chick nor child.' She thought he had plenty of money. We called on him when we went to Galway. I would stand in the shop, smelling the clean smell of brushes and shining new buckets and spades and eye the sweet counter with longing. He would give me a toffee bar and have a few words with my mother in the dusty little parlour behind the shop which was full of yellowing newspapers and piles of bills held together with long sharp stilettos. He showed an interest in Tom and would bring him outside to the shed, a kind of warehouse, while I sat with my mother in the dusty parlour and stared at the Victorian steel engraving of the girl feeding geese by a pond which he had bought in a jumble sale and hung over the mantelpiece. There was an untidy pile of books on the mantelpiece, covers stained and pages dog-eared.

'Can we go soon, Mam?'

'Whisht, child, whisht.'

I told him his picture was nice and he laughed and said 'Aye ...aye ... Sure maybe I'll let ye have it sometime.'

Jack Stapleton's son, Paddy, had a pale thin face with brown eyes and a cow's lick standing up on the crown of his head. He had a stammer, but was good at school, forcing out the words of the lessons with determined passion, ignoring our teacher's occasional taunts. He was particularly good at maths, computed compound interest faster than any of us, and did calculations at speed in his head.

I liked him very much; he sat behind me in school, prompted me when I mixed up the poetry, which I frequently did, and walked home along the rutted boreen with me and Niamh Houlihan. Niamh was one of the brightest pupils in the class. She was pretty, with blue eyes, light brown curly hair and a phenomenal memory for anything with the ghost of a rhyme about it. She would recite endless poetry and passages of prose by heart without any ostensible effort at learning them, her face rapt with pleasure at the cadence of the sounds.

'How do you remember all that stuff?' I asked her one day and she said she was just licking the honey off the words and where was the work in that? I told her she should try for a scholarship and she just shrugged; our teacher accepted her gifts without encouraging her. She was a girl; there was no point in wasting education on a girl.

Niamh's mother was a widow who had a small pension from the British Army and she kept hens, did some dressmaking and had a few acres under vegetables and potatoes. Her father had joined up during the first war and been killed at Ypres.

In winter I would say goodbye to Paddy as soon as we reached my gate, but in summer we fished for pinkeens with jampots and also fished for trout in the Garryogue - the river at the edge of our farm where the fish lazed in dark summer pools. Paddy could tickle trout, the only person I ever knew who could. He would lie flat on his stomach, put his hand gently into quiet pools under the bank and after a minute or two, if luck was with him, there would be a sudden jerk of his arm and a brown trout would be flapping around on the grass.

Further down the river was an old stone bridge which we were warned about. It had been damaged during the Troubles, but we tried our luck from it with kitchen twine and any kind of hooks we could find.

We often rolled down the grassy knoll in the field beside our house in a bet as to who would get to the bottom first. Paddy would let me win and I would arrive at the bottom dirty and dizzy, laughing, my plaits undone.

He told me he would marry me when he grew up. 'We will be rich, and I will give you diamonds as big as thrushes' eggs,' he murmured one day while we were lying back in the long summer grass by the river. He didn't stutter when he was with me.

'Go away with you, Paddy Stapleton. Diamonds is it?' I glanced at my laughing barefoot companion, his long calves sticking out of his badly patched trousers and imagined myself decked in cold shining gems. Paddy evidently disclosed his matrimonial ambition to his father and the latter, by way of a good joke, told this to Tom who repeated it grimly over supper in the kitchen.

'Sure you'd need money in the bank and a university degree to marry Peg Donlon,' Jack claimed to have told his son.

I could see that my brother was annoyed because my name had been bandied by Jack Stapleton in front of a few casual labourers who had been employed to help with the hay. I felt resentful of it myself, imagining the sly laughter of the men and their inescapable prurience.

'That Paddy will never have anything,' Tom warned. 'Anyone who marries him will be marrying poverty,' and I sighed out loud in

14

exasperation. Marriage was for grown-ups who were old.

My mother was a small woman with fine eyes and a high forehead scored from years of anxiety. She had been pretty once, or so the faded wedding photograph in the parlour would have us believe, she standing behind my father as he sat on a photographer's rustic bench, an expression half way between happiness and gravity on her face. Her hair was put up in the fashion of the time and her eyes were full of innocence.

My father, a good deal older, balding, thickset, sat very straight on the rustic bench, suitably grave and moustached, with a high-necked shirt and a waistcoat under his dark suit. He wore the self-important expression men wore for photographs; life was no joking matter - especially when you had to freeze your face for the interminable three minutes the camera needed to capture your image, before returning it to you eventually in monochrome. But there had been kindness in his eyes and laughter.

Whenever my mother spoke of him it was with sorrow and love. I asked to see her wedding ring one day and she prized it off with difficulty, leaving a deep groove in the flesh of her finger. I looked at it carefully and at the hallmark and the words engraved in the back of it - 'Daniel and Maura 16.6.1914' - a legend identical with the one on the ring in her little box upstairs which she had told me had been worn by my father.

'Why didn't you leave the ring on him when he died?' I asked and she said that he was going into a grave and the ring spoke of life and should go to the living. 'You can give it to your husband one day.'

Our house was a modest two storey one, the kind of old farmhouse you would see plenty of in the country in those days, cold pristine sitting-room called 'the parlour' hardly ever used; large kitchen warmed by a big black range; three bedrooms upstairs and a bathroom without running water. The water was carried up by the 'girl' who slept in the small room behind the pantry and who got her board and keep and a very small wage. The 'girl' for most of my childhood was Sadie Murray who had come to my mother shortly after the latter's marriage and who stayed until her own fiancé of seventeen years, a local small farmer, jilted her; then she left and went to England. We got one Christmas card and heard no more from her.

I remember the way my mother would look at me, half evaluating, half proud. She was determined to make a lady out of me; I wasn't to end up with the sort of drudgery associated with a small farm; I was to go to boarding school in Galway for a proper education. Tom was to have the farm, this was clear from my father's will, and I was to be educated 'out of the place'. There was a specific clause in the will about this; the farm was charged with the expense of my education.

My mother thought I might become a teacher or get a job in the bank. And this prospect seemed good to me. Teachers were quasi-gentry and people who worked in banks an employed élite. There was poverty all around us in the countryside - although we hardly identified it as such - enough to eat and a roof, but little money. Children went barefoot in summer and even in winter kept their boots for Sunday. Tom and I always had boots, a new pair every October, although in summer we went barefoot like everyone else.

I enjoyed our lessons at the local National school; we had a colourful and choleric teacher, a Mr Clancy to whom my mother had confided her plans for me. He used to joke continually during my last year and say that I'd show them all when I went away to my fancy boarding school, 'St Catherine's College for young ladies, if you don't mind, boys.' He always addressed the class as 'boys' although half of the pupils were girls.

Mr Clancy was in his fifties at this time. He had wiry grey hair, bad teeth and a tongue like an asp. He had married late in life and had one child - a little boy called Joe who was the apple of his eye. Whenever Mrs Slattery, who taught the infants and first and second classes, wanted more chalk or copybooks from Mr Clancy's cupboard she would send Joe for them and we would watch the way his father's face would soften as the boy came into the room.

But otherwise our teacher was what my mother called 'A Holy Terror.' He drove the class with histrionics and the fear of both tongue and cane. If you stammered he made fun of you. Poor Paddy Stapleton so often endured the jibes, 'Paddy's mouthing, boys, Paddy's mouthing', without flinching as he strove, slamming his hand against the desk, to force the words out of his throat.

If you fidgeted he sent you home, if you were lucky enough to be female, or raised welts on the palms of your hands, if you were not. The cane would be lovingly flexed and would whistle evilly before making contact. It was this kind of stimulus which made it possible for him to galvanise a mixed class of ten to thirteen year olds into learning, without even a hint of rebellion, such esoteric literary ditties as:

'Haste thee nymph and bring with thee,
Jest and youthful jollity.
Quips and cranks and wanton wiles,
Nods and becks and wreathed smiles.'

He loved Milton and Shakespeare and we learned what he gave us to learn and some of us enjoyed it, particularly Niamh Houlihan who would stand up in her bare feet and recite 'To be or not to be. That is the question' or Milton's *Ode on His Blindness* with such passionate pleasure that all of us listened spellbound.

The years followed a pattern, without much that was eventful, save our own inevitable progress out of childhood. Until, in my own case, something happened which would recur in dreams for a long time, right into the horizon of my adult years.

It was the summer of 1932. My mother had sent me for eggs to Mrs Houlihan. There was to be a 'station' at our house the following morning and she was preparing for a big breakfast.

It was a fine Saturday morning in early June and I noted that the tinkers were back in their usual spot on the side of the road where the 'long acre' was at its widest. I was fascinated by the tinkers, living in their colourful caravans, their bright rags stretched out to dry on the bushes, their horses grazing the grass verge of the roadside, their children playing in the shadow of the caravans, the pungent smoke of their wood fires. They lived outside the structures which I took for granted and I feared them a little, interpreting their freedom, perhaps, as some form of contempt. And so I hesitated as I approached their camp. But it was either go home without the extra eggs needed by my mother, or go on. I was nearly thirteen, old enough to have sense.

So I walked on, keeping to the opposite side of the road, watching the little ragged children from the corner of my eye. They stopped their play and stared at me and one of them shouted, 'Hello Miss', and then another one yelled, 'Watch the horses Miss!' in a note of genuine alarm. The next thing I knew three skewbald mares, who had been grazing the ditch a moment before, but who were now dodging the attentions of a stallion, were bearing down on me. The animals, half wild, rolled their ugly eyes; I dodged into a gateway and tried to climb the gate. But to no avail. I was knocked sideways by the shoulder of one of the mares and fell, hitting my head on a gatepost.

I awoke to a dim interior and a terrible headache. I realised that I was inside one of the tinkers' caravans and that the most frightening woman I had ever seen was bending over me. I was aware of the light from the open door and the few pieces of furniture, the pallet on which I was lying, the deal table, the two wooden stools and this terrible woman with the matted hair and the white blind eye.

She looked at me fiercely with the one good eye left to her, an old dark eye surrounded by wrinkles and her mouth smiled and I saw that she had few teeth. The air was heavy with the smell of boiled potato water and smoke.

'Don't upset yourself, little lady,' she said with a cracked voice, putting her hand on my forehead. And as she did so the pain eased. I stared at her, less fearful because of the gentleness of her touch.

19

'You gave your pretty head a wallop, but sure you'll be grand.'

I put my hand up to feel the lump; it was sore, but there didn't seem to be any blood. She turned from me for a moment and came back with a cup of milk. I took the cup and drank the milk, then said thank you and stood up to go. But I was suddenly faint and deposited myself on a stool, willing my head to stop the swimming sensation which made me powerless and willing away the nausea which threatened disgrace.

'Stop here a minute, let you. I'll tell your fortune,' and she reached for my hand. I let her scrutinise the palm and felt her start and look at me strangely. Then she reached for a chipped enamelled basin with a blue rim; the inside was rust because all the enamel was gone. Into this she poured some water from an enamelled jug. She placed this basin between herself and me on the table and bent her head over it, shading it with her hands. She said some sort of prayer - a prayer to Brede it sounded like - and then stared into the water in silence.

'Oh, my little girl,' she said in a low voice after a moment, 'but You will be a great lady some day, and...' and she gesticulated towards the clear water in the rusty basin in some agitation, ... 'the hand of Brede is on you.'

I looked into the basin and saw nothing except the rust. She stared at me and nodded. 'A great lady,' she repeated in tones of wonder. And I stumbled down the wooden steps and made my way home.

I told the story to my mother and she put me to bed, but I could see that the old tinker woman's forecast had stuck in her mind. For days afterwards her speculative, concerned gaze

20

followed me around and she made me repeat the forecast until I was cross and Tom was making a skit of me with 'Here comes the Great Lady. Plain country folk make way!' I shouted at him to shut up and wouldn't speak to him until he came, laughing, to apologise.

I had little thought then, in that last summer of my childhood, of the changes which were imminent. As I wandered down the boreen to my last weeks at the National school, past hawthorn and blackberry hedges with convolvulus and honeysuckle full of perfume, chatting to Paddy or Niamh or any of my classmates, I thought only of the moment; as though there would never be anything except shifting sunshine, a warm dusty road under bare feet, my mother's loving face and a kitchen smelling of freshly baked bread.

The 'fancy boarding school', which had still only a dreamlike reality, would change everything. It was there I met Cissie and Mary and through them the interlude which would stamp and haunt my life.

On a cool September day in 1932 I took the train for Galway and St Catherine's College to begin my new life. Tom came with me to help with my trunk and to see me there safely. I was nervous. The boarding school dream had become reality. For the whole journey my stomach churned in furious resonance with the wheels on the track. I could imagine a world away from home only as a sort of darkness, and into this I was being flung.

When we arrived in Galway, Tom pulled his cap down firmly, hoisted my trunk on his shoulder and strode off to the convent with me trailing nervously behind in my brand new navy uniform which still smelled of the shop. Galway

21

bustled; it was full of country people, men in peaked caps, women in black shawls, donkeys and carts, horses and traps, motor cars, bicycles, and the damp air was full of the smell of horse manure and the salty tang of the sea.

St Catherine's College stood in its own grounds behind a high wall and heavy iron gates. Chestnut trees lined the drive and there were camogie pitches on either side of it. I could see three fenced tennis courts at the top of the field nearest the house. The school itself was a stucco Georgian mansion to which two wings had been added; the wings contained most of the classrooms, the dormitories, the girls' refectory and the assembly hall.

As we walked up the driveway other girls were arriving in black motor-cars - Austin's, Standards, Fords, or pony and trap.

'This is Miss Margaret Donlon,' Tom announced to Sister Barbara, the portress; I saw immediately that she thought he was the hired help and this annoyed me, because Tom carried himself well and was proud. I caught the anger in his own eyes and knew the portress's assumption had not been lost on him.

We were ushered through the main circular hallway with its Italian tiles, ornate ceiling and statue of St Michael and the Serpent, into a long hall with a polished wooden floor and a series of holy pictures with black frames, which decorated the walls from end to end. There were open trunks and cases on the floor; a number of girls were unpacking and the hall was full of their talk and laughter. Tom was shown where to deposit my trunk, while the girls looked him up and down, nudged each other in the ribs and stifled giggles. We said goodbye then; he gripped my

22

hand, the vice-like grip he reserved for important occasions, and his voice became husky.

'God bless you, Peg. We'll miss you at home something awful,' he muttered, uncomfortable with the emotion of the moment and the eyes upon him, and then he was gone and I stood in tears in that long corridor with all those dark holy pictures in their heavy frames. There was a mirror at the far end where I saw my reflection - a gangly creature in a brimmed school hat so typical of the thirties, the ends of my newly cut hair sticking out like the cut edge of a hay rick.

The other girls, dressed in the same navy tunic and white blouse as myself, lost interest in me after Tom's departure and went on unpacking trunks, sucking sweets, talking about the summer holidays and directing the occasional curious glance at any newcomers, greeting old friends with shrieks of delight. 'Did you have a good time?' 'Isn't it ghastly to be back?' 'Which dormitory are you in this year?'

I leant into a window niche from where I could see the drive and watched Tom stride away towards the gate. He turned once to look back at the school and I raised my hand to him, but he didn't see me. Then he was gone through the gateway and I was left with a void in the pit of my stomach, an empty sense of abandonment.

As I was plucking up the courage to ask what I was supposed to do, a tall thin nun appeared. She had a long face and a nose like a beak and she floated down the corridor in her black habit, her head held high. The beads of the rosary hanging from her waist clicked against each other as she moved, and the black and silver crucifix attached to the end of the rosary swung among the folds of her skirts.

This was the headmistress, Mother Mercy, who never twisted her neck. If she turned to speak to someone her whole body swivelled in a movement of studied dignity. She would then bend over the girl she had addressed, her long body curving and her face full of ladylike inquiry, while she adjusted an untidy collar or tie with white hands. Her veil would brush against you in a curious kind of intimacy and you could smell the plain soap she used and the clean black material which made up her habit.

'Sister Barbara told me you had arrived, Margaret,' she said kindly. 'I understand your mother didn't come.'

'No, Sister.'

'My name is Mother Mercy; you can address me as "Mother."' Her voice was modulated with absolute authority. She cast her eyes on the girls all around us.

'Catherine O'Shaughnessy,' she called, raising her voice a fraction and a dark-haired girl of about my own age detached herself from the business of unpacking and came towards us.

'Take Margaret here under your wing - she's in St Teresa's.'

Catherine smiled; she had a shy smile, blue eyes, dark brown hair and an open face with the sort of classical features I had seen in those illustrated plates in Dickens.

Mother Mercy sailed off to talk to someone else and Catherine asked, 'Where's your trunk?' I indicated it, my new brown trunk with the leather handles.

'Take some things out and bring them up. I'll show you where to go.'

She bent to help me and I saw that she had a grey cotton glove on her left hand and that the

24

hand itself had only four fingers, one of them being a stump. I registered a sense of shock, but tried not to show it. Catherine looked at me speculatively for a moment as though daring me to show pity.

I was shown my bed in St Teresa's dormitory; there were fifteen curtained cubicles, each containing a bed, a locker and a basin and ewer. There was a 'cell' in the corner enclosed by a wooden partition where Mother Josephine, the elderly nun in charge of the dormitory, slept. Later I would hear her snoring in the night and would fantasise as to what she would look like without her veil. I imagined a shaven head and a nightcap; but my curiosity was never gratified. Nuns were hardly human; they were brides of Christ and projected such mystery because of their all-enveloping habits and their cloistered lives that they seemed remote from everything ordinary. Even to boarders like ourselves who lived with them they maintained their mystery.

I made my bed and, after several journeys downstairs, emptied my trunk, stacking my belongings in the bedside cabinet and hanging my coat and my spare gym-slip in the big communal wardrobe. It was chilly in the dormitory; thick pipes ran around the wall a few feet above the floor, but they were quite cold. I shivered, fearful of so much newness, bereft of my mother and the hot kitchen and Tom's loud laugh. The tears came in hot prickles; I wiped them away with the back of my hand.

'It won't be so bad here, Margaret,' Catherine said behind me. 'Don't cry. Look, we'll be having cakes an' all for tea this evening!'

I thought of tea at home - my mother's scones and maybe fresh mushrooms picked that morning

25

and fried in butter with a shake of salt, and a grilled rasher or two and a fried egg. I stifled the sobs.

'Where do you come from?' I asked.

'From Ballyharris in County Longford.'

'Never heard of it,' I said. And then she asked me where I came from and I told her about my mother and Tom and she asked if he was the tall fellow she had seen with the trunk and I said yes. She helped me put things away in my locker and then she brought me to her own cubicle on the far side of the dormitory where she showed me a few photographs of her family. I looked at the photographs with passing curiosity, at her parents and brother and the twins - 'They're a right bold pair ' - but found my eyes riveted on her peculiar left hand.

'What happened to your hand?' I asked, whispering because I was in awe of her injury.

She hesitated, stopped what she was doing and then after measuring me with her eyes, removed the glove and held out the hand for my inspection. The little finger was missing as was the top of the ring finger, giving the small hand a peculiar claw-like appearance, like the folded foot of some strange bird.

'I caught it in a rat trap when I was five. I know it's awful.'

'No, it's not,' I insisted. 'It's just a bit different, and if you didn't wear the glove it would hardly be noticed.'

She put the glove back on, smiled at me and shook her head.

'It's nice of you to say so, Margaret. But I just hate it.'

'I'm called 'Peg' at home', I said.

She looked at me from dark blue eyes.

26

'And I'm Cissie!'
So Cissie and I became friends.

The weeks went by, the weather worsened, the flowers died in the convent garden; the nuns had a private garden at the back of the house which was surrounded by a stone wall - probably a former orchard - and we could see into it from the dormitory windows, could watch them on Saturday mornings when we were supposed to be tidying our lockers. They would walk around in pairs, their veils floating a little when the wind caught them.

'You'd think it was recreation hour in a jail,' Rhona Flaherty, who slept in the next cubicle, used to mutter. Rhona was in second year. She had been in trouble in first year for breaking bounds, and was generally regarded as being a bit wild. She showed me two packets of cigarettes hidden under her locker. 'I nip out for supplies when I need them.'

'How do you do that? You'd be caught.'

She smiled, 'Ah ha. This year I have a disguise!'

I didn't believe her. It was only after she was expelled that I learnt about the old raincoat, hat and spectacles hidden in the hollow tree near the gate.

I settled in, learned how to play camogie and became wing on the junior team.

Religion dominated our life at school. We were wakened at seven in the morning by Mother Josephine who came to each cubicle in turn. She would ring a little bell and proffer a container of holy water, intoning 'Benedicamus Domino', and into this small receptacle we had to dip our right hand and intone the response 'Deo Gratias' and make the sign of the Cross. Then there was Mass

27

and then breakfast; in the evening before supper there were more prayers and more prayers again in the dormitory when we were all lined up outside our cubicles and reminded of our mortality. 'Remember man thou art but dust and unto dust thou shalt return,' and we would kiss the wooden floor at this point. I can still feel the dust on my lips.

Then there was the annual Retreat. The Redemptorist priest, in between detailed descriptions of hell - devils with red hot pikes and worms gnawing at your eyeballs - would wax eloquent on the means of getting there. Sex.

There were other ways you could end up in hell, but sex was the primary one. Sex was a sin, tolerated within marriage subject to certain provisos, like doing it for procreation purposes only. Everything to do with sexuality was a sin; we were so young that we hardly knew what the grim-faced priest was talking about; but when he said that touching yourself for pleasure was a mortal sin there would be guilty faces because breasts were growing and were being nocturnally investigated.

The Retreat would last for three days. During this time we had to observe total silence and contemplate our sins. I dredged my conscience, unearthed several crimes and went to Confession. It made me sick with embarrassment but I knew that this was an important sacrament - this middle-aged man sitting behind the grille and questioning pubescent girls about their 'sins'.

Midway through the term a new girl arrived; I watched jealously as Cissie greeted her as an old friend. She had titian hair, green eyes, long slender legs. Her name was Mary McElligott and she came from near Ballyharris in County

28

Longford, from the same parish as Cissie where her father was the local schoolmaster; she and Cissie had known each other for years. She was late coming to school because she had caught pneumonia from some escapade involving the lake near her home. The nuns petted her, treating her as still convalescent, and allowed her second call in the mornings and sent her to bed early as well.

Cissie was obviously delighted to see her. I sulked for a day or two while the two friends consolidated their relationship, feeling very much at the periphery of their world, muttering to myself about 'that one with the red hair' and 'who did she think she was'. I wanted to keep Cissie's friendship and I found Mary polite but distant. She fascinated me all the same with her indifference, the turn of her wit, her command of situations and by the vulnerability which underlay all of this. It was this vulnerability which was the basis of her charisma; she had a kind of magic about her and there evolved among her classmates a tacit agreement that she was someone who must not be hurt. How this had come about I did not know, but it was there.

It was the business of the cigarettes which brought me within the ambit of her friendship. A few of us were trying to smoke in the lavatories - Rhona's cigarettes, which she had pressed on me. Smoking was smart; the film stars did it, albeit with long black holders. We lit up, inhaled, coughed, eyes streaming. The bell went for class; cigarettes were extinguished and everyone fled. I was the last one out and the only one seen by Mother Mercy who came on the scene immediately afterwards and smelt the tell-tale smoke. I got the blame. I admitted the charge, denying that anyone else was involved. Mary confided to me afterwards that if her father had been told that she was smoking he would have removed her from the school. She was grateful, spoke to Cissie of 'our loyal comrade' as though we were partisans in some guerilla war.

I was punished; lines - 'I must not smoke' ad nauseam down four foolscap pages, 'penance for tea', no cakes on Sunday. But it was worth it. Both Cissie and Mary kept pieces of cake for me and the three of us became inseparable.

Cissie suggested one day that we should have a secret name. We mulled for a day or two over what name we should have. In a moment of levity I suggested 'The Three Bears' but this met, for some reason, with paroxysms of derision. 'The Twee Liggle Bears' Mary said; 'Who would be de Mammy and who would be de Daddy; we know who is de Baby,' and she looked at me severely and I laughed at her histrionics, secretly annoyed.

Eventually Cissie decided with the help of the Oxford Dictionary that we were fearless and inconquerable and so we became 'The Invincible Three.' The name conferred power and purpose and we sealed the association in blood one day in the camogie shed, by nicking our palms with the blade from a pencil sharpener and mixing the blood. This made up Blood Sisters, a potent association. We devised a secret handshake, such as we had heard the Freemasons used. However, there was disappointingly little opportunity to benefit from this important means of identification.

Sometimes we talked about boys; about getting married and having babies. There was a lot of speculation as to how exactly the baby came out and where. 'There are cords attached to the baby,'

Rhona, who had set herself up as a sort of oracle, said knowledgeably. 'And if the cords aren't tied together the mother will die, and she told us some story about a woman giving birth on board ship where no one knew about The Cords. Needless to say the mother expired.

We didn't like boys but we knew that if we got married our husbands would adore us.

'Do you know anyone you would like to marry?' I asked Cissie and she blushed when Mary said in a knowing voice, 'Oh yes, she does. The handsome Prince Peter!'

'Who's he?' I demanded.

'Oh, just a local young royal, the heir apparent of Glenallen.'

I tried to get more information but Cissie gave Mary a painful dig in the ribs and the subject was allowed to drop. Later, when I got around to the subject again Cissie said with a sigh that his name was Peter Fitzallen and he lived in a place called Glenallen in County Longford and that Mary was imagining things.

Mary smiled, raising her eyebrows.

'Has he got a brother who would do for you, Mary?' I asked and Mary said he had a brother, God help him. Then she whispered, when Cissie was out of earshot, as though talking to herself, 'Anyway, I hate Glenallen,' and would not be drawn any further.

We had a maths teacher, Miss Sweeney, who also taught us a little science although it was not on the curriculum. She conducted a few simple experiments with materials she brought from home - burning copper and showing us the green residue - copper oxide; growing bluestone crystals and making chemical gardens. Enthralled at the secrets hidden in the everyday, I made up my mind that I would study science when I grew up and become a science teacher. I wanted to unlock all the doors.

Christmas came. There was a decoration hanging in the refectory, made with four candles, one for each of the four weeks of Advent. When three candles were lit the suppressed excitement of end of term had begun to permeate the convent; we sat there in the refectory every night and knew that as soon as the last remaining candle was lit we were as good as home. The nights were black as pitch outside the refectory window which sometimes got steamed up; I drew wheels with spokes and elaborate decorations on to the condensation until Mother Mercy said that whoever was drawing on the windows was to stop as it made them more difficult to clean.

Tom came to take me home for the Christmas holidays. From ten o'clock in the morning the girls had been leaving; some went on the train, some were collected and went off in traps or motor cars.

I introduced my brother to Cissie and Mary.

'Pleased to meet you, Tom', Cissie said.

Tom shook hands awkwardly with them both and I saw that Mary was giving him the Secret Handshake. But Cissie just regarded him shyly, her left hand finding her pocket. There was silence; Tom was not used to girls looking him in the eye. At home they were usually making a play of some kind for him and he had an exalted notion of himself as a result.

I put on the hated school hat and the belted gaberdine coat and gloves and presented myself to the Portress who cast a sharp eye over me and then wished me a happy Christmas. She closed the door behind us, and we set off for Eyre Square and the station. It was a crisp December day, with deceptive noon brightness, darkness only four hours away. Galway was full of pre-Christmas bustle. Bronze and white turkeys, still fully feathered, eyes closed in death, hung in rows in butchers' shops. Shop windows were full of toys, dolls with luxuriant curls and big eyes, Meccano sets, Hornby trainsets, tinsel and holly, boxes of biscuits and chocolates.

Tom glanced at me from time to time with comments like, 'Sure you've got all grandified,' and I tore off the school hat and gloves. 'I see you're still biting your nails anyway,' he said then in an encouraging voice as though there was still hope for me. But I knew that he was pleased with signs of my 'grandification'.

'What did you think of my friends?' I asked him as the train pulled out of Galway station.

'Cissie seemed nice enough,' he said in a grudging voice.

'And what did you think of Mary?'

'That one's a bit of a strap. She didn't even shake hands properly.'

'She was giving you the Secret Handshake.'

He snorted, laughing, and hit his head with his hand. 'The Secret Handshake! Of course! Stupid of me! '

'I'm going to ask Mam if they can come and stay for a while in the summer. Cissie's asked me to her house already!'

'Ummph,' he said absently. Then he burst out after a moment that the economic war with Britain was ruining the country. I had heard about this already - how Dev had refused to pay any further land annuities to England and how

33

our exports to Britain were being cut off in consequence. 'Bad for the cattle farmers,' Tom was fond of saying, 'bad for anyone depending on the British market.'

I asked my mother when I got home if my friends could stay and she wanted to know what their fathers did and when I said that Cissie's father was a doctor her eyes widened a little; doctors as a species were just a few rungs down the ladder from God. And Mary wasn't doing too badly either with a teacher for a father.

On my first day home I met Niamh, coming down the road on her bicycle. I asked her what she was doing with herself and she told me she was working behind the counter in Percivals, the grocery shop in the village, and she laughed, saying it was boring, and studied me keenly.

'You've changed, Peg.' She said it sadly, like one who had expected nothing else.

'Of course I haven't changed.'

On Christmas Day Paddy Stapleton called, ostensibly to deliver a sack of onions. He sat in the kitchen and talked of the new school I was going to and his eyes hardly left my face. Occasionally he stammered, something he never used to do with me. He had changed in the last few months, grown like a weed, and his voice had broken.

'H..h..how do you like your n..n..new school?'

'Are you going to spend the whole day jawin' to Peg?' Tom demanded testily after a while.

When he was gone my mother looked up from her knitting. 'Don't be heedin' the likes of young Paddy,' she said suddenly. 'You can do much better than that!'

I gasped. 'For God's sake, Mam; I'm only thirteen. Anyway, Paddy's a bit of a yob.' I felt ashamed, felt my betrayal of my old friend; he hadn't seemed a 'yob' in the summer; but I had new and sophisticated yardsticks now.

'Anyway I want to go to the Uni', I went on. 'Cissie wants to go too. We want to become scientists. Can I, Mam?'

I loved the word 'scientist'. It imported arcane knowledge and importance for the owner. But all I really wanted at that point was to impress.

Tom looked up at me while he pulled on his boots. 'You'll need more brains than you have for that, and where will the money come from? That's what I'd like to know.'

He left, shutting the door abruptly behind him. There was silence for a while, broken only by the click-click of my mother's knitting needles. I thought perhaps she hadn't heeded me.

'I'll work in the summer holidays and help pay the fees,' I offered.

'I'm proud of you,' she said in a low voice after a moment. 'I don't see why not. It will be nice to have a daughter who is a University graduate. We'll find the money, don't worry. You're a pretty girl. You'll meet the right sort in the University.'

I sighed loudly.

'I don't like boys,' I said crossly. 'And neither does Mary, or Cissie, except for one boy who lives near her in County Longford. His name is Peter and he lives in a big house called Glenallen.'

My mother smiled and nodded absently. What was Glenallen to any of us then?

The next term was the longest, or seemed to be. It was cold in the school; the radiators were hot but the draughts were everywhere, icy little breezes sending shivers up legs despite the heavy lisle stockings. Getting up in the morning became an ordeal; no matter how hard I prayed for actual grace I could never jump out of bed the instant the bell rang. Mother Josephine had preached it as a way to God, this self discipline.

'Prompt rising, prompt rising. Didn't his Grace the Bishop say it himself?'

I wondered if his Grace had to get up at seven.

It was about this time that, bored to death one Sunday afternoon, I made three little dolls as mascots, one for each of us, using cardboard and long strands of our hair, which I plaited together, and crimson silk thread to tie the little figures into shapes.

'They're for good luck,' I said as I presented them to my friends. 'They have something of each of us!'

'Isn't that superstitious?' Cissie asked doubtfully.

'I can feel the luck already!' Mary announced. 'All actors have mascots. I will keep this until I die!'

Mary was in a different dormitory, St Anne's, and, in an attempt to obviate what she called 'the sheer boringness', tried to organise a midnight feast, leaving a note for Cissie and myself at a pre-arranged spot behind a piece of loose skirting. This note was written in invisible ink, the ink being lemon juice, which required heating to be legible.

I found the little note and took it up to St Teresa's dormitory. I had the butt of a candle - the spoils of a few days helping in the sacristy - and Cissie had some matches and before lights out, on the pretext of going out to the lavatory, she slipped into my cubicle and we lit the candle butt to decipher the missive. The wick was long and the acrid smell reached the nostrils of Mother Josephine who came rushing to investigate.

We might as well have been the perpetrators of the Gunpowder Plot. What were we doing in one another's cubicle? What were we doing with the candle? The air was thick with unspoken accusations. Cissie said we wanted to say a special prayer. Mother Josephine looked dubious, working her lips the way she did when deliberating. Cissie had a blameless record. We were mildly penalised but Mary, as usual, got off scot free, although her proposed feast collapsed. I began to realise that she was not happy unless she was involved in some kind of drama. She led us behind the curtains of the assembly hall stage one Sunday when everybody was supposed to be out of doors and arranged us as her supporting cast for some romp of twelve lines she had written.

She strode across the stage, throwing back her thick red curls, pretending to be Sarah Bernhardt whom Mother Xavier had told us about. Cissie and I rebelled at being made to sit and stand to order.

'You're very mean! How can I practise my stage presence if you won't help me?'

'You and your stage presence!' Cissie said, twinkling, 'With a name like Mary McElligott!'

'Sneering now are we?' Mary demanded, her right hand pushing back her hair, her eyes narrowed in laughter. We heard a nun coming into the hall and hopped through a window on to the fire escape.

But as the days lengthened and the snowdrops came up something happened which chastened us, so that we became for a time subdued and frightened.

Rhona, who seemed to have few friends, and who latched on to us from time to time, asked us one day if we had ever tried to contact the dead.

'Don't be stupid,' Mary said. 'That's all eyewash. You can't contact the dead!'

'Oh yes, you can,' Rhona insisted, dropping her voice to a whisper. 'My Auntie Bridie goes to séances, and the spirits come.'

Cissie groaned and I laughed. 'Trickery. They play tricks! It's a racket for money!'

Rhona looked deadly serious for a change.

'It's not always trickery. If you played planchette you would know that. I played it with my auntie once.'

'What's planchette?'

She told us about the circle of letters and numbers - the alphabet, the numbers 0 to 9, the inverted glass and the invocation you made and how the glass would spell out the answers. We began to think as we listened that it might be fun to try it.

So, next day, when we were all supposed to be reading or listening to music on the old gramophone in the assembly hall because it was raining, and Mary had got tired of trying to interest us in her sketch called 'Napoleon's farewell' which she wanted to audition for us, we slipped off to a small deserted room near St Teresa's dormitory which was used occasionally as a sewing room. Rhona produced thirty-six pieces of paper with a letter or number printed on each - the letters of the alphabet - and spaced them in a circle on the table. She produced her glass tooth mug and put it, inverted, in the middle. We sat around the table, put our right

38

index fingers on the inverted glass as directed and Rhona intoned some sort of prayer and then asked in sombre voice, addressing some unseen presence, 'Tell us the future - tell it for each one of us.'

She looked at us and hissed, 'Don't put any pressure on the glass now.'

The glass moved, Mary started giggling and Cissie and I followed suit, snorting and laughing. The glass moved towards one letter and then another and spelt out WOLLY and Cissie said, 'This is ridiculous,' and we all howled with laughter, all except Rhona who pursed her lips in exasperation and said huffily that if we were going to make a skit of it it wouldn't work. 'The Spirits are out for the day,' Cissie suggested innocently and we snorted again and Rhona clicked her tongue angrily, got up and left the room in a huff.

We looked at each other. The rain beat at the window. There was nothing to do except return to the assembly hall until the end of recreation.

Cissie had started to gather up the pieces of paper when Mary said suddenly, 'Wait. Let's give it another go.'

She rearranged the letters, put the glass back in the middle, made us put our fingers on it and then, having warned against any particular pressure being applied to the glass, intoned in the rich dramatic voice she could turn on when she wanted, 'Tell us the future, for each one of us.'

'For Mary, Cissie and me,' I added in a whisper.

We were silent, quiet now because there had been something in Mary's voice that was entirely serious. For a moment the glass did not move and then it started to slide. It moved towards the letter

39

L and then towards the letter O and then towards the letter S and then T. Then it stopped.

'L-O-S-T,' Mary whispered, her face strained and puzzled, but she kept her finger on the glass with the persistence of one making a scientific inquiry. 'Did one of you push it?' she demanded hoarsely, but Cissie and I shook our heads.

'Cissie now,' she breathed.

We waited; the raindrops slipped sadly down the window pane and the wind howled in the empty chimney. I thought the room had become very cold.

The glass moved again, to D, then E, then A, and then D. I glanced at Cissie. Her face was very white. She looked at us accusingly. 'This isn't funny!'

'No. I swear,' I said in a hushed voice. Mary was shaking her head, the pupils of her eyes black and frightened.

'Let's stop now,' I whispered.

'No,' Mary croaked. 'You now, Peg.'

The glass moved, stopped and then exploded with a sound like gunfire. Little shards of glass were embedded in our flesh and blood dripped silently on to the table. I could almost hear the beating of our three hearts in the silence.

We bound up our hands with our hand-kerchiefs, cleared away the mess and went to the infirmary where we told a cock-and-bull story. We never alluded to the incident again, except that Mary said we had pushed the thing around ourselves without realising it, and put too much pressure on the glass. But we were very quiet for weeks after that and the nuns and the girls looked at us curiously, sensing something. We did not tell Rhona the outcome of that afternoon's work.

She was expelled at the end of the term for breaking bounds again.

The drifts of daffodils and narcissi appeared in the nuns' garden; they were arranged on the altar in the chapel and before the statue of the Sacred Heart in the refectory, ushering in the spring of 1933.

Cissie's parents came to see her and she brought me to the parlour to meet them. They invited Mary and myself out for tea and I went off happily in their big Ford car - the first car I had ever sat in. We drove through Salthill and around the bay, and watched the Atlantic rollers crashing on to the Silver Strand. It was pure bliss, I thought, and very posh to sit under rugs in a car like this. Cissie's mother wore a long fur coat and had powder on her face; you could smell the perfumed scent of it and see the tiny flecks of it on her nose and cheekbones. She was a glamorous woman and I fantasised that she was my mother and that Cissie and I were sisters and then I felt guilty. Hadn't I the best mother in the world, even if she did look heavy and old beside Mrs O'Shaughnessy?

Then it was home for Easter. The daffs and narcissi, relics of the gardening once carried out by the big house, were out in their hundreds at home, great sweeps of them along the banks of the Garryogue, which was heavy and dark with floodwater. I remember the Pascal candle in the church, the journey to mass in the trap with Mam and Tom and the way the neighbours would look at me as though I had become someone of consequence. Even Niamh Houlihan was shy with me; the old ease in each other's company was gone. Paddy Stapleton didn't come to the

41

house anymore. His father said he was going to America.

But I could hardly wait to get back to school to my new friends. I told my mother we would be playing tennis the following term and she searched for an old racquet she knew was in the house somewhere; it was warped and I said I'd be the laughing stock of the school. I looked for the newspaper and after going through pages of ads. offering things like ladies' shoes for 16/11d and check gingham for 6d per yard, I found the advertisement for Slazenger racquets and told my mother nothing else would do. She sighed and told Tom to buy me a new one and a press to go with it when he went into Galway for the fair - which he duly did, albeit with bad grace and mutterings about bankruptcy.

There was a lot of talk at the time that the country was facing bankruptcy. Desmond Fitzgerald warned of it and spoke of the necessity of getting our goods back into the British market.

'They should listen to him,' Tom said. 'Do you know what I saw in Eyre Square the other day - a poor man in tears. He had come in from Connemara to sell his calf and had waited all day in the rain and no sign of a buyer. The Long Fellow's pride is driving the country to hell. Maybe O'Duffy and the blueshirts have the answer!'

There was a lot of trouble about the blueshirts, scuffles and stone throwing wherever they paraded. Herr Hitler was in the news too; I recall a photograph in the paper about that time of him being honoured in the German Legation in Dublin. His portrait was given 'The Herr Hitler salute' by visiting Germans in reception rooms draped with the Nazi flag. But I wasn't worried about the country, or the fascist element in politics. I was concerned mainly with my new tennis racquet.

My mother came to see me during term and Tom came with her. She was wearing a new straw hat with a narrow brim and a light grey frock with long sleeves and cotton summer gloves. She looked tired, kind, gentle and a little nervous and I kissed her with only a hint of the sudden surge of love for her which almost overwhelmed me as I came in the door.

Tom twisted his cap around in his hands when Cissie came into the parlour and Cissie shook hands and kept her left hand down by her side. Sometimes her insistence on trying to hide this hand made her appear awkward, which she was not.

Mary was not present. She had been taken out by her Aunt Lily, who had come all the way from Dublin to see her.

We went to Lydons for tea and cakes and looked out the window at the street below, at cars, the donkeys and carts and bicycles and traps. My mother chatted rather garrulously I thought and Tom was strangely shy.

'Mrs Donlon,' Cissie said, 'Peg is invited to my house for a fortnight - beginning of July if that's alright. We're supposed to be going to Kilkee in August.'

'That's very kind of you, Cissie,' my mother said and I knew by the look in her eye that she wouldn't have minded a holiday in Kilkee; she had not had a holiday since the week she had spent in Dunmore East with my father after their marriage in 1914.

43

'You must come and stay with us too, you know, anytime you like,' she said to Cissie.

Cissie reddened.

'I'd like to, very much.' She glanced at Tom under her lashes and he shifted uneasily.

'Maybe you could come and stay with us instead of going to Kilkee? I said.' Cissie looked from me to my mother.

'You'd be welcome as the flowers in May,' my mother said. 'But what would your parents say?'

'Sure they'd be delighted.'

So it was more or less settled. Cissie wrote and told her parents who gave their permission. I invited Mary too and she said she was dying for it. She wrote and asked her father.

The rest of the term was spent in desultory studying for the exams, except for a break one Sunday for an outing to Connemara.

We sat our exams at the beginning of June while the sun blazed outside; when they were over school broke up, except for the older girls who were sitting State exams, the Leaving Certificate and Intermediate Certificate, which went on longer. Did I remember, that June, the old tinker woman who had read my fortune only a year earlier? I think she was never more than a shadow in my mind until years later. Did I treasure the days and hours of an innocent and carefree existence? I wished them away, dreaming of the future.

So ended my first year at St Catherine's. My trunk was duly packed and Tom came to bring me home. He was a little taciturn on the journey although once or twice he asked me obliquely about Cissie and when she would visit us. But all I could think of was the beginning of July when I would set off for County Longford and Bally-harris.

Chapter 2

The day was humid; the sky was overcast and the suffocating closeness promised rain. Cissie met me at the station. Her brother Desmond was with her, a tall youth of sixteen with silken dark hair cut short at the back and sides. He looked at me quizzically over his round spectacles and seized my suitcase.

'This is my brother, Des,' Cissie said. He shook my hand with brusque shyness. A lock of hair flopped on his forehead and he raised his left hand to push it back. He wore a collar and tie and a brown houndstooth jacket. Small beads of perspiration slicked his forehead. How could men stand their clothes in summer? I wondered. Cissie was cool in a summer dress, as I was myself.

'You're welcome, Peg. Her nibs has been talking of nothing except your visit for the past fortnight.' His eyes were blue like Cissie's but without the faraway look she had; he was awkward and forthright and I liked him and felt shy of him because he was so grown up.

Dr O'Shaughnessy's black car was parked outside the station. Des put my case in the boot, opened the back door with a flourish and Cissie and I got in, giggling and setting each other off into peals of laughter about nothing. Then we were off, down through the main street of Ballyharris. It was a large market town about fifteen miles from the principal county town of Longford. It had plenty of shops, seven pubs, one hotel, The Royal Hotel. The spire of the catholic church dominated the market square. The main street ran uphill and at the top of the hill was the protestant church, its spare, square lines visible through the trees. Cissie pointed out various shops, a little café where we could have ice cream, her father's surgery with its brass plate beside a dark green door. Raindrops spattered the windscreen and Des turned on the wipers.

We moved slowly down the main street. A couple of people waved to Des in greeting. We overtook traps and horses and carts and cyclists and then we left the town behind and followed the wet road out into the countryside.

'I thought you lived in the town,' I said.

'Three miles outside it,' Cissie answered. 'But Dad has his surgery in town. Des has to bring the car back to him as soon as we get home. He couldn't come himself so he let us borrow it to collect you.'

'But how will Des get home?'

'Cycle. There's a bike at the surgery. But don't worry. He thinks it's well worth it for the chance to drive the car. Don't you, Des?'

Des nodded. 'You bet.' He put his foot down; we sped along at forty miles per hour.

'Dad said not to go fast,' Cissie reminded her brother. I stared out at the countryside. The fields were bigger than at home, few stone walls, little gorse. Looming in the near distance was a mountain of sorts, a huge mound of a hill very dark and brooding against the grey sky.

'That's Knockshee.'

I translated mentally - The Fairy Mountain - wishing vaguely that this mound did not overshadow us.

We passed a pair of big iron gates and I could see a huge old house at the end of an avenue lined with beech trees.

'What a beautiful house!' I said.

'That's Glenallen. We'll be there next week for the gymkhana.' She turned her head to peer through the rain on the back window until the house was lost to view. I looked back with curiosity, aware that this was the home of 'Prince Peter' of whom Cissie was so fond. And because it was such a beautiful house I stared at it until the trees hid it, glanced for a moment at Cissie who laughed after an embarrassed fashion and shrugged, as though in answer to some unspoken question.

A few minutes later the car slowed and we took a left turn into an open gateway between two concrete pillars, crunched along a short driveway and stopped precipitously, gravel spewing. Cissie and I were bumped against the front seats. 'Good brakes,' Des murmured knowledgeably. Cissie sighed, clicked her tongue and raised her eyes to heaven.

Cissie's home was a square two-storey house, with plastered walls covered in ivy. It faced the road, set back behind a long sloping lawn and a tall hedge. The front door was open. I saw the flagged porch and the tiled hall beyond. Some leafy plants stood on a table in the porch. Climbers clung to bamboo sticks and a few geraniums blazed through the widows into the damp afternoon. A fluffy grey cat picked its way around the side of the house and a cocker spaniel came barking ecstatically from somewhere. Various people appeared at the door, Cissie's mother and her young brother and sister - the twins she had told me so much about. I got out of the car and stood nervously.

'You're very welcome, Peg,' Mrs O'Shaughnessy said, smiling, taking my hand and drawing me into the hall. 'Or should we call you Margaret?

'Only Mother Mercy does that. Everyone calls me Peg.'

I felt very shy, couldn't think of anything to say, looked around me, saw a half-moon hall table with a brass vase full of roses, an umbrella stand with two black umbrellas with leather handles, some prints and watercolours on the walls, a shooting stick in the corner. At the back of the hall was a huge grubby teddybear with a noose around its neck.

The two eight-year-olds thrust themselves forward. 'This is David and this is Barbie,' Cissie said severely. The children, blue eyed and dark haired, regarded me curiously.

'How long will you be staying?' Barbie asked without enthusiasm.

'Till she's hunted,' Des said, bringing in my case and winking at me.

'Her hair's the same colour as Fluff's,' David observed matter of factly, giving weight to my good points.

'You can sleep in my bed,' Barbie confided. 'It has a hole in the mattress.'

Cissie made shooing gestures. 'Scram!' She was laughing, embarrassed, and stared at the twins, her face full of tacit threats.

'Who's Fluff?' I asked. Cissie indicated the golden cocker spaniel. Mrs O'Shaughnessy took charge of the twins and told Cissie to bring me upstairs.

I glanced into the rooms to right and left. To the right was the dining-room, while the room to the left was the sitting-room, a large comfortable room - chesterfield suite covered in flowered chintz, a second sofa by the window, wireless on a table near the marble fireplace, bookshelves painted white, antique occasional table with magazines, a piano with brass candlesticks on top of it. Beside the bundle of sheet music was a goldfish bowl with two bright inmates.

'Oh, you have goldfish,' I breathed. I had read of them, but had never seen them. I went over to inspect them, comparing them with the little pinkeens I used to fish for at home. They were fat and burnished and content. 'They belong to Barbie,' Cissie said. 'God help them.'

I followed Cissie out to the hall, past the doorway to her father's study-cum-surgery and up the old stairway which turned at a tall window and continued in the opposite direction to the landing; it was covered with an oriental style carpet in blues and reds, slightly worn on the treads. The dog hurried up after us full of importance, swinging his ears.

Cissie shared a room with Barbie; I was to have Barbie's bed and she was to be moved to the guest room. It was a bright room, overlooking the back garden and the apple trees trained against an old brick wall. On the other side of the wall grew a tall sycamore, prolific with green seed pods. The bedroom walls were painted cream; the bedspreads were white cotton; the curtains were chintz, with roses and green leaves. I dumped my case on Barbie's bed. There were a few pencil drawings on the wall near the bed head - a series of stick- like figures in skirts and a few figures dangling from gibbets. I looked at them and laughed. Cissie shook her head. 'She's going through a phase.'

Cissie stood beside me at the window. The day had begun to clear; the sun was coming out in snatches.

'That's the back of the stables; we have two loose boxes. I'll bring you down to meet Banner when you're ready.'

I looked at her in envy, feeling the tenor of her life, happy to be permitted to be a part of it. Not that I had been deprived, but the atmosphere in this house spoke of things I had not known, of careless plenty and the warmth and fun of a large family. And above all there was the thrill of friendship, of sharing, of acceptance, and the knowledge that an eternity of time stretched before us, that the world was ours.

'You're so lucky, Cissie.' She looked down at her hand, shrugged, her face suddenly pinched.

'Would you like to go for a ride?' she asked after a second or two and I said I would but warned her I was no rider. I did not mention the fear I had of horses; in my mind was a memory of rolling eyes and powerful bodies rushing to crush me.

'Except for Tom's mares there's only the trap pony at home; and there's no saddle; Tom rides bareback.'

Her eyes widened. 'He must be a terrific rider!'

'Ah, I dunno. He doesn't have much truck with it. He doesn't hunt.'

Cissie snorted. 'Bareback hunting! That would cause a stir! Perhaps I should try it.'

'For God's sake, Cissie, don't do anything stupid.'

'I'm fooling,' she said and we went downstairs and out into the summer.

I had my first riding lesson that evening. We went out to the ten acre field behind the house, which contained two horses, Banner and Tess. Cissie saddled Banner and gave me a leg up and I walked around on him. He endured me with patience but next morning when I was mounted on him yet again he decided that enough was enough, or perhaps he sensed my secret fear, for he suddenly lunged into a canter and I fell off at once into some nettles.

'Peg, are you alright?'

Cissie had her hand over her mouth trying to contain the laughter.

'I'm fine.' I sucked my smarting hand.

'It takes seven falls to make a rider,' she said, eyes twinkling, 'so that's only six to go.'

'I can tell you now - it's none to go! This sport is not for me.' I got up from the nettles, found some dock leaves and scrubbed the white blisters vigorously, leaving green smears. My bottom was sore too and I rubbed it surreptitiously.

Cissie looked contrite and went after the sneering Banner who was happily wrenching the grass in the ditch with long yellow teeth.

'You are a very bad horse,' Cissie told him and he farted noisily - plutt-plutt-plutt - depositing behind him a pungent rope of manure.

She turned to me, unsteady with laughter.

'Let's go for a cycle. I told Mary we'd call over.'

We took off Banner's saddle and bridle and carried it back to the house, shutting the gate of his field carefully. Banner looked after us with sly triumph and gave his chestnut mane a shake to warn off the flies.

When the tack had been restored to its peg Cissie brought me to the big turf shed and prised two bicycles loose from where they were wedged behind a step ladder, a wheelbarrow and a three-

legged kitchen chair. We brought them out to the
road and then we were away with much laughter.

'What time did you tell Mary we'd call? She
may be out,' I said.

'Who cares! We can always come back.' I can
show you a bit of the county. What are you
interested in? Megalithic, prehistoric, early
Christian?'

'None of them,' I said sheepishly.

Mary lived with her father in the teacher's
residence attached to the local National school.
The house was a small square two-storey one,
with dormer windows, built specifically as a
teacher's residence at the end of the last century.

Mr McElligott was a gentle looking man of
medium height, bespectacled, grizzled, and not in
the least like Mr Clancy, the terror of my
childhood. He came to the door of the kitchen as
Cissie poked her head in. Mary was in the garden
he said and we skirted a hedge to find our quarry
spread out on a rug under the shade of an alder,
engrossed in a book.

Cissie put a finger to her lips and we hid
behind the hedge, making soft groaning noises.
Mary looked up, listened, frowning like one who
doubted herself. She pursed her lips as we
jumped out from cover.

'You're the right pair of eejits!' she said. I
glanced at the book she was reading, saw the title
The School by the Sea.

'Any good?'

'Middling.'

She brought us into the house. Her father was
reading and writing at the kitchen table. There
was a small tiled hall and two reception rooms.
The books were everywhere, in bookcases, on
tables, chairs, window-sills. The house felt like the

53

scholar's residence it was, but lacking completely in the kind of warmth I associated with home.

Mary's bedroom was a little room under the eaves with white walls and a dormer window inset into the roof which came down at an angle. Cissie and Mary sat on the bed; I perched on a chair and examined my face in the mirror, comparing it with Cissie's classical features or Mary's luxuriance and giving up the fruitless comparison.

'I hate small rooms,' Mary said. 'When I grow up I'll have a mansion. I shall die in a great chamber.'

'What do you want a mansion for?' I asked.

Mary closed her green eyes. 'For the sheer grandeur.'

'Someplace like Glenallen?' Cissie ventured. Mary hesitated; her face paled a little and the smile died in the corners of her mouth.

'Maybe. I haven't decided.'

We laughed. 'You should marry Brian Fitzallen so,' Cissie said.

Mary thrust back her red hair, letting it ripple through white fingers. 'The falcon does not mate with the curlew,' she muttered dramatically. 'And he'll marry money. They'll make sure of that.'

The pallor was still in her face. 'Anyway Peter's better looking', she added mischievously after a moment in which I tried to work out who was supposed to be the falcon and who the curlew. The falcon was predatory, soared and seized freedom; the curlew was lonely. I had often heard his sad slanting cry across the bogs near us at home. Neither description fitted Mary. She was always throwing out pieces of nonsense to see how they sounded.

Cissie flushed at the mention of her hero's name and Mary nudged her with her elbow and sang softly.

'Guess who loves Peter Fitzallen. Guess who loves Peter Fitzallen.'

Cissie gave an embarrassed, unconvincing laugh.

'Would you ever shut up, Mary,' I muttered.

She glanced at Cissie apologetically. 'Ah, don't mind me.'

But I did mind her. I ached for her, for her life without a mother, for the solitude she had at home. When we came in from the garden I had seen her father engrossed at the kitchen table with his books and notes. He had smiled up at her and at us after a kindly preoccupied fashion and had gone back to his work.

And I had seen too the picture in the hall of the young woman with the same thick curling hair as Mary, looking into the camera with warm, smiling inquiry.

'What happened to Mary's mother?' I had asked Cissie once.

'She died when Mary was five. Some sort of virus infection. She was in hospital for a week, seemed to be recovering, but had a relapse and was suddenly gone. Daddy told me about it. It was terribly sad.

'I think there was some kind of family crisis at that time because, quite recently, I heard Daddy saying something to Mummy about it being responsible for her relapse.'

'What kind of crisis??'

'I don't know. They wouldn't talk about it.'

It was lunch time. We brought Mary back with us to the O'Shaughnessy residence and wandered into the kitchen where Nellie, the housekeeper, had salad waiting for us, hard-boiled eggs and slices of ham with tomatoes and fresh lettuce from the garden. The elegant cat I had seen on my arrival was asleep in her basket by the range and Barbie and David were just finishing their meal. Barbie put her plate in the sink and looked up at us innocently as she sidled from the kitchen. David jumped off his chair to follow her, knocking over his glass and spilling milk on to the floor.

'Clean that up at once, young man,' Nellie said sharply and David immediately grabbed the sleeping cat by the scruff of the neck and wiped the slop with her. The cat spat, stared at her dripping coat and then at us through mortified green slits, before scuttling under the table for a clean up. Cissie, Mary and I laughed till we cried. Nellie went to the back door and shouted for David who had fled into the garden. But there was silence.

'The blackguard,' she muttered. 'The bold little blackguard.'

Mrs O'Shaughnessy came in then with an armful of roses. Nellie fetched her a vase and she began to arrange them, showing them to us with pride.

'They've come on so well.'

'Mummy's exhibiting at the flower show in Glenallen,' Cissie said.

'When is the flower show?' I asked.

'It's the same time as the gymkhana.'

I knew Cissie would be riding in this gymkhana and turned to Mary asking her would she also be a competitor.

'I haven't a horse.'

'Of course you have a horse. You can ride Hector. Mr Whithead is only too happy to lend him to you.'

'Who's he?' I asked.

'The Rector,' Cissie said. 'His horse is always in need of exercise.' But Mary was strangely reluctant; I put it down to diffidence about the horse. Cissie said she would ask the Rector herself, reminding Mary how much she had enjoyed the gymkhana when it had been held at Barnstown and what a good horsewoman she was and how badly Hector needed exercising. Mary sighed as though the fight had gone out of her.

We made sandwiches and took them down to Saleen, the nearby lake, propped our bicycles against some bushes, lit a fire to clear the midges, and sat in the shade of an oak tree to devour our picnic. I looked across the water, saw the shadows of the sky, the shivers on the surface when the breeze blew, the little rippling sounds. I made a mental note that day: I am nearly fourteen and I am happy.

'This lake is treacherous,' Mary said at one stage. 'You must never try to swim here. It's full of drowning weed.'

I shrugged. 'Can't swim.'

I looked around at the warm countryside and up at the shadows playing on Knockshee. The mountain looked cheerful now, the sense of its brooding watchfulness muted, the sunlight picking out the shades of green and brown. It was as though it approved of us, the three young girls picnicking by the lake.

I must be a little mad, I told myself, fighting with the invasive notion that the mountain was a conscious entity, old and amoral. My imagination was over-active. How could a physical feature of

57

the landscape have such a presence? All around us the countryside was lush, miles and miles of verdant Ireland in every direction, torpid with summer and peace. In the distance a donkey brayed, a long sad complaint.

The O'Shaughnessy household in summertime ate when it was hungry, except for the evening meal when Dr O'Shaughnessy was at home and the whole family attended. Sometimes he would be called out in the middle of the meal and Mrs O'Shaughnessy would sigh. 'Can't you finish your meal?' And he might respond wearily that babies didn't wait, all of which was heady stuff to me, to be so close to someone who was involved with real life, birth and death on a daily basis. But what I knew about birth made me embarrassed that a man, even if he was a doctor, should attend such an intimate event in a woman's life. I decided that when I grew up I would not have babies.

He told me stories about the county, the battle fought at nearby Ballinamuck in 1798 between the Irish and French forces under General Humbert and the English under General Lake. He was a mine of historical information, riveting because he projected his own intense interest, so that even Des, who had been looking rather glazed, joined in the discussion to tell me about Gunner Magee who, with his two cousins, used broken pots and pans as replacement ammunition for one of Humbert's guns. 'When one of the gun's wheels broke, the two cousins supported the axle with their backs while Magee fired the last shot. Their backs were broken by the recoil and Magee was killed by the English cavalry.'

He told the story as though it had happened yesterday. Barbie and David listened with their

mouths open until Dr O'Shaughnessy changed the subject.

'How's the riding?' he asked Cissie. 'Going to bring home the Fitzallen cup this year?'

Cissie made a gesture of 'maybe', moving her hand from side to side. She always wore the little glove, winter and summer; I was so used to it now that neither it nor the deformity which it was intended to conceal struck me as anything out of the ordinary.

'What about you, Des?'

'I don't mind competing in the thing - but don't expect me to win on Tess. She's too damned lazy.'

His father studied him for a moment, greying eyebrows tangled over tired eyes.

'I know who's lazy,' Cissie said. 'And it isn't Tess. You only take part in the gymkhana to see Harriet Fitzallen.'

Des flushed. 'Little girls should be seen and not heard,' he said crossly.

And so the banter went on, about the Fitzallen's and Glenallen, which was the local stud farm, where the local flower show and the gymkhana had been held for the past two years, ever since Mrs Fitzallen had become involved on the committee.

There were three children in the Fitzallen family, Des told me; two boys - Peter and Brian and a girl, Harriet, in age like steps of stairs; Peter was seventeen, had just finished school and was going to Dublin to study for the Bar. Harriet was a year younger. 'She's at a boarding school in Dublin; she's a great horsewoman.'

'Fine looking girl,' his father offered, regarding his son quizzically.

I looked from him to Mrs O'Shaughnessy, but she said nothing and looked at her son with a smile.

'I don't like her,' Barbie said suddenly, arranging her mashed potato in a thin layer around the edge of her plate so that her mother would think she had eaten most of it.

'Why not?' Des demanded.

'She called me "darling" when I spoke to her in Gogarty's yesterday when Nellie sent me down for some butter.'

'That's a stupid reason,' David, her twin, said scornfully and Des muttered something under his breath about wishing she'd call him darling.

'No, it's not a stupid reason. She didn't mean it. And her eyes never smile.'

'What about Brian?' I asked.

'He's fourteen,' Cissie said. 'He's a bit of a loner - but he's nice.'

The cat gave David a wide berth that evening. I asked Barbie where they had spent the afternoon and she pointed to a jampot on the window-sill full of swimming stickleback, their silvery flanks catching the light. Then, putting her mouth to my ear she whispered that she had put some of them in with the goldfish - 'for company.' I thought no more of this until later, when the quiet was rent by shrieks of grief and rage and I saw Barbie striding purposefully towards the lavatory with her goldfish bowl. The goldfish were dead; the stickleback had skewered them and now swam around under the red-golden corpses of their victims which floated on their sides.

'You killed my goldfish,' she screamed in a fury of tears. 'You killed my poor goldfish,' and then

we heard the sound of the lavatory being flushed on the guilty.

Chapter 3

I wore my best dress for the gymkhana, a blue frock with a belt and a vee neck with white revers, which Mrs Houlihan had made for me. Cissie rode to Glenallen with Des and her parents brought me in their car, Mrs O'Shaughnessy's roses filling the boot, their perfume surrounding us as soon as we opened it. We entered Glenallen by a back gate, following a signpost directing us to the parking field. Some people were already there with pony and traps and one or two cars. It was a lovely afternoon, rich with summer, although the clouds in the west hinted at a different end to the day.

Cissie arrived on Banner shortly after we did and she dismounted and walked around the jumping arena with me, leading her mount who looked very smart with his clipped coat and freshly plaited mane and tail, pointing out the various courses which would be followed during the competitions. There was a smell of new-mown grass, an aura of excitement. The field was laid out with jumps and obstacles. There was a wooden wall, a bush fence filled with gorse, gates, poles painted red and white.

The arena was bounded by a wire and pine pole fence to protect the spectators. On one side a hay float loaded with white bentwood chairs was reserved for the judges. It had a table in the middle on which the cups were displayed and there was a large box of red, blue and green rosettes for the also-rans.

At one end of the field was a fenced off paddock with an open gate. Cissie led Banner into it and greeted the youth who approached us, leading his horse. He was wearing cavalry twill jodhpurs, tweed hacking jacket and held himself well; he had a preoccupied air and the indefinable aura that goes with privilege. He greeted Cissie a little diffidently as he passed and glanced at me.

'Who's that?' I asked after he had moved away.

'Brian Fitzallen.'

Then the timbre of her voice deepened. 'Look, here's his brother, Peter.'

I turned to see this paragon, the subject of so many innuendos from Mary. About fifty yards from us a young man in riding breeches and black boots was approaching with a fair-haired girl. He was about the same height as his brother, handsome, with a way of holding his head very straight, even while conversing, in an attitude of unyielding pride. He was wearing a black velvet jacket with a snow white stock and, as he walked, he slapped a silver handled riding crop against his polished black boots.

'That's Harry with him,' she added.

'The sister?'

'Yes.'

I studied them covertly. They seemed deep in conversation, but Harriet's eyes moved over the other people present as she talked to her brother. She was a tall girl, dressed in the same immaculate fashion as her brother, and radiated gaiety and confidence.

'Harry's an odd name for a girl, but it sort of suits her.'

Cissie nodded absently. I saw the way her eyes were glued on Peter, how black the pupils were.

They spoke to a few of the contestants and I heard Harriet's laugh tinkle for a moment. Then they strolled towards us. Cissie became engrossed with Banner, stroking his nose insistently, so that he snorted uneasily. She turned sideways. I knew she was nervous and wondered why.

'Hel-lo there!' It was Harriet's voice, genial, comradely.

'Hello, Harry,' Cissie said gravely, continuing to stroke Banner. She glanced at Peter who was directly behind his sister; he smiled at her perfunctorily and looked away.

'This is my friend,' Cissie added, indicating me. 'Peg Donlon.'

'Hello, Peg,' Peter shook my hand. I had the sensation of being examined and rejected as unworthy. Harriet smiled at me - a bright smile, charming me by the sense of contact, by her intention to charm. She radiated an absolute confidence that people were as she perceived them to be; that they existed only in relation to her and that she was at the centre of things. And the charm which accompanied this perception was seductive; it offered rewards; the rewards were her friendship, her recognition; and the price was the remoulding of one's identity to accommodate them. All of this is apparent in retrospect, but at the time, having few personal pretensions, I was simply seduced.

Des suddenly appeared on Tess, dismounted, said a curt hello to Peter, and greeted Harriet eagerly. His eyes dwelt on her in open admiration. I knew at once that she knew he adored her and that this pleased her but left her unimpressed.

'I saw your new horse,' he said. 'Yes, Mister Charming. What did you think of him?'

64

'He's magnificent. You'll walk away with the cup.'

Mary came along then, riding the borrowed Hector, who was fat, unclipped and dripping clots of white foam. She was looking erect and competent, titian hair tamed in a hairnet under the hard black hat. But her hands were clenched tightly as she sat looking down at us and I saw with some amazement that they trembled as she prepared to dismount.

'Good day to you all, my good people,' she said regally, showing no overt sign of the turmoil evinced a second earlier by her shaking hands. She threw one slim leg over the horse's neck and slid off. Everyone laughed. Mary had the gift of not appearing to care what anyone thought of her and was highly regarded in consequence. I saw Harriet look at her measuringly through her fixed smile of welcome, saw her glance at Hector with raised eyebrows.

'If I'd known poor Hector was so out of condition I'd have exercised him for the dear old Rector.'

Then she turned back to Cissie who stood talking to Peter and holding Banner, her left hand in her pocket. Banner rattled the bit, curling his rubbery lips and baring his teeth. I knew from Cissie's face that she was hardly aware of her surroundings; that she had distilled reality into a sharp focus on one human being.

'Cissie darling,' she said, 'don't you find Banner a bit trying?'

Cissie didn't respond for a moment. She turned then and laughed. There was colour in her face and her eyes were very bright.

'Of course not; he's a pet.'

65

'But he's very strong. Don't you find it hard to hold him in at the turns ... with your poor little paw?' She indicated Cissie's left hand which was still in her pocket. Cissie paled, seemed totally at a loss, took her hand out of the pocket and looked at it wretchedly. I saw Peter glance at the gloved left hand. Mary drew a long breath through her nostrils.

'No,' Cissie stammered, mortified that her deformed hand was centre stage, mortified too, I suspected, that Peter Fitzallen was present to witness her humiliation. And as for Peter himself - his face was almost inscrutable, except for the sudden disapproving tightening around his mouth. He glanced at his sister, narrowing his eyes.

'Not at all,' Cissie said shakily.

'A good horsewoman steers with her knees, not her hands,' Mary said sweetly and as Harriet turned her cool blue eyes on her added, 'I see you're using a twisted snaffle on Mr Charming already.'

Harriet's expression of being pleasantly superior became fixed and she gave Mary a look which chilled me. Peter made a pleasant witty comment to Cissie, bending towards her a little with condescending affability, and then his sister put her hand on his arm. 'Darling,' she said brightly to her brother, raising eyes to him with an expression like Bambi: 'It's almost eleven. We'd better get moving. I'm such a scatterpillar.'

He responded to her with a half laugh; his eyes showed sudden delight in her and he seemed almost relieved to be drawn away. And then she and Peter were gone, walking across the field, chatting to some other people, and Cissie stood there still stroking Banner's nose in a kind of shock. I saw the tears start in her eyes, saw the set line around her mouth.

'Don't mind her. She didn't mean anything,' I whispered. 'She's just a bit insensitive.'

'She's just a cow,' Mary said, 'trying to put Cissie off her stroke.' Cissie said nothing, but her mouth trembled and her eyes narrowed on the tears.

'Just who do they think they are?' I whispered angrily to Mary.

She gave a short laugh.

'Royalty ... They think they're royalty, but I bet you anything royalty have better manners!'

The gymkhana began. I watched with Mrs O'Shaughnessy and the twins from the small crowd. There were ten contestants in all, including Des and Mary. Harriet's new horse was a fine chestnut gelding and she rode him with pride, but after an impeccable performance he knocked the top pole on the last fence.

'Goody, goody.' Barbie, who was beside me, and fully recovered from the tragic death of her goldfish, whispered fiercely before being hushed by her mother.

All the competitors were eventually eliminated except Cissie and the three Fitzallens. There was a jump-off against the clock. Peter and Brian went first and knocked a further fence apiece. Then it was Harriet's turn. One could sense the concentration with which she entered the arena, but her horse was strangely skittish this time and knocked the second fence. Now it was up to Cissie. Harriet looked angry as she trotted out of the arena and into the paddock.

Cissie came forward into the enclosure. She had prayed for this position, for which lots had been cast, and came forward on Banner, sitting erect, face set and eyes very black as they always were when she was excited or afraid.

Banner behaved meticulously. The crowd held its breath. I could feel that they were rooting for her, this fourteen-year-old with the poor little hand, God help her. Mrs O'Shaughnessy sat back with feigned relaxation. On the far side of the enclosure I saw the Fitzallen parents. Did they think the day was won already? I wondered. When I knew them better I would realise I had misjudged them; that theirs was a dark fatalism which expected nothing.

First one fence was cleared, then another, the double, the bank, the water jump. There was a tense moment as Banner clattered a top rail with a hind hoof, but it held - wobbling for a moment. He seemed to realise his mistake, because he cleared everything else with inches to spare. And then there was the last fence and it was over. Miss O'Shaughnessy on Banner with a clear round and one time fault had won the event. Everyone clapped and cheered, especially the twins who were screaming with delight. I saw Cissie bend caressingly over Banner's neck, saw her eyes swivel, not towards where her family and myself were sitting, but where Peter and Harriet Fitzallen were watching. I saw the way Peter looked back at her - with a sudden arrested interest, like an ornithologist who has just seen a rare and splendid species. He stood there, this teenager, tall, regal and cold and followed Cissie with his eyes. And perhaps it was a combination of his beauty and his coldness which made me feel uneasy, that and his interest in Cissie, which was unmistakeable.

There was some kind of peril here which I could not understand. Watching the three young Fitzallens in the paddock it occurred to me as strange that Brian was never with his sister and brother; he kept to himself for the most part, but once, when he went to speak to them I saw the way Harriet's head jerked to look away from him and his brother deliberately turned his back.

Then they had the victory parade. The sun came out and blazed on Cissie as she led the parade around the enclosure, and on Mary bringing up the rear, head held high, mouth in a set smile. I studied Harriet Fitzallen for a moment to see how she was taking her defeat; she was smiling a sporting smile, but her eyes, as Barbie had pointed out at an earlier stage, didn't smile at all.

They lined up before the judges for the prizes. A rosette was pinned on Banner and Cissie was handed the silver trophy by a congratulatory judge, the Fitzallen cup, which she could keep for a year, and the smaller replica. She took these with her right hand, holding the reins with her left, smiling happily. And then, suddenly, at the moment of her triumph Harriet Fitzallens horse became restive and backed into Banner and Cissie's instinctive movement to control her horse with her good hand resulted in the silver trophy falling to the ground.

I saw her face whiten with shame, saw her tremble as she prepared to dismount and then Brian Fitzallen was on the ground, scooping up the trophy, and handing it back to Cissie with a bow. Several people clapped. I loved him for that moment of chivalry, loved the hissed inquiry, 'Can't you control that animal?' which was directed at his sister, noted her look of open hatred. And Peter sat there impassively, the onlooker, cold and contemptuous, watching Cissie, his face showing no emotion, other than the same concentrated interest I had read in him while he watched her win.

Then the second and third prizes went to the Fitzallens and they were well cheered and Brian turned as he was given his rosette and caught my eye and smiled. It was an instant of private contact, gone in half a breath.

This was the highlight of my first stay in Ballyharris. Afterwards there was tea in the marquee, which had been erected on the lawn in the shadow of the mansion. I stood at the marquee entrance and stared up, a little awed, at the Georgian windows of that house and drank in the atmosphere of wealth and the benisons it bestowed of confidence and privilege. I looked across the lawn to the small artificial lake and the little wood beyond it. The fields beyond that were dotted with horses, their graceful silhouettes against the sky.

I was wondering where Mary was, anxious to share Cissie's victory with her. But she was not among the crowd in the marquee so I moved outside, where the cool evening breeze was pushing at the canvas and the sky promised rain. I could see that the rain had already started on the mountain. I scanned the front and side of the mansion and then saw Mary approach under the archway from the stableyard. I was about to call, but she moved away towards a clump of trees near the tennis court and there was something in her gait which galvanised me. I ran to the trees and found her in the shadows, bent over, retching.

'What's made you sick?' I gasped and she looked up at me, shaking her head, trembling.

'I don't know, Peg. There's something about this place ...' For a moment I thought she might be joking, but the stubborn lines of endurance in her face spoke for themselves.

'This is the most beautiful place I have ever been in,' I said in wonder, having forgotten for the moment the shadow I had experienced only half an hour before. 'What's wrong with it?'

'I am afraid here,' she whispered then. 'I'm afraid and I'm disgusted and I don't know why.'

She wiped her mouth with the handkerchief she produced from her jodpur pocket and insisted that we go back to the marquee. I walked beside her in silence, feeling the first fine drops of rain, aware of the mountain stalking us under its shroud of grey mist.

Doctor O'Shaughnessy collected us. Mrs O'Shaughnessy's roses had won second prize. She seemed happy enough and we drove home in tired contentment; Cissie and Des walked the horses home while Mary returned her mount to its owner and joined us later for supper.

And what a supper it was! The kitchen reverberated with the laughter, the comparisons, what Harriet's horse must have cost and how cheap Banner had been in comparison. 'I knew he was a good bit of stuff,' Dr O'Shaughnessy said in between mouthfulls, and Des said that Mr Charming was really a skittish horse. 'Did you see the carry on of him at the jump-off?' And he added that Harry was the best horsewoman in the county and David said that 'Mr Charming' was a stupid name for a horse, and Mary who seemed fully recovered said little, but giggled wickedly

71

occasionally. Nellie bustled around serving us, commenting that it was the mercy of God that the rain held off and she put her hand gently on Cissie's head in passing. Cissie had bathed and changed and looked tired and content.

'What were you giggling about all evening?' Cissie asked Mary later on, after we had helped Nellie clear everything away and were alone in Cissie's bedroom. I was looking out the window and the other two were stretched out on the beds. It was wet outside now, blustery puffs of wind driving a fine rain before it, and the sycamore and appletree leaves danced wildly. But the window was securely shut and we were snug and safe. I turned to watch my two friends, glad of the way we could shut out the world.

Mary looked blank. 'What are you talking about?'

'You were cackling to yourself at supper. Share the joke.'

Mary looked from one of us to the other.

'This is for the Invincible Three only.' She paused, bit her lip, while I snorted. Invincible Three! The agony of it! That was nine months ago. We had outgrown all that.

'You see,' she went on, hunching her shoulders, 'I simply prodded a few nettles where they would do the most good.' She laughed again, tears of mirth running down her face like one who was both delighted with her own temerity and glad of the excuse to release some terrible tension.

I didn't know what she was talking about. Cissie looked perplexed for a moment, then launched into a paroxysm of guilty laughter. 'Oh God, I didn't really win at all; it was you!'

Mary turned to me, eyes streaming. 'Don't you see, dear idiot. I rolled some nettles into a ball and before the jump-off, when they were all lined up against the back railing of the paddock, I shoved them up Mr Charming's arse.'

'What did you ...?' I was bewildered.

'It's an old tinker trick,' she added when she was able. 'They use it at horse fairs to make an old horse act young and frisky. Am I very bold?'

'Oh yes,' I said, stuffing a pillow over my face to stifle the shrieks of laughter. No wonder Mr Charming had been skittish.

I said nothing that evening about what I had seen in that little copse near the stableyard. I had been about to mention it at supper but Mary had forestalled me; she had frowned at me in warning and had shaken her head.

When Mary was leaving, Cissie and I went downstairs with her to the front door. I saw that Dr O'Shaughnessy was saying goodbye to a patient - a tired looking sparrow of a woman who had a bandage on her hand. He was refusing the money which she proffered saying, 'Try to take a rest Kate, and follow instructions about the hand. You know yourself that you must prevent the infection taking hold.'

'Divil a hold. Sure haven't I had many a scratch worse than that.'

She looked up at us as we came downstairs.

'Begod, Dr O'Shaughnessy, but young Cissie is getting shockin' tall; we'll have to put a stone on your head, young lady ... And the two grand young friends you have. God bless them.'

I saw her eyes take in Cissie's left hand, anxious eyes despite her chatter.

'Who was that?' I asked Cissie when Mary had left on her bicycle and the patient was a grey outline on the dark road.

'You mean the patient - oh, just poor Mrs Hennigan. They live in a cottage down the road; her husband works for the Fitzallens. They have eleven children.'

As we came back through the hall I noticed that the study door was open and heard Dr O'Shaughnessy saying to his wife who was standing in the doorway, 'Poor woman ... She may lose the hand. Why didn't she come to see me before now? I've lanced it, but that's only a stop gap. She got a splinter under her nail and ... ' He shook his head.

I tripped over the half-throttled Teddy. Mrs O'Shaughnessy looked over at us. 'Where is Barbie? Tell her to take that thing out of the hall.'

'Barbie,' Cissie yelled. 'Get rid of your blasted victim. Peg nearly broke her neck.'

Barbie emerged from the kitchen, a smear of chocolate around her mouth, her twin at her heels. 'But that's the best place for hanging,' she told her mother, indicating the end of the string which was wound around the bannister at the return of the stairs.

'Have you been eating the mousse?' Cissie demanded furiously and was answered by a red-faced Nellie who came storming out of the kitchen.

'I can't turn me back, ma'am. I was in the pantry for a minute and when I came out there were holes in tomorrow's dessert.'

'You little rats!' Cissie hissed at the twins and Barbie glanced guiltily at her mother, picked up her Teddy and ran upstairs; then she furiously untied the knot at the bannisters, while David made faces down at us.

Cissie came to stay with us for most of August that year. Things were worse than ever in the countryside, because of the economic war. Our farm was not as badly affected as were others, for Tom was doing well with the horse breeding and trading and there was a demand for his animals which was not dependent on the British market. But still I knew that things were very tight and that my mother was making do in lots of ways to put the money aside for my school fees.

Mary had been invited to stay with us as well, but she had also received an invitation from her aunt who lived in Sandymount in Dublin and the city had won.

'I'm off to the metropolis, my pets, where I shall map out the lie of the land.'

'You make it sound like some sort of reconnaissance,' Cissie said. Mary laughed.

'Exactly. I must familiarise myself with the scene of my future triumphs.'

Mary tended more and more to the dramatic, appropriate enough for someone who wanted to become a famous actress someday.

'Why do you want to be an actress?' I had asked her once. Her reply had been unusually quiet and considered. 'It's not really that I want to act; but I need to do things that have meaning; I would like to do something wonderful and dangerous, something that would really matter, but this is not possible, so I can pretend instead.'

I was afraid that Cissie would find the farm boring after all the excitement of Ballyharris, but she seemed to like it and to feel at home. Tom and I picked her up with the trap at the station and she was no sooner in the place than she was off out the back to see the mares, Tom hardly able to

75

keep up with her. He had her up on one of them in a minute and the two of them lumbered off, bareback, around the pasture. I worried for her because she was so fragile in comparison with those seventeen hand horses, but she rode with the devotion of the obsessed and returned flushed and laughing.

'You should try it Peg - I can't understand why you haven't.'

'I was cured of bareback riding at a tender age.'

'What happened?'

'Tom put me up in front of him and trotted off - nearly killed me.'

Cissie looked severely at Tom.

'The mare was old,' he explained. 'All spine. Peg could be heard in the next parish. Grand pair of lungs.'

I laughed. 'And then I had a fright about a year ago - with some tinker horses.'

'What happened?'

'Nothing much, just a fright,' and I saw in my mind's eye the skewbald ponies bearing down on me.

'Come up with me,' Cissie said, patting the mare and scowling at Tom who smiled with delight. 'Lila here is very good and a lovely ride.'

The mare looked down at me, huffing indifferently.

'Come on,' Cissie insisted, walking Lila towards the boulder which Tom used as a mounting block. 'It's the best way to learn - without a saddle; it'll give you a good seat.'

'I like my seat the way it is,' I protested, but to please her I got up on the boulder, hitched up my loose cotton skirt and mounted behind her.

'Now hold on to me,' she said and started to walk Lila around. I put my arms around Cissie's waist and held on; she felt slender and strong and when I looked down at Tom I saw that his smile had become fixed and I knew immediately that he envied me, that he would have given much to have sat there with his arms around that waist.

The upshot of this episode was that Tom bought two second-hand saddles and Cissie and I went riding on the two big mares almost every day. Tom came with us for the first day or two but then felt we were safe enough on our own.

We met Paddy Stapleton on one of our rides. He was cycling down the boreen towards our house and when he saw us approaching he dismounted and waited.

'Hello Paddy,' I called. We reined in the horses and I introduced Cissie. He put up his hand to take hers. His face looked strained.

'Is everything alright, Paddy?' I asked.

He glanced from Cissie to me and reddened a little. 'C..c..can I have a word with you, Peg?' He glanced at Cissie again. - 'In private, if you d..d..don't mind.' He took his cap off as he said this and wrung it in embarrassed fashion. He had grown a lot. He was tall now with a shadow on his upper lip, and a face resolute and strong beyond his years.

I looked at Cissie who simply dug Lila in the ribs and trotted away up the road.

'What is it, Paddy?' I asked loftily from my perch on Peg's broad back.

'D..d..did Tom tell you that I'm going to America?'

I nodded. Tom had mentioned it some days earlier, but I had taken little notice. 'He told me you were going out to an uncle in Chicago or somewhere.'

'I'm going to w..w..work hard and make my fortune,' Paddy continued in a rush. 'And then I'll c..c..come back for you, Peg, if you'll h..h..have me.'

I stared at him, thinking he was joking. Somewhere inside me I was giggling. 'Go away out of that!' I said, 'and don't be making a hare of me.'

He looked as though he was about to continue but then changed his mind, smiled at me a little sadly and said in a bantering voice, 'I'll come back for you one way or another - see if I don't.'

He got on his bicycle and pedalled off.

'Good luck in America, Paddy,' I called after him, suddenly touched by something like premonition. 'And don't forget the diamonds you promised me!'

He raised his hand in acknowledgement but didn't look back.

'What was that all about?' Cissie asked when I had caught up with her. She was around the next bend, lying back on Lila's broad rump, sunning herself, while the mare was wrenching mouthfuls of grass from the 'long acre.'

'Just a proposal of marriage,' I said, and laughed with the relief of being able to do so.

Cissie sat up in the saddle and widened her eyes. 'You're not serious?'

'He was joking,' I said. 'He really wanted to say goodbye.'

On the second week of Cissie's stay the weather changed. The heavens opened and we were visited with thunder, lightning and bucketing rain. We sat in the parlour playing cards and talking. Cissie sat on a stool near the hearth, her dark hair shining in the firelight and I saw how

Tom turned to her on every possible pretext and laughed inordinately at her jokes.

'Did you hear the one about the lunatic who had the beetles?' she asked. This dreadful narrative concerned an inmate of a mad house who thought his pet beetles went deaf when he tore their legs off. I groaned, having heard the story many times at school. Tom howled with laughter. Mam laughed too, more at Cissie and Tom than at the joke.

Next day we were glad to get out of the house. Tom saddled Lila and Peg for us. We went down near the Garryogue which was in spate and tearing thunderously along with branches and other debris. Joe Clancy, a little bit taller than I remembered him, was fishing on the old bridge and I could see, even from a distance, that some more of the stones had been washed away. That bridge has been unsafe since the Troubles and had been losing stones every year since.

I felt a kind of paralysed fear for the boy, afraid to move in case I distracted him, swaying backwards and forwards as he cast his line, pushing against a piece of the parapet that stood out like a broken tooth while the river rushed below him. A salmon rose, the boy jerked the rod, and placed a foot on the stone which suddenly gave, toppling him into the river.

It all happened so suddenly - the boy and the stone falling, the river sweeping him down towards us as he flailed and struggled. I thought of the 'Holy Terror' his father, and what this would do to him; his Joe, the apple of his eye to be lost in a needless tragedy in the Garryogue. I screamed at the boy to swim towards the rocks but he couldn't hear anything above the roar of the water and then Cissie was out in the river on Lila.

I held my breath. Cissie could not swim. If she was swept into that river nothing could save her. Her face was white but she urged Lila straight into the boy's path. The mare was working against the current, stumbling. It could not last.

Cissie shouted at Joe, leaned down to take his outstretched hand and would have been swept off the mare but for her firm grip on the mane. She was now drenched to the waist.

Not wishing to be outdone and terrified for both of them I urged Meg into the water but while she took a few steps forward she stubbornly refused to enter the river, despite my kicking. So I sat and watched from her broad back, impotent and useless.

The boy had the sense to grasp Cissie's boot, and Lila, urged by Cissie, turned around and made for the bank. I heard a shout behind me and turned to see Tom riding towards us, just in time to haul the boy peremptorily to safety. Tom wrapped his jacket around him and lifted him on to his horse. He trotted off to the boy's home, one strong arm holding Joe who was now weeping with shock, relief and the humiliation of having been rescued.

'You could have been drowned,' Tom shouted at Cissie when he came back to the house. 'In a river like that!' His face was red and angry. 'And Lila due to foal soon. That brat had been warned a hundred times about the bridge.'

Cissie let him rage. She sat, wrapped in an old warm dressing-gown, by the range, sipping the hot milk my mother had made for her.

'Lila is strong,' she said in a stern voice which I had never heard before, 'and none of us, including you, were free to stand by and let him die.'

The spleen died in Tom; he said nothing but his eyes told me everything.

The following day Mr Clancy arrived, with young Joe in tow, to personally thank the girl who had saved his son's life.

'I had given him the rod for his birthday,' he said gruffly, his voice suddenly breaking. 'But divil a rod he'll get again, unless it's across his backside. You are the bravest young lady in the world.'

Joe looked sheepish and Cissie smiled and blushed with embarrassment and kept her left hand in her pocket. And I watched with new sympathy and understanding the teacher of whom I had been so terrified brusquely wiping the wetness from his face with the palm of his hand.

Chapter 4

The years passed - two years to the Intermediate Examination and then the Leaving and Matriculation two years after that. They crawled, those years, picking up momentum only towards the end.

In the interim I spent a week or so every summer in Ballyharris and Cissie and Mary would visit me for a similar period. My mother always made a fuss when they were coming, cleaning and distempering. 'You'd think it was the Queen of Sheba that was coming,' I'd mutter to myself, annoyed at the work when all I wanted was to escape out of doors if it was sunny, or immerse myself in a good book if it was not.

Initially Paddy wrote to me every few months. 'Don't forget me, Peg,' he would say at the end of his letters. 'I'll be back someday. And I won't forget the diamonds!' He talked of how much he was learning in the Kaiser yards, new techniques, prefabrication. America was leaping out of recession and fortunes were to be made by anyone who could keep up with this new progress.

I replied to these letters only sporadically. Paddy was gone; I felt sorry for him and the life of drudgery I imagined to be his lot in America. I was consumed by the challenges facing me, the prospect of a future which would bend to my will. I would meet Niamh Houlihan from time to time; she was still working in Percival's and seemed sunny as always, although I pitied her, stuck in a dead-end job like that, her life out of her control. She avoided me when Cissie and Mary came to stay and was shy with them when they bought sweets from her across the counter.

Mary sat the Leaving with a sort of bravado. She didn't want to be called to teacher training - which her father had wanted for her; she wanted to become an actress. And she wanted to learn French - 'French as she is spoke, dear girl, not the Galway variety!'

'What earthly use is French?' I had asked.

'Don't be such a philistine ... you're not sophisticated unless you know French.'

'Why do you want to be sophisticated?'

Mary sighed and pursed her mouth.

'I suppose it has to do with power,' she said candidly after a moment. 'And don't ask why I want power. Everyone needs it, including you.'

It was arranged through contacts the nuns had in France that Mary would go to a convent in Paris for the following year; she would teach English to the younger pupils and stay in the convent. I think she had half promised her father that if he let her have a year in France she would come home and go to college. But events, once precipitated, have a momentum of their own.

It was 1937. Mary was eighteen now and Cissie and I would be eighteen in a matter of months. Cissie had fulfilled the promise of her childhood and grown to be beautiful, not the chocolate box variety, but the living beauty of an intense and private soul. She possessed the charm of the authentic; she was genuine, self possessed, but in repose her eyes had the focus of one who is not part of the calculating present but has other perspectives. As always, she kept her left hand in a little black or grey glove, but didn't hide it

83

anymore. In school no one noticed it; if you had dark hair you had dark hair and if your left hand was in a glove it was just a personal detail like any other. She was beloved of everyone, the love that accompanies respect.

And as for Mary - she was the green eyed Lorelei, and she radiated repressed energy and impatience. In school she was always in trouble - questioning everything but getting away with murder as though she had a charmed life. Few people saw her moments of doubt and introspection, but Cissie and I did, sensing in her a core of insecurity, some sort of anxiety which she hid under her flippancy. She liked to wear masks.

The day came when we left St Catherine's for the last time, a lovely June day in 1937 when the white candles on the chestnut trees were being replaced by small green fruit and the camogie pitch, which had been turned into grass courts for the summer term, was bereft, the nets hitched up. I looked around me before I left, imagining the shouts of Miss Greely our games mistress, the summer voices on the now deserted tennis courts and the distant cries of girls playing rounders, like ghosts in the breeze.

Tom did not call for me; he had a crisis with one of the mares and my mother was ill into the bargain, so he sent a wire and the O'Shaughnessys kindly left me, trunk and all, to the station. It was strange saying goodbye to my schooldays, saying goodbye to the nuns, looking back at the tiled hallway, at the statue of St Michael and the Serpent, the Italian ceiling with its lovely plasterwork, and knowing that I would never stand there again as a young girl in a gymslip, knowing that the future I had once glimpsed at the end of a seemingly interminable tunnel was now upon me.

Tom met me at Ballycloghan and I instantly asked him about Mam; she hadn't written for several weeks. I had a cold feeling in my heart about her which overshadowed the momentous nature of the day.

'Not the best, Peg,' he said, quietly. I tried to read his face, but I questioned him no further; I was too full of fear. He was suspiciously quiet and gentle and didn't tease or insult me once on the journey home, confining his comments to the pony - 'H'up there' and 'Whoa' as we turned in the gate. The pony flicked his tail at the flies and I saw the dust in his coat and the sweat at the edge of the harness and all around us the countryside smiling with honeysuckle, dog roses and the burning yellow of the gorse.

I was shocked by the way my mother had failed in the space of six weeks. I had not seen her during the term and now the lines of her face were haggard and her eyes had lost their joie de vivre; their perspective had become internal, a sort of private stock-taking. Whether she knew the full story or not at that point I cannot say, but she used to talk of what we would do when she was well again, how we would go on a holiday together, all three of us, before I set off for the University in the autumn. Then again, she would talk of her death and she gave me her few pieces of jewellery - her gold pin brooch and the gold watch Tom had bought her as a birthday present. 'I won't need them where I'm going,' she said with a small laugh. Her eyes would linger on me hungrily, thoughtfully, as though her mind was full of things she could not say.

85

She had had a breast lump for a couple of years and had ignored it, although she had mentioned it to me once with a disparaging grimace. I know now that she had really been looking for support and advice. What did I know of lumps? But my mother's lump was cancerous and it was killing her because I hadn't insisted that she go to the doctor.

It invaded her and although they operated a few weeks later, it was too late. She faded, shrivelled, and left the kitchen, the house and the farm to emptiness and desolation. We sat with her, spent with grief, all the terrible night of her dying, as she laboured for breath and spoke to us of the care we should have for each other, and never, for an instant, evinced either doubt or fear or concern for herself.

The discovery that the living focus of my life had been my mother's face and that I would never see it again, consumed me with anguish. I had never dreamed such pain existed; I could not escape it and did not know how to endure it.

I was due to go to UCG in October but now I no longer wanted to go; nothing seemed to matter. Tom and I clung together for comfort; he went about the work of the farm like an automaton and spent most of the spare time of the evening in the kitchen with me, not saying much, pretending to read a paper and talking in short isolated bursts. And then again we would talk about Mam at length, long into the night, consolidating memories.

It was during that awful time that Tom came back one evening with a little savaged kitten - a tabby - which he had found on the road. It was half dead, blood matted in the fur, but still breathing. We speculated on what had happened to it. Had its attacker been a dog or a fox? I disinfected its wounds, settled it down in a biscuit tin by the range with an old jumper for a mattress and fed it drops of warm milk on a constant basis. I called it Tiddles. The efforts to restore the bloom of its small life helped in a marginal way to blunt the anguish of my bereavement. I hated death. I willed the little thing to live.

I got another letter from Paddy Stapleton telling me about his life in America. He had not written for almost a year and I thought he had forgotten me. Business was booming, he said. He had managed to form his own company, not in building, but in something called 'Logistics' - supply and demand. The Kaiser yards had begun to get a lot of army and navy contracts and Paddy was supplying both. It seemed incredibly simple. He located what they wanted and collected a commission; he was using his money to stockpile surplus and metal scrap for what he called 'The Big Day.' He believed that if there was war in Europe America would fight in it. He would like to come back to see me - but not until he had made his killing! He supposed I had left school now.

I answered his letter and told him that my mother had died and that I was going to UCG to become a scientist. I thought this might put him off me, but he was delighted, writing back a gentle letter of condolence, and then telling me of people in Germany - the Krupps and Bayers who had risen from nothing because they had applied science to industry. He said I should study metals; new alloys were making people's fortunes.

I had not seen him for four years and found it difficult to imagine him. Whenever I thought of him I saw the face of the boy who had stopped me on the road and said he would come back for me, saw the strong pinched face and the determined mouth. Four years would have changed that boy into a young man; what did he look like now? But I wondered why he felt he had to impress me, sure that his exercise in 'Logistics' couldn't be that much to write home about. How could he be supplying army and navy?

I was unsettled. I cleaned the house feverishly one day, baked like fury, and sat listlessly by the range the next. I knew that Tom dreaded me going away; in a way the strong, brusque Tom, had become like a child; I had become the mother surrogate, the place where he could warm his soul.

I told him I would stay at home and not go to college and he became angry and said I was doing nothing of the sort. 'You're off to Galway this October, my girl. Like it or not.'

Then, after the Leaving and Matriculation results came out, Cisssie came to stay. She had come with Mary at the end of June for my mother's funeral but when I had declined invitations to return with them to Ballyharris, they had left, sensing the need Tom and I had for no company other than our own. The Leaving results were disappointing for me - two honours - maths and English. My own fault. Cissie had got six honours and Mary had failed maths and scraped everything else except English and French where she had scored highly.

Now Cissie told Tom that she was going to take me home with her to Ballyharris - for a rest; would he be alright by himself? Tom said he'd be absolutely fine; did she think he was a child? and the small moustache he had taken to wearing bristled and he smiled at her with his eyes on fire.

Cissie put out her hand and pushed him playfully and didn't even notice that she had used her crippled hand. But Tom did and smiled.

I went back to Ballyharris with Cissie. On the following day, while out cycling with her and Mary, we met Brian Fitzallen. He came by the lane, on horseback, taking a shortcut to Gogarty's shop. He sat a horse well, shoulders straight, heels down. We stopped to let him pass and he smiled at us diffidently. As he exchanged badinage with Mary I saw that his profile was beautiful. I shyly met his eyes, but I don't think he really saw any of us.

'He's actually a better horseman than any of them,' Cissie confided to us later, when we were sitting by the lake eating our picnic of ham sandwiches and lemonade, and watching the reflected shadows in the water.

'You should have seen him this year at the gymkhanas - he cleaned up most of the prizes!'

'Bet that didn't suit the Two Uglies' Mary said.

Cissie looked at her in perplexity for a moment.

'Two uglies? You mean Harry and Peter?'

Mary chuckled, nodding. 'The Two Ugly Sisters! Brian is Buttons - they give him hell - so who is Cinders?'

'Oh I suppose that post can be filled: they could advertise,' I joked weakly.

'What's ugly about ... Peter?' Cissie demanded, reddening.

'Well, he's arrogant, snobbish, dismissive and rude,' Mary said.

I agreed in silence; I was still smarting. I had met him the day before in Gogarty's and had greeted him, to be rewarded with such condescension that I had felt withered.

'He's never done anything to you.'

Mary sighed.

'You're too googly-eyed about that man to notice his little inperfections, she murmured.

Cissie flushed. She was silent for a moment. She flicked a horsefly from her tanned forearm.

'And I suppose the same doesn't go for Brian Fitz?' she said, giving me a sly look.

'Oh 'tis herself has the soft spot for Brian Fitz,' Mary said knowingly. 'Didn't you see the way she looked at him a few minutes ago?'

'And the look he nearly gave her,' Cissie added. 'If he looked at any of us it was at her!'

'How would you like to be Cinders?' Mary asked archly. 'Think of the glowing possibilites; bed, board and the condescension of your betters.'

It was my turn to blush, irritated at the constant verbal attrition which was Mary's stock in trade.

'Jesus, Mary, would you ever shut up!'

She raised her hands, acknowledging reproof, dropping her head and looking up at me in mock contrition.

'And he's going to UCG too next month,' Cissie said.

'Go on!' I was genuinely surprised.

'I'm serious. He wants to study Archeology.'

'Why should he be bothered.- Isn't he getting Glenallen?'

Cissie had told me this once, on the basis that Peter was gone to Dublin and Harry was 'only a girl'.

Now she shook her head. 'Things aren't so good in Glenallen anymore or so Dad was saying. The economic war has hit them too. And Brian was always interested in ruins. He wrote a few articles for *The Chronicle* on the ruins hereabouts. And he also wrote an article on Knockshee, but they wouldn't publish it. Anyway, ask him yourself whether he's going to College.'

'Why wouldn't they publish his article?' I asked.

She shrugged. 'Don't know. Maybe because it wouldn't have been lucky!'

A breeze got up, shivered across the lake. It had the feel of rain. I looked up at the mountain, now sombre and brooding, and it seemed to me that it was waiting, watchful.

'I hate that mountain,' I muttered. 'It's almost like a living presence and I know that's ridiculous.'

There was silence.

'It gets fog bound very suddenly. People have got lost and drowned in the high bog,' Mary said. It has a long history - Knockshee, the fairy mountain. No one hereabouts will go near it.'

'Why not?'

'It's supposed to be haunted. There's an old passage grave inside it. No one grazes on it - except the Fitzallens.'

I scrutinised Knockshee. Right enough there was no sign of sheep - which might have been expected; nothing grazed on it except some horses in the lower slopes.

'Why?'

She shrugged. 'Bad luck, or so they say. But the Fitzallens are above such superstition - even though two German hikers went missing on it five years ago and were never found.'

I felt cold. I saw Cissie look down at her crippled hand, saw the angle of her face, the bitter resignation. We became very quiet, gathered up the rug and found our bicycles.

As we cycled home I asked Mary, who was leaving for Paris the following day if she was nervous.

'I'm a nervous wreck!'

'What will you do when the year is up?' I asked. 'Will you come back and go to college?'

She shook her head. 'I can't. I have neither Maths nor Latin. Anyway I want to act. I want to live.'

'One can live even if one goes to college.'

She turned to me, smiling, innocent, wilful.

'With me nose stuck in a book. Doing everything like a good girl!'

'You mean you want to be a bad girl?' Cissie teased.

Mary shrugged, her face serious.

'I want to be allowed to be myself' I do not want to spend my life as a looker on.'

It began to rain and we parted with a sort of sad levity. 'Where shall we three meet again - in thunder, lightning, or in rain?' Cissie intoned lugubriously and I said that if we met in Ireland the rain could be ar-rain-ged anyway and Mary said my puns were pathetic, but embraced me fiercely as she said goodbye.

We waved to her, Cissie and I, standing there beside our bicycles in the drizzling dusk, and she turned her head at the bend in the road, waved back and was gone.

I did ask Brian Fitzallen about his going to college. I met him next day. I had gone out cycling on my own in an effort to cope with the black depression which had descended upon me and which I ascribed to the parting with Mary and apprehension about the future. Cissie had gone with her father to help with some paperwork in the surgery.

I felt alone, a loneliness of the spirit that did not yield to logic; I needed my mother. I went down to the lake, to the old picnic spot by the oak tree and dismounted. As I sat there watching the water the grief came like a sudden storm and I put my head in my hands and cried until I trembled with exhaustion.

'Mam, Mam,' I heard myself whispering, 'Oh Mam darling, how can I live without you?' I was seventeen and filled with the death wish of the immortal. 'I have lived long enough,' I told myself. I considered the still water with morbid speculation, aware that hidden beneath its limpid innocence was the drowning weed - flowers for Ophelia, for me. I was unaware that I had company.

I didn't know Brian was there until I felt the arms around me. 'Cissie told me. I'm so sorry, Peg.'

He held me, rocked me silently. It did not seem strange that he should do so. He represented warmth and understanding in that moment, compassion, someone who understood suffering. I felt his tweed jacket against the back of my hand and the shaven texture of his chin against my hair and, for the first time, the taste of his breath. I said nothing at all, but we stayed like that for what seemed a long time, although in reality it was probably just one or two minutes.

I asked him later, as we desultorily threw pebbles and twigs into the lake, was it true that he was going to UCG and he confirmed what Cissie had told me.

'I thought you would be staying at home, looking after Glenallen.'

He shrugged, his mouth tensed. 'Glenallen may take my life, but this is for myself.'

'But why archeology? I always thought you'd have to go to Egypt for that,'

'Peg, there were ruins here before the pyramids were built.'

'I heard you wrote an article on Knockshee but it wasn't published.'

'It wasn't about Knockshee. It was about a souterrain that runs into it. There is a stone with Ogham script at the entrance and the same message is carved in Irish on a Celtic Cross in the graveyard. Local tradition has it that both were written when St Patrick converted the area. The bishop ordered *The Chronicle* to suppress it when I pointed out that the Ogham was pre-christian!'

I looked at him. 'Go on! The bishop wouldn't give a damn!'

He smiled. 'Not normally perhaps. But he did in this case!'

'What is the message?'

'*I know mine and mine know me.*'

'But that's in the Bible!'

'I know, but that message was notched into the rock before the New Testament was written.'

I was silent. The bishop did not want the faithful to know that words of power from the New Testament were inscribed into a pre-christian stone at the foot of Knockshee.

'Can I see it?'

'The cross yes. But the entrance to the souterrain was buried in a rockfall some years ago, some time after archeologists had been investigating it.'

He spoke with authority and passion; no sign of his usual diffidence. Now he looked at me, stopped abruptly and smiled. 'This is my hobby horse. Am I boring you?'

'No.'

Cissie and I settled down to life in Galway. We had digs in Salthill. It was an exciting Autumn for us, grown up now, by our own standards at least, and in charge of our own destinies. There was no Mother Mercy to supervise or pester us.

There was an air of relaxed academia about the College; all the students knew each other and the social life went on endlessly, with dances in the aula, parties, boating on the Corrib.

During my first week I went to see Uncle Matt. He had not come to my mother's funeral and had sent a letter of condolence, excusing himself that 'the leg was bad.' 'Scrooge' my mother had called him, because he had avoided any suggestion that he might contribute to the expense of my education. She had hoped he might, but in vain.

Now he brought me into his fusty parlour for a brief moment. The picture of the girl with the geese was still over the mantelpiece. The piles of newspapers had grown and the place had the tired smell of old papers and dust. The leg was bad alright, some sort of circulatory problem, because he muttered about damn doctors telling him he should consider amputation. He hobbled around and was as abrupt as ever.

'So you're a University student now. Well, well, Miss. Do you know what Robert Burns said about those people?' And he reached for a dog-eared old volume on the mantelpiece.

I shook my head and found a hundred reasons why I had to go, but he had already found the page.

'A pack of self conceited hashes,
Confuse their brains in college classes,
They go in stirks and come out asses
Plain truth to speak,
And then they think to climb Parnassus

By dint of Greek.'

He smiled triumphantly. 'Do you know what a 'stirk' is, Miss? It's a bullock! But sure he was writing in the days before they let little lassies like yourself into the universities.'

I was glad I hadn't brought Cissie with me.

'I have to go, Uncle. I have a lecture.'

'Well, 'tis a queer world, Miss. And your brother at home doing the work. He calls to see me when he's in Galway. A fine lump of a man!'

He handed me a penny bar and I escaped, coining insulting ditties in my head like, 'Oh Ebeneezer you're a geezer' and making myself laugh in the street.

'Miss Donlon, Miss Donlon,' the zoology demonstrator said one day, 'Will you please contain yourself.' He looked at me over his glasses, sarcasm at the ready, the unspoken comment about females taking science hanging in the air. The lab was cold, full of varnished benches, high stools, wooden cupboards, engraved glass jars, specimen plates, chipped white sinks, the odour of formalin. We were dissecting dogfish.

'A right sour-smelling yoke,' Jarlath Quinn muttered and for a moment I thought he was referring to our demonstrator. Jarlath was beside me, slicing with distaste. We were both laughing, lips pursed, eyes downcast. My initial revulsion for dissection had left me, and I was no longer sick from the stench of formalin, the guts spilling on to the dissection board, the worms from the stomach and the underlying sweet taint of corruption from the liquefying nervous system.

But it was not Jarlath's asides that had made me giddy that afternoon. It was the meeting with

Brian, the lunch in Lydons, the chat over roast beef and boiled potatoes. I had bumped into him in the quad at lunch time as I went to fetch my bike and go back to the digs. For years we had known each other from a friendly distance. Now, since the day by the lake, the sight of him was enough to paralyse me with shyness. It seemed to me, looking back on it, that we had established some kind of tacit understanding and yet I so seldom saw him that this seemed absurd.

'Hello Peg.'

'Hello Brian'.

'Are you in a hurry? Will you have lunch on me?' He grinned. 'Well, on a table actually!'

He asked it with his shy smile. He was awkward with witticisms.

The blush flooded to my hairline. I hated it venomously; I willed it away; it burned spitefully.

'Thanks.'

'How are you anyway, Peg?' he asked when we were seated upstairs in Lydons and had placed our orders. 'You seem well settled. Everytime I see you, you seem to be dashing somewhere!'

Lydons smelled of soup, roast meat and onions. Outside, the October day was grey and leaden. I wished I was wearing something other than the shapeless grey jumper with the fairisle design, which Niamh had knitted for me as a 'going to college present', cycling over on the eve of my departure with it wrapped in brown paper.

'I'm fine. The digs are alright. '

He was not really listening. He was simply looking at me, smiling from time to time.

'And you?' I asked, desperate for him to take over the conversation.

'Well, you know how I like archeology! I'm doing English as well.'

Silence. His eyes dwelt on me with open warmth. He was at home with silence. He gave me the feeling that he belonged in some different time and space to which he might disappear any moment.

'You like that? I'm sure it must be hard with such a lot of reading.' Shut up Peg, for Gods sake, I told myself.

He smiled. 'I like it very much. But I already know most of what we've done so far in archeology.'

'What will you do afterwards?'

He shrugged.

'Teach perhaps. Or maybe the Civil Service if they'll have me. Foreign Affairs or maybe the Board of Works.'

'When you get your degree do you think the bishop will let you publish your article on the souterrain you were telling me about?' I asked.

'No. The souterrain is really a passage grave and they're still afraid of it.'

I studied him as he ate. He had a handsome open face, although the nose was off-centre. His brown hair was parted above the right temple; he had a tic - a shiver of a tiny muscle in his lower eyelid - from reading too much? His eyes were grey-blue and focussed on me with both interest and detachment. His eyebrows and eyelashes were darker than his hair. His mouth had a quirk at one corner. On his chin he had a shaving cut which was healing. His clothes were warm, well cut tweed jacket with a shirt, tie and pullover.

'But what about Glenallen?' I asked tentatively after a moment. 'I always imagined you as a gentleman farmer.'

The humour left his lips. His eyes were expressionless. 'Glenallen? But there's Peter and Harry as well, you know.'

'But Peter is a barrister - he has a career. And Harry is ... I was going to say 'a woman' and checked myself. I assumed she would get married and clear off elsewhere. Women did not matter in rural Ireland. Land was more valuable than life; land belonged to men and they made sure it stayed that way.

He changed the subject and asked me about myself then. I told him about Ballycloghan and Tom and the mares and he became immediately animated, inquiring about the animals and the number of foals and a host of questions I was ill-equipped to answer. I had never taken too much heed of what Tom was doing and kept away from the horses. But I could see how Brian loved them, how his face lit up when he talked of anything to do with horses.

'Maybe I will meet your brother sometime,' he said and I said he was bound to if he went to the fairs.

I watched him all the time, ready, because I was young and hungry to live, to fit him to my private fantasy, to make of him something larger and greater than life. He was different from any other boy I had met; he gave the impression of being immune to the perspectives of his peers, as though he were a lot older than they, but without, at the same time, possessing any of their cynicism. And because he projected mystery, the sense that he was special, I was filled with desire to make him want me. He had an instant, incisive approach to anything of an intellectual nature, was widely read, urbane one moment and awkwardly shy the next. Most of all, perhaps, I

99

was caught by his vulnerability. This was evident in sudden unexpected moments when he betrayed a lack of confidence where I would have expected certainty, sudden sensitivities unusual in a man. My instinct was to fling myself into whatever breach existed, in his street wisdom, to protect him. And lastly, and more importantly than I would ever have admitted, there was desire. He was terribly attractive sexually, a combination of vibrant masculinity and innocence.

As we left and he helped me on with my coat he looked down at me:

'The fairy princess of where is it? ... Bally-cloghan? And I felt fragile as thistle-down, fairisle jumper or not.

'I'm nearly as tall as you are.' I stood on my toes and he laughed. As we went downstairs he took my hand for a moment in his own.

The hailstones started as we went back to the college and we ran, faces stinging, hair full of tiny melting ice balls.

What was it like to be eighteen and in love? Can I even remember the quality of the ecstasy, the stuffed chambers of the heart, the make believe? The vista of the future, stretching into the mysterious life-that-is-to-come? I know only that it was; its turmoil is gone forever.

'Will you come to the pictures?' he asked as we parted.

'Anna Karenina' was on at the Savoy. I said yes and went to my practical, slipping on the melting hailstones, my heart singing.

For a while we saw each other frequently. We went to debates in the Greek hall together. He came to watch me play camogie down in the

'Swamp'. Later, when the summer came, he would take me boating on the Corrib to visit Menlow Castle. And always I felt with him the sense of the ephemeral, as though he were some sort of manifestation from a more elegant and innocent dimension, who would vanish and leave me forever yearning and unfulfilled. He had a knack of touching me to the quick and then he would be at one remove again, out of range and somehow out of touch with reality. And because of all this he was a challenge of formidable proportions.

He was the last person I wanted to witness my humiliation when, cycling around a corner near Francis Street, I met a donkey and cart approaching on the wrong side of the road and ended up stuck between the shaft and the donkey. Cissie and I had been cycling along, minding our own business and next thing I was catapulted into the shafts of a donkey and cart. I can still smell the donkey, see the dust on his coat, his flattened ears, his bared yellow teeth. Cissie, who was behind me, braked furiously, dismounted and, instead of coming to help me, sat on the kerb, quite useless with laughter. The driver, a wizened little prune with a peaked cap and a nose like a potato, pulled up the donkey, sighed loudly - 'Ye oinseach' - and folded his arms, quite content to sit back and let me extricate myself.

From his perch in the cart he looked around at the other people in the street, with the air of a poor man patient in the face of provocation, nodding his head at my efforts to free myself 'An' fellas marry them,' he complained loudly to the passers-by.

Brian appeared with Jimmy Delahunty on the opposite side of the street and ran to help me.

101

They helped me extricate myself and my bicycle while preventing the donkey from biting me.

They took us to The Magnet for coffee. Brian had managed to restrain his mirth, although his hand shook when he gripped mine and he had to clench his teeth when he asked if I was alright. 'Of course I'm alright,' I said indignantly. 'I'm just furious!' and then he laughed loudly.

'A fat lot of good you were,' I told Cissie.

'It's your own fault. You can't expect people to rescue you when they can't move for laughing.'

Cissie inspired protectiveness among the boys. After the day we had coffee together Jimmy Delahunty pursued her relentlessly, but although she joked with him and sometimes let him accompany her home when I wasn't with her, she refused all his other invitations. Maybe she too had caught the lugubrious expression of compassion which crossed his face whenever he glanced at her left hand.

Sometimes, when we could afford it, she and I had tea in Lydons, an exercise which always reminded me of my mother and the time she had taken us there and, latterly, of Brian and our lunch together on the day of the hailstones. But after the Day of the Donkey, as Cissie called it, I didn't see much of him.

Later I learnt that he was seeing someone from his own class and I was too busy pretending that I was not jealous to apply myself to anything.

Half way through the term I met Brian at a dance in the aula. He was standing, talking to the O'Hagan sisters at the other side of the hall.

'There's your knight,' Cissie whispered in my ear. I looked across at him glumly. Some knight! He was laughing, moving his hands to emphasise a point and Kathie O'Hagan was gazing up at him with those soulful brown eyes. I told myself I didn't care anyway; I knew the girls he was talking to came from well-off families, Galway merchants, and I knew from their general demeanour that they were both out to please, to hook this fish if possible. A young woman of the late twentieth century would say that they were seeking a validator. It was true, it was important to be validated by marriage and a 'good catch'. Young women, not yet twenty, were already afraid - of the shelf, of loneliness, of poverty, of powerlessness, particularly of powerlessness.

Brian took this attention as his due and he seemed to me, staring at him across the room, to be utterly desirable, utterly glamorous and utterly unobtainable.

I was asked to dance then by Jarlath Quinn, someone who could be easily read, easily charmed, someone I found unremarkable by contrast with the fascinating Brian at the other side of the aula. But Jarlath was a good dancer and we did the foxtrot with style and when I looked up I saw Brian watching me. Eventually I retired, breathless, and sought my handkerchief which had fallen out of my sleeve on to the floor.

Brian was beside me in a moment, scooping up the handkerchief and presenting it to me. 'He stoops to conquer,' he murmured. We danced together for the rest of the evening and the O'Hagan sisters who had tried to monopolise him drifted off to dance with other students.

He saw me home, stood on the doorstep and kissed me, suddenly, sweetly, fervently. 'You were the belle of the ball,' he whispered in my ear. 'You're the prettiest girl in college.' And I said, 'Thank you,' and turned and fled, closing the front door behind me, throwing myself into bed in a passion of happiness, embracing the pillow in the darkness.

Tom came to Galway to see me more often than I had anticipated. Whenever there had been a horse fair I could expect his visit in Salthill. I knew that, quite apart from the sales of his own animals, he did a lot of 'on spec' horse dealing, buying and the selling almost immediately. He would come into the digs in a collarless shirt, his pockets bulging, his cloth cap pulled down on his face. I was embarrassed by his dishevelled appearance and told him so. But he just laughed.

'Peg, I can't sell horses if I wear a collar and tie. How could I buy cheap and sell dear? It would be the other way around! And as for the pockets,' he added, surveying them ruefully and then emptying them out on the table, 'that's my float. I have to have money on me in case I see an animal I'm on the look out for.' And I stared at the hundreds of pounds there in a heap on the table.

'Where do you think your college fees come from?' And then he raised his eyebrows, dropped his voice and asked where Cissie was.

'I'm here!' she announced, entering the room, her newly washed hair pulled back with a pair of tortoiseshell combs, laughing as she always did when Tom was around. Her eyes widened as she stared at the table. Tom's expression softened when he saw her, his mouth curving in the way it did for her.

'What would you say to a good feed, the pair of you?'

'Yes, please,' Cissie said primly, 'if you think you can afford it!'

'Sound!' Tom said, laughing, gathering up the money and stuffing it back in his pocket.

I could see that Cissie enjoyed his company; that she was totally relaxed with him. She never tried to hide her hand from him now; she wasn't shy with him. I looked at my brother and tried to see him with her eyes - someone genuine, someone kind. Since our mother's death his face had become older, serious, sensitive.

The farm, he kept telling me, was doing very well now, mostly due of course to the mares; the Economic War was also over - Dev had negotiated a package deal with England and we had a new Constitution. Tom had bought and re-sold over a hundred cobs, mares and ponies that year at a handsome profit and was beginning to get a reputation in the county as the man to go to for a horse. I knew him to be a thrifty and careful farmer, with a sure instinct where his horses were concerned. He seldom lost a foal; now he had acquired a fifth brood mare.

Later on in the term I introduced him to Brian who began talking about horses. He invited all three of us out for dinner (producing a collar and tie from somewhere and putting them on) and spent most of the evening discussing horseflesh, glancing almost reverentially at Cissie from time to time. Cissie enjoyed herself; she sparkled, discussed the ponies they had had at home, while Tom and Brian listened with amused interest.

'Fitzallen is sound,' Tom told me later. 'He certainly knows his business.'

He looked at me consideringly for a moment.

'Do you think he'll marry you?'

'Don't be daft.' I saw the faraway look in his eyes and knew whom he was thinking of.

'What do you fancy are my chances with Cissy?' he asked abruptly after a moment, his eyes full of yearning, an expression so tender that it was hard to believe it was my brother, the scorner of sentiment, I was looking at. What could I tell him? I had seen that self same look in Cissie's eyes often when she spoke of Peter Fitzallen, but I knew she liked Tom, and felt sure that the 'crush' on Peter had to end, that it had no future.

I shrugged.

'I know she likes you, but she's too young to be serious about anyone; she has to get through her exams. '

'Can you see a university graduate marrying me?' he demanded, and I said truthfully there was many a university graduate who couldn't hold a candle to him, that he was as fine a man as I ever saw.

He laughed then, pleased, and pulled a few ribs of my hair playfully.

Christmas came. I went home. The house felt indifferent, impersonal. Tom had gone to some rounds to tidy the place up in anticipation of my arrival, but the furniture was covered with dust and there was a cold dampness in every room except the kitchen. I suspected that he had dispensed with the range while I was away and lived on bread and butter and slabs of bacon. I set about polishing and scrubbing, trying to restore the old sense of home but I was nevertheless filled with resentment that this should have been left there waiting for me. I knew that Tom was prospering; he had bought some more land, about twenty acres adjoining one end of the farm. I told him he needed a housekeeper, that he ought to get married, and he laughed with real mirth and

106

brought me down to the stables to see his latest acquisition and the improvements he had made.

I stood beside him and gazed into the loose boxes at the big, warm, gentle mares, my nostrils full of the smells of horse manure and hay. He introduced me to Pat O'Regan who now worked full-time on the farm, a wiry little man in a peaked cap who took my hand in his tough leathery grasp. 'Pleased to meet you, ma'am!'

'He's very good with horses!' Tom said. 'But I have to watch him; he's fond of the odd drop!'

We had a goose for our Christmas dinner; I had gone to a lot of trouble with it, stuffing it and pricking the breast and basting it as I had seen my mother do. We ate in the parlour. Tom was jovial and preoccupied by turns; he had bought me a gold chain with an amythest pendant for a Christmas present and evinced obvious pleasure at the sight of it around my neck. Occasionally he asked me about Ballyharris and I knew he wanted to hear about Cissie, so I told him what she did during the holidays, and how she hunted in winter; and he became thoughtful again and then said that he was thinking of buying a hunter and that she could use it when she came to visit.

'I've a good bit of money put by now, Peg,' he said with pride after a while, 'despite your attempts to bankrupt me with your fees and your high living.'

'High living! Me?'

We laughed.

'Get married,' I said. 'Niamh Houlihan gave you a great eye this morning at Mass. And there are queues of other girls who would be glad to have you. You're the most eligible bachelor for miles.'

He looked at me for a moment in exasperation.

107

'You know damn well I mean to marry Cissie,' he said quietly after a moment, 'and I'm making sure that I've got something to offer her.'

Then he asked me for the hundreth time what Cissie did during the holidays. And for the hundreth time I told him, secretly anxious.

Some friends of Tom's called after dinner and played cards for a while in the kitchen, drinking whiskey and telling yarns. They tried to include me but I left them and retreated to the parlour and the open turf fire. I stoked it up, re-arranged my cards - one from Cissie, one from Brian, one from Paddy, others from some college friends and from an old nun in school who had taught me drawing and who liked to be remembered.

Mary had written from Paris a couple of weeks earlier, a lovely letter, glamorous with its French stamp, the word 'Irlande' underlined in capitals on the envelope as though by way of reminder that, within the context of some perspectives, our little island was not at the centre of creation, and that there might even be people who would not automatically know the whereabouts of the townland of Ballycloghan in the County of Galway.

Mary said she would be home for Christmas, that she was really getting to grips with French at last and loved Paris. 'It has grace and splendour. I've met a charming man here who is connected with the French Legation in Dublin and apparently has business interests in Ireland - importing wines or something. He may be in Dublin when I get back. He has some contacts in the theatre!'

I kept this letter between the pages of the *The Last of the Mohicans* which I was reading at the time and read it over and over, trying to imagine what Paris was like, what this Frenchman was like, what the convent was like. Mary painted a scenario of the exotic. Even the convent, which seemed stricter than St Catherine's, had a gloss in the recounting that made it magical. 'Paris' I would whisper to myself, letting it linger on the palate. Would I ever get to Paris? I visualised the Frenchman as tall and dark with flashing eyes. But I envied Mary not at all; how could I envy her, when I loved Brian Fitzallen?

Dreaming thus, I sat by the fire in my father's old armchair that Christmas night, longing secretly for the days to pass until I would be off to Ballyharris.

Cissie had asked me for Christmas but that would have left Tom on his own. At the time everyone was talking of the prospect of war and the papers were full of the troubled diplomatic relations between Britain and Germany. Like everyone else I thrilled to the peril of the approaching cataclysm without any real belief in its inevitability.

I went to Ballyharris on 27 December 1937 and was met at the station by Des who shook my hand. 'How are you, Peg?' He explained that Cissie had a cold and was in bed. Cissie indeed had a cold. She was propped up in bed with a red nose and a novel, a woollen bedjacket belonging to her mother tied up with blue ribbons under her chin.

'Isn't this ghastly, Peg? If I'm not better by tomorrow I'll have to miss the party; I won't be fit to be seen!'

'What party?'

'Des is giving it. We've asked everyone. The Fitzallens too, of course.'

'Good,' I said, looking forward to meeting Brian.

'They can't come.'

'Why not?'

She shrugged, reached into the drawer of her little bedside table and threw a piece of paper at me.

'There's the note.' Her voice was full of studied nonchalance.

I opened the missive and read, 'Messrs. Brian and Peter Fitzallen and Miss Harriet Fitzallen regret ... '

'They're having a party themselves on Sunday, or so Mummy's heard on the grapevine,' Cissie went on in the same nonchalant tone.

'And you're not asked?' I whispered.

'No.' She shrugged again. 'They're very grand, you know. I'm only a doctor's daughter.'

I smarted. Cissie had known these people for years. I hated to see her hurt. And I was hurt to the quick myself. If Cissie was only a doctor's daughter where did I fit in? I hated these perspectives which failed to see other people's humanity, or if they did see it, found it valueless. I hated having worthlessness forced upon me; I hated the sense of being measured by some narrow little yardstick.

'Mary's home.' Cissie went on. 'I meant to tell you. She came home on Christmas Eve. She's been over twice. She's in great form and will be here for the party tomorrow.'

Des took me riding the following day. 'To limber you up for the party tonight', was how he put it, but I knew he was trying to cheer me up. Cissie may have said something to him about Brian and me. There was a hunt on, but I was too poor a rider for that and Desmond couldn't hunt that day because of the party preparations.

We went out at about three, just before the light began to fade. In the distance, against the darkening shape of the mountain, I saw stragglers from the hunt returning home. It had begun to rain and I saw Brian and his sister and brother through the bitter drops beating against my face, forcing me to keep my eyes half shut. The reins had become unpleasantly slippery and the steam rose from Banner's neck. They saw us. Harry waved. 'Hello there,' she called and Peter nodded to us in his lordly fashion and they passed us by.

I wondered at the charisma generated by arrogance. There was something hypnotic about people who used presumption to radiate centrality. One wanted to penetrate it, if only to dash it to pieces.

Brian cantered over to us.

'Peg!' He was all smiles. I looked back at him coldly. He was flushed from the hunt and his face was glossy with rain. His pink coat was spattered with lather and mud.

Desmond moved tactfully ahead.

'Why aren't you coming to Cissie's party?' I demanded through the hiss of the downpour.

'What party?'

'Tonight's party.'

He was silent for a moment, trotting beside me. Then he said, 'I take it that we have been invited?'

'Of course.'

'I'm sorry, Peg,' he said slowly. 'Harry must have just sent an answer for all of us. She's an awful boss. We've some boring aunts staying with us who have to be entertained.'

'I see.'

'But I'll come. If I may, for a while.'

111

'Don't incommode yourself. You must have plenty to do preparing for your own celebrations on Sunday!'

Brian raised his eyebrows, then frowned.

'You don't understand, Peg,' he said awkwardly.

'You're right - I think you'd better stay with the aunts.' I felt the rain on my lips. I was cold through and through. I kicked Banner who needed no encouragement, caught up with Des and we headed for home. He raised a hand briefly in Brian's direction and we cantered through the downpour, the horses strong and willful and eager for their warm stable. I was glad to stumble into the house at last and straight into a hot bath.

The party went off well. Cissie attended for a while, then pleaded that she still wasn't fully better and went to bed early. I was introduced to some people and chatted and danced with some friends of Des, watching the door out of the corner of my eye for Mary's arrival, aware of the excitement at the prospect of seeing her again.

She arrived with her father. I hurried to the hall as Des was taking their coats, and embraced her with a lump in my throat. She seemed different somehow, reserved. She was wearing a sheath in blue-green which hugged her figure and picked up the colour of her eyes. Every male eye in the place followed her.

'Tell me about Paris.'

'Oh, it's lovely, Peg, but it's deathly cold in winter. I just had to get home for Christmas.' She looked up at her father and squeezed his arm.

'And how's the French coming along?

'Très bien merci. Maintenant je le trouve très facile.'

I felt that her accent wasn't remotely related to the French we had been taught at school.

Her father smiled at her indulgently and Des drew her into the drawing-room and got them drinks and they chatted with Dr O'Shaughnessy who was full of compliments for Mary. Mrs O'Shaughnessy came over to give her a hug. 'Poor Cissie's still a bit under the weather,' she told her. 'She's gone back to bed.'

We slipped away upstairs then to Cissie's room. Barbie was in the landing in her dressing-gown, staring down through the bannisters at the people moving across the hall. 'I'm old enough for a grown-up party,' she was muttering rebelliously, while she made little paper darts and dropped them into the stairwell.

We found Cissie in bed, reading. Mary hitched up her blue-green dress and sat on the edge of the bed and I lay back on mine and listened as Mary recounted 'for the tenth time' all about her new world, about the French nuns, about the silly mistake she had made when asked at table would she have second helpings - 'Non merci...je suis plein,' which meant, Mary explained to my blank gaze, that she had informed the good ladies that she was pregnant when she merely meant to say she was full.

We laughed heartily. I questioned her then on the Frenchman she had mentioned and she shrugged and said he was an uncle of one of the girls in the school. 'He's ancient, about thirty-two. He has a title. Don't look at me like that, Peg.'

'Is he married?'

'No. Didn't see you in the hunt today, Peg,' she said then, changing the subject. 'Time you gave it a go.'

'You know as well as I do, Mary, that I don't hunt.'

I was aware how Cissie's attention was suddenly concentrated.

'You could try. It would do you good!' Mary persisted.

I sighed.

'I'd come off at the first fence.'

'No, you wouldn't,' Cissie assured me, not for the first time. 'Just hold on tight and let the horse do the work. You're safe enough so long as you don't go over Reilly's Bank.'

'Where's that?' I asked, trying to place it. I had heard of this bank mentioned before but had never been sure of its whereabouts.

'Oh, it's on the boundary between Glenallen and the common. Nobody jumps it since they did the ditch on the far side - it's a death trap now, a drop of twelve feet.'

Why did I feel so suddenly cold?

'Don't worry,' I said, trying to rout the shadow, 'I have every intention of living to be old and troublesome. Has anyone been hurt there?'

'Not seriously. '

'Peter Fitz. made a half-hearted attempt today,' Mary interposed with a disparaging grimace, 'but his horse refused.'

I felt Cissie react, felt how still she became, but Mary went on conversationally, 'I didn't see him here tonight.'

'No,' I said, 'and not for want of asking.'

Mary snorted. She looked at Cissie.

'You're not still sweet on him, are you?'

'I have better things to think about,' Cissie replied.

She changed the subject then; we'd better go back downstairs, she said or Des would say we

114

had ruined his party. So we left her and made our way downstairs, warning Barbie who was still on the landing that anyone who had their eyes put out by paper darts would be looking for her.

'I've used up my paper. I threw the last one at Brain Fitzallen, but it missed him.'

Mary looked at me.

'When did he come?' I asked.

'A minute ago.'

He appeared in the hall as we came downstairs, and came towards us smiling.

'Hello, Mary, Lovely to see you back.' He shook her hand.

'I thought you weren't coming,' I said.

'Why? I was asked, wasn't I?'

He smiled, looking at me innocently. The dance music floated from the dining room.

'Will you dance?'

And suddenly the evening was a glorious success. I danced, drank wine, talked, discovered little pockets of wit I had not known I possessed and caught Mary's surprised eye occasionally.

'I'm sorry about... Harry's regrets note,' he said before he left. 'And I'm sorry I can't ask you and the others to the party on Sunday. It's not really my party. Harry organised it. I'll probably avoid it. I can't stand her friends!'

'Why?'

'Boring as hell! They spend their lives striking attitudes.'

'Does Peter like them?' I asked, thinking of Cissie.

'He adores them. Why wouldn't he? He is the arch attitude striker himself and he loves whatever Harry loves.'

'Like a Siamese twin,' I ventured.

'Exactly. They are joined at the soul and she will do anything to keep it that way.'

I saw Peter and Harriet Fitzallen once more before I left Ballyharris that holiday. They were on the platform when I went to catch the train. Peter was going back to Dublin and Harry was seeing him off. Cissie had come to see me off and we were laughing together over some private joke.

I saw Harry's glance move over us with detached curiosity, fasten on Cissie's left hand for a cold speculative moment and then on to me.

They both turned towards us, smiling, polite. Cissie put her left hand in her pocket.

'Hello there,' Harry said, with her usual bonhomie.

Peter inclined his head smilingly, but his eyes were just as examining as ever, although I thought they stayed on Cissie even longer than usual. I knew my eyes were on him, just as Cissie's were. He had enough presence for ten men, most of it emanating from an attitude so contemptuous that it was breathtaking.

'Peg is going home,' Cissie said. 'New term begins on Monday.'

Harry drew a deep breath through her nose.

'Aren't you the clever things!' she exclaimed. 'I'm far too stupid for college.'

Instantly I felt that college was a dubious place where the lower orders congregated. To be clever, in that way at least, was not an attribute.

Peter turned to Cissie.

'I didn't see you at the last couple of meets.'

'No. I had flu.'

She looked into his eyes and I almost felt the tremor of her heart.

116

The train came puffing in then, lurched, hissing, to a halt; the steam filled the station; I got into a second-class compartment, looked out at the huge hose pipe as the train took on water and at Peter Fitzallen who said goodbye briefly to Cissie and took his own seat in a first-class compartment. Cissie waved to me as the train pulled out, and I sat back in the carriage and wondered what Peter and Harriet Fitzallen possessed that affected me with such foreboding, like the premonition of some inescapable fate.

Chapter 5

When we returned to Galway I expected that Brian would contact me. I longed to see him, to revel in the feeling that we meant something to each other, and the sense this gave me of being buttressed against the world. But a week passed and no Brian. I wondered whether he had actually returned after the holiday; maybe he was ill. But I saw him at the end of the second week, cycling with Jimmy Delahunty in Eyre Square. He saw me, raised a polite hand, and proceeded on his way, leaving me with a sensation of desolate let-down. Cissie, who was with me, raised her eyebrows.

'He's gone off me,' I said.

'Should you care?'

I looked at her, wondering why did I care, why should it matter. I was better off without him. He defied all my perceptions of how people behaved to each other; he treated me one day as though we were soul mates and made me feel invisible the next.

'I do care. It's a kind of contest and I want to win!' It was much more than that, but I young and full of pride.

Cissie laughed. 'There's a terrible stubborn streak in you, Peg. There's one way to wake him up,' she added mischievously. 'Go out with someone else.'

'I don't want anyone else.'

'What's that got to do with it? Go out with someone else; and make sure that Brian knows about it!'

'You're a bit of a Machiaevelli, Cissie O'Shaughnessy.'

She laughed again. 'Except that Machiavelli probably took his own advice.'

But when the experience was repeated a few days later, Brian responding with the same automatic politeness to my hello, as though I were a stranger, my mind was made up. To hell with him. There were other fish in the sea.

So when Jarlath Quinn asked me out I readily agreed. Jarlath flushed under his red hair and his big hands fidgeted. He was terrified of a refusal.

'If you've nothing better to do on Friday, Peg, will you come with me to the pictures?'

'I'd love to, Jarlath, Thanks.'

Relief. He smiled. 'We'll do the town, Peg. I got a cheque from home this morning.'

I left the lab with him when the practical was over and as luck would have it met Brian in the quad.

'Hello,' I said casually. 'Jarlath, do you know Brian Fitzallen? Brian, this is Jarlath Quinn.'

They shook hands and after exchanging a few words I strolled off with my new conquest, enjoying the chagrin I had left behind me.

Brian arrived on the doorstep that evening after supper. He wanted to talk to me, he said, but there was nowhere in the digs one could talk in private. Cissie was studying upstairs and anyway it was certainly out of the question to bring him up to my room.

'Will you come out for a walk?'

'I think it's going to rain,' I demurred, looking past him into the darkness where the street lights shone. 'Will you come in?'

My landlady put her head out of the sitting-room door to see who the caller was and disappeared again. He stood a little uncertainly in the hall. He wore a woollen navy-blue scarf twisted carelessly around his neck. The sea wind had tousled his hair. The light shade in the hall cast a blueish tinge on his face. His eyes focussed on me with a frown.

'Peg, will you come to the pictures on Friday.' he asked with matter-of-fact inquiry.

'Sorry, Brian, I have a date.'

He was silent, his face suddenly vulnerable, surprised.

'I see.'

He turned to go. At the door he said, hunching into his shoulders and smiling, eyebrows raised, 'You could break it, the date?'

'No.'

'Are you angry with me for something, Peg?' he said with so much charm that I wanted to disclaim any date, then or ever.

'No, just instructed. You are like one of those little men they have in funny clocks - who come out on the hour.Unless I happen to meet you when you are out it seems I'm not really visible.'

He was startled, abashed, silent for a moment.

'I'm sorry, Peg. I'm preoccupied sometimes. I have things on my mind.'

'Of course you have. And as I never have a thing on mine I would hate to disturb such lofty meditations,' I said from the depths of the perversity which had begun to rule me as soon as I saw that I had the upper hand. But his expression made me wish I had bitten my tongue.

120

'Have it your own way, Peg,' he murmured politely, hurt, and turned on his heel. I shut the door before he reached the gate, feeling sick, longing to run out after him. I went upstairs and sat at my table, staring at my chemistry textbook with unseeing eyes. Oh, to hell with molecules, periodic tables, keytones, acetones. Where did one get some salve for the heart?

The days that followed were full of misery. I went to the pictures with Jarlath; I cannot remember the film; all I remember is seeing in my mind's eye Brian Fitzallen's suddenly hurt, too sensitive face. My victory had left me empty; I felt mean, petty, bereft.

Jarlath wanted to kiss me. He was rough, caught between his urgent sexual needs and his wish to please me. His bony hand clenched mine. I refused him my lips, pushed him away with a laugh. Jarlath accepted this; nice girls didn't. But I longed for the evening to end so that I could lie in bed and think of Brian, who had now assumed a heroic gloss because he was lost to me.

But Brian was not so easily lost to me. He came into the lab at the end of a demonstration period on the following Monday and asked me out for coffee, nodding to Jarlath with an amiable condescension which irritated me and made me refuse the invitation. I felt he was presumptuous, that he still assumed I was his if he lifted his finger.

He did not lightly take no for an answer. He would wait for me after lectures, leaning against the wall in the corridor outside, his face registering disquiet if I emerged from the lab with Jarlath. I pretended indifference for as long as I could bear it and then, afraid that I really would lose him if I kept it up any longer, I capitulated

121

and was taken out to dinner. I borrowed a dress from Cissie for this dinner, cream coloured with a broad white belt, and sat opposite him in a haze of delight, impressed at his apparent knowledge of wines, his conversation which touched on a myriad topics, his funny asides, his desire to entertain.

He apologised obliquely for his preoccupied behaviour. 'You see, Peg, there are problems concerning Glenallen on my mind. I'm sorry I've been such a boor.'

'I'm sorry I was so rude to you,' I muttered, flushing.

He gave a hearty laugh. 'Do I really remind you of a clockword manikin?'

'Of course you don't.'

'They tell me at home that I live in my own world. At least Harry does. I am bedevilled with all sorts of things. However, from this moment forth I shall think only of Peg Donlon, the fair maid of Salthill!'

He leaned towards me across the table, eyes laughing. 'Now are you going to forgive me my enormities, Peg, or must I sit at your gate in sackcloth and ashes?'

What was I to do with this humility?

'What things?' I asked, to deflect the embarrassment of the moment. 'What things are you bedevilled with?'

He didn't answer my question and changed the subject.

We kissed at the door that evening, a long delicious kiss.

Cissie watched developments with interest

'He's mad about you, Peg. And he'd be a great catch, I think.'

I reddened, angry with her. I hated this assumption that women were all on the make, hunting men as prizes or bread tickets, the insufferable inference being that they were themselves valueless.

'I'm the catch!'

'I know,' Cissie laughed, 'but I think he is too.'

'I'm not interested in whether he is or not. In fact he told me that his "expectations are modest"'.

This was true. Brian, when aimlessly discussing possibilities for the future had said he would like to emigrate to south Africa or Kenya.

'That's a long way off. Why do you want to go out there?'

'There are great possibilities out there. I'd like to see the ruins of Zimbabwe - look for lost Ophir. Africa is the cradle of mankind. And I could make a life there. My expectations are modest, you know,' he added with a short laugh.

What did I care what his expectations were? I gave passion rein. I poured the whole of myself into this gallop of the soul, projecting qualities on to him out of all the books I had ever read. I thought him the answer to every longing, physical or metaphysical. I was a religious person in those days and was shocked at the realisation that I loved him more than God. But nowhere did it occur to me that perhaps he was all of the things I thought him to be only because I had willed it so; that I had, in some private sense, constructed him.

He never asked me to sleep with him. Cissie had warned me that if he did it would mean that Peg Donlon was good enough to bed, but not good enough for a Fitzallen to wed.

Whenever he spoke of Glenallen I wondered at his studied nonchalance, the effort he had to make to sound casual.

'I think you love Glenallen very much,' I ventured after he had talked of the farm.

He looked at me with a half laugh. 'Perceptive, Peg. I love it and I hate it! I would like to be free of it and I could not bear that freedom. Do I sound insane?'

'No. We are never free of the places which formed us! What I find puzzling is that you should want to be.'

I looked up at him. His eyes stared past me for a moment and I realised with surprise that they were full of something hard and speculative, something very much like dread.

He did not seem to mind that I was shy; that my reserve extended to everything.

'I'll find out what makes you tick, Peige ... wait and see.'

He often called me 'Peige' - which made two syllables out of my name and which he told me was common in Aran - the islands to the west.

'I don't come from Aran.'

'I think you come from Tír na nOg, which is out in the same direction', he said referring to the mythical land of the Sidhe, the fairy people, where one never grows old.

'You want me to take you there?' I demanded, 'like Niamh of the Golden Hair took Oisín? Away on my white horse to the land beyond the setting sun?'

He laughed, face creased in mirth, opening his hands in emphasis. 'I do. I do.'

'But then, in the nature of things, you would yearn eventually to come back, and if you set foot on your native soil ...'

His smile faded. He dropped his hands.

'I would wither and die,' he ended for me, his voice very quiet. 'I know.

The prospect of making love with him made me shiver with excitement; but I was afraid of his subsequent contempt and afraid of the mortal sin. I had no wish either for the status of the fallen woman - tart, whore, slag, strumpet, or any of the mean little labels which men, having arrogated to themselves the power to name a woman's experience, were ready to pin on any woman who yielded for an instant to her own humanity. I also had no wish for the crushing weight of moral failure.

And I wondered too why he wanted me. He knew both of my friends, had known them since childhood and they were beautiful. I must have articulated some query along these lines, for he joked, 'Mary is a peacock, Cissie is an icon, and you are a squirrel. I am very partial to squirrels!' He closed his eyes as he said this and breathed in ecstatically through his nose.

'You'd better watch out in that case; they sharpen their teeth on all sorts of things.'

'Are you going to sharpen your little fangs on me?' he demanded, laughing. He kissed me suddenly and I kissed him back, head spinning, and then demanded why he thought I was a squirrel.

'Fastidious, elegant, shy and given to occasional bold forays,' he answered after a moment. 'Disappears into the branches if offended.'

I laughed, but was, as he had said, fastidious, careful of the rules, mindful of all the warnings my mother had ever given me about men; how easily he could destroy me, 'squirrel' as he thought me. I knew only too well how vulnerable squirrels were, having caught a young one once only to have it die during its first night of captivity.

But as the months went by I knew it was only a matter of time before he ask me to marry him and knew also what my answer would be. I could not bear the thought of a future without him; I imagined the years without him, relentless with tedium, without challenge or excitement.

Mary had come back from France at the end of her year but then went to study acting at the Abbey School of Acting in Dublin. Her father did not approve, but he was too besotted with his only child to stand in her way. She came home at Christmas for a couple of days every year and for a week or so in the summer, and she looked almost carelessly glamorous. She never seemed to put on weight, which was not surprising as I never saw her eating; she never seemed to have a spot or a pimple. But now there was a distance between us, as though from some subliminal recognition that we were assuming new and different identities. We were no longer sure of our ground with her and felt curiously childish beside her. Cissie said she had become hard, but I did not think so. There was something about her now, beautiful and young as she was, that smacked simply of endurance.

The War broke out in September 1939. I was at home in Ballycloghan with Tom that Sunday mornings and barely heard on the wireless at eleven fifteen, the metallic voice of Chamberlain, fading in and out, as he told how his efforts for peace had failed. Later we tuned in to the King's broadcast, and I was stirred to tears by the words:

126

'We are called, with our allies, to meet the challenge of a principle which, if it were to prevail, would be fatal to any civilised order in the world. The task will be hard. There may be dark days ahead, and war can no longer be confined to the battlefield. But we can only do the right as we see the right and reverently commit our cause to God.'

When the broadcast was over we sat in the dark sitting-room, with only the embers of the fire, and talked for a while of the awful times now facing Europe. 'We won't be dragged into it,' I said and Tom told me not to be stupid. Nobody, he said, would be untouched by this war; everything would change.

Everyone in the countryside talked about the war. People gathered after Sunday Mass to discuss developments, whether there would be poisoned gas, whether Ireland would stay neutral, whether many of our young men would join up.

I dropped into Percivals for groceries and to speak to Niamh. She was alone in the shop when I entered and I saw her jump and shove a book under the counter, relaxing when she saw who it was. 'I'm supposed to be doing the shelves and I'm fed up,' she announced.

'I'll take to the drink if I see another tin of condensed milk. You're so lucky, Peg! You're privileged and don't know it!'

'I do know it.' I felt for her, the boredom of her life, measuring out pounds of sugar and flour, counting money into a till, day in day out, while her lively mind was starving.

When I returned to Galway a month later I found that some of the students had gone to Belfast to enlist; even though it was their final year several of the boys had gone. We who remained felt guilty, ashamed that Dev was keeping Ireland out of the war, outraged at the rumours that we would be invaded. We read the papers avidly; the talk of gas masks and evacuations sent cold shivers through us and we looked around at placid Galway and its peace and beauty and felt ourselves both blest and deprived. We were young afterall, and the excitement was all elsewhere.

The months came and went thereafter in feverish interest and sporadic studying for the final exams which were facing us in June 1940. I spent most of the Christmas holidays of 1939 again with Cissie in Ballyharris and when Mary came home for a few days from Dublin the three of us got together, but the old ease in one another's company was gone; Mary had moved beyond us in some way, her beauty now taut and disciplined with sophistication. She was really acting now, not just as an extra, but small parts which gave her increasing assurance.

It was after one of these evenings with Mary, in the Christmas holidays of 1939, when she had hinted again of her French Count (whom she had met again in Dublin) - Lucien this and Lucien that - that Cissie broke down as she sat before her dressing table; she tore the glove from her broken hand and belaboured it with her hairbrush, weeping uncontrollably. I rushed to her and tried to stop her, but she threw herself on the bed, stuffed the pillow in her mouth, the muffled howls of 'horrible, horrible, horrible' coming in a torrent of tears.

128

I threw myself beside her and held her, weeping myself. When she had exhausted herself she turned her red eyes on me and said she wished she was dead; she thrust her injured hand with its missing little finger and partially amputated ring finger almost into my face. How could anyone love her, with a mutilation like that? I said that everyone who knew her loved her; that nobody gave a damn about the hand or even noticed it. But I knew she did not believe me.

Mary's father died of a heart attack on New Year's day 1940, a day or two after she had returned to Dublin from her short Christmas break at home, and she came back, attended this time by a foreign looking man, driving a car the like of which had not before been seen in Balyharris.

'This is the Comte de Rais' she said as she introduced him after the funeral; her face was mottled from weeping, bare of makeup, crumpled with loss. She was dressed in a hopelessly expensive black suit, with a black hat and veil, and she looked mysterious and elegant in spite of her grief.

I looked into the brown eyes of this foreigner, knowing that here was the man she had met in Paris, aware of a gaze more intent than any I had ever encountered; certainly Brian had never looked at me with that kind of appraisal - and even though it was Mary's father's funeral and we were standing in the biting cold in the graveyard, skeletal trees creaking in the wind, Knockshee a dark shape in the mist, something shivered in my veins. I wondered about it afterwards - that feeling - the sense of excitement, of some kind of danger which gave life a point.

'My name is Lucien.' He spoke perfect English, but the accent was French. I shook his hand, struck by how warm it was, said how do you do, feeling suddenly young, gauche and inexperienced. Afterwards in the Royal Hotel Brian took him aside and questioned him about the war. I overheard them discussing the RAF - the Count saying he would contact friends in the War Office '- they're looking for pilots' - and I heard Brian speak of his flying lessons at Foynes in County Limerick which he had had while staying with a school friend during the summer following his last year at school. I felt anxious, wishing I had been privy to the whole conversation, afraid that Brian was thinking of enlisting.

Then the Count drove Mary back to Dublin in his big black car and we were left bereft of her, aware that she had become reserved and cool and older and that we were out of our depth with her. I had asked her how things were going for her and she had said 'As well as I can expect' and lapsed back into her grief, emerging from it occasionally to ask us if we thought she had neglected her father in the last few years. We answered no, of course not, but she was not to be comforted.

And what was this foreigner to her? Was she going to marry him? Why hadn't she waited at home for a day or two to be with her old friends?

Meanwhile the war went on. The January and February of 1940 were the bitterest for forty-five years. We heard how the English civilian population were preparing for the worst the war might bring, gas proofing rooms with cellulose sheets and tape, erecting Anderson shelters in their gardens, buying black-out blinds and sticky tape for the windows to minimise the effect of flying glass. We knew the British cities were in darkness, no more neon lights or lighted shop windows, and Ireland observed a black-out too. But still there were no reports of an active war. Then, in April, Denmark and Norway were invaded and the following month the Germans followed suit with Holland, Belgium, Luxembourg. On the same day, 10 May, Churchill became Prime Minister. The end of that month saw the evacuations from Dunkirk and Churchill warning that a miracle of deliverance was not victory.

In the years since we had started college I had seen Cissie become more and more introspective, and I worried about her. The only time her eyes really lit up was at the mention of Peter Fitzallen's name. I still met him occasionally when I went to Ballyharris. He had a priestlike remoteness about him, buttressed by his apparent disdain for others, and by the sudden superb urbanity and charm he could turn on like the drop of a hat and which forgave him everything.

I had stayed with Cissie during part of every holiday since the first time we had met. She still rode in the Ballyharris Gymkhana every summer and her eyes would seek out Peter Fitzallen who was always home for the event. I had met his parents, and Harry, when she noticed me, now greeted me with the same brittle cheeriness which she accorded to all her acquaintances.

Cissie she treated with the same cheerful camaraderie, but I noticed how her glance would frequently stray to Cissie's blighted hand while her eyes became glassy, narrowing coldly, as though in some sort of private recollection or calculation. She had many admirers and exchanged banter with them, but I never saw her for long in the company of any one particular man. She liked older men, whom she flagrantly teased.

One day I saw Des O'Shaughnessy, home from the College of Surgeons in Dublin, present her with a bouquet of flowers with a jocose bravura which only thinly covered his vulnerability.

'Flowers? Oh God, they give me hay fever!'

Des, deeply offended, didn't bother her after that. Now he was talking of enlisting and his father told him bluntly during the Christmas holidays that if he did anything of the sort he would regard him as dead; that England's quarrel was not his affair. To which Des replied angrily that the quarrel belonged to the civilised world; that there was not enough room on the face of the earth for both civilisation and Nazism; that one of them would have to go. He returned to Dublin but went to Belfast shortly after to enlist - to the great anxiety of his parents.

Brian and I never became formally engaged. Marriage had been a tacit thing between us for a long time and I expected that we would get around to it after we graduated. But Brian was now talking of enlisting; he would like to join the RAF, he said; he already had flying hours to his credit from that summer at Foynes and was sure it would all come back. I was filled with terror at this possibility. When he pressed me to marry him he made it clear it was an immediate wedding he was thinking of - with no one from Glenallen present. I was offended by this; was he ashamed of me I asked him and he laughed and said God no, quite the contrary. If I wouldn't marry him he was going to go off and enlist right away.

'Marry me now, Peg. Marry me now! To hell with formalities and waiting and pleasing the family. Do you realise that we are almost finished in Galway, that the big bad world awaits us. I might lose you to the world.'

I thought about it only briefly, crowding all the ifs and buts to the back of my mind. A whirlwind wedding had a romance to it comparable with elopement. But I suddenly realised that Brian had hardly told me he loved me; it was something alluded to occasionally by way of a joke and I wanted his love, his declaration. I was sure of it in my own way, sure that he needed me, needed the purpose and definition he had once told me I gave to his life. So I waited for his avowal.

'Why do you want to marry me?' I asked eventually.

He had looked at me in silence, raised his eyebrows and answered me with surprise.

'How can you ask that? Because I love you, Peige. And I love you because you are real!'

Our wedding took place on 29 June 1940, the end of a pivotal week in the course of the war and, for me, the end of many other things - and the beginning. Our college life was over; the last of the exams a week before; we were still reeling from the relief of being free of them and the frightening reality of being now thrust upon the world, of being no longer cocooned in the privileged status of big children. We were supposed to be adults now, but we were insecure ones looking back over our shoulders at what we had lost.

An armistice had been signed between France and Germany, the French ambassador had resigned in London and the British government had recognised De Gaulle as the leader of the Free French. The Germans seemed to be terrifyingly invincible. But the war might have been taking place on the dark side of the moon, for all I cared, that June Saturday morning. Brian's friend Jimmy Delahunty was best man and Cissie was bridesmaid.

Jimmy had given us the key of a cottage in Lettergesh, which he had recently bought with some inherited money, as a honeymoon retreat and we had prepared a pack of food to take with us.

Most of the final year Science students came to the church. I wore a simple off-white linen costume and carried a small bouquet of roses. Tom, distinguished in his new suit, stood us the wedding breakfast in Emerson's Hotel. He had been deeply shocked by our speed and secrecy and could only attribute it to Brian having 'taken the penalty before the whistle blew' as I had heard Jack Stapleton describe a similar situation. He didn't actually say this, but I knew it must have been on his mind.

'You should have asked Uncle Matt,' he said to me when he saw the guest list.

'I'm not having that fellow hobbling around and insulting everyone.'

'He's very rich, Peg. You should keep in with him.'

'He can leave it all to you.'

Mary arrived on her own, elegant in navy blue, with a wide brimmed hat. She hugged me and told me I looked beautiful; she was perfumed and groomed and smiling and there was about her a passionate loneliness. I had never before imagined that Mary could be lonely, but I felt it now, watching the green eyes which hardly smiled. I had invited her Count as well, but she said he had gone to London to meet de Gaulle and involve himself with the French Volunteer Legion which he was forming there. She said that he had been disgusted about the armistice signed at Compiegne with the Germans on the preceding Saturday.

I longed to ask her if she was going to marry him. Cissie and I were terribly impressed that she should have met someone like him, but Mary remained quietly evasive.

Brian's family were conspicuous by their absence. I had managed to get Brian to send them a telegram with details of church and reception, but no one turned up.

We made plans to go to Dublin after we were married. Brian had been at school at a college in Dublin and had the promise of a teaching job from his old headmaster, dependent of course on his results.

'Where would you like a flat?' he asked me. 'Which part of Dublin would you fancy?' and I said the part we could afford.

'Pragmatic Peige. If we lived in Rathfarnham, for example, we could cycle into the Dublin mountains. Would you like that?'

'And be worn to a thread keeping up with you!'

I thought of the capital with its busy streets, of seeing Mary and being introduced into her world of theatre, of going shopping, of going to the cinema. I imagined our little flat, sitting-room, bedroom, white walls and bright curtains and a fireplace with a blazing fire for winter. And freedom. A life of bliss, with long conversations and long love-making and long languorous Sundays. I would learn how to cook and give parties and when everyone was gone home we would lock the door and leave the mess until the next day and go to bed and make love and fall asleep in each other's arms.

I slipped the wedding ring on to his finger, my father's ring which bore the legend 'Daniel and Maura 16.6.1914' while the priest invoked, as he had while Brian had put a ring on my finger, the name of the Father, the Son and the Holy Ghost.

We left the reception for Connemara and honeymoon. We took the bus to Clifden, our bicycles trussed on to the roof rack. We sat holding hands while a garrulous red-haired driver talked non-stop about the war to the conductor who was seated beside a stack of brown paper parcels in the front seat. On the top of the heap was a box of day-old chicks cheeping and chirping and sticking their little yellow beaks through the ventilation holes.

Occasionally the bus would stop, a parcel would be delivered, a conversation would be had with the recipient of the parcel, and then the journey would resume.

We were at the back of the bus, which was only half full. Oughterard was passed and then we were into the purple wilderness. I leant against this new husband, still dazed from the ramifications of the day's ceremony. The bus rattled over every bump, but we hardly felt them. We alighted at Clifden and the conductor went to get down our bicycles. He climbed the ladder at the back of the bus, untied them and handed them down to Brian. There were bits of confetti still clinging to us and the conductor winked at Brian.

'Good luck to ye now!'

'Thanks. Good luck.'

We put our bags on the carriers, smiled at each other and cycled off to find our cottage. There was a tension between us, and a shyness too. We were in the country again in a moment and deliciously alone.

'Where exactly is the cottage, Brian?'

He halted, one foot on the road, took a map out of his pocket, the one Jimmy Delahunty had drawn for him. I stopped a few yards further on.

'About five miles off.'

I looked around at the majestic wilderness, the heather in bloom, the lonely mountains, the black faced sheep feeding off poor grass, their long baa -aa-ing and the whisper of the wind the only sounds in the stillness. We asked directions from a man cutting turf and he looked at us and at my shiny new ring. He had thick dark curly hair and one brown tooth and a wonderful weathered face. He smiled, gave directions and shouted, 'God bless ye,' as we moved off.

The cottage was two hundred yards from the cliff and a hundred yards down a dirt track. Brian opened the gate.

'Wait here - I'll just check this is the right place'

I saw the sea frothing against the rocks, the white riders racing towards the shore. I looked away into the blue distance towards Aran and imagined I saw the coast of Mayo. Cloud tendrils floated high up, catching the eye and drawing it upwards, reinforcing the sense of panorama.

The immediate landscape itself was broken only by turf clamps and behind me were the awesome Twelve Pins and the country in between was wild with beauty and melancholy.

Brian waved. He had opened the door. I wheeled my bicycle down the little grassy track to my temporary married home. The cottage was traditional, ageing thatch, stone flags, open fireplace with a crane and a pile of sticks and turf in a tea-chest. There was an old woodwormed dresser, a deal table, two chairs and in the little bedroom next door a double bed and a wooden chest with bedclothes protected in oilcloth.

We had brought some provisions with us, milk in a lemonade bottle, bread, butter, eggs and rashers, sausages and a chocolate cake which Cissie had rushed off to get us at the last moment, 'to help keep the wolf from the door!' and Jimmy had laughed and said it was the wolf inside the door I would have to look out for. Brian didn't mind being called a wolf; he raised his eyebrows and smirked innocently, 'Me?'

We stared at each other shyly. Brian pulled me into the bedroom; we grabbed a blanket and lay together in that creaking old bed and consummated our marriage, clumsy with innocence, our clothes in heaps where they fell. The day ebbed outside and when we surfaced Brian turned to look out the window which was on his side, and whispered in my ear, 'Look Peg, look at the sun! 'And I leaned against his back and watched the red gold fire disappear into the sea, my lips against the skin of his shoulder-blade, my breast against his arm.

There was little sleep that night, snatches here and there, and I woke to find his arm under my head, his skin against mine, his hands gentle and demanding, his tense, fervent whispers, 'Little squirrel - I do love you.' And all the night I heard the sea singing for us and, at last, as from a distance, I heard my own song, sharp and sudden in the silence.

In the late morning we lit a small fire to make breakfast; the smoke curled up the chimney and out into the kitchen, making our eyes smart. We opened the door to the summer and through it came the peace of the countryside and the pulse of the Atlantic. I looked at the gold band on my finger and examined myself in the small blotched mirror in the bedroom for signs of maturing and change. My face was the same, but happy. It looked very young in fact, younger than the day before when I had been powdered and lipsticked. I suggested that we take the bikes and explore.

We took some towels and cycled through pot-holed roads, down boreens which were little more than green ruts, and having gone a considerable distance, stopped in the emptiness to swim at an inlet. I found the water bitterly cold and ran back to the rocks, clambered up a slope and sat half naked in the sunshine watching Brian swim, watching the powerful thrust of his arms as though he owned the water. I saw the lonely wilderness stretching away into the distance on every side, the lines of mountain and moorland, the sweep of water down the inlet, the long trails marking the current, the eddies foaming white on blue towards the shore. There were grey rocks, the sound of rushing water, noisy ripples. From nearby came the smell of burnt gorse. I saw the new young growth beside the blackened twigs, heard the cry of sea birds, watched the ants busy beside me in the pink sea thrift, happy in a world full of happiness.

Brian joined me after a few minutes, shivering, towelled himself briskly and lay back looking at the puffy little white clouds.

'I feel like I am lifted to the sky,' he murmured and I lay against him and tried to fit the cavity of a broken grass stem over a single tough spike in his day old beard. The breeze stirred my hair, lifted it in floating strands. 'You are clothed in gossamer,' he murmured, watching me through half-closed lids. He reached over and touched my lips, tracing their contours with his index finger, whispering:

'A bank of tangled briars,
Sloped gently to the south,
Its leaves recalled her mouth,
With its soft hidden fires.'

I stopped tickling him with the grass stem.
'Who wrote that?'
'Gogarty.'
I didn't even know who he was.

Then Brian jumped up and started to tickle me, saying there were some things a man was not going to take lying down and I shrieked with laughter, pleading for him to stop, begging for amnesty when he attacked the soles of my feet, and we ended up in a small dip in the ground making love with a bullock for an audience. I was embarrassed by the bullock, but Brian would not heed my protestations.

What else do I recall of that day? The hunger with which we cycled home to a fry and chocolate cake, the laughter as we cooked together, the sense of wonder I had that this man, whom I adored, was mine.

Later, our fire going, our oil lamp lit and the door open to the evening and the white moths, we talked about the future. I asked him would he miss Glenallen. He was relaxed and happy, but he tensed and hesitated for a moment.

'No. It will be better for us to have our own life.'

'Isn't it queer to think that we'll probably have children some day.'

'A football team,' he suggested.

I pushed him so that he fell off the stool.

'Football team how are you! Not from my dainty person!'

He picked himself up, his laughter filling the kitchen and frightening the moths which fluttered at the lamp.

'I can see I'll have my work cut out with you, Miss,' and he grabbed me around the waist, dragging me off my little wooden perch, one hand dancing up and down my rib cage until I pleaded for mercy and promised reform.

I was in a dream. But when, sitting on the floor, he put his arms around my legs, leant his head on my knee and recited poetry to me, I felt I would sell my soul for the dream.

As we lay in bed that night I kept my hand cold by grasping the iron frame of the bed and used it to cool my sunburnt forehead. But this was only marginally helpful. My thighs were sore too from cycling beyond my pace, trying to keep up with my hard taskmaster who never slowed for me, but we made love all the same. Brian eventually slept and moved and murmured in his sleep and I made out his dark profile against the window and felt the long naked warmth of him against me.

Later that night I heard him call out, words that were meaningless to me, and he seemed terrified and sweating. I woke him and he apologised, his breath coming in short gasps.

'Sorry Peg. It's an old dream.'

The night was very short; the dawn crept over the sea and in through the window and showed me my husband's face, peaceful now, deeply asleep. His arm was thrown over me. It was heavy and I could hardly move, so I lifted it gently and repositioned it, noticing for the first time as I did so the parallel scars at his wrist where the flesh had obviously been cut at one time by something very sharp. How had he come by that? A fall? An accident? I wondered about it for a while before slipping into the heavy sleep which comes at dawn after a restless night.

When I woke in the morning he was already up; I found a note on the kitchen table to say 'Gone for a walk' and three irregular pierced hearts by way of signature. I have it still.

But he did not return for several hours and was short with me when I remonstrated with him.

'I need to be on my own sometimes, Peg.'

He was taciturn for much of that day. I felt hurt, puzzled and put it down to the nightmare of the night before and the anxiety he must feel about his parents, in not having advised them of his marriage until it was almost a *fait accompli*.

I discussed it with him at supper. He agreed that he was anxious, but maintained that we had been right. 'I couldn't run the risk of losing you.'

'You think you would lose me if your parents disapproved of me. Are you so obedient?'

'Not at all, but I might lose you because you might not care for my family or for Glenallen - or even for me - if you got to know us well!'

'Why wouldn't I?'

'You just might not.'

142

There was a wire waiting for us when we returned to Galway five days later. The wire was from Brian's mother and said quite simply:

'Congratulations stop Father very ill stop Come home.'

Chapter 6

Murty, the stud groom, met us at the station. Brian introduced us. 'This is Murty Kavanagh, Peg. Murty, this is Mrs Fitzallen,' and I squirmed at the strange new name which was mine and at the servile way Murty tipped his cloth cap - 'Pleased to meet you, ma'am.'

He drove home with grim concentration, glancing at me from time to time. I was tired; I looked out at the lush summer evening and saw the shadows on Knockshee.

'Poor Katie Hennigan died last week!' Murty said suddenly.

'Oh. What did she die of?' Brian asked.

'She just took a notion. Sure she was never right after she lost part of the arm six years ago. Never right.'

I thought of the woman I had seen with Dr O'Shaughnessy at the time of my first visit to Ballyharris, the woman with the infected hand.

'Mick is terrible cut up, God help him,' Murty added.

I turned to Brian. 'I remember her. She had some infection in her hand.'

'She had, the creature,' Murty said, nodding his head. 'And the mountain has her now.'

I felt Brian start, felt my flesh creep.

'For God's sake, Murty, don't start going on about seeing her on Knockshee; you know that's all rubbish.'

Murty exhaled, his chin settling huffily.

'It is not all rubbish, Master Brian, as you well know. Knockshee has always been taking folk.' He said this in a pained, patient voice and kept quiet for the rest of the short journey.

I became increasingly apprehensive as the car approached the gateway and moved slowly up the avenue of beeches which I had first seen seven years earlier from the O'Shaughnessy's car; it stopped by the front steps.

The house loomed beside us, the same ivory mansion in the evening sunlight. The flight of granite steps to the front door and the curved pillared balustrade now struck me with dread. From one of the great windows on either side of the door, I saw Mrs Fitzallen's anxious face looking out at us and a moment later the door was opened and she came hurriedly down the steps. I got out of the car and stood uncertainly.

Brian's first question concerned his father.

'He had a bad turn, but he's up today and a little better,' Mrs Fitzallen said in the low voice reserved for matters touching mortality. 'He'll need minding for a while now.'

Then Brian introduced us.

'Mummy, you remember Peg?' His voice sounded suddenly hoarse. I looked at my mother-in-law, praying she would like me, suddenly consumed by a sense of guilt as though I had done something shameful.

She had got thin, almost birdlike, and now carried one shoulder slightly higher than the other. Her face was gentle, but there was reproach in her eyes. She looked at me for a moment, a mother's look, assessing this new and radical twist in her son's life and then put out her arms and embraced me.

'You're very welcome, dear,' she said without either warmth or disapproval and then Brian dropped a peck on her cheek and she held his shoulder for a moment and straightened his tie. I saw the light in her eyes as she looked at him, the unmistakable love - more than love - the intense air of someone who is looking at her *raison d'etre*. I did not exist for her at that moment although I stood beside her, as she looked into Brian's face and slowly, slowly, straightened his tie; her fingers lingered on her youngest child, her longing to embrace him and kiss him hanging between us in the air. I felt the lot of mothers, her sense of loss, how it would be with me too some day, and understood the tears she tried to hide as she turned to me with an almost visible effort and took me by the hand.

'You must be exhausted, you poor things. All that awful journey,' and I went with her up the intimidating granite steps and into the hall where Brian's father, frail now, came to meet us. He shook my hand and I felt his keen gaze on me as he ushered us into the drawing-room.

'How are you, Dad?' I heard Brian ask quietly and the old man's slightly querulous reply, 'I'm fine, I'm fine. I have angina.' And then he added in a voice pitched very low, 'Gave us all quite a shock. Is she in the family way?' and I heard Brian's exasperated 'No!' and some sort of embarrassed explanation to do with the war and how you couldn't be sure of the future.

Was this my doing, I wondered, this sick man who jibbed at his son's precipitous marriage? Was he ill because of this marriage? Possibilities which had never occurred to me crowded me now; Brian's parents had become a stark reality, instead of almost ghostly figures on the sidelines.

146

The drawing-room was a big bright room, in shades of cream and gold dominated by a large marble fireplace with a gilt overmantel. Although I had often looked up at the windows of this room I had never before been inside the house and I gazed around me with interest.

The walls were covered in pictures, oil paintings, water colours; there was a worn hearth rug in front of the fireplace by the high brass fender. The furniture consisted of a chesterfield suite in a russet colour, a small chaise longue in gold velvet, a lady's writing desk by the window with a huge vase of roses, and two antique side tables with other vases and family photographs. It was a room full of charm, comfort and an old-world graciousness which emanated not so much from the house or its contents, but from the presence in the room of Brian's parents. I know this because it went with them and never returned.

Mr Fitzallen turned to me, politely urbane.

'Well, well, well; what a lovely girl!'

He turned to Brian. 'Always knew you had a fine eye for a filly, old chap!'

Brian laughed uneasily. He knew that his father had met me before and obviously didn't remember. But it was clear that he was pleased about having a good eye for a filly - and clear also that he was not at home in his reactions. He was different here; he was putting some sort of mask in place, a mask which I instinctively disliked. It was a pretence of a kind. He was oddly unsure what to expect from the people in this place which was his home.

'Patrick!' Mrs Fitzallen expostulated, sighing sharply and shaking her head at her husband, in a voice pitched half way between amusement and annoyance.

'These country boys you know dear!' she murmured to me by way of apology. 'Come with me,' she added conspiratorially; 'I'm sure you'd like to freshen up.'

'Thank you.'

I caught Brian's eye as I left the room with her. He winked at me and followed us upstairs with the suitcases. As we went upstairs Mrs Fitzallen said to me, 'Brian should have brought you home to see us, long ago. It's really too bad of him to have kept you all to himself!'

So she didn't remember me either. Brian had introduced me to her at the Gymkhana the year before.

I looked at myself in the bathroom mirror; I felt less nervous. Brian's parents were all charm. I wanted more than anything else for them to accept me. I longed to be rich, to have something tangible to bring to this marriage with their son. There were so many things I felt myself capable of, I would make them glad of this marriage. Someday I would be rich and they would be glad he had married me. I did not know how these riches were going to materialise, but I decided at that moment that they would.

The bedroom assigned to us was pretty, pale pink bedspread, white French dressing-table, mahogany wardrobe in an alcove and, on the floor, an old Indian carpet in shades of pink and ivory. It was at the front of the house and was filled with the evening sunlight. I looked out the window. The driveway wound in a curve from the gate through the avenue of beech trees. Two horses grazed in the front field. To the right was the lake, a small ornamental mere with a single

148

white swan and beside it two riders, a young woman and young man, walked their horses in the direction of the house. They seemed to be deep in conversation. I identified them at once - Harry and Peter.

Brian came in with our cases, deposited them on the floor of our room and tried to take me in his arms. I pushed him away.

'You're messing my hair!'

He sighed. 'Come down when you're ready. Supper will be ready shortly.'

I pointed out the window. 'There's Peter and Harry!' I said, indicating the two figures by the lake.

'Yes,' he said. He watched them for a moment. I saw the shadow cross his face.

He pushed me back on the bed, nuzzling against my neck. The bed creaked reprovingly.

'Don't,' I whispered in agitation, watching the open door. 'Your mother will hear us!'

'If she doesn't know what it's all about by now,' Brian muttered, 'she must have lived in a state of recurring surprise!'

'Scram. Let me get ready.'

He got up and looked around the room as though seeing it for the first time. 'It will be funny sleeping in the guest room. My old room is at the back.'

He turned at the door. 'Love you,' I whispered. He blew a kiss at me and was gone. Ten minutes later I came downstairs and Brian appeared in the hall. I was wearing the new dress in pale crepe de chine, which had almost bankrupted me, or rather Tom, who had whistled when I told him the price but had stumped up like a good brother.

'You look like a swan,' my husband whispered, a sudden burst of raw pride on his face. And

149

because of him and the light in his eyes I felt suddenly beautiful, powerful with femininity, ecstatic with love and life. He took my hand and brought me into the drawing-room. The only person there was Mr Fitzallen who immediately rose from his armchair.

'Please don't get up,' I murmured awkwardly.

He rose all the same, shakily, and smiled at me.

'Sit down, won't you, Peg. You'll have a sherry, or would you prefer a gin?'

My mother had always warned me never to accept alcohol from anyone. But this was a different world and I was afraid of seeming provincial. 'A sherry, thank you.'

I sat near the fireplace, where two red setters were lying across the hearth rug.

He poured the drink from a decanter on a side table and said, 'Tell me all about yourself.' I looked to Brian and back and warmed to the old man's charm. And he looked really old although he couldn't have been much more than sixty-five. His fingers were gnarled and waxen and he had a pallor to his face and a fragility to his movements which told their own story.

I told him about my life in Galway and about my home and he made much of my university career.

'Never been much of a scholar myself!'

The door opened and Harry and Peter came in. Harry smiled at me, and I saw in Peter's deep-set eyes an expression halfway between hauteur and curiosity. They both ignored Brian.

'Well hello, Peg. Aren't you the dark horse?' Harry said. 'You do believe in doing things quietly - going off and getting married like that!'

Brian turned to her. 'We did send a wire,' and I hated the apology in his voice and the way he adverted to me by way of explanation.

When Harry moved away to pour herself a drink Peter put his two hands gently on my shoulders and gave me a chaste peck. His eyes and lips were cold. The peck was the done thing; it imported no affection.

'Welcome to Glenallen,' he said in a measured voice.

'Will you ride with me tomorrow?' Harry asked then and I said that I would but that I wasn't a great rider.

'She can ride Mara tomorrow,' she said to Brian. 'I assume you'll want to show her the farm?'

'Not Mara, I think,' Brian said uncomfortably.

There was silence then for a moment. Harry poured sherry into old crystal glasses.

'You're from Galway?' she asked. 'Small farm?'

'Hundred and forty acres,' I said, taken aback, but my voice was lost in the noise of the dinner gong which suddenly boomed in the hall.

Mrs Fitzallen came into the room.

'Come along; supper's ready. My two travellers must be starving!'

Harry handed Peter his drink and embraced her mother. 'They're not the only ones, mother darling,' she said. 'Peter and I played tennis until five and have been out riding since then.'

'How you two wear yourselves out!' Mrs Fitzallen said in a low voice, half alarmed, half jocose, and shook her head. But her gaze returned to Brian, traced his face tenderly, the same expression of maternal love I had seen when we arrived, and I saw the sudden fierce expression in her daughter's eyes, fiery with grief and exasperation.

151

Supper was served by Nora, a shy young maid. The meal consisted of soup, roast chicken, boiled potatoes, broccoli, cauliflower and a superb home-made chutney. Dessert was strawberries and cream.

I was introduced to Nora and she blushed and shook my hand and called me 'Ma'am' which made me feel venerable and uncomfortable.

The dining-room had a red carpet, off-white curtains, dark red wallpaper, several enormous fox hunting prints and portraits of horses. I was quizzed about my parents, about Tom and when I would bring him to meet them, but I sensed the absence of any real desire for this encounter. Every time I looked up I caught Peter's evaluating eyes. Harry kept up an intermittent barrage of conversation about what various friends were doing, what So and So was doing with his stables. Peter spoke about Clifden with nostalgia; they had holidayed there as children.

Brian was the only one who said little. He ate his supper and put in the odd comment, speaking like one who knew he lived on sufferance. When he ventured his opinion on some venue in the racing calendar I saw Harry aim a kick at him under the table, half jokingly and wholly in earnest, while Peter registered exasperation. When Brian spoke to his brother the latter answered with the pained patience of one who would not answer at all, except that appearances demanded it. There was some sort of undercurrent here, apparently unnoticed by the parents who seemed to be unaware of how quiet Brian was or how the others rushed to put him down.

I blamed it on myself; we had effectively excluded them from our marriage and must expect some negative reaction. The passionate sense of romance, the pride I felt in my husband, which had bouyed me up, dissipated here and I felt foolish and apologetic. I caught Harry's eye and smiled tentatively. She smiled back. I felt her charm and self assurance and apparent acceptance thawing the ice around my heart.

While the plates were being removed to make way for dessert, Peter, who was sitting beside me, leaned across and said to me in a low, urbane voice, 'You're very lovely, if you don't mind my saying so.'

'Thank you,' I said, flushing. He knew he was attractive, this man. I thought of Cissie and her lonely, single-minded, love.

When supper was over Brian took me by the arm and brought me around the house, from the eight bedrooms and four bathrooms down to the huge kitchen where there was a big Aga cooker. Here I met Eilie the cook, who gave me a searching look and shook my hand warmly. She had been with the family for years and Brian was her pet.

She pursed her lips, put a hand on her hip.

'Oh, now 'tis yourself is the smart boyo - goin' off and gettin' married like that and your poor mother half out of her mind from the minute she got the wire. And the master getting a bad turn and Miss Harriet shouting at everyone!'

I blushed crimson and she glanced at me apologetically. 'Don't mind me, ma'am. We haven't had excitement like this since I don't know when!'

Nora was stacking dishes and smirking and turning around shyly to look at me and then back again to the cupboard, her dark hair tied back and a little white cap on her head. The kitchen had a warm smell of recently baked bread and freshly

153

ironed linen. The windows looked out on the stable yard. The floor was flagged and there were several doors leading into pantries or larders. In the middle of the floor was a big pine table, well scrubbed, and against the wall was a tall old dresser, the shelves laden with platters and dishes. On the walls hung various copper and other utensils. A tiny marmalade kitten was asleep in a basket by the Aga, reminding me of little Tiddles, now grown up.

I picked the kitten up, stroked it, inquired did it have a name, smelling its gentle furry scent.

'Tiny Tim,' Nora said in a rush. 'It's my little cat, ma'am.' She seemed overcome with this boldness for she reddened furiously and rushed into a pantry with a butter dish.

'Runt of the litter,' Eilie explained. 'That poor old yoke, Gracie, had another litter last week in the haybarn; Murty drowned them, but,' she gestured towards the pantry, 'her nibs saved that one.'

'We had fifteen cats at last count,' Brian said by way of explanation, seeing my dismayed face. I looked into the round milky blue eyes of the kitten and put it back in its basket.

Brian brought me into the kitchen hall where there was a coatstand; he indicated a narrow stone stairs going down to lower depths.

'The cellar is down there - gloomy place; no point in showing it to you.'

I leaned over and saw, where the stone stairs ended, a flagged floor and a stack of bottles and various brooms. Then he took me outside to the stable yard.

'It's a palace,' I said. 'You'll never be able to live in a little flat after this.'

'Funny thing,' he said slowly, 'I've never belonged here!'

He said it without rancour. 'I don't care for the endless bloody cant about dogs and horses - where you daren't pretend that you've read a book.'

We went out into the twilight; the summer night was full of warmth; the young swallows swooped, screeching, and soared again to the warm blue evening sky. Brian took me through the upper yard where he greeted the workmen who were around. There were a couple of mares in the loose boxes, their half doors open and we stared in at them, Brian pointing out to me his favourite, Jessie, who gazed down at us with aristocratic patience, flicking her mane and tail. I put up my hand to stroke her velvet nose, but she snorted explosively and shook her head away. In the lower yard were loose boxes with heavy doors and iron bars on 'windows' and in one of these I heard urgent neighing, the sound of plunging hooves and tense voices, one of them being Murty's. I was about to take a look through the barred window but Brian steered me away.

'Just a mare being covered,' he said. 'A bit violent for you, Peige. And dangerous too, even with Old Dickon. Besides,' he added slyly, 'I don't want you making any comparisons!'

I gave him a dig in the ribs. I had never seen a mare being covered. We had no stallions in Ballycloghan and Tom always brought the mares to other farms to be serviced.

Then it was around to see the kitchen garden and we emerged near the tennis court where Harry and Peter had commenced a knock up.

'Like a game?' Harry called, directing the inquiry to me, and I looked to Brian who indicated to the contrary.

'Not at the moment, thanks.'

Harry smiled understandingly and enveloped us in her friendly, curious gaze. Peter came over to the wire mesh. He was wearing tennis whites and looked absurdly handsome.

'I'll find you some tennis shoes if you'd like to play,' he said.

'Leave those lovers alone,' Harry called, laughingly. 'Can't you see they want to be alone?'

Peter, amused by his sister's banter, raised his eyebrows, and Brian and I drew away into the gloaming. Behind us Harry's bright voice and the whack of tennis balls punctuated the evening.

We skirted the house and walked to the artificial lake which I had seen earlier from my bedroom window. The swan had retired to the rushes.

'There used to be a pair,' Brian said. 'The fox got the hen; the cob won't last much longer. They mate for life.'

'Did you want to play that time?' he asked then.

'Tennis? God, no. I'd probably make a show of myself. And they didn't ask you to play?'

He looked at me sharply, his face pale in the waning light. Then he laughed. 'They were being polite to you; they don't have to be polite to me!'

I stared at him in perplexity. 'Why don't you just stand up to them?'

'Of course I have; but then they just upset Mummy and say Brian is causing unpleasantness and she gets worked up. It doesn't occur to her to disbelieve them. Dad then gets at me for upsetting my mother. You see,' he added quietly, 'she is

156

terribly easily upset and it is rather important that she should not be upset.'

I was silent for a while. I wondered how much of what Brian had told me about his brother and sister was his own subjective evaluation, based perhaps on childhood experiences? I could not believe that anyone as charming as Harry could intend any harm. Perhaps there was just some sort of silly sibling rivalry between the three of them? I ruminated for a minute or two and dismissed the whole thing. Glenallen was beautiful; my in-laws were beautiful; Brian was beautiful. All would be wonderful; the future was resplendent; had we not energy and passion enough for everything?

We went for a walk - skirting around by the wood beyond the artificial lake. I looked at the fields, almost all of them with horses grazing, some with a few cows. I saw a hay float containing a huge barrel trundling across a field. 'Water,' Brian explained. 'The troughs have to be filled.'

The wood was full of ash, birch, sally, black shadows and cool woodland smells. Brian knew his way among the shadows and drew me into a little dell, a semicircular drop in the ground and sat down. Overhead, through the branches, was the evening sky, blue-grey with twilight. Beyond the house I could see the mountain, dark with evening shadows, knowledgeable with the twists of Time. I leaned against Brian's shoulder.

'Tell me about Knockshee. I have the absurd notion that the hill watches us.'

Brian laughed, not a genuine convinced laugh, but a piece of dry intellectual mirth. 'You sound like Murty. He is so superstitious it's a wonder he does any work. Knockshee, the work of glaciation, too low now for a mountain, too high for a hill. We graze our horses on the commonage there, although no one else does.'

'Why?'

'Why what?'

'Why does no one else use if for grazing if it is commonage?'

He paused, then fixed me with calm eyes.

'Same reason why no one will plough a fairy fort. They're afraid?'

'What is there to be afraid of?'

'There are a host of stories. But I researched the folklore back as far as I could. Have you heard of the Formorians, Peige, one of the precursors to the Celts?'

'That's going back a long way!'

'I know! About six, maybe seven, thousand years. Legend has it that they had a king called Balor who had a terrible Eye, an evil eye. It was usually shut, because it took four men to open it, but once opened - rather like Pandora's Box - all manner of evil escaped.' He paused. 'Balor is supposed to be buried in that hill.'

I felt cold. It's only a myth, I told myself, remembering what Brian had told me down by the lake that summer after my mother's death.

'Is the writing you told me about - the message on the Ogham Stone - supposed to be linked with him?'

'*I know mine and mine know me*' he recited softly. 'Who knows? There are probably a lot of places like Knockshee. Ireland hardly tossed aside thousands of years of devotion to the ancient religion, to the goddess Brede, just like that! The princes welcomed Christianity because it consolidated their power. So what happened to

158

the Druids and those who would not convert - buried alive, perhaps, in their own temples?'

Then he added, with a short dismissive laugh, 'Once the place was called Súil Balóir - Balor's Eye - and then it became Knockshee because the country people saw fairies there and the ghosts of the dead.' I stood up and turned my back on the mountain.

'You're not superstitious, are you, Peg? It's only a bloody old hill, with a bog at the top. We'll ride up there someday when there's no mist on it, for the view.'

Why did I feel that he was protesting too much?

A little later, as we walked back across the fields we heard heavy breathing behind us and the paddings of heavy feet. I stifled a scream as a horse's head butted Brian gently. He stroked the animal's nose, pushing her head away.

'It's only Mara,' he said laughing at my terror. 'She's looking for sugar.'

I stood back and surveyed the mare; she was barely visible, a presence in the night.

'Is this the one Harry thought I should ride?' I asked, summoning the courage to stroke her nose. 'She's very nice.'

Brian sighed.

'She's a jade actually. She has bad habits!'

'What sort of habits?'

'Well her favourite trick is scraping her rider off on gateposts.'

We came back by the other side of the house. I held on to Brian's arm; it was dusk and he knew the ditches. We passed a construction of brick, circular, with boards nailed across the top.

'Is that a well?'

'It was. Peculiar one too, because it had an iron ladder going down which is now gone. They say that a passage ran under the house and came out half way down the well. If there was such a passage it was bricked up - at this point anyway!'

'Why was there an underground passage?'

He shrugged. 'The house is very old, late eighteenth century. The family was nominally Protestant for a few generations, but priests would come secretly to say mass. This passage, if it really existed, may have been their means of going and coming. And it may have connected with the souterrain at the foot of Knockshee.'

'I see. Where is the entrance to it in the house?'

Again he shrugged, lifting his shoulders.

'I don't know. Harry used to boast that she had found it, and that she would lock me up in it!'

He laughed again, but I heard the pain in it.

I brought up the subject then of when we would leave Glenallen and go to Dublin. How long were we going to stay? A week or two was what I had in mind, but Brian sighed and said it would depend. 'We can go whenever you like, of course, but at the moment Dad needs me here. He's not able to do very much right now; he's under doctor's orders to rest And he will only rest if I am here to look after things. I'm the only one who can run the place. Peter is only interested in his legal career. He has no interest at all in Glenallen.'

'Your sister could run the place. No bother to her, I'd say!'

He turned to look at me in the half dark.

'Yes, she probably could. But she will not be able to convince my father of that.'

'Murty could run it.'

'No! An experienced manager could, but his salary, at the moment, makes it out of the question. It will only be for a while, sweetheart.

Can you bear with me? Once I get the place running properly again we'll be free as the birds. Anyway there'll be no real job in Dublin until September when the new school year starts. And then we'll have a wonderful time, just the two of us!' He squeezed my hand. His own was very warm.

We came back under the arch of the stable yard where I had seen Mary all those years before stumbling off to get sick, and re-entered the house through the kitchen, wiping our shoes carefully at the door to placate Eilie, who was tidying something away in a drawer of the dresser, smiling at us knowingly and indulgently.

'Tis time the pair of ye were in yer bed. Do ye want a bite to eat before ye go?'

Brian laughed and I blushed, shaking my head.

'We're off this minute, Eilie,' he said and took my hand, leading me up the kitchen stairs and into the hall.

There was a polished oak table in the hall with a vase of summer flowers and beside it a lamp spilling light on to the mellow wood. Above it was an antique gilt mirror and near it on the wall was a 'brush', a fox tail mounted in silver. There were a few paintings of horses, and, towards the back of the hall, beside a fox's mask, was a coat-stand with some tweed caps and overcoats hanging from their pegs.

The stairs was at right angles to the tiled hall, a curving staircase with a dark red carpet. As we walked towards the steps I saw that the light was on in the drawing-room. The door was ajar and I thought we should say goodnight. But as I approached the door I heard Harry's voice.

161

'Just like him to marry a goldigger from the bogs without a penny.'

'Well, she's quite lovely, I suppose,' Peter's voice said in his quiet measured tones.

I stopped in my tracks.

'Is she? Maybe. Until she opens her mouth. She's as common as dirt. And I suppose we'll have to have the awful brother here, clutching his forelock. It's too bad, so dreadful for Mummy and Daddy.'

I heard Peter's conspiratorial laugh, the laugh of someone for whom the company is delightful and the conversation amusing, if a little extreme. I didn't look at Brian who was whispering something to me, but wrenched myself free of his arm and walked upstairs, trying to stem the tears. Afterall, I was the ugly duckling and they were the swans. Why should they accept me?

I woke that night when Brian cried out in his sleep. I cradled his head and told him he was only dreaming. He came groggily out of the nightmare, relaxed with terrible relief and we lay for a long while, half talking, half sleeping, while the moonlight came in through the chink in the curtains and silvered a patch of carpet. Why did he have these dreams? Why was he the butt of his sibling's contempt? What was all this business of ghosts on the mountain and his overdone, repeated insistence that the old folklore about it was rubbish? (I knew it was, of course, and consequently did not need such frequent reminders.) Why had he scars on his wrist and why had I been diffident about asking him about them? Just what had been going on in Glenallen?

The 'awful brother,' wrote to me a couple of weeks later, suggesting that he would come to see me when the hay was in; that he would like to visit Ballyharris. But, he stressed, on no account would he stay in Glenallen. 'I'm sure your new family have enough to do without catering for your stray brother! I'll stay in the hotel in Ballyharris.'

I told Brian that Tom was thinking of visiting and he said, 'Good. Tell Mummy and ask Eilie to get a room ready for him,' but he said it hesitantly and I let the subject drop. Tom arrived at the end of July, sooner than anticipated, and without any further warning. He was there on the front doorstep at about three o'clock one lovely afternoon when the house was empty. Harry was playing tennis with Clare de Lacy, a school friend who had come to stay with her, and Mr and Mrs Fitzallen were both resting in a sunny corner of the orchard.

I was in the stable yard talking to Brian over the half door of one of the loose boxes when Eilie emerged through the backdoor.

'Your brother's in the drawing-room, Mrs Peg.'

I ran into the house and, sure enough, there he was, in the fine new suit he had bought for my wedding, wearing collar and tie for a change, standing erect and staring out one of the tall drawing-room windows, his cloth cap in his hand. I embraced him and as I turned around I saw Harry standing in the hall, staring at us.

'Is this your brother?' she asked coldly. 'I saw him from the tennis court.'

Tom shook hands with grave courtesy and looked at her with open admiration. She was wearing tennis whites and was flushed from exercise; the tendrils of hair around her forehead

163

were damp with exertion and her long legs were golden from the sun.

'Pleased to meet you, Miss Fitzallen.'

'Where are you staying?' Harry inquired politely but pointedly while I blushed and Tom said quietly that he was staying at the Royal Hotel in Ballyharris; he would be going home tomorrow he said - five o'clock train.

Harry nodded then, said she would ask Eilie to send in some iced tea and disappeared.

Tom raised his eyebrows and looked at me closely.

'Are you happy here?' he demanded and I said I was very happy and he said I was living in a fine house and I agreed. It was not my place to show him the house; it was not my house. I wished that Brian would come in from the stable yard. From the window Tom and I saw Cissie approach on her bicycle, cycling slowly up the dappled avenue, print cotton dress rippling as she moved, and I saw the leaping pleasure in Tom's face.

'How did you get here?' I asked.

'Hired a bicycle!' He pointed to the stone balustrade and there, resting against it, was a black gent's bike.

I went to the front door to greet Cissie and when I came back Eilie was bringing in a tray with a jug of iced tea and two glasses.

'You'll never guess who I have here!' I said to Cissie as I brought her in and saw the genuine delight in her eyes.

'Tom! How did you get here?'

'Same way you did,' he said with a grin, taking her hand and holding it firmly.

I waited for a while for Brian to put in an appearance, but I waited in vain and gave up some excuse when Tom asked for him. I made

Tom and Cissie quench their thirst with the iced tea and then we set off on bicycles for the O'Shaughnessys, and the three of us ended up having high tea in the Royal Hotel in Ballyharris. Tom asked Cissie would she have lunch with him the following day and I heard her agree and I made my excuses. I knew the real reason why he had come to Ballyharris.

'I'll see you tomorrow, Peg.' Tom said. 'I'll call to say goodbye about four.'

'Better still' I said, 'I'll meet you at the station at half past. That will give us time for a chat before the train.' I did not want him calling to Glenallen again; I could not bear the prospect of him being slighted.

I went home to Glenallen and asked my husband why he had not come in to greet my brother and he stared at me with blank exasperation.

'Christ, Peg. I'm sorry. I was up to my eyes. I wanted to talk to him, but when I looked up you had all gone.'

He seemed genuinely upset.

'We couldn't wait all day.'

'Don't be cross. Ask Tom to excuse me when you write to him. Now stop smouldering and come and kiss me, Peg.' His hair was tousled, his blue eyes teasing, his open face penitent.

The letters arrived from UCG with our results. Brian and I both got good second-class honours - two ones. I felt as though a weight - the spectre of failure and its disgrace - had been lifted from my shoulders.

Brian did not seem overjoyed. 'I should have got a first,' he muttered, looking at me as though it were my fault.

'Maybe you would have if you hadn't spent your time kissing the fair maid of Salthill,' I whispered in his ear, and gave his ear lobe a sharp little nip in the sudden rush of euphoria. We were in the hall. Brain looked at me with a wicked smile, narrowed his eyes, dropped his letter and chased me out the open front door. Down the avenue I ran, my husband in hot pursuit, to be caught near the gate and bundled on to the grass. 'I'll be good, I'll be good,' I shrieked, kicking and thumping and begging him to stop tickling.

'Bite your husband would you?' he said gravely. He sat on me, grabbed my right foot and went over the toes and the sole with terrible teasing fingers.

'Beg for mercy,' he suggested conversationally, when my screams of laughter and outrage had reached new pitches of intensity.

'Mercy, mercy,' I howled.

A shadow fell across us. It was Harriet with her bicycle. I saw the cold curiosity in her eyes, although her lip curled in smiling distaste.

The euphoria, the laughter, died in me.

'You're showing your knickers, Peg!' she said with thin contempt and I smoothed down my skirt, stood up and explained that we had just got our results.

'How did you do?'

'Alright. We both got honours.'

'Good for you,' she said without enthusiasm.

That evening Eilie prepared a celebratory supper. Brian and I played 'footsie' under the table. The future seemed promising; we could now make definite plans. Harry was congratulatory after a flippant fashion and then very quiet. Her silence was powerful, intense, especially as she watched her mother congratulate Brian and heard her father say, 'Well done, my dear old chap. Well done, Peg.'

There was a shadow in Mrs Fitzallen's eyes and I knew that she was afraid of what this portended. She watched Brian's face at table, and although she was smiling and chatting her eyes were full of questions.

And in the weeks that followed he was courted by his parents; his father sought his opinion, had long evening discussions with him in the library - the small room which was really a study, filled with leather backed books and ledgers, the marble mantelpiece smoke stained, the window looking out at the side of the house by the archway to the stable yard. I would hear the discussion in passing whenever the door was open, what mares had 'broken out,' which of them had been covered by what stallion and how often; which of them had slipped foals; how Jessie had foaled a bay colt by Old Dickon and Ida had foaled a filly by Argos. His father would sip his whiskey, which he wasn't supposed to drink, and the two men would be so immersed in the business under discussion that they would hardly notice my shadow passing at the door. His mother would put an arm out whenever she met him to give him a quick, loving hug, and Harriet became quiet and watchful and subdued at table.

Brian blossomed. He strode around the farm with an air of command, was immensely busy, but had little time for me. I tried to immerse myself in reading, undertook the painting of some skirting boards and bedroom doors, occasionally wandered around the house at a loose end trying to imagine it in earlier times, to construct the past with its long dresses and its romance, and in turning a corner would frequently jump when I met Harry who seemed to materialise when I thought she was outside. 'Are you looking for something, Peg?' she might say, making me feel like a burglar caught red handed. I sensed a gathering angry desperation in her and began to feel very ill at ease on the one hand and very bored on the other.

Whenever Peter would come home he and Harriet would ride off together and at mealtime the bond between them was strong enough to send messages across the table in the absence of any speech. You could feel it, the empathy they shared, the pleasure he took in her company, the need she had of his, the necessity to her of his continued delight and admiration. It was as though she were visible only to him. Her parents were both sweet with her, treating her like a child. 'How's my honey?' her mother might say and her father, who had a pet name for her would ask, 'Suzy, will you find me the paper?' both impervious to the force she carried within her. She hid the extent of this force even from Peter; she held him with charm and feminine drollery and the mercurial, biting, turn of her wit.

Peter was more stand-offish than ever with Brian, treating him like some sort of usurper, addressing him with studied, contemptuous patience.

But Brian didn't seem to notice this. He was immersed in running the four hundred acres, in directing the twenty men who worked there. He had bought in several head of cattle, cows and bullocks at about £20.00 apiece and was full of plans for diversification. 'We should go into beef; that's where the money is now!'

I heard him talking to his father about the wages bill and the necessity of trimming back because of the war. Several of the men were let go.

The papers were full of the war; there were German air attacks on Channel convoys; there had also been the first large scale air attack on Britain over the Welsh docks; rationing was introduced in Ireland.

The dinner table in Glenallen buzzed with speculation; Brian and his father would discuss the latest developments, drawing themselves into a mutual rapport from their mutual anxiety, while Harry would interrupt with some bright comment from time to time and would assume a speculative brooding look when she didn't get the attention she expected. She spoke to her mother with gentle raillery; she was always gentle to her. But Mrs Fitzallen looked worried; she tended to get overwrought about anything at all that wasn't going right; she feared the war, the repercussions on the bloodstock industry, she feared the tightened belt which Brian was introducing, seeing in it a harbinger of bankruptcy. She was a pessimist by nature, enforced the blackout rigorously and wondered if Hitler would bomb Glenallen.

One day Brian mentioned the treatment of the Jews in Germany; there had been a newspaper article which had shocked him. He had passed it on to me. I said I thought Hitler was an evil man; for once, there was a war with a right and a wrong side.

'You like the Jews?' Harry asked, looking across the table at me in polite wonder.

I hesitated. 'Why shouldn't I? They're human beings.' I could feel my face redden and willed it to stop but, as usual, made it worse.

'Have you ever met any?'

'I really don't know,' I muttered, so hot in the face I thought I would spontaneously combust.

'They tend to take over everything, Peg dear,' Mrs Fitzallen assured me in subdued serious tones, shaking her head a little to emphasise the point. I retreated, knowing little of the real plight of Europe's Jewry and too shy to assert my viewpoint anyway. I ached to be alone with Brian who drew contemptuous glances from his sister and who seemed not to notice. Only alone with him was I at ease.

But ease or no ease I was half in love with Glenallen, its beauty, its space and peace; although I was haunted by the unspoken message in Harriet's eyes which was there despite her bonhomie. I knew how I stood with her; it did not take little episodes like, 'Open the gate, will you,' in peremptory command when I happened to be outside and she wanted to take the car out, to know how I was with her. I began to long for a place of our own; I wanted Brian to confirm the teaching appointment offered by his old school. But he only became defensive.

'Well, we'll go if you want, but it's not safe in Dublin now. It may be bombed. And they need us still. Dad's not well. It's only for a while.'

So I retreated again. My desires were so trivial compared to the serious family matters at issue. And Brian was happy, with the determined happiness of one who has the recognition, which he had always sought, dangled before him. His father needed him and his mother was ecstatic to have him back at home. I felt that, in their eyes, I was the appendage, the price of his compliance.

I had looked forward to our conferring in UCG. It would have been a day off, a whole day with Brian and Cissie. It also coincided with Cissie's twenty-first birthday. But Brian ended up being conferred in absentia because he claimed that he couldn't spare the time. I went to Galway with the O'Shaughnessys, congratulating Cissie and giving her a gift of a new riding crop with a silver handle, something I had kept money aside for from Tom's wedding gift of £50.00. Mary had written and had sent her a bottle of French perfume. 'I wish you would come and see me in Dublin,' she had said.

Tom turned up for the conferring ceremony and was introduced to Cissie's parents afterwards. When he heard it was Cissie's birthday he insisted on standing us all a good lunch and went off for a while to return with a huge bouquet of flowers for her.

'I'll have a party to celebrate at Christmas,' she told him. 'I hope you'll come.' Tom said he would, delight written all over him.

It was a happy day. I wore my hired mortar board and black gown with a lot of pleasure and went up for my parchment to polite clapping, turning to seek out Tom's eyes in the gathering as I came down from the rostrum. He gave me the thumbs up sign.

We laughed a lot that day, Cissie and Tom and I, like old times. Dr and Mrs O'Shaughnessy were in fine fettle, reminiscing about student days of an earlier period, which sounded to me like ancient history.

The gloom returned in the O'Shaughnessy's car as I saw Knockshee in the distance and

171

approached the gateway to Glenallen. It was a lonely kind of gloom; I was going back to a sort of silence, to being the outsider, and I did not know what to do about it.

Brian came to bed that night in good spirits, waking me when he got in, holding me tightly against him, his mouth against my hair. He was pleased, excited.

'Peg, my darling. Do you think you love me enough to make your home in Glenallen? Dad and I have been talking and he seems intent on leaving the place to me. If I stay.'

I struggled to sit up.

'But what about the others?' I said, trying to conceal my dismay.

'There's some money, Mummy's money, capital that was settled on her when she got married, of which she can only touch the income. But she can dispose of the capital by will. That could be given to Peter and Harry. The farm is mortgaged anyway - so it'll even itself out.'

'Has your mother been asked about this?'

'Of course. She's in full agreement!'

I said little. He was so happy, this man who would rule Glenallen. I loved him and delighted in his happiness. If only I could feel at home; if only I did not feel weighed under by some species of oppression which had become really apparent to me when I had been able to get away for a day. I slept little that night.

Not long after this Brian took me riding with him around the farm, pointing out various places of interest, the fairy well, the remains of an old stone sauna, the 'famine walls' erected by the starving in exchange for money to buy food during the hungry years - so that people on the edge of the grave would not be insulted by charity; a gravel quarry, long disused, gouged into the side of the earth.

'Where's the souterrain, or passage grave, or whatever it is?' I asked. 'I'd like to see the Ogham Stone.'

He pointed towards the foot of the mountain. 'It was covered in the rockfall. The time I saw it was after the archaeologists had uncovered it. And a queer bloody thing happened to me after that.'

His voice dulled and he looked away into the distance, up towards the summit.

'What happened to you?'

He frowned, then turned to look at me, squinting against the sunlight.

'Well, it was shortly after the archaeologists had finished their examination. I was about ten. I had a dog I was fond of, a terrier called Bob. He went missing for some days and I went out calling him. He was important to me because he was the only living thing I had to play with; neither Harry nor Peter would play with me - they were a bit older anyway - and I was forbidden to mix with the local children.

Anyway, I saw him running up towards the place the archaeologists had been examining. I shouted and shot an arrow from the bow I was carrying - one I had made myself with an ash plant and some string; he always ran to retrieve the arrows.

'But he didn't seem to hear me and went past the old Stone into the mouth of the tunnel and I followed him in, wondering why he didn't respond to my call.'

He stopped, silent.

'Go on.'

173

'I ran into the darkness and could not find poor Bob or any sound of him either. And then I realised I could not find my way back. I was in total darkness and silence. I shouted, very frightened, and all I heard were echoes. I cried for my mother, for my father. But there was only the darkness.'

'How did you get out?'

Brian turned to look into my eyes.

'I don't remember. They came looking for me it seems, with torches and found me curled up in one of the tunnels. It's a blank to me now. I had been in there a day and a half and if one of the men hadn't remembered that he had seen me running in that direction and if I hadn't dropped my bow near the entrance I might be in there still.'

'What an awful experience! Why didn't you tell me about this before?'

'I don't like talking about it! I'd rather forget it.'

'What happened to your dog?'

'That was the queerest part of it. One of the workmen had found his body two days earlier and had buried it so as not to have me upset. So whatever I was seeing when I followed it into the tunnel, it wasn't Bob!'

I felt the shiver up my backbone. Oh God, to get away from this place!

'You must have been very upset for some time, after an experience like that?'

'I suppose I was. But I hid it. Ours is a family where you do not show your feelings.'

'But,' I persisted, 'has this experience anything to do with your nightmares?'

He shrugged, looked away.

'Maybe. I dream that I am in dark place, which has at its centre something voracious, timeless, powerful; something seductive too because it

174

seems to offer ultimate satisfaction, ultimate peace.' He laughed, his dry intellectual laugh. 'Don't look at me like that, Peg. It's only a dream!'

'Yes,' I said. 'Eventually even reality itself becomes a figment of the mind. Will you show me the Ogham Stone?'

So he led the way towards the lower slope of the mountain where there was a rockstrewn bulge in the earth overgrown with brambles.

'It's in there.'

'Pity,' I said. I would have liked to have seen it.

I showed my degree parchment to the Fitzallens who were polite but disinterested.

'That means you can teach or something, does it?' Harry asked.

She was usually out for a large portion of the day, training and breaking young horses in the Long Field, a field of about thirty-five acres. She also went cubbing and sometimes came back with one or two friends for a drink. One of them was James Regan who had recently inherited a big place - Conneely House - about eight miles away. He was a big, hearty young man and I think Mrs Fitzallen hoped Harry would marry him. I watched her with him, but could not discern any affection for him, although he was very attentive. If anything his attentions made her irritable, for when he was gone she would become morose. I was in the kitchen one evening and saw Harry talking to him in the yard before he left. Tiny Tim was playing with a rubber ball, pouncing and dancing, the tiny bell which Nora had put on a collar around his neck catching the light. His attention was diverted by a thread that hung from Harriet's skirt. He took a swipe at this, missed and nicked her grey silk stockings.

James Regan left. Harry bent to look at the ladder in her stocking, then raised her eyes to where the kitten was playing. I saw the way they narrowed, the fury in them.

Next day Harry came back at lunchtime with lots of mushrooms strung together on long grass stalks. She left them in the kitchen and I washed and cooked them in milk with a shake of salt and pepper as I had seen my mother do, Eilie looking over my shoulder with a laughing comment, 'There's a cook lost in you, Mrs Peg, ma'am.'

On the following day Harry brought more mushrooms, but this time she seemed to have also brought back a few unusual varieties which she discussed with Murty in the upper stable yard. I saw her talking to him from the landing window, the mushrooms lying in the palm of her hand. Murty seemed to know a thing or two about fungi. He was shaking his head and I saw him prod the mushroom with a stick, turning up the gills and breaking open the flesh before throwing them on the ground and grinding them into the cobbles with the heel of his boot.

At lunch Mr Fitzallen asked Harry were there a lot of mushrooms this year and she said yes. 'Bumper! They're out every morning. I pick them early before the maggots can get into the gills.'

Her father nodded and Brian asked had she seen any of the queer ones that used to come up in the wood.

'If you see any, mash them.'

Harriet's eyes became glassy.

'Destroying Angel, Panther Cap,' her father continued. 'Pretty lethal damn things.'

Harry said she hadn't seen any.

Brian was in good form. 'You see, Peg, Harriet knows all about plants and fungi, but she won't

176

go to college. She'd make a great botanist Are we being lazy or proud?' he asked his sister, with an awkward attempt at brotherly raillery, which he essayed now from time to time in an apparent attempt to break the impasse between them.

Harry's face darkened. 'You idiot! Women lose power once they reveal they have it.'

There was a surprised silence. Her mother looked at her, startled, but Harry smiled and the moment passed.

That evening Nora was very quiet as she served supper and it wasn't until we heard the sniffs that we realised she was in tears.

'What's the matter with you, Nora?' Mrs Fitzallen demanded.

'Oh nothin' ma'am. It's just my poor little cat. He's missing.'

Mrs Fitzallen raised her eyes to heaven.

'That girl is a bit simple,' Harry said when Nora had left the room.

As autumn deepened I realised that I was pregnant. I felt nauseous. I missed two periods. The smell of the dogs, of the horses, of everything, was heightened. I lost my appetite, skipped meals. Mrs Fitzallen expressed anxiety about me and Harry told her I was sulking about something, or so Brian told me later. But as I only suspected my condition I was afraid to tell him in case I was wrong. And if I was right it would be an acknowledgement that my fate was sealed, that my life's course was set and immutable.

The great bonus about living in Glenallen was having Cissie nearby; being able to cycle over to see her in the evenings and at weekends. She was teaching at the girls convent secondary school, a new day school, in Ballyharris and her father took

177

her with him every morning when he drove to his surgery. Being a doctor he was still able to get petrol for his car.

Since our conferring she had begun to talk about Tom occasionally, after a gentle and intrigued fashion. I knew he had written to her, and I suggested that the two of us pay a visit to Ballycloghan after Christmas for a day or two. She agreed, 'If Tom will have us,' she said with a twinkle and I smiled to myself. Tom have us indeed! So I wrote and told him to expect us and got an ecstatic letter back. 'Wonderful - looking forward to the pair of you!'

Cissie got a new horse, a hunter called Ebony, black and beautiful. It was her parents' birthday present and I saw less of her now, because she was so busy exercising him.

Peter came home for one of his occasional weekends and, as we drove back from Mass, happened to see Cissie at the top of the lane waiting to cross the road. He stopped the car and opened the window. Cissie was looking wonderful, flushed from exercise. She was carrying the new crop I had given her and raised it in greeting.

'Congratulations,' Peter said, indicating the new horse. 'How do you find him?'

She laughed.

'He's great - a real eager beaver!'

The horse, as though to prove her right, danced a little under the restraining rein.

'Why don't you come up to Glenallen? I'd like to see how he compares with Bella. Join us for lunch!'

I could see Cissie struggle to keep control of her face. She blushed crimson; joy leapt in her eyes. She looked at me, glowing, half laughing.

'Alright. What time?'

Peter said one thirty and drove on. Harry was sitting beside me in the back and I saw her face, saw the surprised arrested expression, saw her glance swiftly at her brother. And Peter drove on home with a poker face. He rode with Cissie that afternoon and again when he came home for the following weekend. Cissie was welcomed by Mr and Mrs Fitzallen at the lunch table, but Harry always excused herself early. Then, some weeks later, Brian told me that he had seen them dismounted in the wood, in a passionate embrace. I looked out for signs in Peter of this burgeoning romance, imagining his lips in passionate contact with Cissie's, but he struck me as more inscrutable than ever. I waited for Cissie to confide in me, but she said nothing.

Mr Fitzallen's condition worsened. He became increasingly sallow and frail, took to his bed more, talked of making his will. After this I noticed how even more withdrawn Harry became and then suddenly friendly, affable, drawing both Brian and myself within the magnetic circle of her charm. I thought that she had decided to like me after all and to bury whatever hatchet had existed in her relationship with Brian. So when she came into our room one evening - I had gone to bed early and Brian was out at a foaling - I welcomed her. When she questioned me about my health I said I was fine and when she asked me if I was just a teensy weensy little bit pregnant I nodded, laughing a little at her perceptiveness. Her face

179

became instantly inscrutable although the smile played still on her mouth.

'Oh well done, you clever thing!' she said. 'Does Brian know?'

'I haven't told him - yet.'

'Well, we'll keep it our secret for the moment so,' she said.

She asked me about the book I was reading, *Anna Karenina*, and said she had seen the film - and we discussed Garbo; She talked about her school-days then and made me laugh with her funny reminiscences. It was a pleasant evening - one of the pleasantest I had at Glenallen.

The next day, 26 October, was my twenty-first birthday. I knew Brian had forgotten it; I had dropped no hints and he had not mentioned it. I woke up to an empty room as was now usual and as I was going downstairs, I tripped inexplicably. I felt something hard and round under my feet - like marbles or ballbearings. Harry was quickly on the scene, gathering me up at the bottom of the stairs and calling for Nora to fetch the doctor. I could hardly see her. There was nothing except pain.

'There was something on the stairs, marbles, I think,' I gasped, crying.

'You tripped on the loose piece of carpet,' Harry said. 'I was coming down behind you and saw the whole thing.'

I passed out then and came to in bed with my ankle in bandages, Doctor O'Shaughnessy beside me, his face full of concern and compassion. There was a covered basin with blood spots on the cloth. He didn't have to tell me what was under it in the basin. Brian came in, took me in his arms and we both cried for a long time.

'Why didn't you tell me?' he asked.

'I wasn't sure.'

And he made me promise never to do that again. And I promised and cried and said there had been marbles or something on the stairs and I hadn't seen them. He listened and looked perplexed.

'You must be imagining things, Peg. How could marbles get on to the stairs?'

November came, the November of 1940. I got a card from Tom wishing me a happy birthday and apologising for being late. 'I'll save your present till I see you!'

I got a card from Mary too, but no letter, which I had hoped for.

It was almost a week since the miscarriage and I was under doctor's orders to rest as much as possible. Eilie brought me breakfast in bed every morning on a small oval tray with a pretty little embroidered cloth, puffing so much that I suggested she should get into bed and eat it herself.

'Go way outta that with you, Mrs Peg, Ma'am,' she said, plumping the pillows.

She brought me the paper and showed me the picture of Peter in wig and gown taken outside the Four Courts with some notables who had been involved in a civil action and whom he had represented. In his legal regalia he looked haughtier than ever, his handsome face pale against the black gown and white collar and his eyes stern under the anachronistic eighteenth-century wig.

Every day the paper brought more news of bombing raids on London; the blitz was underway in good earnest; the tension reached even us in far away Glenallen, holding our breaths in our own fashion, fearful for the future. I read the papers avidly and got nightmares about wandering lost in a city in flames, groping my way among the dead. Again I dreamed I was underground with corpses all around me, yellow white, decaying, and among them Tom's face; I awoke with terror to find the light still on and Brian not yet in bed. I sat up and wrote a letter to my brother to tell him my news and ask him to write to me.

His reply, which I received a week later, asked if this miscarriage meant I would not be coming with Cissie after Christmas. I did not answer this immediately; at that point I could not imagine myself having the energy to walk down to the end of the avenue, never mind undertake a journey to Ballycloghan.

Peter came home for a few days to hunt and came up to see me one evening after supper.

'How are you, Peg?' he inquired, with grave condescending affability.

I was delighted to see him, because I was fed up being so much alone and he was such superb company when he put his mind to it.

'I'm fine now.' I told him I had seen his photograph in *The Irish Times* in his wig and gown. 'You looked every inch the advocate,' and he seemed pleased.

'You must rest,' he said and searching for something else to converse on, glanced at my book shelf and raised his eyebrows.

'Quite a selection. You read a lot?'

'Voraciously at the moment. Cissie brings me plenty from the library.'

I detected a flicker in his eyes.

'We were hunting today,' he murmured.

182

He leaned back in the chair, looked around the room, relaxed for a moment as I had not seen him relax before.

'Do you find it dull here?' he asked then, watching me, his eyes suddenly gentle.

'No,' I lied. 'Glenallen is such a lovely place, but you must know that better than I do.'

'Lovely? Yes.' He paused, his eyes still on my face. 'Although when I was a child I had such a sense of isolation all the time. We were too much alone. I don't ever want to be trapped here again!'

I tried to conceal my amazement, not at what he had said, but that he should have disclosed himself at all.

'You see,' he went on, 'in a way we are like the Graeae, - the three sisters of Greek mythology who shared a tooth and an eye between them. None of us is whole; - stunted development from a claustrophobic childhood!'

I listened in astonishment, hoping he would go on, but he abruptly changed the subject, favoured me with a polite peck and was gone. The room felt strangely empty. I got out of bed and pulled the curtains against the black night and tried, unsuccessfully, to warm the cold despairing loneliness which now beset me on an almost daily basis, like an enemy waiting for a breach in my defences. I thought of the child I had lost, my son, and made myself ill with weeping for him, mourning his childhood, his adolescence, his manhood, all that might have been. I imagined his face; imagined teaching him to walk, to talk, to discover the world. I did this alone because Brian was so seldom with me.

I knew he was working himself to death, now that so many of the men had been let go, and that he spent most of his spare time with his father.

However, now that Peter was home, my young husband sometimes spent the evening in our room with me and talked about which of the mares was due to foal and about his plans for diversification. I listened with definite, but ill-defined, foreboding. There was no more talk of going to Dublin. He assumed that I had shelved this ambition since the night he had spoken to me of his prospects of inheritance. I had kept silent about it to give him the space he needed. I knew he had been desolated by the miscarriage - so had his parents; even Harry had seemed depressed and consoling. It had brought on one of the migraines she suffered from occasionally, necessitating her staying in bed in a darkened room for two days. She came to see me when she got up, looking so pale and ill that I felt alarmed for her.

'Are you better?' I asked.

She nodded with a half laugh. 'I wish they would invent something. When it's bad it's like a sledgehammer bashing out my brains.'

Cissie called to see me after lunch on the day following Peter's visit. I had seen her only once since the miscarriage and then briefly as she had been under strict instruction from her father not to tire me. Now she came in quietly, her face radiantly happy, and deposited a little gaily wrapped parcel on the bed.

'For your birthday,' she said gently. 'It would have been inappropriate any sooner.'

I took the small parcel and removed the paper carefully to disclose a red morocco box. Inside, on a bed of white satin, was a gold charm bracelet with a single circular charm bearing the initials

MF. The legend on the inside of the lid said 'Oliver Sweeney & Sons, Jewellers, Ballyharris'.

There was also a little white card which read: 'To our darling Peg with best wishes on your Birthday. With love from all the O'Shaughnessys'.

Unable to speak I took out the gold bracelet to put it on my wrist, and burst into tears. Cissie put her cheek against my wet one and whispered, 'Cheer up. There'll be other babies.'

'It's not even the baby.' I sobbed. 'it's everything!'

When I was composed I told her it was beautiful and thanked her and said to thank them all for me and I blew my nose.

'What's up with you anyway?' I asked then. 'You're glowing like a star.'

She laughed, showing her even white teeth.

'Thanks, Peg. It must be the hunting. Ebony is a great ride.'

'Yes. So Peter tells me. I can't tell who he is most impressed by - you or Ebony!'

I saw the quick cloaking of expression in her eyes. She had never told me
romance, or what was between her and Peter.

'There was a downpour yesterday and we sheltered in the old quarry.' She did not meet my eyes as she said this, but smiled to herself with a joy that resisted containment.

'Very romantic,' I said, my heart sinking as I thought of Tom. 'Does he kiss nicely?'

Cissie blushed, avoiding my eyes.

'Oh Peg. How can you be so silly?'

'He's an attractive man,' I said, 'And he knows it.'

The blush deepened. She shrugged, shook her head at me as though I were a precocious child.

'Well, I'll be off. Hope you're back on your feet soon.'

When she was at the door I said 'Cissie' and she turned to me, her face still smiling, although now slightly strained.

'Be careful! Particularly of Peter!'

The smile was shut off. She stared back at me, shock in her eyes, the pupils large and black.

'Why?' she demanded. 'Why should I be careful of Peter?'

'I don't know,' I said miserably. 'He's too deep; too secret; too contained. There's a melancholy in him too.'

'You worry too much, Peg,' she breathed. 'That is precisely what I like in him. I think we have some kinship of spirit.' And she raised her eyebrows to show that she didn't mean to sound ponderous and was gone, shutting the door quietly behind her.

That night Brian told me that he had seen Peter and Cissie riding together in the direction of the old quarry earlier that evening. And Peter, when he appeared for dinner, had been tired and non-communicative.

'I don't know the hell,' Brian said. 'If I didn't know my brother better I'd swear there was something serious going on there!'

'Well, he's only a man after all.'

'Yes. But he's too private to ever disclose himself - physically or emotionally; and if he did he'd never forgive the person responsible.'

I bit my lip. I thought of our little *tête-à-tête*; would he hold that against me? And I thought of Cissie who was a combination of strength and fragility. Where Peter was concerned she was fragility itself.

Brian shrugged, dismissing the whole thing.

'Anyway, Cissie's too sensible for that,' he said.

I did not show him the O'Shaughnessys' present. I was too angry with him for forgetting my birthday. I put it away at the back of a drawer, treasuring the knowledge of it, treasuring the love which had prompted it, taking it out sometimes to reassure myself. And Brian and the rest of the household remained oblivious to my coming of age.

I got up, still a bit shaky, my ankle tender and my back wobbly, and went back to active life in Glenallen. But I was really chafing at the restrictions now, longing to have a job like Cissie, longing to have an income, something I knew was needed in Glenallen. When I mentioned it at dinner table there was silence and Brian frowned at me meaningfully. Apparently (so he explained rather diffidently afterwards) it would not do for a member of the Fitzallen family to so demean herself. I was surprised, because I knew from Brian how tight things were now. Various repairs were needed to the house; there was a leak in the valley in the roof for instance and some of the guttering needed replacing. It would be expensive work, but still I wasn't to get a job. I could make myself useful in the house if I liked, but that made me feel like a servant, especially as neither Harry nor Brian would dream of doing housework. The only light on the horizon was the nearness of Cissie. But she had lost the glow of that day when she had come up to see me; she refused to be drawn about Peter and when I asked her was she still interested in the trip to Ballycloghan she demurred, saying we could put it off until the weather got warmer, that Easter would be a better time. So when I wrote to Tom I broke the news that we would not be coming, giving my own exhaustion after the miscarriage as an excuse.

Cissie, however, became so withdrawn that I resolved to tax her with it at the first opportunity. I wondered was she ill, so pale had she become with dark shadows under her eyes.

But before Christmas came something happened which made me feel that our position in Glenallen was more than precarious. Brian rarely went hunting. Harry, however, had told him that if he wanted to be taken seriously in the neighbourhood he had better be seen and that the exercise would do him good anyway. So he did hunt, mounted on Rufus, a chestnut sixteen hand gelding. It was a December morning, cold mist hanging over everything; the meet was at Glenallen and I watched it from the bedroom window. Cissie was there - she never missed a meet - and the usual hunting fraternity, their voices high with the prospective excitement of the chase, their breath steamy in the cold morning air. As they moved off Cissie turned and waved up at me and Brian did too. Looking after them with their straight backs and equestrian confidence, it occurred to me that Brian should have married Cissie, they made so handsome a couple. I watched Brian's back until he was lost to view.

About an hour after the hunt had left, while I was trying to mend a pair of old tapestry curtains in the green bedroom, I heard raised voices downstairs, and galvanised with some inner dread I hurried down. It seemed that Rufus had returned, riderless and without his saddle. Every eye in the kitchen, Eilie's, Nora's and Murty's (who had come in from the stable yard with the news), turned to me.

'I'm sure he's alright, ma'am,' Murty said, but his eyes were full of fear. I recognised that he was afraid for himself; it was his job to see to the tack and if the girth had broken the blame would lie at his door. I felt a stab of the anguish I had experienced when my mother died, the essential loneliness of the world. But then I knew that Brian was too good a horseman to worry about a toss. He knew how to fall, he was alive - but was he injured?

Cissie galloped into the stable yard a moment later. I saw her through the kitchen window and rushed outside.

'Brian's alright,' she shouted at me. 'The girth broke when he was taking a fence in Jack Ryan's meadow and he came off in the hedge. He's a bit scratched but on his way!'

I laughed in relief and saw the relief in Murty's eyes too.

'But how could the girth break?' I asked.

Cissie raised her shoulders and dropped them again. 'It happens,' she said. 'Old leathers?'

Murty stared at her, indignation written all over him.

'Them leathers were fine ... nothin' perished about them.' And he turned on his heel and went into the tack room, emerging with saddle and bridle for Winny and another saddle for Rufus. When he had saddled the latter he rode off to fetch Brian, holding Rufus by the rein; he didn't throw another glance in our direction.

Cissie made a face at me, rolling her eyes. She dismounted.

'Aren't you going back to the hunt?'

'No. I'll wait with you for the returning wounded. Anyway the hunt will be miles off by now.'

Brian came back on Rufus a little later, looking furious. Behind him came Murty with the offending saddle perched clumsily over Winny's shoulders.

'What happened?' I asked Brian.

'Damn girth snapped.' He glanced at Murty who looked sullen and busied himself removing the saddle and broken girth into the tack room. 'Good thing it didn't happen when I was jumping out on to the road or it might have been serious.'

Murty stayed in the tack room for a few minutes and then came out and calmly unsaddled Rufus and Winny and led them away, their hooves clopping on the cobbles. Then he called Brian aside and spoke to him just out of earshot. I saw Brian's face whiten as he listened and his mouth tightened as he followed the groom into the tack room. Cissie and I made to follow them, but found the door shut in our faces.

I tried to talk to Brian later about the accident, but he was strangely cold and impatient with me and did not want to be questioned. Harry seemed concerned at suppertime, saying that Murty was getting past it, her eyes flickering from one of us to the other, before settling on her mother's anxious face. And Nora was upset again. One of the men had found the corpse of Tiny Tim in the manure heap. It was decomposed, but identifiable by the little bell on its neck.

'You can have another kitten,' Mrs Fitzallen told her.

Nora gulped. 'But it will never be the same one, ma'am; and the poor little thing was smothered, buried in the manure.'

Harriet's eyes narrowed and she hissed at Nora not to be upsetting people about her stupid cat when they were at table.

190

'I'm not that easily killed,' Brian told his mother with a short laugh after supper, when she pressed him about being careful. He put an arm around her shoulders jocosely and tenderly and she looked up at him with pride and love. I looked at Harry and saw the same cold exasperation in her face which I had seen on my first evening at Glenallen.

That night I prayed for Brian and myself as I waited for him to come to bed, prayed for our future, passing the rosary between my fingers under the blankets, full of an unease I could neither elude nor identify.

Chapter 7

The Christmas of 1940 was a quiet one. We went to eleven o'clock mass in the trap. When we returned the house was full of the scents of roasting fowl and Nora was flitting between kitchen and dining-room preparing the dinner table. There were sprigs of holly stuck behind the picture cords in the hall and a red Christmas candle by the window in the drawing-room; it stood up straight in a dried flower arrangement of leaves and gilded acorns.

Brian and I gave small gifts to everyone. Harry distributed her gifts; she pecked Brian on the cheek with barely concealed distaste as she gave him his little box of handkerchiefs and wished him a happy Christmas. Mrs Fitzallen handed him an envelope and I saw that there was a cheque in it. Harry saw this too; her face darkened and she looked at the scarf her mother had given her with cold comparing eyes.

Brian and I had already exchanged our own presents in our room - a jumper for him, knit during the long lone evenings, a silver filigree brooch for me in the shape of a true love knot.

'Peg, my darling,' he had said with a hang dog air, 'I forgot your birthday and you never said a word.'

'It doesn't matter,' I answered, delighted that he had remembered it now. 'We had other things on our minds.'

I kissed him, lingeringly, breathing him in, feeling the rasp of his chin. It was Christmas. We could be together for a while, I thought.

I wanted to go back to bed, but someone called him from downstairs and he went off with a quick apology.

We ate at three, the curtains open to the darkening day, the sun going down like a blood orange behind the trees in the distance. The cold air was heavy with mist. I loved the feeling of the dead year outside and the warmth within.

Peter was not at the dinner table. He was spending Christmas with some friends in Dublin and was expected the following day. Aunt Rita, sister of Mrs Fitzallen and the survivor of the two aunts who usually came after Christmas, was the only guest at the table. She sat up very straight, her yellow-grey hair pulled into a bun.

The dining table was set with silver candleabra, damask, Christmas roses in bowls; there was goose and turkey and plum pudding with brandy butter. The room smelled richly of roast fowl, hot potatoes, vegetables and the last of the wine from the cellar. The talk was, as usual, of the war.

I watched the flames dancing up the chimney, watched the people at the table, candlelight flickering on faces, enjoying the feast. The brass fender was bright with recent polishing; china plates and dishes were stacked on the sideboard; the two red setters, Rex and Roger, slept on the hearth rug, twitching occasionally, their heads snugly between their paws.

I listened to the talk of the blitz, my father-in-law declaiming on the plight of the Londoners; the people queueing for entrance to the underground stations, the horror of living beneath the city with the wind blowing eternally

193

through the tunnels and the bombs crashing overhead. It sounded like something from HG Wells, some sort of fantasy remote from reality.

'The British will stand up to them though; I'd go to fight the Hun myself if I had my youth back,' he announced. Mrs Fitzallen smiled uncomfortably, her grey eyes fixed immediately on her son, and Brian said nothing. His father looked at him, adding hurriedly, 'You can't go, of course. Your first duty is here.' And he went on about how Jerry would be taught a proper lesson this time.

Mr Fitzallen's health was worse; he had failed in the past few months, become thinner, intolerant of his illness, irritable in a way I would hardly have believed of him. He was given to talking about the war as though he were running it. He disliked Aunt Rita and made little secret of the fact. Later, I heard from Brian that he had approached her for a loan of some money to deal with the problem in the roof; she had refused. For this she had not been forgiven.

The old lady was precise in her speech and this monotonous precision grated on my father-in-law's nerves. She said what she thought, told me my hair was nice - the same colour as Danny's; I asked who Danny was and Brian sighed and said in my ear that he was her old spaniel. I laughed, remembering Barbie. I was wearing the same hair up this evening and my crepe de chine dress with my new filigree brooch and the little antique earrings I had got from Aunt Rita for Christmas.

Harry darted me a look of private satisfaction.

'Aunt Rita darling, won't you have some more turkey?' she asked a little too loudly and the old woman, who liked food, and who had already had second helpings, said she would and applied

194

herself to the fresh plateful with gusto. Mr Fitzallen confided to me testily, in a whisper which the whole table could hear, that greed was always disgusting.

Harry gave a stifled snort of laughter and the old lady looked up at me with eyes full of pain. I wanted to disclaim out loud any complicity in this cruelty, but I could say nothing. My father-in-law sat beside me at the head of his table and I dared not say anything which would show a kindness for poor Aunt Rita. It was impossible for me not to like an old lady who had gone to so much trouble with her presents and her pathetic beseeching aura to be liked and accepted as one of the family. I knew that Mrs Fitzallen, her sister, wanted this too; she sat quietly and impotently at the other end of the table, but it was plain at a glance that the contempt for her sister was not lost on her. And so, although the fire blazed merrily, and the lovely old room surrounded us with elegance, the Christmas dinner was fraught with tension and pain.

'How is Mary McElligott getting along in Dublin?' Harry suddenly asked me and I said that she was getting along fine, that she was in demand as an actress and now had a part in 'Strange Guest' by Francis Stuart which was playing at the Abbey. Mary had told me this in one of her letters, but had not stated what part had been given her. I felt a warm pride in her success and was looking forward very much to seeing her after Christmas. Her card had mentioned her proposed visit to the O'Shaughnessys. She would be staying with them for a few days.

Harry leaned back, a little tight from the wine, and giddy perhaps with having, surreptitiously as she thought, baited Aunt Rita for her father's amusement. Her blue eyes were very bright tonight, and the candlelight played on the blond glints in her straight fair hair, and on the string of creamy pearls she was wearing, her Christmas present from Aunt Rita, an heirloom. She looked flushed, very young, very regal.

'Poor old Mary,' she said with a sudden fit of giggling and her mother looked at her, frowning.

Aunt Rita put her head a little sideways, brows creased in recollection.

'She was in the Long Field one day,' Harry went on. 'She was very small at the time - about five - and Peter and I set Billy on her. She thought he was the devil.'

She looked at my blank face.

'Billy was a goat we had then. We used to play bullfighters with him. He butted everyone. Poor Mary was knocked down and every time she tried to get up he butted her again and she had to cross the field on all fours.'

Tears of mirth were streaming down Harry's face. 'It was so funny, but of course he wouldn't really hurt her. Anyway, Jim, that queer fellow who was the assistant stud groom at the time, came and took her out of the field. She was screaming and holding on to him for dear life and we ran away.'

There was sudden silence at the table.

'Was she the little girl ... the time the ... you remember that awful man?' Aunt Rita asked in her precise voice and Mrs Fitzallen's wine glass fell from her hand, spilling the contents across the white cloth. Nora came with a napkin to mop it up.

Harry's mirth suddenly died. She looked at her mother with alarmed concern. Mr Fitzallen pushed back his chair and said something to Nora. There was total silence then. Eilie and Nora busied themselves with cutlery at the sideboard.

Aunt Rita went on eating methodically, swallowed, took a drink of her wine, quite oblivious to the rising tension.

'Then there was the other poor child ... who had that accident,' she said, shaking her head, 'that unfortunate accident.'

I looked around the dinner table at the pale, silent faces. Mrs Fitzallen pushed her plate away. Harry, bereft of laughter, stared at the table-cloth for a moment before directing a forced command to one of the dogs who was scratching his ear, her eyes returning to watch her mother's face. Brian kept his eyes on his plate.

Who was the other child who had an accident? Was it Cissie? Was it at Glenallen that she had lost part of her hand, all of her peace? I caught Brian's eye, but he shook his head almost imperceptibly, glanced at his mother and whispered 'Later.'

Although it was Christmas I determined to seek Cissie out after dinner. Not that I was going to ask her any questions arising out of the exchange at the dinner table in Glenallen, but I needed to talk to her.

She hadn't called for about a fortnight and I couldn't help wondering whether I had become as dull as my circumscribed life - or had she taken umbrage over what I had said about Peter. Things had not been quite the same between us since. I had seen her at mass that morning, looking pale and a little tired, although she had brightened momentarily when I approached.

'Are you hunting tomorrow?' I asked then and her eyes stared past me for a moment and she said she probably would. 'Peter's coming home,' I added. 'Why don't you come back after the hunt for a drink?'

'No thanks, Peg. I don't want to intrude.'

'You intrude? Cissie, are you out of your mind?'

But she just smiled thinly at me and turned away.

Something was definitely wrong. I wanted to confront Cissie and find out what, but at the same time I didn't want to make the rift between us any deeper. So I sat quietly at the dinner table in Glenallen and abstracted myself from the pained silence. I thought of Tom eating his Christmas dinner alone and also thinking of Cissie. His Christmas card had contained a note; he was very busy, he said and hoped I was feeling better and he was sure it wouldn't be long before I was writing to tell him there was another baby on the way and to be careful of stairs the like of which they had in Glenallen. How was Cissie? He was disappointed we wouldn't be coming after Christmas but we must come as soon as we could, for a few days, like old times. Then he had told me that Uncle Matt was poorly and that he was bringing him to stay in Ballycloghan for Christmas.

I had told this to Brian at table. 'Your rich uncle? You should invite him here!' Harry had interjected with a laugh and I had laughed back and said she wouldn't care for him. 'He has a terrible tongue and the only person he likes is Tom. When he dies Tom will be worth a fortune!'

Harry's blue eyes dwelt on me for a moment. 'Is that so?'

Tom's card had a blue ribbon tied in a little bow and two robins sitting on a snowy branch. I was sorry for the disappointment he had sustained over Cissie's visit, sensing the blow it had been to him.

It was very dark after dinner and I got Brian to drive me over to Cissie's. I knew Harry would not approve because of the shortage of petrol and the fact that the tank at the back of the lower stable yard was more than half empty. 'Harry will have a fit,' I murmured.

'She can have all the fits she likes,' Brian answered equably.

Young David, recently tall and broken voiced, opened the door of the O'Shaughnessy residence with 'If it isn't the grand Mrs Fitzallen?' and led us into the sitting-room where the family were all gathered, all that is except Des who was with his squadron at Biggin Hill in England, and Cissie who was not in the room.

After exchanging seasonal greetings, accepting our box of chocolates and pressing a whiskey on Brian, Mrs O'Shaughnessy said to me that Cissie was in her room and to go on up, which I did. The stair carpet was worn through to the weave in places now, but the house still exuded that old warmth, gathering me back to it with faithful love. It was a house where people mattered, an age away from the oppression of petty personal politics and conquest by contempt.

The door of Cissie's room was open and I knocked quickly and stuck my head in, words of cheer ready on my lips. But the room was empty. I walked in, glad to be back in this cocoon where I had spent so many contented nights of my childhood. Cissie's diary was on her bed and on the floor was a typewritten letter. I picked up the letter, caught sight of the signature and, acting on an impulse of which I was later ashamed, I opened it out and read it.

199

'Dear Cissie,

I am in receipt of your letter. I am sure that on reflection you will realise it was a little extravagant. It was kind of you to offer to visit me here, but I will be so busy between now and Christmas that I can't see myself having a single moment to spare!

You are a very attractive young woman, not withstanding your small deformity, and I'm sure you will have no difficulty in attracting some man worthy of you.

And as we can't avoid seeing one another at the meet I'm sure you will have sufficient delicacy to avoid embarrassment.

Every good wish,

Sincerely,

Peter Fitzallen.

I heard the lavatory flush and in a moment Cissie stood in the doorway. I dropped the letter. Cissie looked from me to it, paled and went quietly to pick it up.

She took the letter, folded it carefully and tore it into pieces, throwing the pieces into the waste paper basket in the corner. Then she turned to me, her eyes hot in her white face.

'That wasn't worthy of you, Peg.'

'I'm sorry Cissie. I didn't mean to pry.'

For a moment she looked as though she would burst into tears. I saw the tremor at the corner of her mouth, then the assertion of the pride which denied the release of tears.

'He's not worth it, Cissie.'

Some of the coldness drained out of her face.

'I'm a fool, Peg. But there's really nothing for you to worry about. I'm not the first woman to have made a fool of myself over a man and I won't be the last.'

She glanced down at her injured hand and put it in her pocket. She managed a small stiff smile. 'C'mon,' she added with forced gaiety, 'let's join the others downstairs.'

I took her by the shoulders and sat her down on the bed.

'What happened,' I asked, 'between you and Peter?'

'A lot, and nothing. We got a bit carried away once or twice.' She blushed, put her head in her hands. 'And I was fool enough to think it meant something for him too.'

I was silent. We could hear the others downstairs; someone had told a joke and the laughter bubbled through the house.

'I will have to go away. You see, I'm pregnant!'

I heard these words without understanding, the way one might hear words on the wireless, dramatic in themselves but having nothing much to do with the stuff of real life. But this was real life.

'But he'll have to marry you now!' I whispered.

'No! He would not even give me time to tell him.'

'Oh Cissie ... You can't go away! Where would you go?'

'I don't know yet. Can you imagine what this would do to Mummy and Daddy?'

I was silent. Cissie would need money. If she went away she would have to give up her job.

'Christ, Cissie, I wish I had some money to give you, but I haven't a cent. I have to darn my stockings and mend my knickers and Brian hasn't got a bean either; they work him to death but give him hardly any money.'

She squeezed my hand. 'Thanks, Peg. I have some saved.'

'You contacted him since?' I asked, aware that I had no right to an answer, but consumed with curiosity about the letter I had read.

'Yes. I thought I might do some Christmas shopping in Dublin and wrote to tell him I would be up on the 8th. I sent the letter to Glenallen. He didn't want to see me, of course. I'm deformed you see.' She gave a little forced laugh. 'You saw his letter?'

'Yes. And you still love him?'

She stared at me, her mouth curved. 'Love?' And laughed that little hard laugh again.

She was silent for a while and then she muttered, 'The irony of it too - it was in Glenallen that I had the accident with the hand.'

The dinner table at Glenallen was immediately in my mind, Mrs Fitzallen's wine glass spilling across the cloth.

'What happened? You never told me the full story.'

'Oh - I don't want to talk about it. A stupid prank. They blamed Brian for it, at least Harry and Peter did.'

She heard me gasp. 'Brian?'

'But I have never believed that he was responsible,' she hastened to assure me. 'Never. I heard his father thrashed him horribly over it. I was sorry about that. He was so young and he was too horrified to have had any part in it.'

'Who was responsible so?'

She shrugged.

'I don't know. I don't think the other two were involved either - so it must have been one of the servants - maybe a stable-boy.'

And then she made me swear that I would tell no one about her pregnancy. 'No one, Peg, ever. It's bad enough that I know I've made a fool of myself. I couldn't bear it if other people knew! '

I was aware that Mary was coming to stay with her for a few days, and realised that she did not want even Mary to know. So I swore.

Downstairs Brian was waxing anecdotal under the influence of John Jameson. He sat back expansively in the big armchair, long legs crossed, clutching his whiskey, and the O'Shaughnessys sat around listening and laughing. I could see at a glance how happy he was; how embraced he too was by the happy atmosphere in this place. He did not seem to notice that Cissie was taut and strained. I asked after Des and was shown his Christmas card and letter which was so heavily censored that hardly any of it was left. He sounded cheerful, however. Brian asked a lot of questions about him, about how he was finding the RAF, did they know what make of plane he had, did they know how many sorties he had been involved in, but they had little information.

'You're not thinking of joining up yourself?' David asked and I listened with my heart in my mouth for the answer.

'Not at the moment. Peg won't let me go.' He glanced at me, smiling.

I saw the laughter in his eyes, the quirk of his mouth, the sly smile directed at me and the glass of amber whiskey in his hand. He was tight, lovable, relaxed as he had not been for a long time. I tried to imagine his as a pilot, but failed.

It's Glenallen which will never let you go, I thought, suddenly weary.

Barbie, teenager now, angular and pretty, told me about school. I reminded her of the old days, of the stickleback and the throttled teddybear, and she laughed with embarrassment and said that all the best people had a past. And David laughed, his face scarlet, remembering how he had mopped the floor with the cat.

'Poor old yoke died last week.'

'She got lockjaw,' Dr O'Shaughnessy said sadly. 'I had to put her down.'

We stayed for another while and then wished everyone a happy Christmas once again and left to go home on icy empty roads with threadbare tyres. I did not sleep much that night. I listened to the wind and the sleety sounds at the window and Brian's breathing beside me. He had made love with robotic vigour, as. though part of him were elsewhere. He seldom had nightmares now; he was probably too tired, but I felt the nightmare facing Cissie and wondered what I could do to help her.

Brian was off early next morning to the meet in pink coat and black boots. He kissed me perfunctorily as he left. I went into the landing after him, watched him stride down the stairs, watched the movement of his body; his boots rang on the tiles in the hall as he turned for the kitchen stairs and I ran shivering back to bed and dressed myself under the still warm blankets.

My mind was full of what he had told me the previous night after our return from the O'Shaughnessys. I had asked him to explain what his Aunt had been talking about. He said he knew nothing about Mary and the goat, but did know

204

there had been some sort of trouble many years before over a stablehand. He believed the fellow had been killed by a stallion. He himself had been very young at the time.

I asked him then about Cissie's hand.

'I was very small,' he said, rubbing his hands tiredly through his hair as though he wished I hadn't brought up the topic. The *joie de vivre* which he had acquired in the O'Shaghnessys deserted him and he looked morose. 'It happened at a children's party here. I got the blame - at least Harry and Peter blamed me. Mummy stood up for me and eventually she even convinced Dad that I hadn't done it. He still thinks it was one of the servants. We had one or two peculiar people then.' He looked at me almost fiercely, as though in answer to some question I had not framed.

'No Peg. I didn't bloody do it. If I was half the things that pair would make me out to be I'd have been shut away long ago.'

'Why do they hate you so much?' I whispered, suddenly beset by the pain of it all. 'It's like a physical weight. I live under it with you and I can't bear it. I can't bear it.'

'What makes you think I can bear it?' he demanded testily, taking off his cuff links and pulling up his sleeve, so that I could see the scars on his wrist about which I had often wondered and about which I had been half afraid to ask.

'I was twelve; it was the year before I went away to school; I couldn't bear any more; I wanted to die and I did this with a Max Smiley razor blade.'

I stared at the pale scars and at him and burst into tears.

'Peige, Peige. I'm sorry. Please don't cry.'

205

He hugged me to him. There were tears in his own eyes. 'I have to prove myself every moment here - but I can't bear to be defeated. I want them to see they are wrong. I used to think I didn't care, but now I just want to win.'

'Do they know about that?' I asked, indicating his wrist.

'No. Eilie found me and bandaged it up. She didn't even get the doctor. Poor Eilie, white as a sheet, warning me to tell no one I had done such a thing to myself, talking of mortal sin and hell and how the moutain would get me. Mummy was away at the time - she was ill, in a nursing home - and by the time she came back the scars had died down. It was a stupid thing to do. But it is not indicative of neurosis, Peg, so you can take that look off your face. I was a child; I did a foolish thing. That's all.'

I dried my eyes.

'I think we have to get away,' I said. 'I think you are obsessed. This place will drive us mad. When a situation is beyond redemption the only thing left to do is withdraw. '

He looked at me, head slightly to one side, smiling coaxingly.

'Come on now, Peg, no need for such drama! It is not beyond redemption! People grow up and change. Things always change. I cannot pass up the chance I have to put Glenallen back on its feet; I cannot pass up the chance of inheriting. Dad thinks I am the only one of the family who will really pull the place together. I cannot pass up the chance of actually succeeding here in the end.'

He looked grim suddenly. The coaxing smile was gone.

'I'm not saying you're not right, Peg. But for God's sake give me the chance.'

206

I touched his cheek. 'My darling, I'm on your side; I'm your friend, remember!'

He wrapped his arms around me. 'Thank God for you - Friend.'

Harry did not hunt that morning. She stayed back to pick up Peter from the station. She was annoyed that Brian had used the car the night before; 'There's so little petrol left. It should be kept for emergencies.'

She had smiled then to emphasise that she was being reasonable and Brian had smiled back without comment, so that her truculence hung uncomfortably in the air.

This round to you, Brian, I thought.

When she had left for the station I slipped down to the kitchen. I knew that Nora was busy upstairs making beds and hoped that I would find Eilie alone. She was making pastry at the table, flour up to her wrists, and I came in and hesitated, went into the pantry for a glass of milk to make it look as though I had some business in the place and then blurted out what I wanted to ask her.

'Eilie, were you here when Brian and the others were children?'

She looked at me speculatively.

'Of course I was, Mrs Peg. I've been here since I was eighteen. I was the housemaid then.'

'I was just wondering, did an accident happen to some little girl here a long time ago - when the children were young?'

Eilie stopped kneading and looked at me sharply.

'What sort of accident would that be, ma'am?'

I felt a bit foolish but pressed on.

207

'I know my friend Cissie O'Shaughnessy hurt her hand when she was about five. I know the accident happened here!'

There was silence for a moment. Eilie pursed her lips, sighed, looked back at the pastry and slowly recommenced her work.

'It was a terrible tragedy, Mrs Peg' she said, 'nothin' but tragedy. There was a birthday party for Miss Harry. She was seven and Miss O'Shaughnessy was one of the little girls invited. I remember her well, a little dote with big eyes and curls. Master Peter was there, and Miss Harry in her blue silk frock but young Brian had been sent off to bed by his mother for being bold - he had spilt lemonade all over his little party suit and some had got on to Miss Harry's new silk dress and she started crying and complained to her mother. Everything was grand for a while then until they had the bran dip; The children had been helping to wrap gifts for all the guests the evening before, little presents of pencil boxes, sweets and the like. Anyway, one by one the children put in their hands into the drum for their presents and tore off the paper, squealing as babies will. And then I saw the O'Shaughnessy tot take out a parcel and rush off to open it in the corner and it occurred to me that it looked a bit bigger than the things we had been wrapping the day before, but I paid no further heed until I heard the crack and then the terrible scream.'

Eilie shook her head. She kneaded the pastry silently for a moment, not looking at me, troubled. 'The craythureen had a rat trap sprung on her little hand and it was crushing two of her fingers, had them nearly severed. And then a strange thing happened - didn't young Master Peter, who never normally put himself forward about anything (if the sky fell down, Mrs Peg, he'd just sit there with a look on his face that would curdle new milk), didn't he rush over to her and take the trap off her hand and put his arms around her. It was strange because she was so suddenly comforted, her head buried against his shoulder, blood on his clothes and her crying all stopped in spite of her hurt; and young Peter with an expression on his face like the one Nora used to wear when she was coaxing her little kitten. Not like him at all! He was nine then. But how that rat trap can have got into that bran dip I can't say, ma'am.

'There was an awful fuss about it, but Miss Harry said that Brian had done it and though he denied this I don't think anyone believed him. I believed him of course; he was never a boy to hurt anything.'

Her face was suddenly grim, the muscles working for a moment in her jaw; 'No mean streak there! But sure don't mention it at all, ma'am; they don't like being reminded about it.'

She looked over her shoulder at the door. 'Especially the mistress, they try to protect her - ever since she was sick with her nerves.'

I sat at the kitchen table in silence, miserable, imagining the scene, only too well aware of the years of suffering which it had caused, remembering Peter's letter and his reference to 'your small deformity'.

I was about to ask her what exactly had happened to Mary - the business about the goat and about the stablehand, but I heard the sound of a car engine and knew that Harry and Peter were back. They came in the backdoor in a moment, said Hello very cheerily, Harry's eyes going from me to Eilie and back with cold, smiling inquiry.

'Eilie is showing me the secrets of good pastry,' I said, finishing the milk and putting the glass in the sink.

'There will be two more for lunch, Eilie,' Harry said, 'James Regan and his sister, Kitty. We bumped into them at the station.'

I asked Peter how Dublin was and he said that it was a little dreary thanks to the blackout and the shortage of petrol.

A little later, while I was in the library, looking for something to read, I heard the Regans arriving and then Harry and Peter entertaining them in the drawing-room. I thought of the cruel letter and wondered how anyone capable of writing something like that to someone as vulnerable as Cissie could laugh and chat urbanely with friends. I wished I could talk to Mary about it, could tell her Cissie's trouble; Mary would surely be in a position to help. But I had given my word.

Brian returned from the hunt with a man who wanted to look at some horses, a prospective customer. I met them in the hall. I knew from Brian's face that he had agreed a sale. He was proud of the yearling hunters, particularly Hopscotch, one of Jessie's colts. He introduced me to his customer - a Mr Jackson - tall, grey-haired, fortyish.

'Have a drink with us, Peg,' Brian said, opening the drawing-room door. The buzz of conversation inside ceased and introductions were made. I felt Harry's eyes on me, felt her exasperation. I was too shy to shine in company; the weight of her disapproval pressed too heavily. I was Brian's wife and for this I would not be forgiven.

'Was Cissie at the hunt?' I asked Brian and he said no. Was I expecting her? I saw Peter listen for my answer and then relax when I said no, not this morning. I wanted to shatter his complacency, confront him with what he had done. I hated him for that awful letter. But I did as I had promised and kept my distance, keeping the resentment and anger from my eyes.

Cissie did hunt three days later. The meet was at Glenallen and when I saw her arrive with Mary, who had come to stay with her the day before, I decided to screw my courage to the sticking place and give the hunt a go. I struggled into my boots and breeches, put on my hacking jacket, one of Harry's cast-offs, and took one last look out the window at the company below. I saw Mary turn around to greet the foreign looking man who had just arrived on a chestnut hunter and I realised that this was Mary's French Count whom I had not seen since the day of her father's funeral. I saw him being introduced to several people; shaking hands, chatting for a moment to Cissie, and I found my eyes resting on him as though he represented reality in some way heretofore unknown to me. And as I watched him he suddenly raised his eyes to the window where I stood and looked into my face.

I started, shocked by a sense of having been discovered, and he smiled in recognition and inclined his head and shoulders towards me in an almost imperceptible salute. And I think it was then, for the first time, that I felt that strange sense of conspiracy, as though there was between us some inexplicable complicity.

211

I hurried down to the stables to tell Murty to saddle up Joey for me. I chose Joey deliberately because Murty had frequently described him as a 'lazy hoor'.

Now Murty nodded gloomily.

'That yoke,' he muttered, but he obeyed, telling me pointedly as he gave me a leg up to hold on to the martingale going over the fences.

'Don't worry your head, Murty,' I said. 'Divil a fence I'll take.' I can still see the look in his eyes.

I trotted Joey around to join Cissie and Mary and the others at the front of the house. I leaned over to embrace Mary. I was glad to see her. She looked well, less strained that she had been the last time I had seen her at my wedding.

'How's the old married lady?' she asked, smiling at me, and I said she was okay.

'Should you be riding so soon after the mishap?' she whispered, lowering her voice so that male company could not hear and I said I was fine now.

'You remember Lucien?' she asked and I looked at him, blushing for no reason and said of course I did and felt the pressure of his gaze and his quizzical smile.

I caught Brian's eye, guiltily, because he had repeatedly told me I was not to go hunting until I was a better rider. 'You could be killed, or injured.'

This had accorded so entirely with my own sentiments that I had obeyed. But I had made no effort to become a better rider. I hardly every rode - I had gone round the farm with Brian on horseback once or twice - but that was more for the convenience of seeing the place than from any desire to become a serious horsewoman. I could not lose the fear at the pit of my stomach. The fear was there today too, but overridden by some species of compulsion. I wanted to be with Cissie today.

Brian walked Rufus over to me and told me in a low voice to get off. I stared at him, amazed at the angry look in his eyes and said I wouldn't. Lucien looked on with an inscrutable face and Mary raised her eyebrows and looked from one of us to the other.

'This is a turn up for the books. Peg insisting on hunting.'

Cissie looked worried, holding in Ebony who seemed eager.

'Why did you come, Peg?'

'It's time I did!'

'Well, be careful who you follow. You don't want to be led over big fences.'

'I won't jump anything bigger than a cowpath!'

She laughed in spite of herself and said I wouldn't have much choice. 'But don't follow me.'

Brian looked worried and furious, but didn't dare make a scene, muttering that I had bloody well better be careful.

'You shouldn't be so discouraging, Brian,' Mary said sweetly and she moved away to rescue Peter who was trying to politely shed an elderly gentleman. I was longing to ask her about Lucien, but could see I would have to wait.

'Hello Lord Darlington,' Mary said cheerily. So this was 'Darlington' whom Brian had told me was an awful bore, but whom my father-in-law, who loved titles, always referred to as 'a decent fellow.'

'Hello, Peter,' and they both looked at her, smiling, with the sudden gleam in the eye men have when they are confronted by the beautiful. Then Mr Fitzallen himself came out to meet the hunt and shook hands with Lord Darlington and was introduced to Lucien and Peter was able to make his escape.

I saw Cissie's eyes turn towards Peter; he was now engaged in conversation with Mary; he sat erect on his mount, handsome in his 'pink' and his snow white stock, and although he did throw a glance in her direction it was so contained that it was unreadable; it seemed to me that he was conscious of Harriet's eyes beside him. In the melée prepartory to the draw, Cissie passed beside him, said 'Hello, Peter,' in a voice so small and fragile I wanted to put my arms around her and he turned and looked at her guardedly, said 'Hello there' pleasantly, as politeness demanded, and turned back to Mary. Mary looked at Cissie and then sharply at me, and her eyes when she returned them to Peter's face were full of speculation. It was only when Cissie's back was turned that I saw, for an instant, Peter's eyes dwelling on her with an absolute, concentrated intensity as though he would burn her image on his retinas.

Cissie stiffened under her idol's politeness and rode out smartly with her usual style, her chin up, but with her face now set in such grim desperate lines that I was afraid without knowing why. I tried to catch her eye, called out something to her and she turned and looked at me without really seeing me; the focus of her attention was elsewhere. I tried to keep abreast of her, but it was no use; Joey, 'the lazy hoor,' was living down to his name. The draw was slow; Joey was slower, and Cissie had urged Ebony away from me and to the left.

214

And then everything happened so quickly. A fox broke cover and then the hunt was away in full cry, the hounds ululating, the fieldmaster souding the view halloo. Joey was now transformed into a power-house of energy that I couldn't contain. The movement of the hunt had stirred something in his blood, and I held on grimly, grasping the mane and praying under my breath. The wind whistled in my ears; my nose ran. I passed Lord Darlington, the master of the hunt, without knowing it; I heard the Field Master and Whipper In shouting 'Get behind the hunt,' but they could roar for all they were worth, there was nothing I could do. I looked back at Brian; he was galloping after me, his face a mixture of exasperation and concern. I just wanted the horse to stop. But it was I and not Joey who stopped; I lost a stirrup, lost my balance, tried desperately to secure myself to the mane, and next thing hit the ground with a thump. Bits of mud hit me in the face from the flailing hooves which passed me by.

I saw Brian look back over his shoulder to see if I were still alive. I was aware that one of the horses had been steered off to the right, wheeled around and was returning to me. It was the Count. He dismounted and helped me up. 'Are you alright?' I said yes, it was just that I was a terrible rider. As I spoke to him I saw the hunt tear in a crimson dash through the gate that had been opened to avoid Reilly's bank and then I saw Cissie, galloping like a fury, head for the bank itself. I saw some people staring after her, resisting their mounts' urgency to follow her; someone shouted something. I heard male words of command and then Brian's voice roaring, 'Don't, Cissie!' coming back to me on the wind. His voice trailed away as Ebony rose to the challenge and I held my breath as Cissie cleared the bank, but I couldn't see the other side where the steep drop was, or know whether she had landed safely. Neither did I know that one of Ebony's forelegs had caught on the barbed wire on top of the bank.

All I knew was that the hunt was converging on the spot; Lucien, muttering 'There is trouble,' re-mounted and headed for the bank where everyone had gathered. People were dismounting and I ran, my heart labouring, my legs like logs. I saw Mary, now dismounted, jump over the bank and into the ditch and then I was there myself and I knew it all.

Ebony was in the ditch lying on his back, his head twisted in an impossible angle, his legs held up by a fetter of barbed wire and lashing out spasmodically; Cissie was pinned beneath him in the brackish water that covered his back. The horse was quivering and blood trickled from his nostrils and Cissie's legs were moving, and her right hand, her good hand, thrashed convulsively. I couldn't see her face which was under the horse, but there was a stream of bubbles where it should have been. I heard myself screaming. 'She's drowning, she's drowning - get the horse up.' And then someone told me to shut up and I saw Brian, Peter and Lucien trying to pull the horse off her. Ebony's legs were kicking and I saw an iron shod hind hoof catch Lucien a glancing blow to the side of the head which instantly poured blood. But once the wire pinning the foreleg and baring the bone was cut off, one leg swung away, bent where there was no joint. The horse did not get up. I saw Peter's face, white and vulnerable, and Lucien standing very still, dazed from the blow to his head, being supported by an ashen Mary

216

while the blood trickled thickly down the side of his face and stained his white stock with scarlet.

I jumped into the ditch, my heart hammering and pounding against the inevitability of what was happening and against which all my will was futile, and beat Ebony's rump with my crop, caught Cissie's hand and tried to pull her out from under her dead mount. Nine minutes, I thought. Nine minutes to die of drowning! Then I knelt, the water up to my thighs, and talked to Cissie, while the hunt dragged Ebony out of the ditch, telling her, through a torrent of tears, how I loved her, uncaring that everyone could hear, holding her small hand and, after a little while, it became very still in mine and she died beside me there in the ditch.

I can't remember who or how many tried to revive her with artificial respiration. They stopped only when rigor mortis had set in.

I remember only snatches of the rest of that day. We waited, shaking and frozen, while the light faded and they came with a stretcher for Cissie and a team of plough horses to remove Ebony. The parish priest anointed Cissie and went to tell the family. Cissie's father came and waited with us for the ambulance. He bent over her, his head bowed, the grey hairs thin on the crown, his fingers reaching automatically for his child's pulse. Then he dropped her wrist and gathered her up in his arms.

Mary and Lucien and Brian and I held on to each other in an agony of grief and disbelief. It was bitterly cold and sleet began to lash us, darkening the winter sky as it swept in from the black bulk of Knockshee.

Everyone went over to the O'Shaughnessys then and everyone hugged everyone and cried.

217

David held on to Barbie and they rocked together while she screamed and wept and Dr and Mrs O'Shaughnessy trembled and sat holding hands, greeting everyone, like people in a dream. Harry was wonderfully efficient; she organised things in the kitchen - Nellie was only able to rock herself backwards and forwards, murmuring in great wrenching sobs, 'My poor little cushla child.' Harry made tea and produced a tray of biscuits and scones, but Peter was very quiet, his tearless eyes glassy, his face the colour of old putty. Someone suggested that we say the rosary and we all knelt and poured out the muted Hail Marys like mantras, joining in together at the 'trimmings'. 'And do thou, oh Prince of the Heavenly Host, by the power of God thrust Satan down to hell and with him the other wicked spirits who wander through the world for the ruin of souls.' I looked around at the white faces, my eyes stiff with salt, Mr and Mrs O'Shaughnessy very close together, Mary kneeling beside Lucien who seemed less interested in the rosary than he was in her, watching her with compassionate concern as the tears poured continuously down her face.

Next day I sent a telegram to Tom to tell him what had happened. He turned up for the removal of the remains that evening, very quiet, very non-communicative, stiff in all his words and gestures as though his body was being operated from a distance by someone pulling strings.

There was a huge funeral two days later. I was with Brian and Tom in the pew behind Peter and watched his back as he stood and knelt, and I felt nothing, nothing at all except numb, bitter grief. The memory of my interview with Mrs

O'Shaughnessy the day before was still fresh and still terrible.

I had gone over to their house on the morning following the accident. Cissie was laid out on her bed, waxen, peaceful, her hands crossed on her breast. I stood beside Mary and looked down at her. I saw the little grey glove through a storm of tears. The house was full of whispers; most of the parish had come to pay their respects. The curtains were drawn and Mrs O'Shaughnessy was white and ravaged with grief. She drew both Mary and myself into her own bedroom and asked was there someone in Cissie's life she did not know of, some relationship which had been making her unhappy. I lied and said that I didn't know; Mary said she didn't think so. Mrs O'Shaughnessy then took a piece of paper out of a drawer and handed it to me.

'I found that in her waste paper basket.'

I smoothed the crumpled sheet to read it. It was in Cissie's handwriting.

'What can I say of you? I was doomed to a blind passion and I lived it, endured it, burned in it. It isn't over; it's unlikely to end even with my death because if there's life elsewhere I'm bound to be still looking for you even if I can't remember who you are.

'You are blind. You are without compassion or judgement, but I can't escape from you.

'You are chains and I put out my feet.

'I despise so much in you, but put out my heart and soul for your merest touch. I am a fool, but can't make myself wise. Wisdom is a poor substitute for you. I am diseased with love and there is no remedy. The disease inhabits my life; it is possession.

You consume me, bind me, and are only half aware of me. Do something finally ugly and irretrievable and let me go.'

We read it in a silence punctuated by the sounds of passionate sobbing from the next bedroom, Barbie breaking her heart. Mrs O'Shaughnessy excused herself to go to her and I put the little note, the last thing, perhaps, that Cissie had written, into my pocket.

Without Cissie life was empty. Glenallen had become a cage. Brian had become even more immersed in his plans for the farm and was working day and night. The war was ruining what was left of the bloodstock industry; the Economic War had long since put a stop to the annual journeys to Doncaster with the yearlings, and when that war had ended in 1938 the real War had arrived hot on its heels. The result was that no longer were any interested buyers coming from England and only the home market was left. So Brian was trying even harder to interest his father in alternative forms of farming. A dairy herd was one proposal. He was still breeding hunters and that side of things was going quite well and he had started keeping beef cattle. But the money was tight and the sums he wanted to invest were not available. The Fitzallens were on their uppers.

After Cissie's funeral Peter went back to his law practice in Dublin and I never got around to telling him exactly what I thought of him, or of what I knew. 'No one ... ever,' Cisse had said.

He spoke to me once or twice before his departure, in the same assured, condescending tones as ever; he was sorry about poor Cissie; he knew what a friend she had been to me; she would be sadly missed by everyone. I looked into his eyes and thought for a moment that I detected there more than polite regret, a momentary hesitation, a momentary black expansion of the pupils like a hurt child, or like someone hoping for some emotional crumb.

I said she wouldn't be sadly missed by me and he stared at me, frowning, taken aback. No, I said savagely, not 'sadly missed' or anything so trite. I had been robbed of her; she had been robbed of her life.

I can still see the shocked jerk of his shoulders. His expression became haughty, remote, pained with distaste; I had transgressed the canon of behaviour which dictated an absolute reserve in the matter of one's feelings. I reasoned that he had rationalised his relationship with Cissie, now that she was safely out of the way, as some sort of romantic interlude; that he even mourned her in a deliberate way, because it was proper that one should mourn one's friends. But I noticed that he became withdrawn, that he looked haggard and that he had been unable to hide the expression of anguish when I had disturbed him in the study, where he was supposed to be working on legal papers, on the day after her funeral. His head had been propped on his elbows, fists against his forehead, eyes closed, conveying the impression of a mind's battle for control.

I had excused myself and crept away. It might not have had anything to do with Cissie I told myself. And yet, for a while, I was haunted by the sense of a tormented will asserting ascendancy over emotions too powerful to be released.

Harry, on the other hand, made no secret of the fact that she had recovered from the shock.

'You're not still grieving?' she greeted me cheerfully one morning about a week after the accident, regarding my swollen eyes with

221

surprise, and the force of her unspoken assertion that I was in such dreadfully bad taste made me try for a moment to put my anguish behind me. Whenever I saw myself through her eyes I tried to amend whatever it was in me she found offensive, so weak was my self image, so powerful her disdain. But, in truth, I was haunted by Cissie, longed to see her, asked her to come to me as a ghost, that I wouldn't mind her being a ghost. But she never came, although I did dream of her, dreams where she came to visit and I said how weird it was that she was dead and she said it was very strange and she stood up and said that she had to go. And I felt in the dream the compulsion on her to leave, the impossibility of holding on to her for another minute. Not like real life, where one has some sovereignty in the matter of one's time. Cissie had no such discretion and I woke up to desolation.

Now, the matter of my father-in-law's will was mooted again. He had another bad turn early in the new year and this had precipitated new talk of his will. Harry got that old look in her eyes again, the look of speculative desperation. She became pleasant to Brian and myself, asking our opinion on assorted matters, involved us in her plan to visit Dublin.

'Maybe you'd like to come too, Peg. The break would do you good!'

A solicitor was sent for from Ballyharris and he arrived by car is his tweed suit, with a brief case, and was with the old man for upwards of half an hour. It was understood that he was taking instructions for the will and would bring it back for signing the following week.

I was at the front of the house when he came out and he raised his hat to me very politely before he got back in his car and drove away. This happened on a Friday and Peter arrived home that evening for the weekend. He spent most of the time with his sister, walking around the farm, and made no attempt to socialise locally. He had little appetite for his meals and I would find his eyes on me when he thought I wasn't looking. On Sunday Harry drove him to the station in the trap and he went back to Dublin.

At breakfast the following day Harry announced that her pearl necklace was missing. This was the present which Aunt Rita had given her at Christmas. I asked her where she had been wearing it last and she said she hadn't worn it since Christmas Day. It was very valuable she said, and she asked Eilie to get Nora to look out for it while doing the cleaning. I helped in the search, looked under the cushions in the drawing-room, under the rugs in the dining-room and in going along the landing to our room during the course of the morning I paused at the open door to Harry's room where Nora was cleaning and asked her if she had found the necklace.

'No, Miss Peg,'
'Have you checked everywhere.'
Nora shook her head and said she supposed Miss Harry would have checked through her drawers herself, but she pulled out one of the top drawers of the chest beside the door.

I looked in and saw an assembly of bric a brac; diaries, letters tied with a ribbon, an autograph album and in the corner of the drawer small round objects - marbles; small, red clay marbles. My mind shot instantly to the day I had fallen on the stairs and Harriet's assurance that there were no marbles in the house.

I stood at the door while Nora opened the other drawers which were full of neatly folded clothing and left her to search. I went out into the stable yard, stroked a few warm noses in the loose boxes, while the men helping Murty stared at me. Murty came along in his old brown tweed jacket to ask did I want to go riding.

'No, Murty ... '

Marbles in Harriet's drawer did not mean a thing, I told myself. She probably didn't even know they were there. And I was no longer so sure that I had stepped on anything like marbles when I had fallen on the stairs that morning. I had probably tripped on a loose shoelace, like Harriet had said. Anything else was now inconceivable.

When I came back into the house Nora, who seemed very agitated, met me in the hall. She was opening and closing her hands in a spasmodic nervous way.

'Mrs Fitzallen wants to see you in the drawing-room, ma'am.'

The drawing-room door was of varnished mahogany, panelled, with a brass handle. I felt my heart start to thump as though I had been summoned to Mother Mercy's office and I resented this. What did Mrs Fitzallen want to see me about that could not wait until supper, or that she could not come and see me about herself?

I opened the heavy door and let myself into the room. My mother-in-law was sitting on the couch and Harry was pouring herself a pre-lunch drink from the sherry decanter on the sofa table. She glanced at me as I came in, a kind of aloof half smile that spoke of power and contempt and curiosity.

Mrs Fitzallen said in her low, rather nervous voice, 'Ah, Peg dear, there you are.'

224

I waited. I felt, rather than saw, Harry take a sip from her drink. She stayed by the table, just on the periphery of my vision. Mrs Fitzallen seemed frail sitting on the large sofa. She gestured to a chair.

'Sit down for a moment.'

I sat, half sick with the sudden rush of adrenalin.

'Yes?' I said with a voice I could have killed, so full was it of tremor. I always hated confrontation and the atmosphere in this room made no doubt about the nature of the interview.

'You know Harriet lost her pearl necklace?' my mother-in-law said nervously, but with stern undertones.

'Yes, of course. I helped search for it.'

'It's been found now.'

She was watching me, not with the acuity of someone who is trying to piece the truth together, but with the mournful accusation of one who knows the truth.

'Oh, good,' I croaked, knowing I had something to defend myself against, but not sure what.

'In your room.'

'My room?'

'Yes.'

Her voice was now strong with sad accusation. 'In a box on your dressing-table.'

'That's impossible.'

'I thought you would have more grace than that, Peg,' she said in a thin reproachful voice. 'The best thing is to make a clean breast of it. Perhaps you only meant to borrow it?'

The blood rose to my face. I strode across the room and rang the bell. Nora appeared at the door in a moment.

'Yes, ma'am?'

'Nora, where did you find Miss Harry's necklace?'

Nora hesitated. Then she looked me straight in the eye.

'I found it in your room, ma'am. It was in the little tin box, the one with the deer on it.'

She was referring to a small tin sweet box which I had from my childhood and had brought with me to Glenallen.

'It fell off your dressing-table while I was dusting, ma'am, and the lid fell off.'

I stared at her. I saw that she was shaking.

'The only thing I keep in that box are things which belonged to my mother - her wedding ring and a brooch.'

'They fell out too, ma'am. But the necklace was at the bottom in a paper bag.'

She was the picture of reluctant candour, pale, clenching and unclenching her hands. Mrs Fitzallen nodded to her and she left the room, quietly closing the door. 'Well, I didn't put it there,' I protested, my voice quivering on the verge of tears, unable to meet my mother-in-law's patient gaze.

She shook her head, murmured 'It's really too bad,' and turned to look at her daughter.

Harry examined me with weary superiority. 'I'm just glad to get it back....' she said with a sigh. 'It's not as though I intend to bother the Guards or anything.' And she walked out of the room, throwing me as she passed a look of contempt as if to say that she had thought better of me and I had failed her. I ran into the hall after her, my walking shoes ringing on the tiles.

'Harry, you don't think I stole it?'

226

She was half way up the stairs and gazed down at me haughtily, a statuesque young woman with blue eyes and a taut mouth.

'Well, what do you call it when someone takes a necklace without any permission and keeps it?'

I felt the tears sting and overflow.

'I didn't take it, Harry.'

She shrugged, narrowing her eyes.

'Well, what were you doing in my room?'

'I didn't go into your room.'

'Nora said you were there this morning.'

'You mean ... when I helped her to look for the necklace?

'So now you admit being in my room?'

I studied her for a moment, sudden incautious anger thick inside me. 'Yes, and I saw the marbles in your drawer, the ones you used to make me fall. You said there were none in the house!'

She paled and stood stock still, gripping the bannister. Her voice came out with a low hiss.

'You're either mad or bad or both.'

She turned on her heel and left me standing there shaking in the middle of the hall, wondering why I had said what I had when I did not believe it myself. Or did I? I crept off to our bedroom, stared with unseeing eyes out across the wet, cold lawn, picking up the familiar tin box with the dancing fawns, opening and closing the lid.

When Brian came in I told him the story and said I would not be coming down for lunch. He divested himself of his damp jacket, gave an exasperated sigh, and donned a jumper in silence. He quietly asked me a few more details about the incident and then, when the gong sounded, gripped my arm and said I most certainly was coming down for lunch; I wasn't going to hide upstairs and let them all think I was guilty. I knew he was right so I reluctantly went downstairs with him and took my seat at the table. It was virtually a silent meal; talk stopped when we came into the room and there was no further spontaneous conversation, just requests for the salt or pepper or whatever. Mr Fitzallen sat as usual at the top of the table, and looked at me with cold politeness; my mother-in-law gave me a smile, half stern, half forgiving and Harry glanced at me but did not meet my eyes. She launched into a cheerfully brittle conversation with her father, occasionally including her mother, but otherwise behaving as though there was no one else at the table. She was wearing a pale blue twinset and the pearls; the blue of her eyes seemed deeper than ever and there was a faint flush in her face. She did not look at Brian who sat silently for the most part, the usual animated conversation with his father absent. Nor did his father throw a word in his direction.

I could not eat but I stayed at the table because Brian insisted I should and because I knew myself that anything else was cowardice. I saw that Mrs Fitzallen was upset and she eyed Brian nervously as though he were a factor that hadn't been taken into account. But Brian ate away solidly, seemingly impervious to the tense atmosphere and made the occasional contribution to the conversation, which was, for the most part, ignored. I saw the way his face set, the ripple of muscle in his jaw, felt his anger.

When the meal was over and Harry about to leave the table, Brian said he would be glad if she would stay. He looked around and asked Nora to leave the room, which she did, looking nervous and jittery, her sturdy young hands shaking a little as she took up the dirty dishes from the sideboard. Outside the window a few flakes of snow fell, hit the ground and melted. The fire settled, sending a shower of sparks up the chimney. One or two small puffs of turf smoke made the room aromatic.

When the door had closed behind Nora Brian looked from his mother to Harry and asked,

'What's this I hear about your necklace, Harry?'

Harry started. She went to stand up.

'I'm too upset to talk about it,' she said.

'I want to know why you accused Peg, my wife, of theft,' Brian said, raising his voice.

Harry looked as though she would burst into tears. She turned to her father.

'You see the way he thinks he can talk to me? I didn't accuse anyone of being a thief, did I, Mummy?'

Mrs Fitzallen was pale and strained and had tears in her eyes. 'It's really too bad,' she said. 'Poor Harry missed her necklace and I had the house searched. Nora found it among Peg's things. I'm sure there's a perfectly good explanation.'

'Peg couldn't account for it,' Harry said sadly, 'so it remains a mystery.' She winced as though in sudden pain, put finger and thumb to the bridge of her nose, squeezing it the way she did when a migraine threatened.

I tried and failed to meet my father-in-law's cold speculative eyes; I felt Harry's triumph, knew that Brian was aware his confrontation was not succeeding. There could be no possibility of success where both his parents were swayed by his sister who could make him appear, by dint of a few words and a confident dismissive attitude, to be a cross between a fool and a troublemaker.

229

'If this is the way my wife is treated ...' He paused, breathing rapidly.

Harry was silent. She was waiting for him to finish, to say what would happen if this was the way his wife was treated. However, my father-in-law forestalled this. He glared at his son, colour staining his thin cheeks, his eyes pale with anger.

'How dare you upset your mother over this contemptible business?' he shouted and I saw that Mrs Fitzallen was quietly sobbing, her shoulders trembling in agitation.

'Mummy darling,' Harry said, and rushed to put her arm around her mother; the latter, however, pushed her away, stood up shakily and left the room.

Father and son stared at each other.

'I think you had better go and apologise to your mother,' the old man commanded angrily.

Brian stood his ground. 'I want to discuss this, Dad; Peg did not take that necklace.'

'No,' I whispered. 'I really didn't.'

My voice trailed away as the old man's fist banged the table, making the coffee cups jump.

'I've heard enough of this miserable business. Never heard anything like it in our family. I don't want to hear another word about it,' and he too suddenly stood and left the room, his tall spareness, the offended angle of his chin, an indictment. Harry left the room behind him with an injured air.

Brian looked at me with a white face, in which anger and impotence were at odds with each other.

'God blast the lot of them,' he muttered under his breath. He went out, leaving me sitting at the big dining table on my own, shaking, hypnotised, a sort of latter-day Alice in Wonderland, helpless in a nightmare where the rules were known to everyone except me. I knew that he was angry with me, unreasonably so, but angry all the same. Had he not just lost the ground he had so carefully cultivated since our return to Glenallen?

I wept then, my head in my hands and Nora came in to clear the coffee cups.

'Don't heed them, Miss Peg,' she whispered looking over her shoulder. She stacked the dishes while I tried to control myself, then murmured in my ear that there was a hot pot of tea in the kitchen and that a cup would do me good.

I picked up a few items from the table and brought them down to the kitchen. Eilie was there, buxom in her wrap-around apron, and Murty was finishing his meal at the kitchen table. There was compassion in both their eyes. Eilie poured a cup from the teapot, steered me into a chair and put the cup in front of me.

'Drink that up, ma'am.'

I took a sip of the scalding liquid while I struggled for control. I tried to ask Nora one or two questions about how she had found the necklace, but had to abandon the attempt.

When I had mastered myself I thanked Eilie for the tea and left the kitchen. Murty came out into the lower hall behind me.

'Be careful, ma'am,' he whispered.

I turned to look at him; he glanced around nervously.

'You remember the day, ma'am, when Master Brian's girth broke in the hunt?'

'Of course I do.'

'I think you should know, ma'am, that the same girth didn't break!'

I stood stock still. 'What do you mean, Murty?'

231

'I mean that it was cut, ma'am; someone half sawed it through beforehand.'

He vanished out of sight through the back door.

Chapter 8

I challenged Brian on the question of his hunting accident and he admitted that yes, something or someone had apparently interfered with the girth.

'Who do you think that could have been?' I demanded.

He shrugged. 'It could have been my spurs, a piece of glass, a kick from a horse with a worn shoe. It need not have been a person. Why? Who do you think it was?'

'Your precious sister of course.'

I stopped abruptly, chilled by his expression.

'Well, look at the carry on of her, this business of the necklace.'

'You really do have it up the nose for Harry!' He lowered his voice. 'Did you take that necklace, Peg?'

I looked into his face. Was this Brian, this man with the cold, hard eyes? Was this the same person who had held me in his arms and comforted me that day years before down by the lake, the man who had called me his "squirrel", who liked to tease me with love and courtship? The man so special to me that I had dreaded losing him above everything? He had changed in a matter of weeks, gradually at first so that I hardly noticed it, until he had become tense and remote, polite like a good neighbour, pre-occupied.

I knew that in his heart he blamed me for the loss of ground he had suffered over the 'stolen' necklace. I felt that I should go away for a while, but did not want to do anything that smacked of histrionics. The trouble was that I was still tied to the dream; I felt we could have it if we could have ourselves. I remembered our honeymoon, proof enough of what could be ours. I cultivated patience; I was optimistic and depressed by turns; I needed him, especially now while my heart was sick with Cissie's loss. But he seemed unaware of all of this. I began to wonder if he had married me to make some sort of point; I realised how important his family were, their recognition of him a necessity. Already I had discovered that little differences between us were dealt with by him with increasing dismissiveness. I was not to make my point of view prevail; whatever the context, he had to be right. He was like a man who sees something he absolutely needs almost within his reach and will do whatever is necessary to reach it, even elbow everyone else out of his way. I could no longer make him listen to my desire to leave Glenallen. I was a "squirrel", the loved one, only while I was pleasing. But I always made excuses for him to myself. He was worried, under stress to produce the sort of results that would save Glenallen.

But now I had been asked if I had taken Harry's rotten necklace. I stared back at him, confronting the look in his eyes.

'I don't mean did you steal it, Peg. I just want to know if you took it.'

'How dare you, Brian! What do you take me for? But since you need reassurance - No. I did not take the necklace. And no, I am not a thief.'

He looked suddenly horrified, murmured that he had not accused me of being one.

'There's a lot of very odd things going on in this place,' I hissed at him. 'Girths break for no reason, necklaces are "stolen" and I fall on the stairs, on marbles or something and now discover your sister keeps marbles in one of her drawers '

He laughed coldly.

'What are you implying, Peg?'

'What the hell do you think? The day I tripped on the stairs I was sure it was on something small and round - like marbles, and when I said it to Harry she said I was imagining things - that there were none in the house! But she keeps them in her room.'

Brian was silent for a moment, his jaw tightening. 'How do you know what she keeps in her room, - in her chest of drawers?' he asked softly.

I turned around angrily and headed for the stairs, but he came after me and grabbed me by the wrist, leading me to the end of the landing to the door of Harry's room. The door was open and he pulled me into the room behind him.

'Alright. Show me the marbles,' he said.

With a shaking hand I indicated the chest of drawers between the fireplace and the door.

'Top left-hand drawer.'

He pulled it open and looked inside.

'I see no marbles, Peg,' he said very quietly. It was true. The drawer was tidy, letters tied with ribbon, a few pens, an old autograph album, but no marbles. I opened the other drawer, but it contained only gloves and scarves.

'She's taken them out.'

'I see,' he said. 'Well, if you think I'm going to go through my sister's room bit by bit, you're mistaken.' Brian ushered me into the landing and closed Harry's door behind him, then strode off down the stairs. I listened to the receding sound of his shoes on the tiles as he went down to the kitchen stairs.

'Where are you going?' I called after him shakily.

'Shooting,' he said and was gone.

I would have to leave Glenallen. But how? I spent the rest of the hours of daylight out walking, trying to debate with myself what was best to do. I wore an old raincoat over two jumpers, a pair of warm trousers and wellington boots. I wound an old knitted woollen muffler belonging to Brian around my hair; it was long enough to keep the wind out from the top of my coat.

Walking was therapeutic and helped me put things into perspective, which I needed now because I had no one to talk to. Cissie was dead, Brian had turned against me, his family despised me. I had no money; I couldn't ride; I was common as dirt; I was a thief.

I tried to tell myself that Harry would realise the truth, would apologise and all would be well. I was still young enough to believe that all one had to do to effect change was to deliver the truth.

It must have been Nora who had taken the necklace and then tried to pin it on me. I should have confronted her about it. And then I thought of Murty's warning. Nora could hardly have involved herself in interfering with the girth. The only people who would have benefited, had Brian been killed, were Harry and Peter. They would then be the only heirs. But Peter had been miles away in Dublin on the date in question.

The alternative to killing Brian would be to discredit him and his wife in his father's eyes. I wondered was I mad to suspect such hatred.

236

I felt I was losing him. He was supposed to be my friend, my lover, my husband. Instead he was becoming a sort of inquisitor, increasingly leagued with people who felt my presence to be an imposition. We had not made love for several weeks - since the night after Cissie's funeral when we had clung together, hearing the wind howl along the roof valley. Sometimes I longed to reach out for him at night, but pride asserted itself. If he would not reach for me he would find I had more staying power than he evidently imagined.

I loved him; it was a love I could not let go without making my life meaningless. And I felt that somehow matters would resolve themselves; I expected this because I could not conceive of a life, of years and years of expectation, which would never be fulfilled. The moment when everything would come right was always just around the corner.

I longed to be accepted by his family; up to this point in time I had got along well with his father and mother; Peter had been pleasant; Harriet had been as changeable as a weather vane. I had hoped they had begun to see me in terms of my own identity and not according to pre-conceived notions. But after today I had lost some sort of credibility, had been undermined in a way I did not know how to defend myself against. I wondered who could give me some disinterested advice, but could think of no one, except perhaps Mrs O'Shaughnessy. But she was still prostrated by the death of Cissie; the whole family had turned inwards for comfort, shutting themselves against the world. I could not intrude on that privacy with my absurd problem. And as I had no money for a train ticket the only thing to do would be to walk home to Ballycloghan; go back

237

to Tom and lick my wounds. I calculated how long it would take me to make the journey - if I walked all day and all night I would be there. I could start walking right now, never go back to that house. I had nothing much belonging to me there anyway, except the few pieces of jewellery and some clothes. I was wearing the gold charm bracelet; I had put it on before coming downstairs for lunch. I liked to feel it on my wrist and to know that it had once been in Cissie's hands; it made me feel in some way close to her.

I walked around the farm, skirting the woods where I could hear the sounds of gunshot; that would be Brian I thought. The snow was still coming intermittently, as though it couldn't quite make up its mind, and it crunched underfoot and collected in powdery patches here and there where the wind drove it. The horses stood out in silhouette against the sky, plump with their thick, winter coats and behind me the mountain, 'Balor's Eye,' was hoar white.

As I left the farm by way of a stile and crossed over to the bank where Cissie had died I saw Harry crossing the lower pasture field. She was keeping close to the hedgerows and walking slowly, as though she were burdened with something, although I could see nothing in her arms. She was wearing what looked like the old gaberdine raincoat which I had often seen on the peg in the tack room, but I could not be absolutely sure of this because of the distance and the snow.

I heard the sounds of gunshots echo through the wood again and yet again and wondered had Brian bagged anything, thinking, despite my resolve to leave, what could I do to make things alright with him, without surrendering.

I thought about him intently for a while, how much he had changed. He wanted so desperately to hang on to the perspective that he could save the farm. I could sense his hunger for the place, now that it was almost within his grasp. He knew of course that his father had given his instructions for his will; he felt those instructions had favoured him and he didn't want anything to change that. And I suppose he felt, consciously or unconsciously, that if he could get on good terms with his sister and have her accept him as the heir to Glenallen, all would be well. If he had her acceptance Peter's would follow.

Well, I told myself, I was a graduate, I could teach and England was crying out for teachers with the men away at war, particularly in science subjects which had been traditionally a male preserve. I was not without resource. And if I went home Tom would be glad to see me.

Then it occurred to me that it would be such a coward's way out, to run away, without confronting Brian. They all thought I was a push-over; was I to prove them right? And again the thought came that I must not act in anger, must not overreact.

And as I thought of all these things the short winter's day drew in and it became bitterly cold. And soon I found myself back at the manor, glad to be in the warmth, determined that I would bring matters with Brian to a head.

I forced myself to go down to supper that evening, although I ate and spoke little. I expected Harry, now that she had monopolised the situation, to carry on her usual cheerful conversation with her father, but instead there was an air of gloom at the table and I could see at

239

once that Brian was in trouble of some sort. Nora crept around serving us as though she was afraid to open her mouth. I wanted to ask Brian what was wrong, but dared not.

Mrs Fitzallen cornered me after supper and said that I should really apologise to Harry and then everything would be alright. I looked at the nervous old lady who wanted things to be harmonious and said I would accept Harry's apologies anytime she cared to make them. She just shook her head and walked sadly away. Looking after her I had a mad impulse to go to Harry and say I was sorry; but I could not endure the prospect of her gratified forgiveness and I went wearily up to bed. I heard voices coming from the library - Mr Fitzallen's and Brian's, both raised in altercation.

'You're a bloody fool,' the old man was shouting. 'What sort of a clown would blind a horse? The criminal carelessness of it.'

I listened at the top of the stairs and heard Brian's voice raised in denial.

'I was in the middle of the wood; I was nowhere near the lower pasture field. Do you take me for an idiot?'

'How dare you raise your voice to me, sir,' his father roared croakily, querulous with illness and I stood, rooted, hearing the door slam behind Brian who came storming up the stairs, glared at me in passing and tore into our room.

I tip-toed downstairs to the kitchen and asked Eilie what was wrong; she was drying dishes and looked frightened. She had the blackout curtains drawn and the kitchen was sombre.

'There was a shooting accident, ma'am. One of the mares has been blinded in one eye, poor Jessie.'

'Blinded? Jessie? How did that happen?'

She shrugged. 'Master Brian was out shooting at the time. No one else was shooting.'

Murty came in for his tea then, looking grim and shaking his head.

I turned away. I had seen Harry cross the lower pasture field near the edge of the woods. But she had been carrying nothing, wearing that old raincoat. She hadn't been shooting. Or had she?

I let myself out into the night. There was a biting wind in the yard and I slipped on the cobbles as I headed for the tack room. The snow had turned into watery slush, hiding little icy pockets. I passed Jessie's stable and peered inside. There was a storm lantern in the corner and I could see that the vet had been and that the mare's eye had been bandaged. She was standing quietly, and I felt my heart turn over for her and her dumb, patient stoicism.

I went into the tack room, lit the lamp and looked around; everything was neatly in place; leathers were bright with saddle soap; saddle irons and bits were scoured and glinting and the room smelt of dubbin and leather.

There in the corner, on its usual peg, was the old raincoat. I went over to it and felt inside; the quilted lining was torn and there were two big pockets on the inside, but they were empty, except for a spent cartridge case, which I removed. The coat itself reeked of fresh cordite.

Upstairs I confronted Brian. He was sitting in the armchair in our room with his head in his hands. He barely glanced up when I came in. For a moment I was tempted to ignore him; after what he had said to me earlier that day I was tense with resentment. But the terrible event which had supervened, his distress and the news I had for him made me forget all that.

'I know who blinded poor Jessie,' I said.

He raised his head, frowned at me as though my presence irritated him.

'Yes,' I continued, 'it was the same person who wore the old gaberdine in the tack room.'

'What are you talking about, Peg?' he demanded testily.

'I saw Harry crossing the lower pasture field this afternoon and she was wearing that raincoat, and big rubber boots.'

He sighed, put his hand to his forehead like Harriet sometimes did, spoke in a voice of abrupt command.

'Please, Peg. I can't take much more of this.'

'Well then, go down and smell the bloody coat yourself,' I hissed at him, 'and you'll see what I'm talking about. And I found this in the pocket.'

I threw the spent cartridge case down on the bed. He picked it up, examined it.

His eyes narrowed.

'What do you mean ... smell?'

'Look Brian, if someone had carried a gun and an empty cartridge - hidden under a coat after the gun had been fired - wouldn't the coat smell of cordite? And I found that in the pocket!'

He didn't answer. He looked almost frightened, then turned on me angrily.

'That blasted coat must have been out on a hundred shoots - why shouldn't it smell of cordite? Why shouldn't it have a cartridge case in the pocket?'

'Damn you,' I said, 'Damn you for your wilful blindness. The tack room is damp, the coat is damp; but look at that cartridge; the brass ring and copper cap are not tarnished; the paper isn't swollen.

He was silent.

'Look,' I went on. 'What shot were you carrying?'

'No. 5.'

'Well, this is a No. 8!'

'So what, Peg?

'Well - what would you use a No. 8 for?'

'Snipe.'

'Or a horse you only wanted to wound and not kill?'

He looked at me wearily, rage gradually building up.

'You are as impossible as they are! How do I know that it wasn't you who shot Jessie, just to get your own back on Harry!'

I looked back into his face. There were hollows under his eyes; his gestures were angry and defensive.

'No,' I said, 'I suppose you couldn't tell. This place may be a lunatic asylum, but I am not one of the lunatics.'

I wished I had somewhere to go, but there was only the little dressing-room so I went in there, shutting the door. I heard him leave the bedroom and I sat down and thought carefully of what I must do. I did not want to force Brian to choose between Glenallen and me. But I was becoming something I had never foreseen, an irritating afterthought, no longer a partner, lover, or wife. As long as he believed he had me trapped that was how it would go on.

I went back to the bedroom. Brian was gone and there was no sign of the cartridge case. His wallet was lying on his bedside table. I picked it up, found five pounds in it and put the money in my pocket. Then I went to the box room for a bag and started packing. I could cycle to Ballyharris, stay in the hotel for the night and go home tomorrow.

I left Brian a note under his pillow; he would not find it immediately.

'Dear Brian,
I am sorry about this course and would not take it if I thought there was an alternative. The situation here is irredeemable and I am withdrawing from it. I am going home. If I can get a job I will go to England.
Peg.'

I slipped out of the house through the front door, took a bicycle and set off along the dark winter road for Ballyharris, keeping my head down against the sleet. I got a room in the hotel for the night and next morning sent a wire to Tom. He met me at the station in Ballycloghan. I had been longing to see him, to be home again, one place where I could be loved and accepted without question or calculation, where I could just be myself.

But oh God, how he had changed. Where was the debonair Tom I used to know, who would poke fun at me? The man who met me was almost a stranger; his eyes were bloodshot; he hadn't shaved for several days; he was taciturn and he stank of whiskey.

I threw my arms around him and his eyes filled with tears.

'It's good to see you, Peg,' he said.

I found the house cold; the range was unlit; there was a pile of dirty dishes in the sink, with mould growing on them. My heart sank. I looked at him, angrily. Is this your monument to Cissie? I wanted to scream at him, but he would hardly have heard me, so morose had he become.

I realised I would have to get the fire lit and clean up this mess and I was suddenly angry at the whole world of men who never for a moment gave real thought to anything or anyone except themselves. Brian had betrayed me by his disbelief. He had allowed his family to destroy us. I could not understand why life, which had promised so much, had become so dark and bitter.

Chapter 9

I sat by the kitchen range in Ballycloghan surveying the flagged floor, the table I scrubbed every morning, the pine dresser with my mother's china, the old chipped enamelled sink, the creel full of turf and Tiddles the cat who had become very big and scrawny and who sat with me by the range. Tiddles purred when I spoke to him and would rub his length against my legs, tail held up sternly like a flag pole. For days I was angry, disturbed, afraid that everything was over between Brian and me. I imagined his face when he found my letter, imagined his angry reaction, imagined the reaction of the rest of the household. In retrospect it seemed to me that I had acted precipitously, and yet there was no going back. I wanted to hear Brian's voice, I yearned for the companionship we had once had, the long conversations, the laughter, the lovemaking, the happiness which had been ours before so much subtle poison had been dripped into the heart of our marriage.

I wandered around the farm, trying to recapture the secure, crystal quality of childhood. I walked down the road, past the spot where the tinkers used to have their encampments and thought of the old woman who had told my fortune, pursing my lips against such nonsense. Great lady indeed! Here I was with a marriage in tatters and burdened by an enormous, shapeless guilt.

I went over and over in my mind the sequence of events at Glenallen and I felt, as I had before when I had got away for a day, the weight of the formless oppression which had overlain everything there.

I wished I had my friends to talk to, but Cissie was gone and Mary was immersed in her career in Dublin. I thought of the planchette board in St Catherine's and realised with horror that one part of the prophecies had come true; and another part of it, the shattering of the glass, the shattering of my life, was in the process of being realised. But at least Mary was safe in Dublin.

I met Niamh Houlihan after mass on Sundays. I could see that she was still angling after Tom, but that she was disillusioned by his indifference. She spoke of emigrating to America and I thought of Paddy and wondered how he was doing.

'It's either America or marry Packey Rafferty,' she confided, indicating the latter with her eyes. Packey Rafferty was a small farmer, thirty years older than Niamh, whose mother had recently died and who was now 'looking out' for a wife. He struck me, standing there in his Sunday suit and boots while he talked with the men, as solid, hardworking, but crass.

'There are worse things than staying here,' I said and then she asked me curiously why I was staying so long and what my husband thought of me being away for several weeks.

I grabbed at the first thought that occurred to me and told her he had gone to enlist and saw her puzzled blue eyes rest on me for a moment in speculation.

Mr Clancy, still every inch the pedagogue, was conspicuous at mass, the shock of his white hair visible above the rest of the congregation because of the way he held himself so erect. Beside him his little nervous wife would pass the rosary through her fingers and his son, Joe, now a big lad of sixteen or so, followed the mass in his missal, his eyes swivelling now and then to the women's side of the church where the pretty teenage daughter of one of the local farmers knelt with her mother.

Keeping house for Tom made me feel I had fallen from the frying pan into the fire. I had lost a husband who had been too busy to talk to me, and found a brother who hardly talked at all. He accepted that I had come back for a holiday and did not question me, being too immersed in his private torment to suspect that anything was wrong. The dullness of every day became intolerable, waiting for the morning post with suppressed expectancy (Brian would surely write. Surely he would come after me ...) and then spending the rest of the day in desultory housekeeping, reading the paper, cooking, while Tom would appear for his meals and disappear to the pub for the evening. He accepted without question that if there was a woman in the house she would make his life comfortable; this was his right; this her destiny. He busied himself with the ploughing and farrowing and seemed tired, getting up later than he should, his eyes red, his breath acrid from the previous night's whiskey.

'For the love of God, will you stop drinking so much?' I shouted at him one morning. 'I know Cissie is dead, but there's no point in destroying yourself over it.' And he had looked at me angrily, without answering. Later, at supper, he asked suddenly if it had been an accident - or had she...? No one, he said, would have tried that bank unless they were trying to kill themselves, that or an exhibitionist, and she was too fine a horsewoman to risk her horse in that sort of caper.

I told him he was mad; Cissie had died by accident. I cried as I spoke, and then wept convulsively, crushed suddenly by the weight of the recent past. Tom tried to solace me and stayed at home that night, making me tea and hovering around solicitously, his grey eyes full of concern. I longed to unburden to him the true events surrounding her death, but did not because I knew how it would devastate him. So I drank the tea and wiped my burning face and eyes with a cold wet cloth and took some comfort from the comfort which was offered me.

Brian's letter came at last. I recognised his writing and was almost afraid to open it, imagining the worst, the cool acceptance of our separation, the end of our marriage.

'My Peige,

Forgive me for being so long - but I have had to think. And now I need to act at once on the clarity of vision that I possess at this moment.

You were right. We should withdraw from situations which cannot be redeemed. No matter what I do here everything turns to ashes. And there is more to it than that, as your comment about the "lunatic asylum" implied. We are all haunted and damned in this house and it will take more than me to defeat it. It's almost as though something is watching us, watching me. Something is sucking the life out of me.

You and I were being destroyed in this mill of the spirit. If I go now, I'll have made the break. If I stay, it will be harder each time. Even if you came back - what would be the next debacle, the next little incident to

249

make us defend our position here, to make us justify the fact that we exist?

If you did not come back, how could I go on? Since your departure I have felt colder every day, like a corpse.

This place has a draw for me that I cannot explain; I think it is more than just family connection. And I hate to fail, but the odds seem stacked against me. And these odds defy coincidence or the rules of chance.

Harry is only a tool; she does not even know it. I have felt this presence here most of my life, since the day I got lost in the passage grave under the mountain. I think I may have brought something out with me. There! That sounds a little mad and I hope it is!

I will send for you as soon as I can - assuming that you still want us to be together. I am going to Belfast to enlist. I want to join the RAF. Millions are being butchered in Europe while I struggle here with shadows. Maybe the war will free us in the end!

I told the family that you had gone home for a break. I have not told them what I intend to do and will write to them from England.

I am sorry our plans went so much awry, but I think I am doing the right thing in joining up. We can come back to Dublin after the war.

I love you.

Brian.'

I read it and re-read it, this letter which affirmed what was between us, while parting us in a way I had not expected. He was going to England and to dangers I could only guess at. And I was going too. I would not wait for him to 'send' for me.

Shortly after this I received two further letters, one had an American stamp and was addressed to Miss Margaret Donlon and the other was addressed to Mrs B Fitzallen and was from Mary.

Shortly after this I received two further letters, one had an American stamp and was addressed to Miss Margaret Donlon and the other was addressed to Mrs B Fitzallen and was from Mary.

Paddy's letter was full of the war and how sure he was that America would be drawn into it. He wished he could come home to see me. He was longing to see me again, and longing too for the sight of green fields and a wild lonely sky. He was quite well off now, he said, and would have something to offer me if I would consider him.

Touched, I thought of 'Paddy the yob' and flinched at my own unkindness. He had never been a 'yob'; he had been clever, gauche and poor, but good, and goodness was something I was beginning to learn the value of.

I wrote back to tell him that I was delighted to hear from him, but that I was married now. I wished him well and gave him a few pieces of local news I felt would interest him. I said that Brian, my husband, had gone to England to the war and that Niamh was undecided between the boat to America - as soon as it was safe to take one - or a husband in the shape of Packy Rafferty.

I was horrified by the prospect of her marrying him, so much older than her, so married already to his bit of land.

Mary's letter came the day after Paddy's. She said that Brian had called to her flat en route to Belfast. He had asked her to tell me he was fine, that he would write soon. The letter had been sent to Glenallen and was postmarked early February, almost ten days earlier.

Mary's letter decided matters. Brian had gone to England and that was where I would go. I wrote to Mary asking if I could come to stay for a while in Dublin - that I wanted to arrange my passage

251

to England. She replied by return to tell me I would be welcome any time. If Brian was in England, I reasoned, we would meet there. Anyway I needed a job and a life of my own and some sort of new beginning. I answered advertisements in the *Irish Times* looking for teachers for schools in England. One of them was for a school called Highcombe in Nottingham.

Mary's flat was in Merrion Square, in a five-storey Georgian house. The ground floor and basement consisted of medical consulting rooms and Mary's flat was on the first floor. I arrived in the evening, by taxi from Westland Row station, with the one big leather case, tied around the middle with a strap, which I had brought with me from Ballycloghan. It was cold with a flaying east wind and I was full of a nervous nausea. The taxi was unheated, a big black austin with the spare wheel on the back.

I paid off the taxi and rang the bell under the legend 'Miss M McElligott.' The door was opened a moment later by a smiling Mary, who embraced me, drew me into an echoing tiled hall and led me up a staircase with a curved mahogany balustrade.

The flat had high ceilings with the original cornices, marble fireplace in the drawing-room, a chandelier scattering light, oriental carpet and porcelain vases. Mary was dressed in jade green and stood out like a jewel against the peach and ivory of her sitting-room, her vivid hair flaming around her face and her green eyes full of delight at seeing me.

'My God, Mary, but you must be doing very well.' I looked around me with delight, comparing the reality of Mary's lifestyle to the

252

notion I had of her inhabiting some garret with not enough room to swing a cat. There were two windows in the room reaching almost to the ceiling. I pulled back a curtain and found I was looking out into a darkened Merrion Square. Dublin was outside, traffic sparse and slow moving. Because of the blackout, there was little sense of being in the middle of a city.

Mary laughed and showed me the small spare bedroom with a window looking out over the narrow garden and the mews beyond. I took off my coat, aware of the ambience of wealth. It was evident in the rugs on the floor, the damask curtains which were tied back with satin tassels, the thick white antique bedspread.

Mary put her head around the door.

'How hungry are you? I ask because we will be dining out later, but if you're starving we can have something now.'

I shook my head. 'I'm not fit to eat out. I look awful and feel worse..But don' let me spoil your evening. I'd rather go to bed.'

She looked at me for a moment.

'Alright. I can understand how you feel,' and she retreated. I heard her clanking in the kitchen.

I put on slippers and joined her there. She had started to cook, something delicious - chicken with some sort of wine sauce. I protested at the trouble I was causing and she said I was a terrible burden alright and to sit down for God's sake and talk to her. I was longing for news of Brian, but did not have to ask.

Mary told me about the evening when he had arrived at her door, looking at me as she spoke with a mixture of sympathy and curiosity.

'What's happened in Glenallen, Peg?' she asked suddenly. 'I know something must have, but Brian wasn't giving anything away.'

I shook my head.

'Do you mind if I don't talk about it right now?'

'I'm sorry. I've always been a nosey parker.'

Mary set the little kitchen table and we sat down to eat. I found that the nausea went with eating so I did justice to the meal. Mary, on the other hand, barely picked at the food.

'Mary, you don't eat enough for a sparrow.'

'I'll eat later. Have to keep the figure somehow or other,' she said ruefully.

'You look wonderful,' I said truthfully. 'A real film star; and you must be a great actress too to be able to afford all this.'

I gestured at our surroundings. Mary snorted.

'Dearest girl! It should be obvious to anyone with eyes in their head that I'm a kept woman. There is no way on earth that an actress in Dublin could earn enough for a place like this.'

I sat there like a fool, my mouth full, staring at her. She raised her eyebrows.

'You don't approve?'

I swallowed. What could I say? Of course I didn't approve. I had been brought up to believe in marriage, in one permanent relationship which would defy the possibility of change, or ennui, or incompatibility. I had been brought up to believe in rigorous chastity. Any discretion as to whether or where one would give oneself otherwise was inconceivable, mortally sinful, depriving one of reputation and consequently of credibility. I felt fear for Mary now, as I sat looking at her lovely clever face.

She shrugged. 'Don't look at me like that Peg, for God's sake. I'm still me, the same old Mary. I can see "Scarlet Woman" written all over you!'

She sounded annoyed.

'You always said you would suit yourself, Mary,' I smiled. 'But I didn't believe you.'

'Neither did I!'

'Is it still Lucien?'

Mary made an eloquent face; she had learnt gallic mannerisms.

'Of course. You'll see him later.'

'And this is his flat?'

She sighed. 'It's mine. But he pays for it. He's very rich. His family own leadmines in the Pyrenees and vineyards in the Loire valley - so he can afford all this.'

I remembered him very well, his face raised to my window, the sense he invoked in me of some strange kinship between us, his kindness after I had fallen off during the hunt and his face dripping blood where Ebony's hoof had caught him.

'What's a French Count doing in Dublin?'

'He's attached to the French Legation. I told you that before.'

'Do you love him?'

She paused. Her face became serious, the expression in her eyes almost hard.

'I wonder if I can love any man.'

I stared at her in perplexity.

'Why not?'

She shrugged. 'It has to do with power. I could not bear to be powerless. It would destroy me.'

I stared at her in astonishment and she smiled as though she had been joking, the almost grim expression of a moment before giving way to one of charm and urbanity.

'He's not married already, is he?'

'No.'

'What happens if ...'

'If I get pregnant?'

She shrugged. 'I won't. He's ... considerate. Because of him I can continue to do the work I love. And, who knows, when the war is over I might make it to London. In fact,' she added as a sort of afterthought, 'if I play my cards right I may even make it to London before then. He has the right connections. He knows Sir John Maffey. Now, tell me about Glenallen,' she said softly, 'if it doesn't upset you.'

She offered me a Gold Flake, gave me a light and drew on her cigarette through a long black cigarette holder. And I told her. I told her about the hunting accident and the shooting incident and my miscarriage and the affair of the necklace and the constant little slights and the way Brian was treated by Harry and Peter, but I did not tell her about Peter's letter to Cissie or what she had confided to me that Christmas night in her bedroom. All of that was Cissie's business, alive or dead.

When I had finished she leaned back in the chair and exhaled smoke delicately. I noticed that her nails were surprisingly short and unpainted. Her hands were slim and white, the fingers long and tapering.

'I could see from the beginning, Peg,' she said, 'that there was no way Harry was going to let you have an innings there. You see, she wants to close Glenallen around herself, her parents and Peter - a little kingdom where she is queen. Brian can't be ruled and so must be excluded. And you're ...'

'I know,' I said. 'I am an interloper from the common little world of real people. But there's a

256

bit more to it. The place itself is peculiar. Haven't you felt it?'

She stared at me for a moment, then lowered her voice. 'My dear girl, for years I could never go into that place without getting the shakes. You were right to get away. I used to wonder how you stuck it.'

And then she asked about Peter and I simply said that I hadn't seen him since his return to Dublin after Cissie's funeral. We talked about Cissie for a while, both of us in tears, Mary speculating as to why she had tried to jump that bank. 'She knew, Peg, how dangerous it was.'

And then after a moment I summoned the courage to ask her something that had been with me since that Christmas dinner.

'Mary, do you remember, when you were very small, being chased by a goat at Glenallen?'

She looked at me.

'What a question! Chased by a goat?' She laughed out loud. 'Why do you ask?'

'Oh, just something Harry said. She said you were five at the time and that they set the goat on you.'

She shrugged. 'I don't remember. I used to play in Glenallen sometimes when I was small, but after a while I didn't go there anymore.'

She changed the subject then, and chatted brightly, but I saw her forehead knit when she thought I wasn't looking at her, like someone trying to remember something long buried.

   . I met Lucien again that evening. He came into the flat with a bunch of daffodils. He wore a dark grey suit with a white shirt and red silk tie and looked foreign, dynamic, rich and very much in control of his destiny. This time I examined him

257

carefully. His eyes were brown and his hair, which receded on the temples, was black. His face was intense, but his long firm mouth was full of strength and humour. He projected command; I felt that his perceptions were his own; that no external dogma would dictate them.

Mary emerged from her bedroom looking stunning in a simple black dress. She was wearing green earrings which shimmered. Emeralds? He looked at her with the sort of appreciation I would have associated with an art connoisseur, pecked her cheek and came towards me, smiling, while Mary brought the daffs into the kitchen to put them in water, her high heels tapping on the kichen floor. I was seated nervously on the peach coloured couch and, smiling awkwardly, gave him my hand which he raised to his lips.

'Madame!' he said, inclining his head after a courtly fashion, 'I am delighted to see you again!'

I saw his eyes study me closely.

He turned as Mary emerged from the kitchen with the vase full of flowers, said something in rapid French in which I distinguished the word 'elle' and the word 'Botticelli' and little else.

Mary glanced at me apologetically.

'Yes,' she said. 'Peg was always lovely but you could never persuade her of it.'

He paid her some compliment then, again in French, and she smiled and brushed his face affectionately with the back of her hand.

'I have booked a table in Jammets,' he said. 'We can't leave your beautiful young guest to her own devices. She must come with us.'

'Oh no,' I protested. 'Thank you very much. I've eaten and I'd rather just go to bed. I'm dead tired.'

It was true. I was suddenly exhausted; the nausea was back again, the fear of the future, and

I wanted to have Brian back and lie in his arms and retrieve some old certainties.

'Before we go anywhere,' Mary said, 'I think you should talk to Peg. She wants to go to England. She wants to teach there. She's a science graduate, but she'll need a passport.'

He sat beside me on the couch and his presence reached out to me and when I looked at him again I saw that he was kind; that he was very strong and ruthless but that he was capable of kindness.

'You have an unusual name.'

'It's short for Margaret,' Mary explained.

He smiled at me, inclining his head.

'A noble name, Margaret. But why do you want to go to England? You know there is a war? It is not safe. It is no place for a young woman with alternatives.'

'Her husband is there,' Mary intervened. 'He left recently to join the RAF!'

'Ah! Do you know where he is stationed?'

I blushed again, mortified because I could not say. I saw Mary shake her head at the Count in a sudden slight movement.

'I don't know where he is,' I admitted. 'I am waiting to hear.'

'You will not be told that in a letter! The Censor would cut it. Can you not wait for him here?'

'No,' I said, 'I cannot. I must go to England; I must get a job.'

He raised his hands in acceptance.

'Well, I will do what I can. I have friends who may be able to help.' He smiled at me and turned to Mary and she rose.

'I'll get my coat,' she said and went into her bedroom.

When she was gone Lucien turned to me, brown eyes fixed on me with concern and appraisal.

'It is a dangerous venture, going alone to England at such a time - a young beautiful woman - you will need to take great care.'

And suddenly I wished that I had someone who would look at me with that solicitude, would caress me with words as this stranger did, would make my pulse race as he did. He made me feel that womanhood was magical, different, powerful; not something devalued as I had so often seen it; not something to be jettisoned in order to acquire the indomitable strength necessary to survive the aggressive, selfish wills of husbands, fathers, sons.

Mary came back then with her coat over her arm, perfume wafting before her. Lucien helped her into the coat. She said they would be back about midnight and they left immediately, shutting the door gently behind them.

I got up to look in the mirror, examining my face from different angles. My face looked back at me; my eyes shone as they had not for a long time and there was a colour in the cheeks which the warmth of the room alone could not account for. I buried my nose in Lucien's daffodils; they smelt only of spring.

BOOK 11

Chapter 10

The journey was exhausting. I had taken the boat to Holyhead; a choppy sea, the possibility of mines, the unknown quantity ahead all made me sick with dread.

I changed trains at Crewe and again at Derby. There were posters, *Careless talk costs lives*, and another one that seemed to address itself to me - *Is your journey really necessary?*, a soldier in uniform with a tin hat and a question mark, his right arm outstretched to the reader in urgent admonition, his left arm holding his rifle upright on the ground.

There were real soldiers waiting on the platforms, young women in uniform, wives or girl friends leaning on their men's arms, a sense of drama, a sense that real business was afoot here. Behind me was the world of shadowy dread; before me was the world of action. I felt a bit like the hero in Wells' novel *The Sleeper Awakes*, so strange and so different was the ambience in which I found myself.

There were interminable delays, with the result that I spent seven hours on that train before getting into Nottingham's Victoria Station at eleven o'clock at night. The black blinds on the windows shut out the outside world; inside the lighting was dim. The carriage was full - two women in felt hats and overcoats, an elderly man with a moustache sitting opposite who engaged me in occasional polite conversation, and four officers in uniform who played cards for most of the journey. The door would open from time to time with a rattle as people looked for seats, letting in the noise and cigarette smoke outside. The corridor was crammed with soldiers, smoking and laughing, full of the burly confidence of men concerned about some common masculine end.

I sat by the window pretending to read *Without My Cloak*, the novel by Kate O'Brien which Lucien had thrust into my hands at Dun Laoghaire as he and Mary had seen me off. Mary had embraced me. 'See you in London,' she whispered. Lucien had taken my hand in his warm grip, whispered 'Bon courage,' his brown eyes kind. I thought of him now, in this furious machine labouring through the wartime night. I had become so used to him, spoilt by both him and Mary; I was still shocked by their relationship, still wary of this foreigner who dared to set up my beautiful friend as his mistress, still astonished at his presumption that life was not only there for the taking, but that it must neither be sidestepped nor allowed to escape. I missed him on this train to the blank future. I had in my handbag the card he had procured for me - *Travel permit for Britain, Éire and Northern Ireland* with its 5/- stamp.

And thinking about him, I remembered that he had never spent a night in the flat while I was there. Perhaps he and Mary got together in his flat; perhaps he only slept with her when there was no one about. And I recalled with shocked disbelief the words he had whispered into my ear when he had come into my room to take my case on the day of my departure, 'Sometime, perhaps, you will be mine?' watching my face for reaction, his dark eyes unabashed, staring into mine as though it was the most normal thing in the world

266

to ask a woman you hardly knew to sleep with you, as though he knew something about me I didn't know myself.

I had turned away, leaving him to carry the case, not sure that I had heard correctly, dismissing the involuntary, excited shiver. Who the hell did he think he was - some sort of oriental Pasha? I felt sorry for Mary that the man in her life knew so little about loyalty. And I thought, with a mixture of excitement and dread, of Highcombe School in Nottingham where I was to present myself for interview. I said a prayer, a reflex kind of prayer, but a prayer all the same.

Mostly I thought of Brian. I thought about him with the ache which had become part of my life, sure that if we could only be together for a while everything would work out. Life did not have to be lived as it was lived at Glenallen. I remembered the night Jessie was shot, Knockshee scooping the snow to itself, as though nothing should come between the mountain and its shadow.

Brian and I would find each other in England, find our own pace, our own peace. But England was a big place, huge numbers of people, and at war. I had known these things all along but now they had concrete significance, now that I was in this carriage being swept towards a city which, to me, was only a name. It had featured in *Robin Hood*, the first book I had read, and that was all I knew about it. I wished now that I had waited for Brian to have sent for me; then at least I would have had a sure destination, would have had someone to meet me, would not have had this sense of being cast out on the mercy of the world. But I knew at the same time that this was generated by fear of the unknown. Action was better than the torment of waiting. Brian's letter, when it came, would be forwarded by Tom. And in the meantime I might be able to locate his whereabouts myself and surprise him. But all of this depended on my being successful in getting myself a job.

As we neared Nottingham the lights in the carriage were suddenly extinguished. One of the officers said 'damn,' more in annoyance at the interruption of the game than concern at the prospect of danger; there were mutterings among the other passengers. I waited for the lights to come back on, but the stygian darkness stayed with us, except for the two glowing points of light, cigarettes being smoked by the two women who spoke together nervously and then lapsed into silence.

'Why have all the lights gone out?' I asked nervously.

'Jerry is overhead.'

It was the old man who answered; his voice was amused, kindly, matter of fact, whatever strain he felt well disguised, or perhaps he was too old to care. I understood him with surprised clarity. The Germans were flying bombers overhead; they would bomb the railway, the train. All they needed was light. I felt the fear choking in my chest, but nobody made any move indicative of the least trepidation. The quiet voices around me went on talking, in whispers now, as though they might otherwise be heard by the enemy in the sky.

The train drew into Nottingham in total darkness. I struggled to pull my case from the overhead rack and dragged it to the door and on to the platform. It was only then I realised that I was totally alone. From being jostled a moment before, from being surrounded by the presence of other travellers, I was now in a world of silence. The station was deserted. It was so dark I could not see my hand in front of my face. All those people who had been on that train had vanished; there was no one, it seemed, but myself on the platform and I was afraid to move, not knowing which step would throw me on to the railway.

After what seemed a very long time, although in reality it was probably five or ten minutes, I heard the rumble of a trolley in the distance.

'Hello,' I called, 'Hello. Can you help me?' My voice echoed in the emptiness.

A voice answered, a man's voice. 'Hold on, luv.'

The rumble of the trolley got nearer and then the man was beside me. I told him that I didn't know my way around and asked why had everyone disappeared. He explained that with the Jerries overhead the station was a target.

'Are they bombing Nottingham?'

'No, Miss; it's Derby; you can see the glow in the sky outside!'

He asked me what was a nice Irish girl doing in Nottingham and where was I staying and I explained that I had nowhere to stay and would he direct me to a good hotel. He seemed taken aback and told me what nearby hotels to try and which ones to avoid and he took charge of my case and said I could collect it next day in the left-luggage, if the station was still standing.

So, clutching my overnight bag, I ventured out into the night and saw, in the distance, as the porter had told me, a dull red glow in the sky. There were no street lights and there were few people about. I followed the directions I had been given, found the hotel, 'The Wickerley Arms', and rang the bell.

The door was opened in a moment by a man who looked at me suspiciously. It had not occurred to me until that moment that anyone could suspect me of being a prostitute, so I explained in confusion that I had just arrived in Nottingham, that I was a teacher and needed somewhere to stay for the night.

'You're Irish?'

'Yes.'

He stood aside to let me enter. I was brought into a dark hall and then through another door into a second hall. To my right was the lounge where there was light and several people, officers in uniform for the most part, sitting at tables, lounging against the bar; some couples pressed close together as they talked, holding hands, oblivious to the world.

The air was close, smelling of spirits and beer, cloudy drifts of cigarette smoke visible against the low lighting. The black blinds on the windows shut out the night and the sickly red glow in the sky. I was conducted upstairs and shown a small single room, No. 13, vacant only because of the number on the door. I was ravenously hungry; I had eaten nothing since midday, but I did not dare venture any further than the bathroom, so intimidated was I by the uniformed presence in the hotel. However, even my trip to the bathroom was not without incident. I was stopped by an officer, a Canadian, drunk, unsteady. Could he buy me a drink. No? He was going to the front, he said, he might never come back. He had blue bloodshot eyes. He smelt of whisky. He was about twenty five. I said I was terribly tired and he insisted on escorting me to the door of my room.

Later that night I heard the doorknob of my room turn and rattle for an instant and listened to the urgent whispers of 'Miss ... Miss ... ' But the door was bolted on the inside and the chair jammed under the handle for good measure and eventually my would-be bedmate went away.

I came down for breakfast late the next morning, hoping to avoid the men in uniform and particularly the Canadian of the night before. It was ten o'clock and I had the dining-room to myself. I feasted on tea and toast and a couple of sausages. I spread my toast with margarine and marmalade remembering that England was facing shortages which I, who had lived in the Irish countryside and fed off the fat of the land, had not experienced.

After breakfast I questioned the receptionist about buses to Highcome School and she gave me directions. My Irish brogue sounded heavy and foreign against her clipped English voice and I felt my perceptions were gauche and innocent, framed by Galway and Glenallen and Ballyharris and Ballycloghan - places strange and dreamlike in the context of this immediate, desperately pragmatic, present.

I got a trolley bus and alighted near the school building, a big red bricked edifice, set among playing fields. The grounds were empty. I went into the hall through the unlocked main door, but the place was deserted. There was a school smell, a combination of chalk dust, pencil shavings, paper, ink. The classroom doors were wide open; scrawls decorated blackboards, maths problems, science formulas, English figures of speech -

everything, books, pencils, pens, copybooks, but neither pupils nor teachers. I felt as I had at the station the night before. What if the school was actually closed down? Where would I go? I had very little money; Tom had forgotten about it because he was drinking and I had lied to Lucien when he had tried to press some on me.

Then I heard the sound of footsteps behind me in the hall.

'Can I help you?'

The voice was polite and a little suspicious. The young man to whom it belonged was dressed in a blazer and grey trousers. He was tall, good looking, about eighteen years old.

'I've come to see Mr Dencher. I'm the new Science teacher.'

'Really!' Polite scrutiny. 'Well, the headmaster is at home; the school is closed for the day. Shall I show you where he lives?'

'Thank you.'

He introduced himself - Paul Smithers; he said he would probably be in my science class; Mr Rogers, his former science master, had been called up. He would be joining the RAF himself at the end of the school year.

He examined me covertly; I sensed his reservations; I was too young to be his teacher; I was Irish and weren't the Irish all navvies or German sympathisers. I was a woman.

I said my husband was in the RAF and felt at once how this drew me within some familial circle, for his eyes brightened and his politeness lost its distance. He inquired where he was based. I explained that he had gone recently and that I wasn't sure yet.

I was escorted out through the school gates, past the big elms on the avenue and down the

272

suburban road. After about ten minutes my escort indicated a white house set among trees at the end of a cul de sac.

'That's it!' I thanked him and he smiled down at me and said in a half whisper. 'Old boy looks like a lion, but his teeth and claws have been drawn long since. Smile at him, Mrs Fitzallen. He likes the ladies!'

He turned and headed back the way we had come.

The 'lion' was planting rose trees. He had a shock of untidy white hair, tangled eyebrows, mournful jowls like a spaniel. He was wearing a dark grey jumper full of holes. His fingers were dirty with clay. I thought he was the gardener.

'Is Mr Dencher at home?'

He started up, stared at me, raising white eyebrows. 'Who wants to see him?'

'I do. I'm Mrs Fitzallen, the new science teacher.'

'Indeed!'

I saw the sudden quirk at the edge of his mouth. He was a tall man, mid-fifties, lines etched in twin curves from his nose to his lower lip, close set shrewd eyes.

'You'd better come into the house.'

I sat in the drawing-room and waited, noting the tidy heap of books and papers on the table, the coal fire glowing in the hearth, the chesterfield suite covered in blue-grey velour. The windows were criss-crossed with sticking tape and the blackout curtains were pulled back to show the garden. I heard his voice from upstairs and a woman's response and then he reappeared, having changed into a dark grey pin-striped suit, transformed; his white hair had been combed and his stern eyes regarded me dispassionately.

'I wasn't expecting you until tomorrow, Mrs Fitzallen.'

I reddened, tried to explain that I hadn't realised that he was the headmaster, cursing myself for an idiot with my 'I'm the new science teacher' and I just attending for interview.

He stood by the fire. I watched the set of his stooped shoulders, his reflection in the mirror on the mantelpiece, his serious authoritarian face. What if he decided against me; what if I was too young or inexperienced?

Smile at him, Mrs, Fitzallen. So I leaned back and smiled at him as he turned around, the same confident smile that I had seen Harry use a hundred times, the smile that said - I am in control of my destiny; I understand the world.

'Know your stuff, do you?'

'Yes.'

He inquired about my husband then and I told him he was in the RAF and again, this intelligence brought me within the charmed circle of some warm and protective freemasonry which he instantly radiated. 'My son is a pilot too.'

The following day marked the start of my new life. I was now Mrs Fitzallen, a science mistress in Highcome Boys' Public School. Glenallen and Ballycloghan might have been on the dark side of the moon, so remote and so different did they seem. But I was homesick, not so much for either of those two homes I had known, but for Ireland, for the subtle social conventions I knew, for the humour, the irreverence. And, most of all, for Mary, with whom I had re-established the empathy of our school days and for Lucien who was not easily forgotten.

England was pragmatic, sensible, set, with her back to the wall; and the English were kind, polite, unquestioning, and possessed a courage which was the more invincible for being devoid of bravura. But what was most astonishing to someone from a country where snobbery was covert, was the absolute acceptance of social stratification as though divinely ordained.

In my case I was invested with a definite mantle by virtue of my profession; and this mantle brought with it obligations and respect. My name was Margaret now; Peg was gone, a ghost who haunted Ballycloghan and the beautiful, painful, confines of Glenallen.

There were six hundred boys in the school. Some of them were the equivalent of first year university students. The universities in safe areas were crammed to overflowing; Nottingham was a 'reception area' and considered relatively safe and students from London, Oxford and Cambridge had come to swell the numbers. Senior boys who had planned a university education were staying on pending call up. I met Mr Warren, whom I was supposed to be replacing. He was waiting for his call he said; it could come anytime now. He was about thirty eight years old, serious, bespectacled.

'I applied for the RAF but was turned down - eyesight not up to scratch,' he told me. 'Can't stand the idea of the navy. Not a good sailor ... seasick ... so it will be the army.'

He explained the curriculum to me and brought me around the school, introducing me to the teachers and the classes which I was to take. The boys all examined me curiously, standing up politely with loud scraping of chairs when we came into the room.

'This is Mrs Fitzallen, boys. She will be taking you for Botany.'

There were smiles, a few smirks; I caught a whispered 'Not bad!' Mr Warren looked at the boys over the top of his horn-rimmed spectacles, and something in his gaze commanded instant silence. I wondered how he did this and tried to copy him; I schooled my face into what I hoped was a competent seriousness and narrowed my eyes. I don't know whether I fooled the boys, but I did not fool myself.

My first class, the 3As, comprised twenty three fourteen-year-old boys. The room was in uproar. Assorted paper missiles were in transit across the room; the blackboard was dotted with little chewed papier mache pellets which had been fired at a cartoon face drawn in chalk - a man with a moustache and a swastika in the middle of his forehead. I stood at the door for a moment, was ignored, moved to the desk, but the noise continued. I turned and strode from the room. Almost instantly there was silence. I re-entered 'my' form room to a small sea of expectant faces, their attention momentarily arrested. Someone hurried to shut the door; someone else ran up to remove the paper dart lying on the seat of my chair.

'Please stand up.' They stood up and muttered 'Good morning, Mrs Fitzallen,' and then I told them that I was giving them an assessment test and to sit down and write an essay on transpiration. I knew from Mr Warren that he had covered it with them already.

While they worked I made a map of the desk arrangements in the room and gave one of the boys in the front row the task of filling in the names, so that I would know who was sitting where, until I had learned to pin the names to the faces.

I repeated this procedure with variations for all the classes during that first day and emerged into the staffroom at the day's end laden with copy books for marking. Mr Warren had made arrangements at lunch hour to take me to the house where he had organised 'digs' for me and so, after school, I went with him to the red-brick house in Stanhope Boulevard which was to become my home.

My landlady was a Mrs Burton, a woman with brown hair and varicosed legs. She showed me up a polished lino staircase to a small room with pink curtains where there was a single bed, a table and chair, a wardrobe and chest of drawers with a mirror. The window looked out on the back garden with its few rows of vegetables and a wooden shed which housed the entrance to an Anderson shelter. She said there were three other people, a professional gentleman and two university students, residing in the house and that the charge for bed and half board was £2.00 per week. As my salary was to be £6.00 per week, a fortune to me, this was acceptable. Mr Warren then said goodbye and left and Mrs Burton brought me into the kitchen, made tea with a tea bag, which she pulled out of the cup almost immediately, and asked did I have a ration book. I said I didn't have one and she said she would get one for me. She made me wait until 'the gentleman' came home to go for my case which was still at the station. It wasn't safe for a girl to be out on her own, she said, with the evenings still dark. So I waited and at six o'clock a young man of medium height, dressed in a belted gaberdine coat, appeared in the hall, looked into the sitting-room, said hello with some surprise and was introduced by Mrs Burton who came hurrying from the kitchen, her cat Queenie behind her.

His name was John Eyreton. He was a civil engineer working on the new airport at Castle Donnington outside Nottingham. Mrs Burton explained to him that my luggage was at the station and he escorted me there, telling me on the way about the military encampment in Gregory Boulevard and to be careful about being out alone after dark. I asked him why he was not in uniform; men involved in essential war work were not conscripted, he said. He spoke defensively. Later I learnt that he had recently received two white feathers in the post.

I told him about Brian and he said I must write to the War Office and I did this next day, under his supervision. On the following day Mrs Burton applied for a ration book for me and I registered with the police.

I also met the other lodgers, two women students - Claire Stonebridge and Ellen Warrell - both of them serious young women, one studying natural sciences and the other reading law. I dashed off a letter to Mary in Dublin to tell her of my safe arrival and that I had landed the job in Highcombe school.

Unpacking my case that first night I found an envelope tucked into a side pocket which I certainly had not put there. I opened it to find five ten pounds notes and a few lines on a piece of paper, 'A gift from a friend which he hopes you will accept, to help with your new life. L'

278

I let the notes fall on the bed, unable to avoid the sudden sense of security from the sight of so much wealth, and then ill at ease. Why had he given me this? I would treat it as a loan and return it at the first opportunity. 'Sometime, perhaps, you will be mine?' he had said. I snorted. I certainly would not. Judas might have sold himself for thirty pieces of silver, but I wasn't going to do it, not even for fifty quid. I was not for sale.

I met Paul Smithers again next day. He was among the boys of the higher sixth, young men who had taken their A levels the year before and who, in peacetime, would have been attending university. But because of the influx of students, Boots University had requested the school to take the first years and so I had first year university dental students.

I found Paul and indeed the others in that class a considerable challenge, and studied the textbooks into the night to ensure that I was a match for them. I sensed at the beginning that my competence was being tested, but with their acceptance of me and the gradual acceptance of the whole school I began to feel secure and at home. And most of all I began to lose the sense that I was worthless, the secret dread of my insignificance which had never really left me since I had overheard Harry discussing me on that first evening in Glenallen.

The teachers took turns to do fire watching duty at the school; we were all issued with tin hats and gas masks; the latter had in fact been issued to the civilian population at large in the fear that Hitler would resort to chemical warfare.

Every single night there was a fire watch duty at the school, in case there was an air raid. This entailed looking out for incendiary bombs and shovelling sand on top of them before they exploded. Nottingham was bombed on one occasion when I was on fire duty and my tin hat was blown off, but the dreaded chemical warfare never materialised.

I stood like a statute that night, paralysed by the unearthly despairing cry of the siren; watching the explosions and sudden leaping flames from the city, the answering steady barking of the Ack Ack, feeling the hat torn from my head and the hot wind which propelled it over the flat roof where I was standing and into the grounds, while the senior pupil on fire duty with me disappeared to the air raid shelter. I went back into the school and waited there; eventually the bombing stopped and the long whine of the 'all clear' sounded and he came back from the shelter. 'You could have been killed, Mrs Fitzallen', he said. I was too shocked to reply, but I could see from his expression that he had misinterpreted my inaction, that he thought me defiant, brave.

On moonlit nights the Trent was covered by a smoke screen to disguise it from the air. The siren would sound, the steady menacing whine growing louder and louder and dying away and I wondered if I would ever live to see the night when I could sleep the old trusting sleep of my childhood again. The first siren indicated that the bombers were sixty miles away and the second siren that they were overhead, by which point, of course, everybody was supposed to have found their shelter. And then the all clear would come, usually without incident. One's nerves grew accustomed to this.

And I was happy. I had got a letter from Brian. At last.

'My dearest Peg,
They tell me you are in England. I wrote to you at Ballycloghan but got no reply. You had probably left by the time the letter arrived. It is safe in Ireland and you should have stayed there but, having said that, I am thrilled at the prospect of seeing you soon. I have some leave coming up - first weekend of next month. Will I go to see you in Nottingham or would you like a trip to London? Write as soon as you can.'

He sent me love and kisses and three little pierced hearts at the bottom of the page, reminding me of Lettergesh and two lovers alone in the wilderness by the sea.

And then Mary's letter came, a letter with a London postmark.

'Dearest Peg,
Wonderful news! Lucien has taken me to London (do I sound like a parcel?) We are staying in Knightsbridge, in a house belonging to people L knows who have fled the war. The house comes complete with maid who thinks we are a little bizarre, a Paddy living with a Frog, but she makes the best of it like the good Devonshire lass she is.

Have you and Brian managed to make contact yet?

L and I will be staying in London for some time. He wants to be with De G. He's out a lot. For God's sake come and visit. I am trying to get some work and have two auditions lined up.

*We have air raids on a regular basis but there is a
shelter in the cellar so we're really quite safe. I don't
know why the war makes one feel so alive; there is
something absolute in all that sound and fury.*
    Fond love,
    Mary.'

Two weeks following receipt of this letter I
travelled to London, taking the train from the
Midland Station to St. Pancras. How strange life
was; I would be with Brian again in a few hours.
We were to stay with Mary and Lucien, now
installed in Knightsbridge, wherever that was.

I had splurged on clothes - a new black costume
with a belt and a pale pink blouse of crepe de
chine and my hair was newly washed and waved.
A wicked little black hat completed the ensemble.
I painted my nails scarlet, put some panstick
make-up on my face, smeared on red lipstick,
straightened the seams in my stockings and
surveyed my transformed reflection with delight.
'Myrna Loy, eat your heart out,' I told the person
in the mirror. To hell with austerity; I had a date
with love and life. And in a pocket specially sewn
into my corset I had Lucien's fifty pounds which I
would restore to him. I had my own money; I was
deliciously independent and I was proud.

St Pancras was crammed, smelt of train smoke,
was deafening with loud-speakers advising of
departures and arrivals, with clanking and
lurching of locomotives, hissing steam, and
somewhere under it all the murmur of ordinary
human voices.

Even before the train got in, I was nervous. What if he wasn't there? I had never been to London; where would I get a taxi? They had underground tube trains. I could travel on those, but where did one find the tube?

I got my small weekend case down from the luggage rack, hung back a little from the throng waiting to alight and eventually found myself on the platform, my coat over one arm, holding my case in the other, walking slowly behind the other passengers towards the barrier. I repressed the nervousness. I wondered would he be glad to see me; I felt embarrassed that the last time I had seen him was the night we had a row. By walking out that night I had precipitated a major change in our lives. Was he still sure in his mind of his own subsequent action, or did he hold it against me?

I was hungry for the sight of him and full of anticipation that we could now reclaim our own world together despite the war. But part of me was still angry; he had allowed things to come to such a pass; he had not apologized for what he had said that night - 'How do I know it wasn't you who shot Jessie ...'

He came towards me, the officer in the grey blue uniform of the RAF, the crowned wings sewn above the pocket, the gilt buttons bright. He was a little thinner, his face wearing an expression of eager expectancy, scanning the people approaching the barrier with a half frown. He looked at me, the young woman in the black costume and hat with the bright lips and his eyes passed me by, to return immediately, his own suddenly appraising, laughing.

He lifted me off my feet, hugged me against his face, kissed me, held me back from him at arms length.

283

'Peige!'

The station, the people, the war, melted away like mist. There were only the two of us in a private space. All reservations were gone.

' You look absolutely wonderful,' he whispered in my ear, picked up my weekend bag and put his arm around me so tightly that he hurt my ribcage.

I caught the kind, sad smile of a middle-aged woman who passed beside us dragging a heavy case. I smiled back. There was love in the air in England then, an emotional rallying which made up for the terror of the nights and the long, onerous workday. Brian looked at her and asked if he could carry her case. She talked in rapid bursts; her home had been destroyed and her husband killed. She was on the wrong platform; she should be on platform 4. Brian carried her case, found platform 4, helped her on to the train, steering her through the soldiers sitting on kit bags, the couples holding on to each other and trying with frantic kisses to postpone the inevitable moment of departure.

Later in a cafeteria near the station, Brian and I sat back and looked at each other. The world was still out of focus; the noise of cutlery and dishes and talk an irrelevant background blur. I drank him in, his old frown as he looked at me, his way of crinkling his eyes as he laughed, his charm and his gentlemanly ingenuousness. There was no sign of the impatient, harassed Brian who had begun to make his appearance before I had left Glenallen.

'You look as though you can't make up your mind whether to be stern and unyielding, or be nice to your husband,' he said, the corners of his mouth holding back the smile.

'I'm not talking to you. You took off without me,' but I smiled as I said it. I was only too well aware that I was the one who had taken off first.

It was paradisiacal, to be here with him, in an anonymous café in the middle of London. It was like seeing each other again for the first time. The weight of uncertainty, of disapproval, of dread, was gone. We were simply a young couple with no one to please but ourselves, prisoners who had not known what they were missing until someone had unlocked the door.

'What could I do, Peg? We had little money, no jobs. There was no guarantee they would accept me in the service. I wanted to get myself established before we made decisions about the future. I didn't want to drag you into danger.'

'Do I have a say in the future?'

'Of course you do.'

'Well then ... you might have included me in your deliberations.'

He leant forward, his face serious. 'You are in all my deliberations; I think about you all the time! I was afraid you had left me for good. If I had come to Ballycloghan after you, with nothing different to offer, what good would that have been?'

'Good enough for me to have known where I stood!'

He took my hand. 'Glenallen is behind us, Peg.' He squeezed my fingers.

'We can do whatever we want now and this weekend we'll give you the casting vote.' His eyes dwelt on me with admiration and desire, the eyes of a lover. 'And you're all fixed up with a job?' he asked then. 'And thriving on it by the looks of things.'

I nodded. 'Six pounds a week. Burnham scale. Beat that!'

He chuckled. 'I can't.'

'Where are you stationed?'

'Manston - Kent.' And he talked of his training, that it had been curtailed because he had flying hours under his belt already from his flying lessons at Foynes. He had just commenced operational duties.

The waitress came with the tea and sandwiches and I studied him while she put the things on the table.

I poured the tea.

'Do you like it ... flying?'

'I do. There's an indescribable excitement in the sky, a bit like hunting - only more so because the danger is real. But the funny thing - it's easier to live in wartime England than it is to live in Glenallen, to fight in the war than farm Glenallen.' He spoke musingly. 'Glenallen has defeated me, Peg!'

I felt the old unease. 'It didn't defeat you, for God's sake. Look at yourself; handsome, brave, clever, young, with a really nice wife!'

His laughter burst like sunshine and people at the nearby table turned to look at us.

I asked him if he had told his parents where he was and he said he had written. 'I haven't actually given an address, just said that I was fine and in the RAF. I want to give them some time to get used to it. I know Mummy must be hysterical. I hate upsetting her and I dread getting an overwrought letter from her. But I can't live my life only doing what she wants!'

'Do you miss Glenallen?'

He raised his hand to my cheek.

'I miss Knockshee! Queer, isn't it? And most of all, I miss you.'

'What happened to Jessie?'

'We had to put her down.'

I saw him look at my nails and I held them out, splaying the fingers.

'Sinful Red.' I thought the shade was good. 'It's hard to get.'

He shook his head. 'I do not know this Peige. She has assumed a sovereignty tinged with decadence.'

Why did you have to go away to enlist? I persisted silently, not to be mollified now that I knew he was safe. We could have gone to Dublin and taken our chance.

But I didn't ask these questions. I was here and it didn't matter anymore. We had a lot of ground to make up, a lot of building to do together. 'We're together now and that's what matters,' I said. 'When the war is over we'll buy a little house, have children, be our own family!'

He smiled at me teasingly, leant over suddenly and kissed me on the mouth.

I saw the angle of his face, the set of his shoulders, the mystery of him, belonging to his man's world of war and aeroplanes, and his terrible vulnerability. And I felt in him again the elusive quality which had first attracted me.

'I love you,' I blurted. 'I love you so much.'

I told him then about Mary's invitation to stay with her and Lucien.

'Do they have a double bed in this place in Knightsbridge?' he inquired conversationally after a moment. I said they might have something like that alright and we smiled at each other conspiratorially. Then he paid the bill and we took a taxi to the address Mary had given me.

The house in Knightsbridge turned out to be a regency mansion, with a pillared front door painted glossy yellow. It was not far from the French Consulate at 58 Knightsbridge, which was at that time still in the hands of the puppet Vichy government. Brian rang the bell and I looked around at the busy London street, the dogged tired faces, smelt the taint in the air of dust and burnt buildings, the sense of being at the centre of the nation's effort to overcome and live. We had passed so much devastation on our journey from the station, ruined blocks of what had been shops and offices, cordoned off areas of rubble where gaunt shells of buildings looked about to topple.

The door was opened by a maid in uniform with a white cap, her hair tucked up neatly, her skin too pale, like someone who hasn't been out of doors for a long time. I heard a hoot of delight from the landing and Mary came running down the stairs, slim legs in black court shoes, and drew us into the tiled hall, which was furnished with rugs, gilt mirror, an antique table with bent baroque legs and marble top, sporting an aspidistra in a brass pot. She was wearing a simple blue dress with shoulder pads. Her red hair was full of waves and sat abundantly on her shoulders. She embraced me laughingly and then held me at arms length.

'God, Peg. Is this really you? Is this our Peg? You look splendid, you look chic!'

'Don't sound so surprised,' I said laughing. 'You'll give me an inferiority complex.'

She pecked Brian's cheek and said he was looking dangerously handsome.

'We'll have tea in the drawing-room, Janet,' she told the maid who said 'Yes Madam,' and disappeared.

288

Lucien emerged from a door at the back of the hall, wearing an open necked shirt and a cardigan. It was the first time I had seen him informally dressed. He looked older, a little tired, kissed me on each cheek with a formality which belied the expression in his eyes. He took me in from top to toe.

'You are lovelier than ever, Madame.' He shook hands with Brian who remembered him well. I could sense that Brian did not really approve of Lucien. 'Why can't she find someone who will marry her?' he said to me later, 'instead of wasting her time with a fast fellow like him?' Brian believed that marriage was the ultimate compliment you could pay a woman and that if she was paid that compliment she was forever fulfilled. My mother had had much the same notion, but Mary McElligott was cut of different cloth. She looked at men with a kind of careless interest. 'Why should she marry anyone?' I asked Brian; 'She makes her own rules,' and he sniffed and said that was all very well but she wouldn't be young and beautiful forever. Anyway, he said, it was immoral.

Lucien was assiduous in his hospitality. We had plenty of precious rationed tea and little cakes with chocolate icing and when I commented on this with wonder and gratitude our host smiled and murmured something about the black market, while Brian raised his eyebrows. He explained that the house belonged to some friends who had repaired to their house in Scotland for the duration, in order to be near their son who was with the fleet at Scappa Floe. 'There's more than enough room for you!'

'And we've plenty of food so you can stop worrying,' Mary added, pouring the tea. I saw how Lucien's eyes dwelt on her, the gentle respect he showed her, and I was impressed. The nuns had always given us to understand that if you gave a man what he was looking for without marriage as the price tag, he had only contempt for you. Yet here was Mary being treated like some sort of princess by the man she had been living with for two years.

'I have been offered the part of Titania in *A Midsummers Night Dream*. It's in a little theatre in Kensington, 'The Walpole', but it's a start,' she murmured, when I asked her if she'd found any work yet.

I clapped. 'Well done. You'll be in the West End next!'

She pooh-poohed this, saying there was always an initial inertia in any career, but she seemed pleased.

She showed us around, from the huge kitchen in the basement to a quick glimpse of the upper storeys. I was surprised that Mary and Lucien had separate bedrooms, albeit with adjoining doors.

Mary left us at the door of our room. 'I'm sure you'd like to have a rest,' he said quite seriously and Brian, taken off balance, blushed. She looked at me then, smiling, and added that dinner was at eight.

'Is that bed big enough for you?' I asked my husband as he shut the door. I put my hat on the dressing-table and sat down on the bed. He pulled the curtains across the windows, and began to unbutton his jacket. Then he threw himself beside me, kissing me between each word.

'Come-here-and-stop-giving-guff.'

Silence. We spoke then without words, with touch and lips, with the aura rising around us like a mist, the sensual and the spiritual becoming one. He was very urgent, but gentle. I was hungry for him and desperate to re-establish old parameters. And then we slept.

Mary knocked about seven thirty. I put on the dressing-gown hanging at the back of the door and answered the knock. She looked at me, taking in my dishevelled state. Her face registered embarrassment. She apologised, handing me a letter.

'It's from Glenallen,' she said. 'I went to see the O'Shaugnessys before I left and I met Harry. I gave her this address. This letter came for Brian yesterday. I forgot about it in all the excitement of your arrival.'

I left the door open and handed the letter to Brian who was still in bed. He sat up immediately, took the letter, tore it open, and turned to me with a curiously expressionless face from which all colour had been drained.

'Mummy's dead!'

I took the letter from him. I recognised Harry's writing.

'Dear Brian,
Mary McElligott had gone to England and says she will try to look you up. I thought you should know that Mummy is dead. She died on 23 March. She never recovered from you having left us. She asked for you when she was dying, but of course we didn't know where you were. She always loved you so much and you had to do this to her.

Daddy is very poorly. You managed to break both their hearts. I cannot help blaming you for what has happened to them. Just when things were beginning to pull up again you deserted us all.

291

I hope you are satisfied with what you have done. Things could have been so good. We could all have been a happy family, but of course you had to spoil everything. If you care anything about Daddy you should come back to see him. Dr O'Shaughnessy is very concerned about him.

Harriet.

I read the letter through, my heart sinking down through my feet. The room was invaded by silence, a silence which had nothing to do with the noise of traffic from the street below. My perky little hat, which I had placed on the dressing-table, was suddenly obscenely decadent. I reached over and took Brian's hand. He was very still, like something carved in marble. I heard Mary move away from the door and I brought the letter out to her, left it with her. I heard her exclaim under her breath 'That bitch!' and then I heard Lucien's footsteps on the stairs and her whispered communication with him and then one of them closed the door.

But Brian sat there in bed and wept, his arm across his eyes. I tried to embrace him, but he stiffened, ashamed of his tears, and would not let me touch him; and I felt his grief and guilt and the destruction caused in him by his rejected love for these people, his family.

I cannot bear the pain in you, I wanted to scream. You have me. I love you. I need you.

The whole power of the missive, apart from its bad news, was the suggestion that Harry actually missed Brian, that she loved him in her way and that he had betrayed her as well as his parents. I began to wonder if she had changed, or if I had

292

got her wrong. There was some inherent inconsistency in her behaviour which I could not understand. But I cursed her silently for her letter.

We got dressed and went downstairs. Mary and Lucien were in the hall.

'I must go home!' Brian said.

Lucien put a hand on his shoulder, murmuring words of condolence. He brought him into the drawing-room and poured brandies, handing them around to each of us. His face was sympathetic, but firm.

'You can't. There is no reason to now. Her funeral is over. You won't get permission!'

'I could fly home!'

Lucien looked at him. 'If you do that, without permission, you will have nothing. You could be court martialled, shot.'

'I would come back at once.'

Lucien gestured. 'The best way to honour your mother is by killing the enemy.'

Brian became silent, drank his brandy, his trembling hand the only sign of the emotion within him.

'I must see my father,' he said after a moment. 'I don't want him to die as well before I have had a chance to talk to him!'

Lucien just shook his head. 'This country is dying. Everyone is in mourning, but they fight on!'

The weekend had lost its momentum. Brian became remote and polite and read the letter several times. Lovemaking, when I tried to initiate it, degenerated into a statutory coupling. Gone was the fervour of that passionate contact where we could lose the world. There was passion of a sort, but it addressed something I could not reach, something dark, insoluble and unjust.

293

Brian was due to rejoin his squadron early on Sunday evening. I could not bear to part from him; I felt the dread of some impending chance concerning him. I couldn't give voice to my apprehensions, but neither could I still them.

Mary and I set the table for Saturday evening supper with the help of Janet who tried to stifle her occasional chirp of a laugh at things we said, colloquial expressions she found quaint. We dined in the breakfast-room beside the kitchen and Janet served us and Mary tried to take Brian's mind off his bereavement by asking him about his life in the RAF.

'How do you feel when you are up there in the sky?'

'Free,' he answered and Lucien leant forward to listen, watching the narrator with intent interest. 'We fly in formation going out; there are eight Browning machine guns on the Hurricane, four in each wing and when they're fired the plane bucks like a horse. Then there's the smell of cordite and also the smell of the fuel - high octane stuff that's quite unpleasant initially, but you get used to it. And when we sight the enemy we attack, strike and run. You can turn around and the sky which might have been full a moment before will be empty. It's quite incredible, eerie.'

Lucien asked him some questions then and technical terms about liquid cooled Rolls Royce engines and 1030 horse power and speed of 335 miles per hour were mentioned and in the middle of all this the air raid alert started wailing and Lucien ordered us all down to the cellar. Janet came down and sat shyly among us and shivered in her thin uniform until Lucien gave her a rug.

Part of the cellar had a corrugated aluminium shelter, with sandbags - an Anderson shelter - and we crept into this. The place was cold. Lucien had a torch with him and shone it around to disclose chairs, an old card table and a kerosene lantern. He took a box of matches from his pocket and lit the lantern.

There were a couple of crates of wine stacked carefully on the floor and our host selected a bottle, took some glasses which were on the table under a tea towel and proceeded to entertain us. It was evident that he had spent some time down here because there were also some rugs wrapped in an oil cloth which he put about our knees and we sat and drank Burgundy by candlelight while the bombs fell not too far off; we could hear the steady dull throb of explosions through the walls and floor. I didn't care, and I knew that Brian didn't care either, whether the house came down on top of us or not. And later when the air raid was over and we came up the cellar stairs, I preceded Lucien who was behind me and felt, for an instant, his hand brush my cheek in the dark.

Chapter 11

Brian and I left London, he to his base at Manston, I to Nottingham. Lucien drove us to the station in a Daimler, making some wry comment about using a German car, explaining that it wasn't his, that it was on loan to the Free French.

Mary had bade me goodbye at the door, telling me to keep my chin up and not to worry about Brian. 'He'll be alright, Peg.' But I saw that there was little conviction in her eyes. She had divined the frame of mind in which he had made his departure.

As for Mary herself - I felt there was in her life some shrouded element, something covert which she did not want anyone to know about. This was apparent in little ways, an absent mindedness, a tendency to drift into a world of her own when people were absorbed in conversation and she thought herself unobserved. Once or twice I had come across her staring out the window, her face tense and far away. I think Lucien noticed this too, because I would catch him looking at her sometimes with concern and perplexity.

I tried to talk to her when Lucien and Brian had gone out together on Sunday morning to examine the extent of the night's bombing. We were in the drawing-room, tall bright windows looking out on the street, red buses passing, the muted roar of traffic reaching into the still house.

'How are things with you, Mary? I've hardly had a chance to talk to you on our own.'

She offered me a cigarette, lit up, inhaled, rested her head on the back of the armchair.

'Ah, sure things are fine. I'm delighted to have got to London. We'll be starting rehearsals soon.' She smiled over at me. 'It's been great to see you - and Brian. It's terrible about his mother. I wish he didn't get the bad news here. I think he's taking it very badly?'

'Yes. He blames himself.'

I did not speak of the guilt I felt myself: it was I who had been responsible for his departure from Glenallen.

Mary sighed. 'I don't remember my mother. I suppose you never find love like that again!'

I nodded. 'The weekend started off with such bliss and then this had to happen. It's a pity he can't go home. Things seem unfinished unless you can go through a ritual of some kind to mark the passage, to see the person laid out, to say goodbye. I can do so little for him, especially as he's going back to his base today.'

Mary was silent. Then she said: 'Poor old Peg; you've had a tough ride between one thing and another. I wonder how many marriages there would be if people considered all the ramifications beforehand, the struggle to be all things to someone, the end of personal peace!'

'You're a cynic, Mary. It's not like that!'

'Is it not? Has he brought you peace?'

It was my turn to be silent.

'No,' I said after a moment. 'He has brought me many things, but he has not brought me peace!'

297

'I should keep my big mouth shut!' Mary said, sensing the tension in me. 'But I'm a spinster and curious!'

I laughed. 'Some spinster! You are a gifted woman and some day you will have the world at your feet! And you'll make a great Titania. Do you remember reading it in fourth year and Mother Benedict? - "Now, Mary McElligott, there's no need to pretend you're on the stage."' I tried to imitate our teacher, pitching my voice higher in a see-saw Cork accent and gave up the attempt. ' I'll come down to see you when the play opens.'

She chuckled, a genuine mirthful laugh, the light of recollection in her face. 'Poor old Benedict! She was a nice poor divil, even if she did subscribe to an eminently decent, one gender, order, where women clung like good little shadows to the periphery.'

She tapped her fingers on the arm of the chair.

'I wish you could stay here longer. I wish you didn't have to go back to Nottingham! It will be lonely without you.'

I stared at her, surprised, touched.

'But you have everything! You are talented, beautiful. And you have Lucien.'

Her smile became fixed.

'Do I?' she whispered.

'You know you do. He loves you. Anyone can see that.'

She continued smoking, looking up at the ceiling and it was only after a moment or two that I detected the tears. They coursed quietly down her face.

'He does love you,' I insisted, aghast, 'and I thought you loved him too.'

She dashed away the tears angrily.

'Poor little Peg. You love Brian and you know that you are the only woman in his life. But as for Lucien ... one loves a man like that at one's peril. He is impervious to anything which fails to please or interest him. How secure do you think is my tenure in his life? As secure as the next woman who fascinates him! He sees other women from time to time as it is, but he comes back to me and keeps me here with him,' she gestured with her hands 'in luxury, simply because I am ... a challenge. So, to answer your question - I don't love him. I appreciate him but, no, I don't love him!'

'But you live with him,' I blurted. 'How can you live with someone you don't love ... take his gifts ... sleep with him?'

She glared at me and stood up.

'For God's sake, Peg,' she hissed angrily. 'Can't you see I am incapable of love. I am a freak!'

She walked out of the room. I was about to follow when I heard the front door open and Lucien and Brian came in.

'You look pale; is everything alright?' Lucien never missed a cue where people were concerned. He was smiling at me now, a questioning smile, dark eyes narrowed, mouth curved, sensing something. He was smaller than Brian, but looking at them there was no question as to which of the two radiated energy and direction. Of course Brian was much younger, with all ideals intact.

'Where's Mary?'

'Upstairs, I think.'

Brian sat beside me on the couch and reached for my hand. I heard Lucien's footsteps on the stairs, heard his voice. 'Cherie, Où es-tu?' His tone was different, very gentle, almost careful.

I gripped my husband's arm, aware that Mary's life was not what I had imagined, that the indifference she projected was as much a mask as it had ever been.

Brian pulled me against him and I laid my head on the blue airforce jacket, traced the single stripe at his cuff, heard the beating of his heart. The gilt buttons had the Air Force eagle, wings outstretched in flight, and above the eagle the crown.

'I wish you didn't have to go.'

I could feel the tension in him, the grief for his mother which he was not going to display or share, and his preoccupation with things I could only guess at. His eyes were fixed on something outside my vision, probing and unravelling some dark skein of the soul.

I looked up at his face; his eyes met mine.

'I want you to know,' he said, 'that you are the best thing that has ever happened to me. I want you to know it, Peg!'

There was silence. I heard someone walking on the floor above us. The traffic droned outside.

'Brian, please don't be so unhappy. It is very sad about your mother but Harry wrote a rotten letter and it's a reflection on her, not on you.'

'I wish to God,' he burst out, 'that I could extirpate that place out of my bones.'

'You're out of it now!'

He looked at me.

'Am I out of it now? It's there all the time! I'm rooted to the place. I try to make sense of it. I cannot let it go before I have made sense of it. Can you understand that?'

I understood it only too well.

Lucien came into the room and said something about the necessity of leaving if we wanted to catch our trains. We stood, collected our bags and coats and Mary embraced us both at the door.

Lucien drove Brian to Victoria and I went with him to the train and stood on the platform and waved as the train drew out. 'See you soon, my darling,' he promised. 'See you very soon.'

I watched until the train had disappeared down the track, my eyes trying to rivet on the window where he sat and then all I could see was the back of the last carriage until it was hidden by an incoming train.

My host then conducted me to St. Pancras. I was silent and he looked at me occasionally, making the odd comment, speaking softly. I took little heed of Lucien. I was worrying about Brian and I answered in monosyllables.

I was not prepared, when Lucien had parked the car near the station, for the movement he made in my direction and the sensual contact of his mouth on mine.

I felt as though my bones had turned to water. I was restored to the world of reality, of flesh and blood. Shock and the rush of sexual arousal such as I had never experienced fixed me rigidly into the leather seat. He did not attempt to otherwise caress me, except to cup my cheek with his palm, and this gesture of tenderness made the kiss almost unendurably sweet. When he withdrew from me I stared into my lap and then into his face and saw there a bemused expression, half way between amusement and curiosity and, in his eyes, dark greedy desire. He smiled.

'Well, Madame,' he said in a low voice. 'We have had our moment of togetherness.'

He opened his door and got out. As he took my case from the boot I put the envelope containing his fifty pounds in the glove compartment. Then I

301

got out and walked beside him into the station. He purchased my ticket despite my protestations and saw me on to the train.

'Au revoir, sweet Peg,' he said as he handed me into the train. 'We shall meet again.'

'Lucien,' I said, 'look in the glove compartment of the car. I have returned some property belonging to you.'

I saw his frown, and then heard the half laugh through the window of the compartment where I had found my seat. He put out both hands, palm upwards in a gesture of mock defeat, raised his hat to me from where he stood on the platform and disappeared into the crowd.

Back in Nottingham I threw myself into my work; I spent hours every evening preparing the next day's lessons. I was now the Botany specialist of the science department as Mr Warren, my predecessor, had gone in response to his 'call'. The first year dental students I taught were expecting their call also, and awaiting it, for the most part, quite eagerly. I asked some of the boys sadly one day why they were so anxious to go out to fight, to die as many already had and was informed that they were doing it for a brave new world.

'It will be a wonderfully different world, Mrs Fitzallen. No more war, a greatly enhanced standard of living for everyone and air travel will be commonplace.'

I doubted this latter piece of augury, so little did I know.

I wrote a long letter to Brian. At least I knew where he was now, I comforted myself, but wished he would write. Was he still sunk in the depression which had succeeded the arrival of Harry's letter? Would we ever live to get Glenallen and the pain associated with everyone

302

there out of our systems? I wrote a short letter to Harry, telling her that I was sorry to hear of her mother's death and explaining that Brian and I were now settled in England, that I was teaching and that he was now involved in operational duties in the RAF and had been greatly upset by her letter. I don't know how much of that letter was cut by the official Censor but I got a reply about ten days later thanking me for writing and that it had been such an upsetting time and that she was glad to have had word from me. I wondered if she had told her father that I had written. I knew he would look kindly on Brian having joined the RAF. Judging by his comments about the war it was just the sort of thing he would have done himself. But she didn't mention the old man at all.

John Eyreton took me to the pictures.

'You're working too hard, Peg,' he announced. 'I'm taking you out tonight. What would you say to seeing *The Little Foxes*?'

I liked Bette Davis and was delighted with the suggestion, but hesitated, afraid of giving him any ideas incompatible with my married state. But there was only kindness in his eyes.

We went to the cinema, but the air raid siren went off half way through the film. Being so central Nottingham was overflown by German bombers on a regular basis and then the sirens would blare, but we were in fact bombed only twice during my stay in the city.

'Hold on,' John said. 'I'll go and see what's going on.'

He left and came back a short while later. The second siren did not go off. So we watched the rest of the film and then walked home along by the smoke screened river and John talked of the war, his work on the new airport, and what Hitler was doing to the Jews. He hated Hitler as I did, as everyone did. It was simply something in the air at the time, this unearthly detestation. What was being done to the Jews was frequently discussed; they often spoke of it in the staffroom at school although some teachers thought that it couldn't possibly be true, that it was mostly propaganda.

I asked John if he thought it was mostly propaganda and he started slightly and looked at me as if to reassure himself.

'Certainly not. It's quite true. I'm quarter Jewish myself,' he added, almost defensively, 'On my mother's side. If the Jerries invade I'll be for it!'

And then,very tentatively, he began to ask me about Brian and about my home in Ireland and I told him a little in general terms about the events leading up to our coming to England.

I asked him what he would do after the war.

'I'd like my own firm, Eyreton Consulting Engineers. How does that sound?' He laughed. 'I suppose you'll have gone back to your island with your husband?'

I was going to answer that we might buy a little house and stay in England, but didn't. I felt the cold premonition that this would remain a dream.

When we got back to the house Claire made some tea. 'The Wizard of Half Oz,' as she called Mrs Burton, was out with her boyfriend, a warden in the ARP who had called around after the all clear. They had gone to the pub.

Later, when I was in my room saying the rosary, begging whatever powers there were to keep Brian safe, I heard the knock on the door. I thought it was Claire and called 'Come in.'

It was John, in his dressing-gown, book in hand.

'I thought you might be amused by this.'

The book was Lowe's cartoons. He left it down on the table and stood uncertainly, then saw the rosary beads in my hands.

'I'm sorry,' he said uncomfortably. 'I didn't know you were praying.'

'It's for Brian.'

'Of course.'

He shut the door behind him very quietly.

The following Sunday afternoon I went for a walk in Wooloton Park with Claire and John. We had taken some sandwiches and spent a pleasant time in the gardens and down by the lake. John was a mine of information; he pointed out the ruined Camellia House with its polygonal floor plan and filled us in on some historical details concerning the house itself. It was always a pleasure being shown the sights by my new friends; I had seen Nottingham Castle as well, the very place where the wicked Sheriff had schemed the destruction of Robin Hood, whose escapades I had once dreamed of in the summer days by the Garryogue.

It was a fine day and there were a lot of families there, old and young, enjoying the walks and the spring sunshine.

When we got back to the digs I found that a gentleman had called to see me, 'a Frenchie by the look of him,' Mrs Burton said suspiciously. He would call around again at five o'clock. 'He had a French accent and was very disappointed that you were out.'

'That must have been Lucien,' I said in hurried explanation, 'my friend's ... boyfriend. I stayed with them while I was in London.'

The 'Frenchie' arrived punctually at five o'clock, looking pale and strangely disinclined to socialise. I introduced him.

'Lucien, this is Mr Eyreton and this is Mrs Burton.' This is the Comte de Rais.'

John shook hands, said 'How do you do' while Mrs Burton murmured 'Pleased to meet you, I'm sure,' electric with delight that she was being visited by aristocracy. Lucien spoke with humorous quizzicality to John, who I could see was amused at his accent and disarmed by his charm. But all the time I could see how detached Lucien really was and how his eyes took in the house and the people around me.

'I have some news for you, Peg,' he said. 'May I be permitted to take you out for some tea? I must catch the late train back to London.'

I collected my coat on the way out. Lucien took me to the Black Boy Hotel. We boarded a trolley bus and, when alighting, he took my hand and held it in his own. I liked the feel of his hand, liked his closeness and mistrusted it. It had nothing at all to do with my feelings for Brian; it was more like a chemical reaction. It angered me too, because this was Mary's man and he had no business making up to me. And I remembered what she had said - that her tenure in his life was as secure as the next woman who fascinated him. Mary was part of my life, almost of my identity; Lucien did not feature in comparison. But what could he possibly have to tell me that he had come this distance?

The Black Boy was the smartest hotel in Nottingham. We sat over the silver tea service in the sitting-room and I felt my mouth water as I stared at the little sandwiches and the iced cakes and knew that my host must be paying heavily for this treat. I always demolished my quarter pound ration of sweets as soon as I got them and my last ration had been two days earlier. I had developed a terrible sweet tooth thanks to the war.

I stared over the cakes and into his eyes.

'How is Mary?' I asked.

'Mary has gone,' he said quietly. 'I went to collect her after rehearsals on Friday and she wasn't there. They said she had just left. She hasn't been back since. Do you know where she is?'

He said all this very quickly, with an almost expressionless face, except for the intent scrutiny with which he assessed my reaction.

I was stunned.

'But where could she have gone? Do you mean she's gone back to Ireland?'

'I thought that if anyone would know, you would,' he said with a sigh after a moment. 'But I can see that I was wrong.' He seemed suddenly tired.

I made him repeat the story, what time had he come to pick her up, whom had he questioned about her.

'I asked everyone, the whole cast, the porter, nearby shopkeepers, taxi drivers, bus conductors. To no avail. I told the police of course,' he added with the ghost of a smile, 'but they just looked at me and took particulars and reminded me that a woman of full age can go where she likes; I asked the Air Raid Wardens in the area and they said no one answering her description had been found.'

'Was there a raid that night, the night she disappeared?'

'Yes.'

'She could have been lost in the blitz. She could be dead,' I whispered feeling my eyes smart with the sudden tears, and he nodded, tears in his own eyes. 'But I do not believe she is.'

I wept shamelessly and after some time went to the ladies room and sat and cried until I had recovered some composure. 'Oh Mary,' I thought, 'I cannot lose you as well as Cissie. Where are you? Oh, please God! Look after her. Don't let her be dead.'

There were so many questions I wanted to ask Lucien. What was his part in this affair? Why had she left? Had he any idea where she had gone?

He sighed and shook his head.'

'So you had nothing to do with it?' I demanded.

He looked at me with his half smile.

'You become aggressive, sweet Peg.'

'You love her, don't you?'

'Certainly.'

Then he said, 'Mary behaved very peculiarly one night recently during rehearsals. She became hysterical when she saw the mask worn by one of the actors. It was very strange and not like Mary to behave like that!'

'What mask was it?'

'It was the mask for the character Puck - the mask of a goat.'

Lucien saw me back to Stanhope Boulevard in virtual silence. En route the air raid siren started screaming and I wanted to scream back, to shake my fist at the sky and the war and the horrors visited upon the world by the deadly games of men.

Lucien drew me into the nearest shelter and we stood there with about two dozen other people waiting for the all clear. No bombs fell; evidently they were destined for somewhere else; it was another false alarm.

I felt his hand on mine again, felt the way he tucked it inside his arm and was strangely comforted. We had drawn together in some way, walking back up Stanhope Boulevard in the gathering dusk.

At the front door he kissed my hand.

'You have power, sweet Peg, much more than you know.' He said it sadly and then he was gone.

It was some days later that the dreams started. I saw Cissie on the mountain, saw her come and go like a shadow, as though she were part of the lonely play of the light. And then Mary came into the dream and suddenly we were back at St. Catherine's with the January day outside and the glass exploding on the planchette board. And I woke with the sense that I was suffocating, that I was pressed down by the weight of something malevolent and intangible which Cissie, Mary and I had unwittingly invoked.

Chapter 12

There were two letters on the hallstand when I got back from school on the following Friday, one with an Irish stamp. I snatched it up, looked at the other one and, with a surge of hope, recognising Mary's impatient writing, tore it open.

> *'Dearest Peg,*
> *I'm sure Lucien has told you that I've gone. I've decided to stop playing games, or to play them where they may be of use.*
> *Don't worry about me.*
> *Love,*
> *Mary.'*

I turned over the letter, feeling full of conflicting emotions, angry that she gave no address, relieved that she was alive. The letter had a London postmark of four days earlier. I examined the envelope carefully in mounting frustration, as though trying to force from it some greater intelligence. It was maddeningly dumb. I felt that the thing knew where she was; it had felt the pressure of her hand.

Mrs Burton appeared in the hall, her handbag under her arms. She glanced at the letter and at my face.

'Everything alright, dear?'

'Yes. It's from my friend Mary.'

In desperate need of a sympathetic ear, I had told Mrs Burton and John about Mary's disappearance. Now her face registered pleasure at my news.

'The one who went AWOL?'

'Yes. But she doesn't give her address.'

Mrs Burton put on her coat, looked at herself in the hallstand mirror, took her compact out of her handbag, dabbed at her nose with the powder puff.

'I can tell you now, dear,' she said in low confiding tones, 'your friend wanted to get away from that Frenchie. Foreign men are a bit ... you know' and she widened her eyes. 'Well, they're not British, if you take my meaning, dear!'

Some fragrant motes of powder floated to the polished lino as she shut the compact with a snap.

Mrs Burton's cat Queenie came waddling downstairs from her favourite sunny spot by the landing window. My landlady bent to stroke her, cooing.

'Puss, puss, puss. Look at the lovely face, look at that lovely face,' and the cat smiled up at her out of feral green eyes, purring throatily and raising her tail.

I brought the letter from Ireland upstairs to my room. When I had seen the Irish stamp I had hoped it was from Tom, but the writing was not his, although it was familiar. Then I remembered Peter's contained writing. It seemed strange to receive a letter from him addressed to me as Mrs Fitzallen. It was almost a recognition and it filled me with something like fear.

I did not want to open the letter. I left it on the table in my room while I dealt with a score or more exercises of the lower V. I had almost finished them when Mrs Burton called everyone for supper.

311

John was in good form at the table that evening; Claire and Ellen joined in the conversation about the war.

There was a kind of shepherds' pie for supper. I looked at it in dismay; I was hungry but it was Friday.

'Just give me some of the potato, Mrs Burton.'

She put her hand to her mouth.

'I'm sorry, dear. I forgot. But there's very little meat in it.'

'You can rely on that,' John said in my ear, indicating fat old Quennie who was lying in her basket in the corner, licking her chops and looking smug. 'It's nearly all in Pussy wussy.'

'So hard to get meat anymore, except horse flesh,' Mrs Burton went on. 'But I told Mr Tinsley, "My lodgers wouldn't care for that," I told him.' She carefully scraped off some potato from the top and handed it to me, passing me some bread and margarine as well. John gave me his potato, shaking his head at Irish Catholicism.

Dessert was jelly, saccharine sweetened, whipped 'cream' made with milk and crushed eggshells.

John had heard the news about Mary's letter from Mrs Burton. I took it out of my pocket and showed it to him. He frowned as he read it and then said it was obvious that she was alright.

'She is probably in a temporary address, or between addresses.'

His certainty cheered me. Mary's letter had been definite in tone, that much was true. And she was alive.

As we helped bring the plates to the scullery John gestured towards the window and the sunlit evening; he said that he and Claire was going out

312

for a walk and would I come. I demurred. I said I had too much work on hand so he said maybe tomorrow. Tomorrow seemed far away when I had a letter from Peter Fitzallen waiting for me upstairs and which I did not want to open.

But I did open it. I went back upstairs after supper and slipped my nail file under the flap and tore the envelope open. The folded piece of stiff paper was tidily written, bearing a printed letterhead, The Law Library, Four Courts, Dublin.

'Dear Peg,

Harriet showed me your letter of condolence on Mother's death. I'm afraid I have further bad news. Father died suddenly on 2 May. Brian must be told. We have had only one letter from him and he did not give his address.

There are matters to be discussed with him now and I would be obliged if you would let me have his address.

I hope all is going well for you.

Yours sincerely,

Peter.'

I spent some time thinking about the letter and then I wrote to Brian.

'My darling,

I am sending you Peter's letter which I received today. I am very sorry at his news and wish I could be with you. I love you very much. Please don't be too unhappy at this sad news. Your father had the Brown Scapular, so he's safe in Heaven now. I am having a mass said for him by the curate here, who is a Father Riordan from Galway! He has already said one for your mother.

313

*We can be together when you get your next leave
and the thought of it is keeping me going. I hate this
horrible war and long for it to end, so we can be
together.*

*Please write to me. I know you are very busy, but I
would love to get a letter.*

'I need to hear from you,' I was going to add,
but crossed it out. It sounded clinging and weak,
so I wiped my eyes and ended on a note of cheer
which I was far from feeling, telling him that I
would write again soon. And I decided not to tell
him about Mary, not yet. The letter contained
enough bad news as it was.

John went out with Claire for a walk and Ellen
went with some friends to the pictures and the
house became silent. I went to bed early with a
book by Damon Runyon, but could not read. As I
was drifting to sleep I heard Mrs Burton's
footsteps on the stairs followed by those of her
boyfriend Jack and listened to the sounds of their
lovemaking in the next room, the rhythmic
creaking and gasping and sudden laughter.

The next day was Saturday and I went with
John and Claire on an outing to Newstead Abbey,
the home of Lord Byron.

'It was built by Henry 11 for the Augustinian
Monks in expiation of the murder of Thomas a
Beckett,' Claire told me as we walked around the
Abbey and the ruined church. Afterwards John
took us for afternoon tea in The Hut, an old
hostelry by the gate.

John was, as usual, the epitome of English
courtesy and I found peace in the emotional quiet
he represented, in the distance from psychological
war games. Claire talked volubly; I could see how
her eyes turned to John and lingered. She was a

handsome, rather serious girl, her looks marred by the round spectacles she wore.

John made some comment about Ireland and how he would like to go there sometime and Claire said she had been to Dublin once, 'Rather depressing town I thought.'

'When you go back with your husband after the war, perhaps you'll send us an invitation to stay for a couple of days?' John suggested.

I said I would of course - if we were there, but that I thought we might be staying in England.

'I don't know why you would want to stay here with a country estate waiting for you in somewhere as lovely as Ireland,' John said and I thought of Glenallen and Balor's Eye and Cissie and Mary gone and Brian an increasingly unknown quantity, too vulnerable, fixated. My hand started shaking uncontrollably; my teacup rattled and slopped into the saucer.

'I will never go back to Glenallen, never, never!' I said through clenched teeth, hearing my voice shrill, closing my eyes and hunting for the control which was about to escape me, my elbows on the table, my clenched fists against my forehead.

Claire put her arm around my shoulder and I could sense her chagrin and John's and they spoke in quiet sensible tones of getting back and Claire took me outside while John settled the bill.

I longed for the emotional security of a family, I thought of Harry and Peter and how I had once hoped to have had in them at least goodwill, if not affection. But they were part of the bizarre scenario into which I had intruded with my life, a scenario which seemed incapable of any kind of rationalisation.

Outside my two English friends sat me between them on a bench and asked me was something the

315

matter, was there anything they could do. I told them, when I had collected myself, that Glenallen was a very strange place and that I would not want to live there. They knew that my father-in-law had died and that I had written to tell Brian and I said I was upset for him.

'It's been such a strain,' I said and Claire said 'Poor old you,' and kindly John brought us off to a pub for a brandy. 'It's just what you need to buck you up!'

That evening I went to confession and told Father Riordan that I was sick with worry about my husband and he asked me in his flat Galway accent why my husband had left me, why had he gone away to the war. Had I refused him? Had I been in breach of my wifely duty? And I thought guiltily of a few occasions when I had pleaded a headache or, being very sleepy, had not responded to the sudden demanding hands in the middle of the night. So I told this man from Galway that on occasion I had refused my husband, and blushed in the embarrassment of telling it, feeling suddenly naked, guilty of everything that had happened, and he listened piously and absolved me from the sin of it, his hairy right hand raised in front of my bowed head - in Nomine Patris et Filii et Spiritus Sancti - the male words of power. I cooled my hot mortified face with cold hands as I knelt to say my penance and remembered with a start that I had forgotten to tell him about the kiss with Lucien at the station and, fearful that I would not now be able to go to communion in the morning, I returned to the box.

Father Riordan sounded weary, muttered something about scruples and warned me to be careful of foreigners, especially French ones.

316

And I wrote to Brian again on Sunday after mass, a long letter filled with pieces about the school and the children and the digs and Mrs Burton's horrible spoilt cat; I was trying to be cheerful. But he did not answer and I became morose, torn between the desire to find his base and call on him directly and the anger which had begun to brim in me where he was concerned. I was sick to death of eternally playing second fiddle to his vagaries and that of his family. Now that we had got away from Glenallen I had thought everything would work out - if we could survive the war. But it was becoming clear that Glenallen was as much a state of mind as it was a place. I prayed into the night for his safety. 'Please look after him, God. Don't let him be killed.'

I could only imagine in general terms what his life in the RAF must be like, but I knew, from hearing the Ack Ack, the barking terror of guns, and I was familiar with the steady drone of bombers in the night sky. The thought of Brian in a similar situation, up there with the enemy, was real and when I thought about it long enough, unbearable. I tried to look into the future with whatever inspiration I could muster, but was met with a blank wall.

The telegram came one Monday afternoon when I had just returned from school. I was in my room, having divested myself of the bag of books and my jacket and was sitting back in the old brown armchair with a cigarette. I had begun to smoke more heavily; they were like gold dust, but calmed my nerves. I heard the ring of the doorbell below and Mrs Burton's voice in the hall and the closing of the front door and a moment's silence before her heavy footfall sounded on the stairs. I don't know why I was so aware of that moment or why I listened with increasing terror as her footsteps came nearer. She knocked, entered, her face nervous, and handed me the telegram in its HMS envelope. My hands shook. I put down the cigarette, conscious in a curious detached way of the little spiral of smoke, of the brown bakelite ash tray, of a door slamming next door. I tore the telegram open.

Regret to inform you Fighter Pilot Brian Fitzallen missing in action.

I sat and stared at the piece of paper in my hands with its abrupt words. The sounds continued from next door, but muffled now as though a glass barrier had been raised between me and the world, the smoke continued to curl from the cigarette and the light form the window was strangely undiminished. The whole force of my being gathered around this moment in denial. I felt the telegram being taken from my fingers and remember the hot tea with powdered milk and sugar and biscuits which appeared from somewhere. And Mrs Burton's kind voice and then John's who knelt on the floor beside me when he came home and wrapped his arms around me until the storm in my heart broke into sobs.

I went to see Father Riordan the next day and gave him five pounds for masses for Brian. He took the money and promised the masses and told me to trust in God's purpose. 'And pray to our Blessed Mother to intercede for him.'

'Missing in Action.' What did that mean? I asked John who said that only the War office

318

could help me. I sent a wire to Lucien. 'Brian missing in action STOP Must check War Office STOP May I stay Knightsbridge? STOP

He replied immediately telling me to come at once, that he would meet me at St Pancras.

The headmaster, Mr Dencher, was sitting behind his mahogany desk when I went to his office to tell him the news. The stern lines left his face as he listened and he came around to where I sat and put a kindly hand on my shoulder, addressing me with sudden uncharacteristic informality. 'Don't throw in the sponge yet, Peg: he may be alright.' He gave me the rest of the week off and, having sent a wire to Lucien to advise him of my time of arrival, I packed a bag and went to the Midland Station for the London train. Lucien met me at St Pancras as promised.

It was dark when we got back to Knightsbridge; we drove through the blackout; the traffic signals had only horizontal slits of light and headlamps had special masks to prevent more than the minimum light escaping. Here and there sandbags were piled high by the entrances to buildings. Pedestrians who had torches had covered them in tissue paper and there were helmeted ARP wardens like busy ghouls in the gloom. Lucien commiserated without many words; he communicated warmth and sympathy through the sudden firm grasp of his hand reaching for mine in the darkness.

I found I was alone in the house with Lucien. The place was full of packing cases, crates, rolled-up carpets. 'I'll be leaving soon and the owners are putting the stuff into storage.'

He drew the heavy black curtains in the drawing-room, lit a lamp and I sat back on the

319

damask sofa, looking around me in the half light, remembering the last time I had been in this room. He took a bottle of cognac from a box, poured two measures - 'Drink that Peg; you need it' - and then, sitting beside me, he asked, almost tentatively, if I had heard from Mary.

'She sent me a note.'

His dark eyes brightened with hope, expectancy, eyebrows raised. 'You have it with you?'

'No,' I lied, knowing that it was beside me in my bag, remembering what she had said about playing games, unwilling to cause him pain. 'But she said that she was alright and would contact me again. She gave no address.'

'Did she mention me?'

'No. It was a very short note.'

He leaned back and sipped his drink. After a moment he sighed and said, 'If I could even be sure she was safe.' He brushed his hand against my wet cheek. 'Courage, courage.' He said it tiredly, without his usual gallant command. Then he excused himself and reappeared in a little while with a tray.

'You must forgive the fare, sweet Peg. I'm a bit like Mother Hubbard at the moment.'

He deposited the tray on the coffee table and put an omelette with some toast before me. He had brought a bottle of wine too, but I refused a glass.

'Where's Janet?' I asked.

'Janet is gone. She is in munitions now, cooking for the enemy you might say. You know they have begun to conscript women?'

'Yes. They are mobilising the nation.'

I slept that night in the same room I had shared with Brian. The bed was too big for me. I felt cold

320

although it was May, cold through and through; my feet were like ice blocks. I woke several times, my hand out for the presence I was used to in a double bed.

The following morning Lucien escorted me to the War Office. We were interviewed by an officer who told me sympathetically that Officer Pilot Fitzallen had not come back from a patrol. He could not be prevailed upon to give further details. 'I'm sorry, Mrs Fitzallen, we cannot divulge such information.' He refused to be specific as to where Brian was based; stating only that he was lost out at sea and that they had not recovered his body or his aircraft.

'Don't worry, Peg.' Lucien assured me as soon as we were outside, 'I'll make inquiries. There are French officers in the RAF.'

He brought me back to Knightsbridge and left me there. But first he brought me up to Mary's room. He opened her wardrobe, indicated her chest of drawers. 'You should take her things. I won't be here much longer. I could not bear to disturb them,' and then he left, promising that he would come back as soon as possible.

I looked around at Mary's room, at her shoes in a neat row, her dresses hanging in the wardrobe, her perfumes and lipsticks on the Victorian dressing-table, and the silver backed hairbrush which lay as though awaiting the touch of her hand. There was a brass bed, an antique French armchair covered in tapestry. A cream silk dressing-gown hung from a peg behind the door. I buried my face in this; it surrounded me with her favourite scent - Chanel - so impossible to get since the war began. 'Where are you, Mary? Why did you go away?' I asked out loud, but there was no answer, only the noise of traffic from the street below.

Lucien came back some hours later. He had managed to make telephone contact with a French RAF pilot based in a squadron near Dover who had known Brian.

'Sit down, Peg.' He took me by the shoulders and made me sit on the bed and then he sat beside me, taking my hands.

Brian was based at Manston and had taken part in a Channel patrol during the course of which some German E Boats had been spotted and attacked. He had flown almost into their guns, sinking one of them. The inevitable squadron of Messerschmidts had arrived too late and most of Brian's flight had got away in a running dogfight back to base. But Brian Fitzallen's plane had not returned. They thought he went down over the Channel.

Lucien told me this hesitantly, trying to draw me to him, his face full of sympathy.

'This contact of yours, was he involved in this?'

'No, but that is the story in the service.'

There was silence.

'I need to be alone!' I said.

'They haven't found his body, or his plane. There is a chance,' he insisted, but I looked into his eyes and he became silent. He left, shutting the door quietly.

I sat on the edge of the bed, seeing myself in the mirror across the room, a young woman with fashionably waved fair hair and a face white and rigid with grief. The room seemed vast; the loneliness filled it like a solid thing, something cold and hard and empty. How could Brian be gone? How could the world continue as though nothing had happened?

Later, after the river of tears, came the anger. Brian and his brave manoeuvre; he had killed himself without thought of me, without thought of what it would do to me. I lay on the bed, quite still except to convulsively wipe my face with the sheet, remembering his words, 'You are the best thing that has ever happened to me.' remembering how I had loved those words. Now, with new and bitter cynicism, I saw that I was a 'thing' that had happened to him. The sentence had been all about him. He was the person in that statement; I was the thing.

The night came. Through windows latticed with sticking tape I watched the light fade from the sky, lit a cigarette, noticing like a disinterested observer that my hands trembled. From below came the ring of the doorbell, then insistent knocking.

Lucien appeared in a moment, entering the room with just a cursory knock, glanced at my cigarette, strode across to the windows and drew the black curtains.

'That was the Air Raid Warden. He must have seen the light when you lit up. These people can be a bit officious, little nonentities mad with power. And they don't like Frogs,' he added ruefully.

'I'm sorry. I forgot. Is there a fine? I'll pay it.'

'Shhh,' he said.

He turned on the dim bedside light and bent down beside me.

'Ma pauvre, come down for supper. You must eat something. There is a piece of incomparable French cheese which I got today in Carlton Gardens and there is some fresh bread and wine.'

'I can't bear the thought of food. It would make me sick.'

'You would like tea,' he said with certainty and went away, returning soon after with a tray. On the tray was a pot of tea, a bowl of marshmallows and some bread and cheese. He poured the tea, put in a marshmallow, handed me the cup and as he did so we heard the eerie alert whining across the city, gathering crescendo and dying away. I registered only a savage delight; let them bomb the whole bloody world; I would be glad to die.

'We must go to the basement!'

'You go.'

'I will not go without you, Peg!'

'Please yourself!'

I finished the tea, refusing the cheese which was ripe and rather smelly. He turned off the bedside lamp, sat on the bed beside me in the dark and traced the contours of my face. The second siren wailed and he slid his hand inside my blouse, confident fingers cupping a breast, transmitting shock waves through my body. And then, in the darkness, I felt his mouth on mine, hard and searching. Like the kiss in the car the day he had brought me to the station; now it was powerful with possible death. I heard the wail of the siren fade away, heard, above the drone of the aircraft engines, the whistle of the bombs and the first explosions somewhere towards the east, heard the answering ack ack fire, heard the furious jangling of fire engine bells. Beyond the curtains were the flashes of white light, the billowing smoke, the floating debris, the yellow splashes of the exploding ack ack in the night sky. Outside was the theatre of death. But I had contacted an

324

immediacy of life, as though he possessed all the life in the world.

A dream, floating in the utter darkness, aware of the scent of him, his breath and cologne and borne up with anger and sudden wrathful desire. With cynicism I felt my clothes being teased off, aware of hands and lips on my skin and gave myself to it bitterly and utterly, until my strength was spent. I knew that outside the searchlights probed the sky and that the mad delirium followed its course.

'Tu me donnes la paix,' he murmured eventually, lips brushing my cheek, lying back, his body moist and sweet against mine. I listened to the drama unfolding not far away. 'You are a whore,' a voice inside me said conversationally and another voice within me answered crisply, 'Better a whore than a shadow.'

'Are all Frenchmen like you?' I felt the rumble of his silent laugh against me.

'No, my sweet Peg. I am unique. And so are you.' And then he asked, diffidently, almost anxiously, 'Did I fulfil you, little Peg?'

And I didn't answer the question, which touched me both by its solicitude and its arrogance. Fulfilment was not the issue. And I thought angrily, 'There will be no guilt; I will not have guilt. I too must vent the passion of my life.' But, rationalise as I might, once anger was spent all that was left was grief.

However, the instinct for survival was there undiminished; the sleep that waited on exhaustion was shattered by a pattern of explosions not far off, the whistle of bombs coming nearer and nearer. I felt myself being

325

pulled on to the floor and I scrambled under the bed. Lucien had acted on some sudden instinct just before the window came in on top of us. We raced then for the shelter of the cellar, wrapped in sheets, trailing shards of glass, feathers and plasterdust. I was aware of a nosebleed, but no pain.

In the morning brown clouds obscured the sun; the air was full of the smell of burnt brick, timber, and charred pieces of paper floated here and there in the wasteland created overnight.

Most of the windows in the Knightsbridge house had been blown in. The bed I had lain with Lucien the night before and my clothes were covered in fragments of glass. Lucien gave me a pair of men's shoes so that I could walk into the room without tearing my feet. I retrieved my case and my clothes. My blouse of yesterday was torn where a jagged shard had pierced it. We got dressed, bolted the shutters on the windows and went out.

The devastation was terrible. Westminster Abbey, the Law Courts, the House of Commons, the Mint and the Tower had been hit. A quarter of a million books had been burnt in the British Museum. Nearly 1,500 people had been killed and more were seriously injured.

We wandered through the destruction and helped where we could. At Westminster Abbey I saw among the crowd the small rotund man with the hat, cigar and cane. There were tears on his face. 'Give it back to 'em, Winnie,' someone shouted and he raised a hand in acknowledgment, two fingers in V formation in his clenched right fist.

I did not go back to Nottingham as I had intended but stayed with Lucien for three more days. He took me with him to Carlton Gardens in St James, one day, the headquarters of the Free French, and I met there a Frenchman in uniform, so tall that he seemed to go on forever, black hair parted on the left, moustached, uniformed, courteous and filling the room with his presence. He said 'Enchantée Madame' very politely when Lucien introduced us. 'Peg, this is General de Gaulle.'

Sometimes Lucien dropped some bitter comment about the Consulate building at 58 Knightsbridge, a stone's throw from where we were, which was now in the hands of the Vichy government.

He took me to lunch at the Ritz and dinner at the Savoy and to a nightclub and I wore an evening dress borrowed from Mary's wardrobe, which I had to adjust, a prussian blue dress which Lucien said made me look like a vision. I put on dark red lipstick, curled my hair so that it framed my face, listened to his compliments in an orgy of self-hatred. I was in a dream; numb from several factors which I could barely disentangle. Brian was dead; my marriage was gone; the place I had been trying to keep warm for him was void. I felt as though everything I had striven for was a joke; the standards I had thought to embrace of love and loyalty and restraint had failed me. I made no attempt to fend off Lucien's overtures; the habits of my life were allowed to sleep. All I wanted was some real, formidable human contact. I did not even advert to the price.

I heard two officers near us talk about 'whores'; they were discussing a brothel in loud, drunken camaraderie and for a moment I thought they were talking about animals, they sounded so cruel and stupid.

'Did you ever go to a brothel?' I asked Lucien angrily and he shrugged and said 'I am a man,' and a private smile lurked for a moment in the corner of his mouth.

'That means you exploit as of right, does it?' I demanded and he looked at me, a frown of annoyance between his eyes and the contained exasperation I had seen before on men's faces when the female company had ceased to be pleasing. When the waitress came to take our orders I asked for gin and lime and told Lucien with brittle gaiety that I wanted to dance and we drifted, body to body amidst the cigarette haze to the sounds of 'We'll meet again.' I felt his desire erect against me and I played the femme fatale with secret rage and went back to Knightsbridge to make furious love. Anything to keep the darkness at bay.

He would knock softly and come it at once, slipping in beside me. Sometimes we talked but the talk would die and then the whole night would be ours and in this strange dream world I forgot every inhibition, every stricture, loosed the angry torrent of my life. I didn't give a damn what he would think of me; let him think what he liked. Nor did I ever advert to what the future would bring. It didn't seem likely that there would be one for any of us.

He usually went out early, but I would be awake before him and would lie still, looking at him, the thick set of his neck and shoulders, the dark fuzz on his arms and poll of his head with the thinning hair vulnerable and strangely touching. He looked so different to Brian and I

328

was glad he was. I knew I had to focus elsewhere if I was to go on.

I felt his eyes upon me sometimes when he thought I didn't notice and if I looked up I would find them full of perplexed inquiry.

On our last night he told me in bed of a chateau in France, sandstone, in the middle of a forest. And a room in blue and white with white shutters overlooking a lawn with a small lake. 'There is a terrace below the window with geraniums, jasmine and heliotrope and the room is full of perfume at night. The Germans occupy it now.'

'Are there swans in the lake?' I asked and he said that there used to be. 'It is not at all like Glenallen,' he added after a moment, sensing the direction of my thoughts, but the name conjured such wrack of soul that my false equanimity deserted me and the hot tears came back. He made love to me then, kissing them away.

'The chateau is within a hundred kilometres of La Belle au Bois Dormant, the Sleeping Beauty's Castle,' he said later, 'and has turrets like a fairytale!'

'You miss this fairyland?'

'It was my home,' he answered after a moment. 'But when I think of it now I think more of the legend of The Sleeping Beauty, because of the idea of that long wasted sleep. I loved her, the Beauty who slept, but my kiss did not awaken her.'

'Women need more than kisses,' I said tartly, suddenly jealous. He had just made love to me and yet he spoke of Mary - who else but Mary - with unmistakeable longing. 'The Beauty who slept', though why he should refer to her in such terms I did not know. But I told myself that I did not covet him; he was a playboy, a man so

329

experienced with women that I could sense the taint of promiscuity in his every move.

'Maybe she wasn't asleep,' I added. 'Maybe she was just very wide awake.'

I felt him start, felt the wound I had inflicted.

'I think you are a very angry young woman,' he murmured coolly after a moment.

But later I had a dream. I saw Knockshee and the house in its shadow. And I awoke in terror. What had I to be afraid of? Just a dream of a hill and a house - but they seemed in the dream to be invested with some brooding resentment I could not elude or understand. And I had heard Brian's voice, muffled, anguished, in which he had called my name.

Lucien woke and held me and I did not sleep for the rest of the night; he dozed off again and I lay awake listening to his breathing.

Once when he was out, I wandered into his study, a room overlooking the garden, sat at his desk for a moment, trying to imagine his life, his interior world, his perspective on reality. There were maps on the desk, an ink pot, a letter opener, sheafs of papers written in French. To the right, under a glass paper weight was a document bearing the heading *Forces Francaises Libres* and underneath *Acte D'Engagement* - Officier. I read this document with guilty curiosity, saw that it bore Lucien's name and that he had engaged himself 'A servir avec Honneur, Fidelité et Discipline dans les Forces Francaises pour la durée de la guerre'. A page sticking out from under the blotter bore some geometric doodles and some notes in French. Even as I read them I was touched by them; although I couldn't speak

330

French I could read it, courtesy of St Catherine's Convent and Mother Xavier's pounding:

'Que la vie est courte! Sans elle je m'eteindrai. Les jours sans elle sont le néant et les jours avec elle la vie.' And further down: 'Mon Dieu, laissez moi revenir dans le sein de mon pays bien aimé.'

I replaced the piece of paper under the blotter and went away, lonely with the knowledge that I had intruded into some rich scenario of the spirit where I did not belong.

Ah Mary, I thought, here is a man who feels himself extinguished without you; a man who feels the days without you are nothing and the days with you are life. How could you leave that kind of devotion? There was a passion here I would have given anything to have inspired; instead I had played second fiddle to a piece of mythology, to petty family politics, to introversion.

The thought of Brian and his vulnerability, his bewilderment before the family emotions he aroused, came swiftly and I wanted to reach back and protect him, cocoon him with love and sanity. But the past was dead, I knew he was gone, and yet I was haunted by his memory and by that place in Ireland which had so hypnotised him. And what of my own sanity? Was I never to find peace?

Every morning Lucien checked the postbox carefully. But there was no letter from Mary. On the Sunday, the day of my departure, he told me again that I must take her things back with me, or as many of them as I could. 'I must go away soon and the house will be locked up.'

'Where are you going?'

331

He smiled. 'There is a war on. You can always reach me at Carlton Garden if you need me.'

And, offended, I swore to myself that I would never seek him out.

When we were packing Mary's things I put some books of hers down beside my handbag and knocked the latter to the floor. Mary's letter fell out of my bag along with small change, matches, a packet of Players, hairpins. Lucien, as though moved by some sixth sense, picked it up before I could reach it and read it immediately, his face becoming very set.

'So,' he murmured. 'She thought it was a game.'

'She didn't,' I assured him because I could not bear the hurt in him. 'She was upset about something. At least I got that impression when I was here with Brian. I am amazed that she did not write to you. I know you meant a lot to her, Lucien. Are you sure she did not leave you a note? Have you searched for one?'

'She left an explanatory note,' he said drily.

He reached into his breast pocket and handed me a folded piece of paper. I opened it out. In the centre of the page were three lines in Mary's writing:

> *In the midst of my life's journey*
> *I found myself in a dark wood*
> *Where the straight path was lost.*

I stared at it in some perplexity and then at him. 'Dante's *Inferno*,' he said. And at the bottom of the page were two words, 'Forgive me.'

'Maybe she's gone to be a nun,' I muttered, because the poem seemed almost religious, with its talk of straight paths having been lost.

He laughed shortly.

332

'I'm serious,' I continued. 'Maybe she needs to be with women. She was happy with women.'

I watched the tension in his face, the tightening of the muscle in his jaw and cursed whatever devil had taken possession of me since Brian's death. He became taciturn and did not talk much on the way to the station. And the goodbye kiss this time was perfunctory.

In the hubbub of the station he thanked me. I felt his thanks like a lash; it was the kind of thing a man would say to a courtesan.

'Shall I come to Nottingham to see you?' he asked, sensing my discomfiture.

'No,' I said, smarting at the 'thanks'.

I climbed into the train, past an embracing couple at the door, and he followed me, saw me to a seat and was gone. I stared through the window at the now familiar poster showing a soldier in combat fatigues, his right hand raised peremptorily - the caption above his head demanding *Is your journey really necessary?* until the train pulled out of the station.

Chapter 13

I notified Glenallen by telegram on my return to Nottingham.

'Regret to tell you Brian reported missing in action. Peg'.

And I sent a letter to Tom to break the news.

Mrs Burton was kind when I got back and tried to be comforting.

She was curious too. 'Where did you stay in London dear?' and I said with a friend and she asked was it the Frenchie and gave me a queer look when I said yes. Was there any news of my friend Mary, she inquired then and I said no.

John was gone home for a fortnight to Bristol. His mother was ill and he had taken leave to be with her.

Nottingham had been bombed on 9 May in my absence. Belvoir Castle and surrounding areas, Moot Hall, Lace Market, the old university in Shakespeare Street to name but a few locations; there were many casualties.

Mrs Burton looked sad as she told me of the damage, particularly the damage to the lace market and the old university. 'That Hitler is a devil. I hope they get him and kill him!' she said; and I, in my fresh young widowhood, agreed in silence. But I did not even hate Hitler; I was too empty to hate.

Claire and Ellen went out of their way to be kind, tried to get me to go out with them, tried to give me their sweets. I wanted only to work. I attacked the books in a way I had not done since the weeks leading up to my degree examination. I stayed late at school marking homework until one evening I was accidentally locked in by the caretaker and had to get out through a window.

John came back from Bristol with the news that his mother had cancer and was in hospital. He would have to go down to Bristol every weekend. They had given her only six months to live. He told me this with matter of fact sadness, shadows under his eyes. 'I can't believe it; it just doesn't make any sense,' he said. I felt for him, knowing the hollow time ahead of him now.

One night I woke to find Claire and Mrs Burton in my room in their dressing-gowns, and John's voice in the landing saying 'Is she alright?'

Claire was bending over me.

'Peg. Peg. It's only a dream.' I pulled myself out of the thick heavy sleep and found that I was trembling and that the sheets were damp with sweat.

'You were shouting and crying in your sleep, Peg! You were having a nightmare.'

But the gossamer nightmare was already eluding me, leaving me only the taste of its terror and the echo of my husband's voice. I apologised to everybody. Claire offered to stay with me for a while but I said I was fine. I left the light on for the rest of the night.

And as the days went by without word from Lucien I found myself missing him. I had told myself not to miss him, but could not avoid it. He hadn't contacted me. He hadn't written. I told myself I didn't want to see him. I told myself that I despised him, a man who honed in on vulnerability and then treated the whole business as though it were merely a casual interlude in the rich drama of his life. I imagined his perspective.

335

The woman had succumbed; therefore the woman was of no further interest. But I also felt that I had hurt his feelings about Mary, and wished I had not.

Why were women so vulnerable? Why could we not express our humanity, desires, without courting destruction. Why should we have to pretend so much in order to survive? The pain astonished me. It rolled through me in waves, paralysing my will.

I also thought of the casual way he had occasionally touched me in passing during those days in Knightsbridge, when his mind was elsewhere, as though he had acquired a right to easy, patronising familiarity, as though I had become a possession. I was angry that he should have dared to perceive me as a plaything, that he should have used pain, that he should have been blind to the racing of my mind; his kindness was nauseating in retrospect because it came with a price tag. The rules he lived by evidently prescribed gallantry for playthings, but there had at all times been the wall of his self protection. Or so I reasoned.

So, when I came out of school one Friday evening about two weeks later, it took me a minute to realise that it was he who was sitting on a bench in the school grounds, reading a newspaper.

'I have taken a great liking to Nottingham,' he announced, getting to his feet as I approached. 'I think it must be the air!'

I laughed. The delight at seeing him could not be suppressed. It surged with its own joy, displacing every reservation. He kissed my hand.

'I have the weekend. And you?' he murmured.

Tell this presumptuous little man to go away, I told myself. Tell him to take himself off. But I did not. The voice of reason seemed the voice of the commonplace, thrown in the face of glorious life.

He accepted my silence and we went together to the Black Boy 'for a drink' he said. 'We should talk,' he said. 'We have many things to talk about.'

He got me a gin and lime. We talked of everything, of Brian and Mary and the war and of the nightmares I was having.

'You will have none tonight. I will keep them away.'

I looked into his face. 'Tonight?' I whispered, aghast. 'Lucien, I don't know what you must think of me, but I am not used to doing ... what I did in London.'

'I know.'

After a moment he added - 'You would like to turn your strength back on itself. You would use passion to contain passion - which is a terrible waste. But you will at least allow me to keep away the nightmares?'

Where was my willpower? Why did I send a message to Mrs Burton advising her I would be staying with a friend for the weekend. He had already booked a double room and after we had eaten we went there and I gave myself to him - this time without anger or fury; without emotional barriers; with only the fragility of my self.

The following weekend he came again. We spent it in bed.

'Is there a St. Lucien?' I asked him, lying beside him in the summer twilight.

'Of course there is,' he answered gravely. 'He was an early Christian martyr; he died of starvation. I don't take after him!'

I laughed. Later he told me that he was going away and would not be coming to Nottingham for some time. 'I don't know when I'll be back. I'm going to France, to help the Resistance.'

In the early weeks of June, I got a letter from Harry.

'Dear Peg,
I'm sorry for taking so long to write to you. It's very sad about Brian; Peter and I have had a mass said for him. Wasn't he very brave? I'm sure you must be very upset, but of course you have friends in England who will look after you. You know you are very welcome to stay here in Glenallen anytime you like.
I suppose it won't take you long to find someone else - not with your looks, Peg; you'll be remarried before you can turn around!
And time heals you know.
It is sad that Brian died so young; Peter and I will miss him.
On another subject - I'm sure you don't mind me mentioning it - but as things are a bit hard up here at the moment I was wondering if you could lend me some money. I suppose you have some saved. You must have a good salary and (I assume) a war widow's pension so you probably have some to spare. The roof here has got to the point where something radical must be done. Unfortunately dry rot started in some wall plates and it has spread - so the matter is terribly serious if the house is to be saved. I'm at my wits end with worry over it.
There's no credit to be had in the Bank, but you can be assured that I'll pay you back after the War.

Your fond sister-in-law,
Harriet.'

I wrote back to say that I was pregnant and that any money I had was needed and that I was sure she would manage. She answered immediately telling me to come 'home'; 'You will need taking care of, Peg, and Brian's child should be born in Glenallen.'

I didn't reply. The only person in Glenallen I wanted to talk to was Murty, to ask him if he had seen Brian's ghost on the mountain. I would go back to Glenallen if I thought I could find Brian, if I could talk to him long enough to say goodbye.

And my mind was preoccupied with something I had hardly adverted to, so confident I had been that that the 'safe period' was safe. I was pregnant! I had gone for a pregnancy test which was positive.

'Congratulations, Mrs Fitzallen,' the doctor said. 'I'm sure your husband will be pleased.'

I told him I had been recently widowed and the corners of his eyes contracted in sympathy. He listened to my heart and lungs, took the stethoscope out of his ears, pronounced me fit. 'Get whatever rest you can and come back and see me in four weeks. Your blood pressure is a little on the high side and we'll have to watch that.'

Then he asked, 'Have you someone to look after you? Your mother?'

'No. She's dead.'

I was stunned by the news of my pregnancy. I had been trying to work up the courage to go to confession and now I had the concrete proof of my mortal sin. I knew that Brian could not have been the father and that meant only one thing. I

339

would wake in the mornings wondering why I felt so terrible and then remember, and feel the weight of it descend for another day, this punishment that I could not escape, the sin for which atonement was too late.

I went to confession and Father Riordan glanced sideways at me from the grille and then froze as he listened.

'Oh God Almighty! How could you have strayed so terribly? To fornicate with that foreigner and your husband just killed. To mock God like that. To let yourself be used by a mountebank.'

Mortified, I watched his head shake above his round white collar. His voice was so loud I was sure everyone in the Church could hear him.

'It was life, when I needed life.' I hissed. 'You do not understand. And you will never, ever, be pregnant.'

'None of that, now, none of that. Bring the child up as your husband's, for the child's sake. God Almighty will know the difference between a bastard and a legitimate child, but the world needn't. And pray to the holy Mother of God that the child will look like you and not the father. I suppose he wasn't a black? Because you'd have no hope there at all, at all!'

I came out of the box, pale, shaking, penitent, aware of the curious faces of the waiting woman and the averted faces of the men.

But confession made no difference to the facts. I tried to re-write them in my mind; Brian would come back; the child was his and we would have a little house with a garden. But did I want a little house with a garden? I was not too sure anymore.

And did I admit in my guilt that my experience with Lucien had been formidable? Did I have the

340

courage to recognise its spiritual and physical gifts? No. I was too caught up in the hearsay voice of God. But even through the guilt I missed him, missed his dynamism, missed the mutual complicity. I had imagined friendship and trust in this complicity and I missed it more than love.

'Contact me at Carlton Garden if you need me,' he had said again when we were parting. I realised now that the possibility of pregnancy had probably been on his mind. I found this humiliating; I could be angry with him again because he was far away, telling myself that he would deal with the problem in terms of how it affected *him*. My co-operation would be presumed.

I knew he would 'stand by me'; he would give me money; suggest an abortion perhaps; do what he thought the 'right thing'; but I didn't want the 'right thing,' the jerking of my life to the strings of anyone's presumption. And if he knew the truth I would lose sovereignty. He would acquire rights - the child was his too - and would almost certainly try to assume control of the situation himself.

Mrs Burton inquired as to why I was so peaky.

'I'm pregnant!'

She looked at me sideways.

'Poor you. And your poor husband gone. When is it due?'

And I lied, flushing crimson, sure there was suspicion in her steady gaze.

Later she asked me, 'Do you want this baby, dear? Because if you don't, I know someone. She's a midwife and all. And if you get it done quickly you'll hardly notice. It's hard to get married again if there's a child in the way.'

There was powder in the pores by her nose and her mouth had a matter of fact pinch to the lips. I stifled the leaping surge of hope. It would be a sin.

'I don't think so, Mrs Burton.'

But I did think about it. It represented the only way out. I dared not debate the issue with myself for too long; defiance dictated the solution. I was already a thorough-going sinner; but abortion was a different matter, an even greater sin. God would damn me for it.

I remembered the conversation I had had with Claire and Ellen and John one evening after supper, a conversation precipitated by my adherence to the Friday fast. I had thought them pagan. They had asked - why make your life miserable when there is no proof that God demands anything of you? There is no proof that God even exists.

Claire had looked at me over her spectacles. 'Religions don't need proof; they colonise the mind!' I had found this very shocking; but I thought about it now. Where had God been when I needed him, when Brian needed him? What if there was no God? What if there was no absolute right and wrong, but only the best people could do, given the circumstances? Anyway there was always confession. No matter what my crimes were all I had to do was go to confession afterwards and I would start again with a clean slate. But I imagined Father Riordan roaring and shouting in the box and knew I would have to get a different confessor.

So I told Mrs Burton quietly, one evening, after supper, that I would be interested in her suggestion and she just nodded and put a finger to her lips, indicating Claire and Ellen who had

finished their meal and gone into the sitting-
room.

Later she came upstairs to my room. She sat
down on the bed. Through the window behind
her I saw the July evening, the warm blue of the
sky. Since May the nights had been relatively
calm; Hitler was concentrating his energies on
Russia and leaving us in comparative peace.

'Let me ask you straight out, dear ... You want
to get rid of this baby?'

Her voice was perfectly pragmatic. Her face,
bare of powder, was serious and credible. 'It's not
cheap, dear, £25.00.' She lowered her voice, as
though the walls might hear, 'It's a criminal
offence, you see.'

My face fell. My entire savings amounted to
£30.00.

'Usually the man pays,' my landlady went on.
'But she might do it for less in your case, with
your husband gone and all.'

'Ask her.'

She studied me for a moment.

'I'll talk to her tomorrow.'

The following evening she came to my room to
discuss the matter in hushed tones. She had seen
the midwife and she would perform an abortion
for £20.00, but I must come within the week. And
I must bring my own towels.

'I told her I'd bring you over on Friday evening.
You'll have the weekend to get over it.'

I nodded.

Mrs Burton patted my hand. 'It'll be over before
you know it and then you'll be free as the birds.'

Friday came. After school I boarded a bus with
Mrs Burton. I paid the fares, envying the young
conductress, who smiled and made some remark
about the heat. We travelled in silence, except that

my landlady would nod encouragingly and smile whenever I caught her eye. We left the city behind and were soon in the suburbs, the coal mining district of Easthorp.

There were streets and streets of mean little houses, built for coal miners, the windows shining, the doorsteps well scrubbed, worn with generations of pride, poverty and grinding work.

No. 43 Eastanglian Terrace was no different from the others. The lace curtain on the downstairs window moved as we approached and I sensed the eyes of the hidden watcher. I felt conspicuous, guilty, afraid. Some children played hop scotch on the pavement and some young girls in sandals who had a skipping robe tied to a lampost, jumped in and out of it to an old children's rhyme. I heard the slap of our shoes on the pavement and the noise of a baby wailing in one of the nearby houses. I had brought a rain coat as directed, for the homeward journey, and also a bag with two thick hand towels.

The woman who let us in was thin and tired-looking with dried yellowing skin. She wore a white blouse, a black skirt and a cardigan and brought us into her sitting-room, a small room with three porcelain wild geese flying up her wall. I produced the money; it was in a manilla envelope and she took it out and counted it. Then she took Mrs Burton aside and whispered to her, something about getting me home quickly afterwards, something about the bleeding. Then she assumed her normal voice and told Mrs Burton to wait. She brought me upstairs.

The bedroom to which she conducted me was at the back of the house. It had a single bed spread with a rubber sheet; a bucket stuck out menacingly from under the bed. There was cracked linoleum on the floor. To one side was a table with a white enamelled basin and some harsh, faded towels folded in a heap. The window was covered with greying lace curtains and looked out on a small back yard, on a row of small back yards stretching as far as the eye could see. Two doors down I saw a woman in a wrap-around apron visit the outside lavatory, slamming the door behind her. I saw boys in short trousers in the laneway behind, pretending to be soldiers, wooden rifles at the ready, shouting 'Bang. You're dead.' The chimneys, with identical terra cotta pots, marched in military formation down the slate roofs and into the distance. There was a wireless in the corner of the room. She turned it on. Vera Lynn was telling the world there would be blue birds over the white cliffs of Dover, and her voice soared with yearning.

The woman, who had not given her name, drew the blackout curtains and locked the door. Without the perspective from the window the room seemed very small, like a cell. There was an odour of disinfectant and of something else which reminded me of the days I had dissected dog fish in the lab in Galway. The room also smelt of pain and nausea and fear.

I backed nervously, knocking the towels off the table and with them something fell to the floor, ringing metallically. The gaunt woman picked it up hurriedly, but not before I had seen that it was a long steel knitting needle, sharp and shiny. She thrust it into a drawer in the table, in which I cought a glimpse of some rubber tubing and a syringe. 'Take your skirt and panties off, love, and get on to the bed.'

The room seemed to swim. I stared at her, saw the beads of sweat on her upper lip, smelt the fishy smell overlain with disinfectant and dread, saw the cynicism on her world-weary face. Here, in this room,with its smells of despair, I was to kill the life which Lucien and I had made together.

'I can't. I just can't. Give me back the money.'

I went back to the digs with Mrs Burton in silence. I did not look at her on the journey home but knew from my peripheral vision that she shook her head from time to time and that her mouth was compressed. Queenie met us in the hall and I wanted to embrace her, so smug and selfish and normal did she seem.

I threw myself into my work. The end of year exams had started and I was busy marking scripts. No one at school had noticed anything of my condition and there was nothing yet to notice. If anything I had become thinner. I continued to do fire watching duty with the others, read the papers avidly, followed the course of the War. And all the time there was a self hatred which nothing could obliterate.

I longed to hear from Mary. I wondered if she had gone back to Knightsbridge to find the house shut up; but surely she would contact me; she knew where I was. Would she forgive me for Lucien? 'I do not love him,' she had said, but that did not absolve me. How could I tell her that I was pregnant by the man who had loved her and loved her still? The two cases full of her things took up one corner of my little room. I had not even opened them.

But one evening, I dragged one of the cases on to my bed, took out some of her blouses smelling of Chanel and the sense of her was there, almost tangible.

And then, taking out one of her books, some sheets of folded paper fell out, ragged pages torn from a copybook as though someone had intended to destroy them. The sheets contained her handwriting; it was quickly apparent that these were pages of some sort of diary, but an undated one and incomplete. I searched among her other books for more of this journal, but without success. I put the sheets of paper back into the book and left it in the drawer of my table.

When John came back from Bristol after one of his visits to see his mother I went to the station with Claire to meet him and saw among the throng on the platform a slim young woman with a mass of red curls. I saw the way she put her hand to her hair, a nervy defiant gesture, and my heart lurched and I ran down the platform, pushing and shoving, oblivious to the voices enjoining me to 'Steady on.' From behind the young woman looked just like Mary - the same way of holding her head. There was an older woman with her, who took her by the arm as I pushed against the crowd and managed at last to look into her face.

'Mary!'

She was beautiful, blue eyes staring at me blankly, but she was not Mary. 'Blinded in the blitz' murmured the woman who was with her, looking at me with the expression I had seen so much of in England, the look which said, 'The war is terrible, but we'll soldier on.' I apologised. 'I thought she was someone I knew,' speaking of her in the third person as though she were deaf or insane. And as soon as we were home I went upstairs and opened the drawer to find the four sheets of paper in Mary's writing. I sat on the bed and read them slowly; they filled me with sorrow and astonishment and I read them again and again.

Then the nightmares came back. I dreamt of Brian, one night and then another night, almost identical dreams, walking towards me down Knockshee. It was dark. I saw the branches of above his head. He was wearing a flying jacket in the first dream, but in the second he was a walking cadaver, wrapped in a shroud. I waited for him each time, but he turned and headed for the house and I saw the outline of Glenallen House, a single light burning in an upstairs window, in Harry's bedroom. I woke with terror, the nameless terror of dreams.

Shortly after this I received a letter from Tom in his crisp masculine writing.

'Dear Peg,

I'm very sorry indeed to hear about poor Brian; he was a fine decent man and deserved a long life. I know you loved him very much. I've asked Father O'Dea to say a mass for him. I hear you are expecting and wish you as much joy as the circumstances allow.

Poor old Uncle Matt died; he left everything to me, except for the picture of the goose girl you used to be fond of. That is for you!

I have some other news which I cannot tell you in a letter. I hope you'll come home - it's the sensible thing in your condition.

Your loving brother,
Tom.'

I looked at this letter for a long time. So Uncle Matt had died and, as expected, left his all to Tom

- except the steel engraving of the goose girl. Apt enough, I thought. I wondered how much his estate had been worth, but knew that this would almost certainly make Tom very well off.

The school year was almost at an end and I wrote to my brother to say I would be coming home for the holdiays at the end of July.

I told the headmaster at the end of term that I was pregnant and inquired if this would make any difference for the new term; in effect, did he want me back? He sat me down on the old horsehair sofa in his office and said the job was mine as long I wanted it. The staff would help wherever they could. What plans did I have once the baby was born? Of course it might be better for me to stay in Ireland, with a new baby to look after. But having said that I would be welcome back. I was a good teacher and teachers were hard to come by. Would I confirm as soon as I could? He would understand.

Mr Dencher's face was paternal, no sign at all of the 'lion,' a man striving to be helpful and kind. I looked around the booklined study with its photographs of cricket teams and its masculine paraphernalia and its 'roll of honour'.

But before I could make up my mind about the future I was handed a letter by Mrs Burton. It had a smear of dust and was crinkled.

'I'm sorry, dear. It came while you were in London in May, and it must have fallen down behind the hall stand! I hope it wasn't important.'

I did not reply. I recognised my husband's writing and took the letter to my room. The note inside was very short.

My dearest Peg,

Thanks for your letter. I will be in touch with you as soon as I can. I have to go home. Dad wrote to me care of the RAF and has asked me to go home for a visit. He seems to be very poorly.

I will contact you as soon as I get back.

Love, Brian'

The date was the day before Brian had disappeared in action, the same day in fact that I had written to him to tell him of his father's death.

I went back to Ballycloghan. The train journey to Crewe seemed interminable; delays and more delays. The boat was again delayed at Holyhead. There were whispers among some passengers about U Boats in the Irish Sea. I looked at the blue sky and the sea and thought of the past and wondered about the future.

I did not understand Brian's last letter. Did it mean that he had actually gone home? He could have flown home on the day he wrote the letter and returned immediately to his squadron. But, if so, Harriet would have said so in her letter. Instead she had simply commiserated with me about his loss. Maybe it was just an intention he had had for his next leave, but that events had superseded him? Or maybe, and this thought took my breath away, he had not been lost in action but had gone back to Glenallen. But I dismissed this possibility. The RAF said that he was missing in action and he would have contacted me himself had he lived.

And as for Tom. What news could he have that he did not want to tell me in a letter? What would he think of me if he knew the truth about the pregnancy around which my body was arranging ᵗᵉlf, waist bands already too tight, nausea,

tenderness in the breasts, veins swelling in my
legs. But I was determined to brazen things out.
What was the use of weakness or failure? I
already knew where the one blindly thoughtless
episode in my life had got me. Whatever belief I
had left me about the nature of my relationship
with Lucien had been scotched by Mary's diary. I
was jealous of her. I acknowledged it. I loved her
and was jealous of her. And I pitied her too - to
have inspired so much love and to have been so
crippled.

I had put the undated pages of her diary into
what seemed to be chronological order and re-
read them until I was cold. I would obliterate
Lucien, destroy whatever grip he had on me. He
was committed elsewhere - the diary made that
abundantly clear, four pages of crystal clarity:

*'I wish to God Mags would stop going around like a
rabbit. She's let the awful Fitzallens get her down -
looked wretched when she arrived last night.*

*Why must she pour herself into other people's
perspectives, especially people like them? Why couldn't
Brian have taken her with him? He leaves her,
breaking her heart, and calls to tell me he's alright.
Men!*

*I can see that L finds her attractive; nothing new in
that - he thinks he can't help himself with women; they
all fall for his direct charm, they think it's a form of
recognition.*

*Peg would be shocked if she knew how carefully her
sexual potential is being summed up. She responds to
him, despite herself, despite all that shock and horror at
my being a kept woman. If she only knew!*

351

He asked me again today to marry him - but I told him again how things are for me. He does not believe it. I think it would be hard to be his wife, always wondering. Should I warn Peg? I could not bear for him to hurt her. But she's off to England soon, out of harm's way one might say (terrible thing to say and England at war); L will help her get the visa and I will hint about some money. He is so good really, would be a wonderful man if he wasn't so dissolute.'

The page with its torn edges had looked like some piece of school work discarded from the year before which had escaped the bonfire. The three other tattered pages did not look like much either, until they were read.

'London here I come. Over the moon. Lucien was going on about the bombing and that I was safer in Dublin, but I said that I would expire with ennui and that danger excited me and that if he didn't take me with him I'd run away with the bellman. He likes the thought of me being excited (but didn't believe me about the bellman). So do I. Perhaps the change will make things work for us, for me rather. I would like to be normal, whatever that is.

And I shall be seeing dear old Peg who sounds so sensible and happy now - and why wouldn't she be with her own good job and Brian back in the offing (somewhere) and Glenallen a thousand miles away.

L says we'll have a house in Knightsbridge. Friends of his, the Daven-Warrens, have skipped off to Scotland for the duration.

Oh God, if you exist somewhere, make it alright; make me love him.'

'London! It would be impossible to imagine this reality without experiencing it. I have started reading Dante. I wonder if he had been here what inspiration would he have had - London blitzed by night and sometimes by day; the vapour trails in the sky; the total blackout; the inferno of noise and flames and smell of burning; the fear and the humour and everyone wonderful. All that is lacking is Satan coiled up in the seventh circle, but he is in Germany and will be defeated. I am sure of it.

Last night L took me to the Savoy threatre, The Man who came to Dinner. Robert Morley; wonderful. Afterwards we had supper in the Savoy itself and traipsed back to Knightsbridge in the Daimler. Tight as an owl - excitement and wine, and fell on to my bed. L beside me in a moment; evening dress undone; bra tugged off, knickers gone; such perfect gentle kisses, hardly there at all. Not afraid anymore. Knew he was taking off his clothes; kept my eyes shut, letting the vertigo spin me away. It was nice being tipsy, like something in a dream; reality had become the abstract whorls in my head; then his hands became heavy, broke the spell; suddenly I was wide awake and there was only desire and power and someone with so slick a sexual experience that I felt sick and had to turn away. He thought it was coquetry, followed me, hands now too rough at my breasts, the half thrust of his body behind. 'I will not get sick,' I told myself and made myself think of the garden at home and the wind blowing in from Sandymount in winter and wanted to scream out the obvious which he will never see. He sensed the tension and covered me with the bedspread.

353

"You are like someone bound in chains," he murmured in my ear after a moment. "Will you not let me set you free, my darling? I will not hurt you."

"I cannot bear it that you have been with so many women." But I knew it was not just other women, although that was a part of it; it is something in me.

"There is only you. The others are nothing. There would only ever be you, if ..."

He was lying, but perhaps he did not know that he lied. And then he said all would be well in time, but that it would have to come from me.

"From now on I will not trouble you. Come to me when you are ready. I only want to be with you. I ask for nothing." He sounded very grave, like someone making an official pronouncement.

His attitude always amazes me; he does not treat sex as a shameful thing. I do not believe he even thinks it.

I'm to audition for A Midsummers Night's Dream - a small new company are putting it on in Kensington, a little theatre called The Walpole. It may be my chance!'

I thought I could act; God, I thought I could act. We had read the Midsummer Night's Dream in school; I knew most of the lines before we even started rehearsals; I enjoy the role of Titania. So, why did I have to muck up the dress rehearsal, screaming like that! Am I going mad? But when Puck came on I could not bear that goat face, the mask. Poor Simon took if off and rushed over to me. 'Are you alright? Have you a pain? What's wrong?'

I cannot bear to think of the horrible thing. They brought me home; I clung to L and he told me everything was alright and brought me up to bed, treating me like a child.

354

I asked him was I mad; he got the doctor who wanted to sedate me, he had his horrible hypodermic out and ready, but I said no and Lucien wouldn't let him. But I did take one of the pills he left and slept a little and when I woke L was there still, holding my hand, his face so full of love. It is always full of love when I catch him unawares.

"What frightened you, my darling?" he asked and I tried to tell him and cried because it seemed to me that the face of Puck was demonic. So stupid because I knew it was only poor Simon in a mask. And I don't even believe in the devil.

I'm sure L believes that he has burdened himself with a hysteric. There is something sitting at the bottom of my mind, something horrible. But I can remember nothing. I wish Daddy were alive; I want to talk to him...'

I looked out at the sea, the choppy summer waves, at the people around me with tired, eager faces, Irish people going home, their Exit Visas in their pockets. They were taking a holiday from the munitions factories and the schools and the armed services. I looked back at the last surviving page of the destroyed diary and wished I could roll back the clock.

'I think L begins to accept there is no hope for us. I should not be here. But I too expected change; I thought it would come right. I think I am cursed with innocence.

355

Made a real effort tonight; wanted to thank him. We had gone up late after the all clear. Put on that silk and lace extravaganza he bought me recently and went into his room; the room smelt pleasantly of his cologne; his body was a dark hump in that big bed. I was afraid immediately. Forced myself to sit on the edge of the bed, trying to be calm.

He lay quite still, apparently asleep, but in a moment his hand reached for mine. He raised the bedclothes, drew me towards him and replaced the covers. The bed was warm; his body was naked; we were silent, but I could sense his delight. He held me against him without a word, without moving, caressed me gently, whispering words of love in my ear; he spoke of homage while he caressed me, squeezing my lips one by one between his, kissing my neck, shoulders, breasts. I tried to relax, but I sensed something like violence beneath his restraint and I gritted my teeth, praying he would get it over with quickly. He lay back after a minute, his disappointment deep and silent.

"Ma chere, I cannot accept your gift because you cannot give it." He has a dramatic way with him sometimes. He sighed, his hand stroking my hair as one would a child's. I felt only relief. But since coming back to my room I have sat in the armchair in the dark, listening to fire engine bells in the distance. It is dawn now. London is stirring. What is wrong with me? I feel inadequate and ashamed. There are things I should do to end this waste of my life.'

Tom met me at the station. I saw him through the window as the train screeched to a halt. He started, smiled, his eyes lighting up with delight. He was shaven, clean and tidy. I drew a sigh of relief as he jumped on board to help me with my heavy cases. 'You're a sight for sore eyes, Peg. Welcome home.'

Chapter 14

Tom had the pony and trap waiting at the station. He put in my cases and we squeezed in beside them. He took the reins, said an abrupt 'H'up' to the pony and we were on our way. I watched everything as we went along, the new-mown meadows, the intermittent sunshine, the white and grey clouds piled like the Alps in the distance. I was struck by the atmosphere, the sense of space and liberty missing in England, and above all by the freedom from sirens, from the drone of aircraft, from the threat of sudden death. The air was different; it was soft and moist, foreboding rain. It smelt faintly of furze bushes and new mown hay.

'It's grand to be back.'

He looked at me sideways and smiled.

'You're different.'

'No, I'm not!'

He was the one who was different - some subtle kind of change - perhaps in the way he spoke, sure and deliberate in a manner untypical of him. He radiated confidence. He had always been confident, except for the period after Cissie's death when everything in him had seemed shattered; but now his confidence had become a kind of certainty.

'How are things at home?'

'Couldn't be better.'

They were bringing in the hay at home. Tom kept three meadows; a good crop this year, he said. The men were working against time; it

might rain that evening and they had to finish.
Several of them raised their hands in salute as we
passed down the avenue in the trap. One of the
men, Pat O'Regan, whom Tom now employed full
time, was coming through a gate to the avenue
and he smiled at me as Tom pulled up the pony,
showing his bad teeth. 'The very grass has been
askin' for yeh, ma'am.'

'Thanks, Pat.'

'And I'm sorry for yer trouble,' he added.

I noticed the way he looked at Tom, the
guarded wary glance.

'Did you bring Mella to the stallion?' Tom asked
in business-like tones.

'Aye.'

The house was clean. I had been dreading the
kitchen, remembering the state it had been in the
last time I had come home, dirty dishes choking
the sink and the table and dresser littered with
rubbish of one sort or another. Even the picture of
the Sacred Heart beside the dresser had had the
glass cleaned; the wick had been trimmed in the
little red lamp and burned brightly. The table had
been laid with tea things; the cloth was white and
fresh. There was a new green cushion in the
fireside chair and new curtains on the window.
The range had been blacked and the kettles were
scoured.

'Who did you get to do all this?'

'Niamh Houlihan. I give her a few bob and she
comes in every week!'

'How is she?'

'She's grand. She's expectin', like yourself.'

'So she got married to Packy Rafferty?'

'She did!'

'You missed your chance there, Tom!'

359

He smiled.

'Sit down there now, Peg, and don't be always givin' out to me,' he said with affected meekness.

He put my cases into the hall out of the way, commenting on the weight.

'She goes off with one case and comes back with two, and the weight of them fit to break a man's back.'

He made tea then and unceremoniously put a loaf of brown bread on the table with butter and jam.

'Would you like to come out with me when you're finished? I've something to show you.'

When I had finished the tea and the hunk of bread and jam which my brother had cut for me, I changed into a pair of old slacks, found a pair of wellingtons under the stairs and clumped off with Tom to the stables. The doors to the loose boxes were all open; the mound of manure and straw in the corner of the yard gave off a powerful aroma. The cart house door was open. I saw Pat moving inside. I put my head in. 'Hello there, Pat,' I said as I smelt the bins of nuts, and saw the light from the door catch the hay knife which hung from the opposite wall.

'Nice to hear yer voice around the place, ma'am!'

There were voices in the haggard where the hay was being brought on a hay float and made into a big rick.

I noticed that there were a lot of new cattle in the two big fields which ran down towards the river, red Hereford bullocks. I followed Tom to the pasture where he had the horses, six of them I noticed.

'You've bought another horse.'

He laughed his old loud laugh.

'I have. Come and meet him.'

I followed him across the field. The horse was a bay hunter with a white blaze on his forehead, slightly skittish; he danced archly away from Tom's outstretched hand.

'What do you call him?'

'Jupiter.'

I laughed. 'Very Olympian.'

'Is there something wrong with that?'

'No. You've been busy, Tom. The place looks prosperous and so do you. And congratulations on your inheritance!'

He seemed pleased. 'Wasn't it decent of Uncle Matt?'

'It was,' I said. 'And terrible decent of him to leave me the picture.'

He glanced at me. 'Is that a bitter comment?'

'No. Sure I knew from the beginning that he was only interested in you. You must be very well off now, quite a rich man in fact.'

He laughed, the closed secret laugh of someone who is not going to give anything away. 'I'm not stuck for a few bob!'

'Well maybe you'd tell me what you were talking about in your letter ... the news you didn't want to write?' I glanced at his face, which registered nothing for a moment and then creased in a sly smile.

'I'm thinking of getting married.'

I looked at him in surprise;

'Great! Why didn't you say so? Who is she?'

He smiled again, the smile of someone about to deliver a surprise. 'You'll never guess this one, Peg, with all your brains!'

I laughed, scanned the countryside in my mind, but couldn't think who was the bride to be.

'Come on. Spill the beans. How can I guess?'
'Harriet Fitzallen!'

I turned to look at him. He stood there with his hands in his pocket, gazing around at his acres, his animals, his stables, listening to the voices from the meadows and the haggard, the rumble of the hay float, the rattle of the harness, the occasional snorting of the horses. He was not drunk or mad, nor did he have the old look when he was teasing me.

'You can't possibly be serious. You hardly know her.'

He turned. 'I do know her. She's been here several times in the past couple of months. We see each other at least once a week! We have even been to Dublin together! Why do you think I bought Jupiter?'

'You used to say you would buy a hunter for Cissie,' I said accusingly.

He was silent; his eyes seemed to focus on the distance.

'Cissie is with God, Peg,' he said then with a sigh. 'She's gone, but I'm still here and I have my life to live! Harriet and I get on like a house on fire; she's a great girl. Wants to save that great big place of hers. And she's right. I wouldn't let a place like that go! I'd live on the boards first!'

'You mean Glenallen?'

'Where else? It's a fine thing in her, the way she loves it. It's a passion with her!'

'And what about the passion she should have for you?'

He laughed. 'Ah, don't worry about that; don't worry about that at all!'

Later he told me how Harriet had written not long after Brian had been lost, asking if she could pay a visit. He had shown her the farm. She had asked advice about breeding Irish Draught horses and he had told her about crossing them with thoroughbreds to make good show jumpers and then she had invited him back to Glenallen where he had gone the following week. It had progressed from there.

'Glenallen is going to wreck and ruin and needs a man's hand,' she had told him. He recounted this with a deprecatory laugh and ill-concealed pleasure at the implied compliment. Eventually, after some weeks of to-ing and fro-ing and because he 'wasn't a man to beat about the bush' he had told her how much he was worth, what he had in the bank and had proposed over dinner in 'that grand red dining-room in Glenallen'.

I wondered as to the mode of proposal. 'What would you say to the two of us getting hitched?' or something of that sort. Knowing Tom, it would have been pragmatic. He had always been pragmatic about everything - except Cissie.

'I went for a ride with her after the dinner; we went out near the hill there behind the house.'

'You mean Knockshee?'

'Yes. Good view. You can see right across the townland.'

'Did you go all the way to the top?'

'Ah no. I had a train to catch.'

'Did you know that there's a lot of superstition about Knockshee? Apparently the area has various druidic associations.'

'Is that so? Place had an odd kind of atmosphere right enough.'

There was silence.

'Is she coming here soon?' I asked then.

'One of the days. Quite soon.'

'Have you set the date for the wedding?'

'Next month.'

I made some excuse and went back to the house. As I came in the kitchen door I heard the kettle hissing on the range, the lid rattling, drops exploding as they hit the hot surface and I pushed it to the back. Tiddles was asleep by the turf creel, curled up, his head tucked against his chest. He'd evidently been involved in an argument; part of his right ear was torn and ragged and the fur around it was gone. 'I hope you won, you silly cat,' I told him.

Outside it was still bright although the clouds were lowering; the voices from the haggard came faintly through the door, shouts and laughter on the breeze.

I wandered around the house, my childhood home, looking for the small remembered things. I looked for the diamond pattern in the hall tiles where I had sometimes played surreptitious hop scotch, with the constant dread of Annie looming from the kitchen and swiping at me with the tea towel. 'Get out outta that. Me poor hall that I only just polished this minute.'

I approached the door of the parlour; here, in the old leather armchair, my barely remembered father had taken me on his knee, and here my mother would sit on Christmas day while Tom and I did the washing up. She would knit as she sat by the fire and drink a glass of stout or sometimes sherry and radiate guilt that she was resting. My bedroom was unchanged, old white handworked bedspread, walls in need of a fresh coat of distemper, plain varnished deal dressing-table and wardrobe. I sat on the edge of the old iron bed and heard the springs squeak, just as they would do when my mother came to say goodnight, sitting beside me for a moment and then her kiss - Goodnight a stór - goodnight Mam - and her footsteps moving away, leaving the door open and the lamp lit in the landing because I was afraid of the dark.

And now I was back, widowed, pregnant by a short-term affair, and determined to brazen the whole thing out. Where was the idealistic adolescent who had slept and dreamed here and read endless Victorian novels so full of virtuous female endurance and incorrigible, magnified men? I looked over at the statue of Our Lady of Lourdes on the mantlepiece, the eyes raised to the power system in the sky, and went to it in sudden irritation and turned it around so that it faced the wall.

I was nostalgic for the past which was slipping out of reach, the past when everything was still possible, before time had etched anything much at all across the pages of my life.

It was a strange, bittersweet, evening, that evening of my homecoming. It began to rain as the night drew in and I heard Tom's footsteps in the kitchen and his voice calling me. Pe..g. Pe..g.

So I left the darkened bedroom and went downstairs to the kitchen, blinking as I came into the light. Tom said the men had gone home and all the hay was in.

I gave Tom the present I had brought him, a dark blue silk tie with which he professed himself delighted. 'I'll wear it for my wedding,' and then made supper, rashers and sausages and brown bread and butter - gluttonous plenty by English standards - and, for a while, did not advert to Glenallen or Harriet. I was subsumed with a sense of fatalism. I talked about the war and the air raids and about my friends in Nottingham and about Brian, and Tom listened intently, interjecting occasionally

'D'you tell me?' in tones of gravity and compassion, shaking his head. I told him Mary had strangely disappeared. I mentioned nothing about the disturbing pages of her journal which I had found among her things. I longed to question him further about his engagement, and waited my chance. My head reeled with the news, with what I wanted to say to him about Harriet, about the impossibility of what he was doing, but did not want him to think me begrudging or jealous.

'This is great food,' I ventured after a long silence; 'It would be hard to find food like this in England,' and Tom said that a lot of German U Boats thought so too. They put in for supplies on the west coast and a lot of food was going to England. 'God help the craythurs there.'

'And the odd German plane "crashes" here too. The pilots are interned in the military camp in the Curragh. By all accounts they have the life of Riley. They're even let go up to Dublin to the pictures if they give their word of honour.'

'Have any of them tried to escape?'

'Divil a one! They know a good thing when they find it!'

I smiled, imagining Germans in the Curragh.

'Well, Peg, you haven't said a word of congratulation. I know it's a surprise, and hard on you too. But you'll always have a home with us, you know. I mean that, girl.'

He leaned over and patted my hand.

'She'll probably want me out!'

'Indeed then she won't. There'll be none of that.'

He said this with authority and decision. He would be master. But he didn't know what he was dealing with. And if I tried to tell him he would think me jealous or lying or both.

Later, Tom got out the whiskey and offered me a drink. I took it, letting the fire of it burn through me, feeling the hazy recklessness surge in my head. I took another, which was not wise.

'I suppose you think she's very fond of you?' I asked bitterly and I could hear that my voice was a little unsteady.

He turned to me. 'Come on Peg. Of course she's fond of me!'

I laughed cynically, thinking of 'The awful brother, clutching his forelock.'

'She thought you were a joke,' I hissed in sudden angry desperation. Tom gave me a sharp angry look. 'What do you mean, a joke?' he demanded taking both arms off the table.

'Oh, for Christ's sake. They think anyone is a joke who wasn't born with the privileges they have. Do you think for one minute that Harriet Fitzallen is going to marry you?'

Tom stood up. 'What's the matter with you at all? You're like an asp with piles. The blood in our veins, Miss, is as good as anything the Fitzallens can boast of, with all their airs and graces. Where did you get your bitter tongue?'

He reached into the drawer of the dresser behind him and extracted a letter.

'Read that!'

I took the proferred missive, saw the writing on the envelope and knew who it was from.

'Dear Tom,

I hope you are keeping very well. I am looking forward to seeing you soon. We are very busy here at

367

*the moment with the hay and I'm sure you must be up
to your eyes as usual in Ballycloghan.*

*The Bank says that if you guarantee the loan for the
repairs they'll give me the money. All you'll have to do
is sign a form. I've got the work in hand, as we agreed;
delay would be fatal. I've given the builder the last of
my ready cash as a down payment, which includes the
money I inherited from my mother.*

*Rebecca is lame at the moment and needs your
healing touch. The poor darling looks so fed up. The vet
has bandaged the leg.*

*Peter will be home soon for the Long Vacation.
These barristers have the life of Riley while we must
slave all the year around. But I'll be up to see you soon
so that we can finalise plans. There's still a drop of
petrol in the tank, which is a great bonus.*

Affectionately,
Harriet.'

I read this letter twice, with the sinking sensation
of one who knows the boat is about to go down
under her.

'Is that the letter of a woman who thinks me a
joke?' Tom demanded triumphantly.

'No. Not a joke. A blank cheque! What's this
bank guarantee? You could lose the farm over it!'

Tom glared at me. 'Are you trying to tell me my
business? I know what I'm doing. You seem to
forget I'm marrying this woman?'

'Well, I hope you won't sign any guarantee until
the knot is tied!'

Tom laughed, breaking the tension.

'Peg, Peg, you have a mind like a rat-trap. You
should have been a lawyer.'

368

But he frowned and was quiet for a moment before adding, very soberly, 'Of course I won't; I didn't come down in the last shower! But she's a grand girl and there's no reason why I shouldn't invest in Glenallen as soon as I am married to her. It would make very poor business sense to let the place go to ruin. I'll have a good look, of course, at everything that I'm putting money into. I'll know where it all goes, you needn't worry about that!'

'Is she in love with you?' I demanded, anxious to know how he assessed the situation. He turned to me and smiled.

'Peg, we suit each other. We are fond of each other. We'll make a good team. What more do you want? I'm not fooling myself that it's love's young dream for her, but she's practical enough.'

As he stood up to go to bed I said, 'Tom, you have the right to do whatever you like. It's your life and your farm. But tell me one thing.'

I lowered my voice, fearful of what I was asking him. 'When you were in Glenallen, when you were on the hill, did you see any sign of Brian?'

Tom stopped in his tracks, turned, stood stock still. 'Did I see any sign of Brian?' he repeated, his voice almost a whisper. 'What sort of a question is that? Brian was killed, wasn't he?'

'Just answer, Tom. Please.'

'No. There was no sign of Brian. Why do you ask such a question? You don't think he's still alive, do you?'

He sounded alarmed, wary, suddenly suspicious.

I waved my hand because I could hardly speak.

'No, no. He left a note saying he was going home to visit his father, and I have these awful dreams where I see him on Knockshee.'

Tom looked at the tears spilling down my face. His face softened. He drew up a chair beside me, put an arm around my shoulder, squeezing it tightly.

'Don't be upsetting yourself now, Peg. It makes me feel very badly, - especially as Brian and not Harriet would have inherited Glenallen if he hadn't been lost. She told me that.'

He rose and stood beside me for a moment, half ashamed. 'You would have done alright if he had lived.'

Chapter 15

That night I dreamed again of Knockshee. I saw Brian coming towards me down the dark bulk of the mountain and then turn away towards the house. But this time there was another presence in the night. My brother's face loomed out of the darkness, stared in my direction and then followed Brian in the direction of Glenallen. I woke in the moonless dark, my heart racing, not knowing where I was and lay for a long time listening to the pattering of the rain on the window.

When I finally got back to sleep I must have slept like the dead, for I woke late. The room was dim although it was nearly midday. The rain was still hissing outside. I got up, found that the fire in the range was almost out and that there was no sign of Tom.

I stoked up the range, made some tea, my head full of my brother and the extraordinary news of his engagement to Harriet Fitzallen. I heard the tinny sound of the rain dancing on the galvanised roof of the turf shed and the gushing of the water from the eaveshoot into the barrel by the backdoor.

Niamh called at two o'clock. She was obviously pregnant, a little round pot which she carried in front of her. I made her sit in the fireside chair, and she sat down with a sigh. She looked tired.

'I'm terrible sorry about your poor husband, Peg.'

'Thanks.'

'An' I hear you're expectin' like meself?'

'I am!'

'Do you remember the old days? God, we didn't know how good we had things. Not a bother on us'?

'Go on! We had plenty of bother. Little bothers, but they mattered then!'

She laughed, patting her tummy.

'And more little bothers on the way!'

'When is your baby due?' I asked.

'About five months. Packey is looking forward to it. He wants a boy.'

I looked at her pale tired face and lank hair and thought of the bright, smiling girl I had known. 'One thing is sure. You can't be doing any more housework here..not in your condition. You need to rest.'

'Rest is it? Peg, I need the money now that I no longer have the job in Percival's. Sure you know what men are like. "Do this, woman. Do that, woman," and never a penny. I have the hens, of course, and I put a bit aside from the eggs.' She sighed and muttered, half to herself, 'But sure haven't I a roof over my head and enough to eat! Amn't I alright.'

'Does he treat you badly?' I asked indignantly and she shook her head, suddenly anxious that I should not think ill of her man.

'In his own way he's the best in the world. Only he gets drunk the odd time.' She smiled a self-deprecatory smile. 'I have no dowry, you know, and I'm not in any position to make complaints.'

'*Is fearr bean ná spraoi*' I answered, quoting the old Irish maxim that a woman is better than a dowry. I knew the worth of this particular woman.

'Do you remember all that stuff you used to learn so easily by heart, the poetry that Mr Clancy gave us? *Paradise Lost* and Shakespeare and we only children?'

Niamh nodded smiling at me. 'Sure I loved it. It keeps me sane sometimes. I let it go around and around in my head like a drug ...'

'When to the sessions of sweet silent thought
I summon up remembrance of things past.'

I watched her recite, encouraging her with a smile, and thought of someone who had also rolled poetry off the tip of his tongue, in Connemara, one summer's day.

'Are you glad to be back here, Peg? You must miss your fine life beyond in England?'

I looked around the kitchen, heard the fire catching, the roar up the chimney, and from outside the lonely song of the rain.

I got up to close the damper.

'I miss my friends. I had some good friends in England.'

She put her head slightly on to one side, sympathy in her eyes.

'I remember the two nice friends you used to bring home in the summer. You told me how the dark haired one died. Where is the other girl, the red head?'

'I don't know, Niamh. I haven't heard from her for several months. She disappeared during the blitz and no one has heard from her since.'

I made some more tea and she asked me diffidently had I noticed a change in Tom.

'Yes. He's very happy now I think. I suppose you know he thinking of getting married?'

She looked away, hiding the hurt in her eyes.

'Yes. He mentioned it. And to your sister-in-law, Peg. Isn't that a bit queer? I saw her down here a couple of times and, no disrespect to her or anything, but the place didn't feel the same.'

I studied her face. 'Why didn't it feel the same?'

'Sure I don't know. Different!' She blushed. 'And I don't think she loves him, Peg. She's a grabber if ever I saw one.'

Niamh left after about an hour. She wanted to do her usual cleaning work but I wouldn't let her. I gave her a pound when she left. 'It's alright. Put it on account.' And I also gave her Palgrave's *Golden Treasury* which I had bought one day in Nottingham when I was wandering around a bookshop and she had come into my head.

She opened the little book in delight and then embraced me. 'God bless you Peg for the kind thought.' Then she was gone, scarf over her hair, wellingtons on her legs, the *Golden Treasury* in her pocket. I watched her from the window, saw her stop by the gate to shake a pebble out of her boot, taking it off and turning it upside down before putting her bare foot back into it.

Tom came in at lunch time, looking around expectantly as though his lunch should have been steaming there on the table and finding instead his sister in the old fireside chair nursing the cat and gazing into space.

'Is there a bite to eat?'

The force of his disappointment made me feel guilty. 'God, I'm sorry, Tom. I don't know. Look, I'll make you a boiled egg and I'll do bacon and cabbage for the supper.'

'A man can't work on an empty stomach,' Tom muttered quite crossly, and I felt, as I always did when a man evinced any spleen in my direction, a clawing fear, as though violence, which could so easily pulverise me, was only a hair's breadth away. It was not that I thought Tom would hit me; it was something deeper and older than that, the instinctive rush to pacify by whatever means, in order to be allowed to live.

Tom reached into the dresser for a loaf of brown bread, put it down on the table with a half-hearted thump and cut a thick slice which he covered with half an inch of butter. His boots left a muddy track on the floor.

I got up, made the third pot of tea of the morning and put it down in front of him. We would have to go easy on tea. I wished now that Tom had hoarded more before the war started.

When Tom had gone back to the stables I cleaned the muddy floor, washed the dishes and cycled into the village for some groceries. I had left the bacon soaking in water and needed only some flour and sugar from the shop. I had Tom's ration book with me and would have to apply for my own.

There was a new assistant in Percival's - a young girl of about sixteen - and she served me with some curiosity, asking me if I wasn't Miss Donlon that got married and went off to the war. She was thinking of going to England herself - she had heard the pay was great in the factories.

I told her a bit about England and she listened eagerly. I did not go back to Ballycloghan immediately. I rode for miles, pedalling harder and harder as though I could penetrate some barrier of space and time which would provide the answers I needed to the questions I hardly dared to ask. The bicycle tyres swished on the wet

375

road. The rain had stopped and the air was very cool and fresh. All around me were wet fields shaved of hay; the hay had been collected into cocks and tied down with straw ropes.

I passed a couple of red haired girls carrying buckets. They were laughing. Their hair was lighter in colour than Mary's, a red gold, and they were speckled with small brown freckles, like trout.

When I got back to the house I put the bacon down to boil, went upstairs, dragged my heavy case into the middle of the floor and took out the four folded pages of Mary's diary and read them again. Then I brought them down to the kitchen and put them into the fire. They were private to Mary; they had no business in my possession. And they were a link with Lucien which I angrily wanted to obliterate.

Was it a couple of days later, or was it a week, that Harriet arrived?

I was in the kitchen when I heard the sound of a car engine, the squeak of the gate, the footsteps crossing the yard towards the open door.

'Hello there! Anyone at home?' Her eyes bulged with speculative surprise when she saw me, wiping my hands and in the act of going to the door to see who could have stopped by the gate in a car.

'Peg,' she cried. 'How absolutley wonderful to see you! I thought you were still in England.'

She was dressed in a two-piece costume with a coachman's jacket, a floral design on an off-white background. Her hair was smooth, the light catching its silken strands; she was wearing lipstick and powder.

'I came down to see Tom.'

I could hardly speak to her. I had expected her to arrive sometime, but without really believing it. Now her presence filled the kitchen of my old home like some sort of invasion.

'Please go away, Harriet. Go away.'

'But my dear girl ... what have I done? Why are you so cross ... Where's Tom?'

'Leave my brother alone.'

There was silence except for the ticking of the clock on the dresser and the breeze soughing outside and the sudden staccato sound of Tiddles scratching. Harriet's eyes were pale blue and very cold. She stood perfectly still for a moment, staring at me, and then she laughed, a melodious confident laugh which sounded foreign here and which wafted through the house. I was aghast at what I had said; I had not meant to disclose myself, but the element of surprise and the sudden unreasoning fear had betrayed me.

'My dear Peg, you do seem a bit under the weather, you poor old thing. I'm sorry if I gave your a start. In your condition and everything.'

She said this anxiously, glancing at my stomach as if to assess the state of my pregnancy, looking around the kitchen as though she expected Tom to materialise and then back at me with a slightly lugubrious expression.

'Peg - nothing stays the same forever! I know that Tom and I must have come as a shock. Lots of things have changed. Try to understand.'

I heard the sound of boots in the yard. Tom had heard the car. He came into the kitchen, delight on his face. He put his arm around Harry's shoulder, squeezing her.

'How's my handsome baggage?'

Why could he not sense her reaction, the electric current of outrage that was as clear to me

377

as if she had screamed it aloud? But she smiled and inclined her head towards him and he kissed her cheek awkwardly, one eye watching me, reddening slightly.

'I'm dead tired, Tom Donlon'. She glanced at me. 'Do you mind if I sit down? I think I've upset Peg by barging in.' Tom pushed a chair forward, raising his eyebrows at me.

'Make some tea?'

The demand was arrogant enough, but his eyes were pleading. I moved the kettle over the hot plate and put out cups and saucers on the table.

'You'll be staying for a day or two?' Tom inquired eagerly and she shrugged and looked at me.

'I think I'm intruding. It's not fair on Peg.'

I blushed. I made the tea. Tom said I was delighted to see her and whispered in my ear that I ought to make up a bed for her. So I took the hint and made some excuse about things I had to do upstairs.

'Have you decided on the day?' Tom asked sotto-voce as I left the room and I waited outside the door for her reply.

'I don't see why it shouldn't be as soon as possible. I thought it would be nice to get married in Dublin'.' She lowered her voice then and I heard Tom's laugh, loud and hearty.

I made up the bed for Harriet in my mother's old room. I opened the door of the wardrobe to get out the patchwork quilt and breathed in the rush of camphor, reminiscent of my childhood. I opened the window, struggling with the sash. The windows had recently been repainted and were stiff. I heard Harriet's footsteps and those of Tom on the stairs. She came into the room, looked out at the sunny afternoon, said something about the view - which was only of flat fields with stone walls, the river and the sweep of the sky. She insisted on helping me make up the bed.

'Thank you very much, Peg.'

She glanced at me, looking almost vulnerable for a moment. Tom put her small suitcase on the chair.

'I'll just get changed and be with you in a jiffy,' she said, and Tom and I went out, shutting the door. I felt how the atmosphere in the house had changed, become charged with some sort of excitement, with the grip she had on life.

She came down shortly afterwards dressed in shirt and jodhpurs and Tom's eyes followed her around as they had once followed Cissie.

'Well, ma'am,' he said, 'your wedding present is outside waiting for you!' She stared at him, mouth opening to show white teeth.

'My dear Tom. What have you been up to?'

Tom evidently loved being called 'My dear Tom'. He beamed. 'Well, are you coming or not?'

She turned to me. 'Come on Peg. Come and see what this brother of yours has been up to!'

'I already have a fair idea.'

I found it hard to preserve intact my spleen of an hour before; the Ballycloghan Harriet seemed different to the Glenallen Harriet, and Tom was looking at me with a beseeching expression. So I got my wellingtons and went with them through the stables, past the haggard now full of the new hay which was stacked in a high rick, and out to the pasture where Jupiter was grazing and shaking his mane, an aristocratic presence among the other horses.

'Oh, he's lovely. How old is he; how many hands?'

'Seventeen hand, three year old American hunter,' Tom murmured proudly.

Her eyes were alive with genuine pleasure. She leant towards Tom, touched his cheek with her lips hastily while she breathed that she was dying to try him out, and when Tom reacted stiffly she added on a note of exasperation - 'The horse Silly - not you!'.

Tom jerked like someone who had been stung and looked at me. But I pretended I was deaf.

The two of them went to catch the bay hunter. Tom took a potato out of his pocket and offered it as bait. He made sure he did this without the horse seeing where the potato came from and then he walked the animal back to the stable yard, leading him by the forelock. Harriet walked on the other side, making comments on Jupiter's chest, checking to see if he was shod and asked Tom if he had studs. Jupiter slobbered and dropped a piece of potato and Harriet picked it up and pushed it back into his mouth on the palm of her hand, wiping the froth from his mouth on his neck.

Tom saddled him up for her in the stable yard and she mounted, cantering off gently around the pasture. The mares looked after her, lifted their hocks and took to their heels, running diagonally across her path from behind and Jupiter tried to bite their rumps as they passed, while they flicked their tails at him contemptuously.

'Well, Miss?' Tom demanded when she was out of earshot. 'What's wrong with her?'

I shook my head.

'Him you mean. He's too big.'

Tom clicked his tongue in annoyance and looked at me sharply.

'I'm talking about Harriet!'

380

'I don't want her as a sister-in-law again!'

Tom gave a snort of exasperation.

'Why?'

'She hates me!'

Tom harrumped derisively, then glanced down at my stomach with the unspoken comment about my condition having unhinged me. 'I'll talk to you about her when you come to your senses!'

When she returned, trotting to the gate where we were standing, Tom went jokingly to help her down, acting the clown and tipping his cap to her, and I saw for an instant as she looked down at him the weary contempt in her eyes and the curl of her lip.

That night I wrote to Mr Dencher confirming my intention to return to Nottingham, but received a few days later a letter from him which had crossed with mine in the post. In it he said that Mr Warren had been demobilised due to a leg injury which had left him lame; he would be returning to his job and consequently I would not be needed. He enclosed a glowing reference and wished me luck. 'I will write to you again if a vacancy presents itself.' Mr Dencher added by way of postscript.

I put the reference away and screwed up the letter. There were other schools. But would they take on an obviously pregnant woman? I was beginning to show, a little round pot where a new person was growing, the child of Lucien wherever he might be now, and mine.

Tom and Harriet were married quietly on 16 September 1941 in University Church, Stephen's Green and there was a small wedding breakfast afterwards in the Shelbourne Hotel. Harriet wore a wool dress the colour of old rose and a small hat with a brim. She looked very calm, except for the nervous light in her eyes. Claire de Lacy - Harriet's old friend who was now married and living in Dublin - was matron of honour. Tom's friend Christy Moran was best man; Peter was there. The O'Shaughnessys had been asked but had sent regrets. Afterwards we walked into the Green and had some photographs taken. Tom was happy, but too straight-laced to evince either tenderness or desire, so the newly married pair walked along side by side, exchanging a word or two, like acquaintances. Harriet's face became a little set and she abandoned her new husband during this walk to converse with her brother in the close, intent, fashion they had. Tom talked awkwardly to his best man and then exchanged a few words with Claire de Lacy. We posed for the photographers, smiled, commented on how nice the day was.

Later, Peter spoke to me very courteously, said how sorry he was about Brian, asked after my health and hoped he would see me sometime in Glenallen. I said 'of course' with cold politeness. My heart said, 'Never, never, never!' But he did not have to know that. I thought he had got very thin and pale and put it down to overwork.

Before we left the newly-weds to their married bliss Harriet took me aside, thanked me for being 'so wonderful' and said she was relying on me.

'You're the only sister I have. Tom tells me you were thinking of going back to England. Why should you do that? You have two homes in Ireland; you need someone to look after you now,' and she kissed my cheek. 'Please stay, Peg.'

She had her head slightly to one side, smiled a rueful supplicating smile, and for a moment, in spite of everything, I almost loved her.

The newly married pair were to stay for the week - in the Shelbourne Hotel, because this was Harry's choice. Pat O'Regan was to run the farm during this time under my supervision.

It was strange and lonely in Ballycloghan without Tom and strange and lonely because I could not feel the same way about my old home. Harriet would be coming there as mistress - when she came - and because of this the place had acquired a patina of sorts, become a little foreign and glamorous.

Tom had had a serious talk with me the day before his wedding, telling me that I must stay for as long as I wanted, whenever I wanted; that it was there for me, my home.

'I have to get a job, Tom; I must be independent.'

'You have your widow's pension. And you're pregnant, for God's sake. Who'll employ you?'

'I can't stay here; it's your wife's home now too.'

He glared at me, moustache a-bristle.

'Give up this nonsense, Peg. It's not lucky. You have some sort of set on the girl. Maybe she's a little bit different from us; maybe she was born with privileges we weren't. But she's sound!'

He paused 'Anyway, this is my house.'

So you think you'll be master, I had thought. You think it's as simple as that. You think Harriet Fitzallen will knuckle down to your bidding.

'You don't know what she's done, what she's like!'

Tom exhaled angrily, folding his arms. 'Well, what has she done. Tell me her terrible crimes.'

'There's quite a list!'

I itemised them on the fingers of my left hand.

'She caused my miscarriage. She accused me of being a thief. She tried to kill Brian by cutting the girths of his saddle. She blinded one of the mares and blamed it on Brian.' My voice lost its impetus. I knew how I sounded.

My brother was watching me with his brows gathered together and his mouth pinched.

'Anything else?' he said softly.

I banged my hand on the table.

'What's the use? You don't believe me.'

'Do you have proof for even one of these monstrous allegations?'

I shook my head. Tom spoke in a stern voice, a man protecting his bride-to-be from calumny.

'I'd be more careful if I were you, Peg. There are laws against character assassination!'

Pat did the work on the farm. I had little to do except keep the house, so I decided to give it a thorough going over, cleaning out drawers and cupboards - a job I loathed, but it passed the time. The drawers in the dresser were a mess, various pieces of string, brown paper, old corres- pondence, vets' bills, blacksmiths' receipts, saddlers' accounts, bills for bran, sealing wax. I took them out, sorted the rubbish into separate little heaps on the table and then, at the back of the drawer I found a letter addressed to myself in Paddy Stapleton's writing. It was crinkled and creased and had been caught between the back of the drawer and the frame. For a moment I thought it was an old letter, but realised that it had not been opened. It was postmarked 13th March 1941. It had arrived after my departure to England and had not been forwarded.

I took it with me to the fireside chair, displaced Tiddles who Meowed peevishly and who immediately jumped back on to my lap. I opened the envelope. It was a response to my last letter to him telling him about my marriage.

'My dear Peg,
Congratulations! I am sorry for myself, but glad for you if this is what you want and if you are happy. Your husband is a lucky fellow and I hope he knows it. All I can say is that there is a little corner of my heart which will always be yours.

The navy are forming a construction brigade and I've been put on the reserves for it. If America joins the war I'll probably see action.
God bless you,
Paddy.'

The familiar signature filled me with a yearning for the simplicity of summer afternoons down by the Garryogue. How to turn back the clock, restore my mother to life, reclaim my childhood? I got out pen and paper and wrote a letter to Paddy, telling him that my husband had been lost in action, that I was pregnant, that Tom had married my sister-in-law and that I did not know what direction to give my life. 'It's murder being a woman, because if you're pregnant no one will employ you. Which means I'm stuck here, absolutely supernumary. I hope America does not go into the war and that you will be safe.'

I thought a lot about Tom and Harriet and her talk with me after the wedding, and Tom's pointed comment that I had no proof. I felt a confusion of doubt. Could I have been wrong about her? She seemed to have changed, become

385

softer, human. Perhaps it was time to let the past go.

Father O'Dea, the parish priest, called one day and asked me how I was getting on in my brother's absence. How did I like my sister-in-law? Wasn't it strange that my brother should marry my husband's sister? She was a grand looking girl; he'd had a word with her once, told her that he had been curate in Ballyharris before she was born.

'You were curate in Ballyharris once? You know Glenallen then?' I asked in surprise.

'I remember it well. A good Catholic family the Fitzallens, although their history is a little colourful.'

He was sipping the little glass of sherry, and I turned to stare at him.

'How do you mean - colourful?'

He hesitated. 'Sure you ought to know that better than me! Isn't there that strange old souterrain there - did they not tell you about it; it goes back to pagan times. The druids built it they say and a quantity of human bones were found there some years before I came to the parish.'

I put my glass down. 'I didn't hear about the bones. Brian told me that archaeologists had been working there and that they had opened it up.'

Father O'Dea nodded. 'That's right. There may also have been an entry point into it from the house. But there's an old Ogham Stone on the mountain which sealed the souterrain entrance. They found the bones behind it.'

'I know about the stone. Brian told me about it and the queer inscription on it. He had a bad experience as a child - lost inside the tunnels for a day and a half; and afterwards he had recurring nightmares which I always put down to that.'

386

I shivered as I spoke; the echoing darkness was still vivid from Brian's description - the child alone and mad with fear.

'Did you know there was a message on the Stone?'

The priest nodded his head. 'I can't remember now, but I heard it was something strange.'

'I know mine and mine know me,' I whispered.

He started. 'They must have made a mistake in the translation; that's in the New Testament - the words of Our Lord. There was a second stone - which the archaeologists actually removed to the museum in Dublin. It also had an inscription.'

'What did it say?'

He shrugged slowly. 'It warned against the place being opened.'

We sat in silence for a while. I was glad of the sunshine coming through the window and the sound of a dog barking in the distance. Oh God, I thought, what do I have to do to get rid of Glenallen?

'Of course the local people went mad when the stone was removed and said the bad luck - the *mi-ádh* - would escape now, so old man Fitzallen had the men set off a rockfall which blocked the entrance completely. But sure you wouldn't want to heed all the pishogues you hear in this country, Peg. Just say your prayers and go to the sacraments and live a good christian life. That's all anyone can do.'

As he rose to leave he turned back to me and said, 'I suppose you know that Mrs Fitzallen had been unwell, on and off, for a long time, ill with her nerves; one breakdown after another. Too much inbreeding did nothing for that family! But your blood and Tom's will fix all that!'

He glanced at my swollen stomach.

'I don't suppose it's the kind of thing people advert to at all when they're getting married!'

'They certainly don't!' I said, flushing.

I talked to Niamh from time to time, called down to her cottage, saw the improvement she had been responsible for, the fresh coat of whitewash, the flowers in the garden she had created, the little hedge of escalonia now growing along the wall near the gate. Packey would turn up for his meals and sometimes sit in the settle, puffing his clay pipe and asking questions about England and the war. My heart turned over for Niamh, to be tied to a man pushing sixty. 'I had no dowry, you see,' she had said. Was there no love in the world?

One day I brought a couple of bottles of Guinness with me, on the basis that it was good for pregnant women. Niamh had confided to me that she liked it. I put one bottle down on the hob and opened the other, pouring it guiltily into tea cups Niamh produced, the two of us laughing like schoolgirls.

'He'd get an awful surprise if he saw me,' Niamh said. 'The men think they're the only ones who are entitled to the odd drop!'

Packey arrived in the door unexpectedly, stooped a little at the shoulders from a lifetime of working in the fields, his greasy cloth cap firmly down on his forehead. I prayed that he would not smell the stout. He glanced sourly at the pair of us and at the cold teapot which Niamh had left on the table to deceive him; then he turned and headed outdoors again.

'Suppin' tea from mornin' till' night and the price of it!' he muttered darkly. Just at this moment the cork popped on the bottle of stout on the hob with a sound like gunfire and I felt Niamh quiver beside me, - anticipation, trepidation, suppressed laughter.

Packey didn't react immediatley. He stopped at the door, looked around.

'Did ye hear a shot?'

'It was one of the Caseys shooting rabbits,' I said in a very even voice, pointing through the open door to the fields beyond.

'Musha, musha, musha,' Packey said querulously, 'Was that what it was?' I thought he was a little deaf, that maybe he did not hear the laughter which filled the kitchen as he crossed the yard.

While we sipped our illicit drink of stout I told Niamh that I would be staying in Ballycloghan to have the baby.

'So you won't be going back to England?'

'Not for the moment.'

'Sure, what do you need a job for anyway, Peg? Didn't your husband, God rest him - leave you something. Hadn't he a few bob?'

I looked at her and laughed.

'He hadn't a brass farthing!'

'But, weren't his parents dead?' she demanded, brows creased in perplexity. 'And didn't they have something to leave him?'

'They had just the farm, Glenallen, and they left that to Harriet.'

Niamh nodded. 'Oh, I see,' adding after a moment, 'Queer thing enough to do and he a son and married!'

I shrugged.

'And Tom will have it now!'

'He's welcome to it,' I said. I looked out at our quiet countryside, far from Knockshee, where Balor lay in his eternal half sleep. 'He's more than welcome to it!'

Packy came back as I was leaving, his pockets bulging. 'I brought ye back a brace of rabbits,' he announced in a dull serious voice, taking out two bottles of stout, putting them down on the table and looking at the two of us with sly satisfaction.

Chapter 16

While Tom and Harriet were away I tried to forcibly distract myself from the thoughts that preyed on my mind by conducting a scientific experiment. If I was going to be stuck in Ballycloghan for the next year or so I wanted to have something to show for my time.

I found some old beakers and a max-min thermometer I had from my student days and rigged up a kind of weather station in an exposed spot on the far side of the haggard. I had the idea of trying to grow tomatoes out of doors - they would be a great source of vitamin C. I was thinking of the rickets which one saw so much of, particularly in the towns.

I decided to start by measuring maximum and minimum temperatures and rainfall, intending to keep up this weather check over the winter and into the summer. It would be something to keep my mind busy until the baby was born, something to keep away the thoughts of Brian and of Lucien, thoughts which were really draining me.

The memory of my husband, the sense of him, would descend on me at sudden intervals during the day. I remembered the way he moved and spoke and his vulnerability, the tension between him and his family. I wished they had recovered his body. It would have closed our account in some way, to have actually seen him dead. As it was I was dogged by him, the sense of tragedy and the feeling that there were matters unresolved. I had asked Harriet if he had returned to Glenallen to see his father before he died and she had answered in the negative, looking surprised and compassionate. And yet I could not divest myself of the nagging doubt, the need to find something which would definitively close the chapter.

The dreams did not help. Again and again I saw him walking down Knockshee towards the house and each time the sense of being watched by something powerful and strange made me wake up sweating with terror. Even though I was a voyeur from the waking world I knew in the dreams that I was perfectly visible to whatever watched me. I dreaded these dreams so much that I forbade myself as I went to sleep to have any, but this prohibition was of little efficacy.

And as for Lucien, the guilt kept him at bay. Certain scents, like my mother's bottle of 4711, invoked his cologne and then he would be there, representing a powerful reality, strong-minded, alive and sexual. In the context of the Catholic Irish countryside he also seemed a dream. How could I possibly have sinned as I had, given myself with such abandon? It did not seem possible in the sleepy parish of Ballycloghan that such a scarlet woman could live and breathe. I longed for my pregnancy to be over so that I could find normality again, get a job again, leave all dreams behind me. The determination to effect this was badly shaken when a letter, cut by the Censor, arrived. It was a letter from Lucien, forwarded from Nottingham.

'I am back in ------ for a while and think of you, my dear Peg.

Unfortunately I have no time to go to ------ to see you, but hope that you remember me. Perhaps we could have a weekend in ----- sometime, if that would please you. Meanwhile I hope that all the fires you might play with shall not burn you.

I embrace you,

Lucien.'

I looked down at myself, the bulge of pregnancy, the months ahead, the life before me. 'All the fires you might play with.' God, but he had a nerve!

Did he think I 'played' like that as a common occurrence? Was he telling me the true standing of our relationship? To him it was a game, one which amused him, and which he hoped also amused me. Again I felt like a courtesan, a mistress, a usable, disposable, woman of sex. I crunched the letter into a ball and threw it into the fire, angry at the spurt of tears. Had Mary felt the same? 'I have decided to stop playing games,' she had written, 'Or to play them where they may be of use.' But I knew, from her diary, from the way Lucien had spoken of her, that the 'game' she referred to was in her mind, not his. I was jealous and hated it. You cannot help what you feel, I told myself eventually; but you can help what you do!

The newly married pair arrived back in Ballycloghan one week after their marriage. Tom sent a wire from Dublin to tell me and I got Pat to meet them at the station in the pony and trap.

Pat set off in good time for the train, fussing importantly about 'the missus'. He had the pony groomed and the trap shining and was quite obviously excited at the prospect of bringing 'the missus' home. He even had on his good jacket for the expedition and put a foxford rug into the trap to protect her from the rigours of the weather. It was an ordinary overcast day, quite warm, and I felt that Harry would survive even without a rug. But in spite of myself and my sour reflections, I too half looked forward to seeing her, to the sense she brought with her of life and excitement. It was time I made my peace with her, I told myself. She obviously wanted it and it was not Christian, or indeed possible, to keep up old antagonisms with someone who tried to heal old wounds. The possibility that I could have been wrong about her shamed me. With the passage of time and meeting her again it seemed more and more unlikely that she could have been the architect of all the bizarre events which had taken place at Glenallen. It would have taken someone very sick in mind to have orchestrated all of that.

Pat was gone a long time; the train was late; the journey from Dublin had taken eight hours as the trains all ran on turf now, because of the war.

I watched from the window of my bedroom as the trap returned from the station, approached the gate and turned into it. I saw Tom leaning forward a little to look at the farm and the house, his face serious and tired, and then Harry said something to him and he brightened and made some quip and they both laughed and the trap swayed beneath the chestnut trees near the house, which were already sporting the yellow gold of autumn. I went downstairs to meet them.

She came into the kitchen, embraced me, gave a weary 'aah' and sank into the fireside chair. She was dressed in slacks and a brown jigger I had seen her wear in Glenallen.

'Darling! It's so nice to be back. The train was like a dead man's coach!'

Tom brought in the bags, looked around the kitchen and sighed with the pleasure and relief of being home. 'Everything been alright?' he demanded and would not wait for a cup of tea before going down to the stables to see the horses and talk to Pat. Harry looked up at him as he went to get his wellingtons and smiled at him, but as soon as his back was turned the smile died on her lips. Tom looked at her with sudden vulnerability and chucked her under the chin as he turned to leave the kitchen.

She examined me languidly, head thrown back against the chair. 'Make me a cup of tea and I'll tell you all the news!'

I obeyed, scalded the pot and put the tea down in front of her with some biscuits I had bought in anticipation of their return. She opened her case and produced a parcel wrapped in brown paper. She handed it to me.

'A present for poor little you. Or should I say, for your little passenger.'

I took off the string, opened the brown paper and found within a box containing a baby's white shawl. I held it up. It was soft and fine with a satin ribbon threaded through the edging.

'For the christening. There's a lovely christening robe in Glenallen, but the shawl with it has yellowed.'

'You shouldn't have, Harriet. Thank you.'

I blushed, folded the shawl and put it back in its box, then busied myself with lighting the lamp. The evening was drawing in. Why did I feel so nervous? Harry sipped her tea, her long legs stretched out in front of her, coaxing the cat with her index finger, scratching his chin. Tiddles loved her, spoke to her with narrow slitted eyes, mopped up biscuit crumbs from her hand.

I met her eyes and she smiled.

'Have you seen a doctor lately?'

'No.'

'You should, you know. You're not looking too well. You have to mind yourself when you're pregnant.'

'I'm fine.'

She leaned over, took my hand, squeezed my nail and studied it. 'You're anaemic!'

I snorted. 'No raw liver for me, thank you!'

There was silence for a while. I busied myself getting supper. She filled the kitchen with a restless, brooding presence.

'How was Dublin?' I asked.

'Much the same. Too many people; so few of them look either well fed or well dressed. I bought some clothes in Countywear. I met James Regan in Grafton Street. He's full of proposals for Conneely, but it will have to await the end of the war and the winning the sweepstake ticket! He's in debt up to his ears.'

She laughed, then lapsed back into silence.

'Will you be going to Glenallen soon?' I asked.

'Am I in your way here, Peg?' She smiled to show she was joking. 'Of course I have to go to Glenallen. Tom promised to guarantee the bank loan for the repairs to the house - the new roof, but he hasn't done a thing about it. And the work must be finished very soon, if the place is to be saved.'

She clenched and unclenched her hand, seeming suddenly upset.

'Will you tell him to hurry up, Peg? He might listen to you! All he says to me is, "I will. Where's the hurry. I want to see the builder first," and she mimicked Tom's voice with its flat pragmatic accent. 'You see, dry rot goes through a place. It's a kind of creeping evil in a house - long cobwebby tendrils hugging walls, seeking every piece of wood, ceiling joists, floors. I'm afraid it will be too late. The builder won't do any more if he isn't paid. The place will be beyond redemption. The rain will get in too because the re-roofing is only partially done.'

'I'll talk to him.'

I saw Glenallen in my mind's eye as a ruined shell covered with creeping grey tendrils against the timeless mound of Knockshee. It seemed a sort of memorial and not one that wrung my withers unduly.

'Are you still dreaming about Brian?' she asked softly and I answered truthfully that I was and that the worst part of the dream was the sense of being visible to something I couldn't see myself.

'I wish he hadn't told me so many stories about the place. About Balor and the rest. That's what's giving me nightmares! And Father O'Dea didn't help!'

'Why? What did he have to say for himself?'

'He dropped in the other day. He said that human bones had been found in the souterrain at Knockshee.'

She started, staring at me, her eyes narrowed and wary, her mouth a cruel thin line. I thought it was a trick of the light because she smiled then, showing her lovely white teeth and snorting in derision. 'Isn't he the dreadful old woman! That was ages ago.'

I was silent, irritated. I had plans to be an old woman myself.

'You know he was the curate in Ballyharris many years ago?' she said.

'Yes. He told me. He seems to know a lot about your family.'

'Does he indeed? What did he tell you?'

'Just that you had a colourful history! Anyway, if I could forget about Knockshee, maybe the dreams would stop.'

She was silent for a moment and then she said, her voice very soft, 'Poor little Peg. Do you think it's as simple as that? Do you think that you can escape Glenallen?'

'What do you mean?' I demanded. 'I have left Glenallen; I do not intend to go back.'

She smiled. 'But you will come back, if only to say goodbye. You need that.'

How did she know? It had been on my mind that I would never be free of a place I tried so hard to elude.

'Did Brian leave a will?' Harriet suddenly inquired in the same soft voice and I turned to her in surprise.

'No, at least I don't think so. Sure he had nothing to leave!'

She dropped her eyes. 'Poor Brian,' she murmured, with a kind of half laugh and when I turned to look at her face I saw that her eyes were just like Tiddles', feral and calculating, except that Tiddles' eyes had never glittered with so much intelligence.

That night, while I lay awake in the darkness I heard the newly weds in their room, heard their bed creaking. I imagined them together, naked, lost. I tried to stop the flight of my mind and the loneliness. My door was ajar because it didn't close properly thanks to a defective catch.

'Harriet,' Tom's low voice came suddenly through the silence. 'What's wrong? We're supposed to be married!'

398

And then I heard Harriet's muffled voice hiss something which sounded like 'What about ... You promised.'

Silence. 'I won't be held to ransom,' my brother said then, quite crossly and I knew from his tone that he was trying to contain his temper.

I heard their door opening and the sound of footsteps going down the stairs, followed by the rattle of the key in the back door and then the footsteps were outside, under my window, walking around the side of the house and down towards the road. I got out of bed and pulled back the curtain. Tom was striding down the avenue. He had a blackthorn in his hand and was swiping at the bushes in the moonlight.

Next day the atmosphere in the house was tense. Harry came down for breakfast, looking pale, and barely glanced at Tom. She went out to ride Jupiter and did not appear again until midday. Tom recovered his good humour during the morning, came into the kitchen at eleven for a cup of milk and said in some jest that herself was off around the countryside. I heard the pride in his voice and also the perplexity.

'She's on about Glenallen,' he said. 'She wants me to guarantee that huge loan for repairs.'

'I know. She's worried sick about the dry rot!'

'I don't want to guarantee anything until I've had a good look at exactly what I'm putting money into,' Tom said. 'I don't want to leave the farm at the moment. Winnie is due to foal.'

He sat morosely by the range for a while.

'She a queer girl,' he muttered. 'She won't relax for a moment, or think of anything except that house.'

He looked up at me, frowning, dragged his fingers across his forehead as though to erase incipient wrinkles.

'There's a streak in her that I can't fathom, Peg. Do you think she's fond of me at all?'

What could I say? 'She fond of Glenallen, like you said. She's obsessed with it at the moment!'

He was very gentle and coaxing when she came in for lunch, but she was not to be appeased.

The evening came. I lit the kitchen lamp. Harriet helped me prepare the meal in virtual silence. Tom came in, removed his boots, sat in the fireside chair with a grunt of delight, reached a hand out to his wife and pulled her on to his knee. He was in good form, laughing, telling us about some joke Pat O'Regan had passed on. The smell of frying bacon filled the kitchen.

Harriet sat on Tom's knee for a moment, stiff as an icon, wearing much the same expression as the O'Shaughnessy's cat the day David had used her to wipe the floor. Then she pushed his arms aside and jumped up.

'What's wrong?' Tom demanded, taken aback.

Harry turned on him, eyes flashing, furious.

'What do you think? You make promises you don't keep! And I wait and wait and wait and nothing happens.' Her voice rose, shrill and desperate. She picked up a delph cup from the table and smashed it to smithereens on the floor.

There was silence. Tom seemed dazed. He watched her in sudden anger and then in growing perplexity. 'For God's sake, I can't just drop everything, Harriet!'

She turned and fled from the kitchen, slamming the door so that the jamb trembled. Tom and I looked at each other without speaking.

400

'She's a bit overwrought,' Tom said, at a complete loss as to how to deal with the situation. His initial automatic response had been anger, mastery, but he knew instinctively that Harriet, in her present state, would pit every sinew and fibre in her being against him if he tried any form of coercion. He knew now as well as I did that she would not be mastered, no matter what the cost, no matter if she died in proving it.

Tom slept downstairs that night. He was very quiet in the morning and hardly spoke at breakfast. Harriet appeared as he was about to go out. 'I'm going home to Glenallen,' she announced. Her face was white, her eyes burning. I discovered I had something to do upstairs, and left the raised voices behind me.

'You're my wife! You can't take off just like that!' There was more dismay in his voice now than anger.

'Do you think you own me? You can't even keep a simple promise!'

'For the love of God, woman,' Tom shouted, 'Will you leave me be! I'll attend to Glenallen as soon as I can.'

The kitchen door opened and Harriet rushed upstairs. I heard her go into their room, heard her drag a suitcase from the top of the wardrobe. Then Tom's footsteps followed. His voice came, angry, surprised and then, after a moment or two, placatory.

'Come on Harriet. There's no need to get yourself in such a state. I told you I just wanted to look at things in Glenallen before I backed the loan. I have a stake in this too now, you know. Be reasonable.'

'I am reasonable. I don't think you understand the urgency of the situation!'

Was it tears I heard in Harry's voice? The ensuing silence surged over the house, broken by murmurs. He couldn't bear it if she cried. I knew this; she had evidently learnt it too.

'Don't cry. I'll go today. Will that be enough? Are you happy now? Don't cry!'

There were squeaking sounds; the bedsprings chattered for a moment. Then their door was firmly shut.

Over lunch Harriet looked brighter. She ate little. Tom was relaxed, happy as I had not seen him for a long time.

'The train is at two thirty. We'd better get going,' Harriet announced, jumping up from the table.

'I want you to stay here,' Tom said slowly, looking at her with a maudlin expression. 'Winnie is due to foal and I need you here to keep an eye on her.'

She turned to me. 'Peg could do that; and there's Pat.'

'No,' Tom said. 'Peg knows nothing about horses and Pat is too fond of the drop!'

Harry's face darkened; her eyes dropped but I sensed in her a new carefulness.

'Cheer up,' Tom went on. 'I'll be back in a day or two and I'll see the Bank in Ballyharris in the meantime. There's a promise! Everything will be alright!'

Tom left for the afternoon train and his wife drove him to the station. She was affectionate and playful with him as they got into the trap, but she returned to the farm in a thoughtful mood and spoke little during the evening.

That night I had another nightmare, the first for some time; like most dreams it melted on awakening, but this time I found Harriet bending over me with a candle, asking me was I alright and what had I dreamt of and I said that Tom had been in it and that something terrible had happened to him, but that I couldn't remember what; the event in the dream was on the very tip of my mind but as I tried to grasp it it eluded me and was lost. Harry was wearing a dark wool dressing-gown and her face above the candle hardly seemed her own, so grotesque was it with shadows.

Was it two days later that Tom came back? It was evening; the day was beginning to fade. Harriet had been exercising Jupiter and had gone back to the stable to unsaddle him. The horse had then escaped to the pasture for a good roll and Harry was in the haggard where she was picking some apples from the few trees forming a natural fence. I was in the garden on the other side of the appletrees, in my homemade weather station, checking to see if some cuttings I had aimlessly planted at the end of July had struck.

I heard the gate squeak peremptorily and the sound of boots striding down towards the stables and I heard Harry raise her voice eagerly.

'Oh hello, darling. Why didn't you send a wire? Is everything alright? Did you go to the Bank?'

I was about to join them when I heard Tom's voice, slurred with drink, asking loudly why she hadn't bloody well told him the truth, that he hated lies and I crept to the wall and looked between the branches to see what was going on. Harry had put the apples in a little pile on the ground and was standing, legs apart, hands on her hips and Tom was approaching her angrily, red faced.

'You told me Brian had not come back to Glenallen,' he said in a raised voice. 'But sure there's no doubt about it!'

Harriet did not reply. She stood quite still as he came towards her and he lifted his hand and slapped her. The blow connected with her face with a clap; I almost felt the sting of it and the humiliation. She staggered, dodged out of sight behind the far end of the hay rick and Tom followed her shouting that she wanted him to put a fortune into Glenallen. 'Where would that have left me?' he demanded. I heard Harriet answer something inaudible and Tom roar: 'Sure wasn't I up at the top of the bloody hill; didn't I see for myself? Is he in this with you? What kind of people are you?'

I heard Harry's contemptuous answer and then heard her gasp and there were the sounds of a struggle and her voice, very cold, 'Don't you dare!' and I galvanised myself and climbed over the wall, wriggled between the apple trees and into the haggard, running through the ankle deep hay around to the front of the rick. Time seemed to stand still; I heard Tom's angry voice, 'You'll tell me the truth Missus; I'll have the truth.' Then there was a guttural male sound of surprise and pain and suddenly all was quiet.

I reached the scene of the struggle to find my brother lying against the rick, his right elbow clenched against him where the hay knife had entered his side. The huge knife now lay on the ground with a tell-tale red smear along its blade and a sticky crimson stream dripped from Tom's clothes and down on to the hay. Then he slid to the ground, face screwed up with pain and Harriet who had sunk to her knees, her head in her hands, went towards him, her expression one of ashen disbelief.

'Get the doctor; tell Pat,' I shouted at her and she turned and fled towards the stables.

I tore off my cardigan, knelt beside my brother and tried to stem the bleeding by making a sort of pressure bandage, but could see my efforts were futile. Tom had started to tremble and was becoming cold.

'It was an accident,' he whispered. 'I fell on the hay knife.' His teeth started to chatter and his breath came in laboured moans. I said the act of contrition into his ear, weeping and trembling, begging him silently not to die.

Tom tried to say something more, but the words bubbled incomprehensibly in his throat. He opened his eyes which were already glazing in death, looked at me and tried to move his head. The pupils dilated into black pools and the moaning ceased.

When the doctor came it was already over for quite some time. I went into the house and saw myself in the mirror, the Maenad of Ballycloghan, streaked with blood and tears. I looked for Harriet who had disappeared as soon as the doctor had pronounced Tom dead. I found her in my mother's room. The room was darkened, the curtains drawn; she was lying face down on the bed, a pillow over her head. She neither moved nor made any sound, but when I touched her she raised her head and looked at me from wild red eyes, her face screwed up with pain.

'I should kill you now,' I said. 'But I need to know what Tom was talking about. What is there you have not told me about my husband?'

She looked up at me in anguish, her hand to her head. 'He was drunk, Peg. I don't know what he

405

was talking about. It was an accident. He slipped and fell on the hay knife. It was an accident. Oh God,' she cried in pain, 'my head is killing me!'

'I hope it does!' I said through clenched teeth.

We buried Tom three days later in my parents' grave. The coffin was borne on a hearse drawn by two horses with black plumes. It rained. The rain hissed into the grave as the clods were thrown in. They thumped sickeningly against the polished oak. Father O'Dea intoned the rosary, a kind of chant, H-ol-y Mary Mother of God, the prayer dying away and the response beginning again, H-ol-y Mary Mother of God. We stood in the long wet grass among the dripping gravestones, the celtic crosses, the weeping angels pointing heavenward, the statues of Our Lady, the old unpretentious slabs leaning askew like broken teeth. Everyone I knew in the parish, including Niamh, was present and afterwards shook Harriet's hand and mine, telling us how sorry they were for our trouble. I loved the feel of those kind warm hands that took my own; I had begun to feel that I was standing on some kind of tectonic fault line of the spirit and that everything I knew was going to shudder and disappear, that I had nowhere solid on which to plant my feet.

A lot of people came back to the house and drank whiskey. Mr Clancy talked to me of Tom's first days at school. 'A bossy little pup; the makings of a scholar. A great head on him. 'Tis a terrible tragedy.' Mr Clancy had a mesh of wrinkles under his eyes now and his face had fallen in a bit. I could not understand how he had ever terrified me.

I found Father O'Dea who was talking to Harriet about God's will, drew him away and said what I needed to say: 'It's that accursed place; everyone who has anything to do with Glenallen is destroyed. You should get them to exorcise it.'

I was about to tell him what I had overhead Tom saying to Harriet that fateful evening, what he had said about Brian, but thought better of it. This was neither the time nor the place. I could see from the priest's face that he regarded me as seriously overwrought.

'Now Peg. You have to mind yourself. You have your child to think of.'

The sergeant questioned Harriet and myself about Tom's death and I told him what I had seen and that there had been words between him and Harriet and also his assurance as he lay dying that it had been an accident. Harriet watched me carefully as I told my story. Then she said that he had drink taken, was overwrought about something and that he had tripped and fallen against the hay knife. They asked her a few more questions about how the knife had been in a position where it was likely to cause injury and she said she didn't know, that everything had happened so quickly.

'They're always sticking the knife back into the rick instead of taking it away with them,' Sergeant Duffy said, commiserating. 'He's not the first man to be killed by his own hay-knife.'

Harriet left about a week after Tom's death. She tried to be helpful in that interim, cooking, tidying the house. Now she held out her hand as she stood on the kitchen doorstep. Pat was waiting outside to take her to the station in the trap.

I declined her hand.

'I know you've always hated me,' she said sadly. 'I know you came into our family and I know that everything went wrong after you did. It's almost as though something unlucky follows you around. You should be very careful, especially as you're pregnant!'

'My life was happy until I went to live at Glenallen,' I said.

'Maybe you're the jinx,' she whispered. 'Have you thought of that?'

Her tone was jocose, looking at me teasingly as though she did not want this conversation to be held against her. So why did the day in the old sewing room with the wind crying in the chimney and the glass shattering on the planchette board return to me with such sudden force?

'Come back to Glenallen,' she whispered. 'It's waiting for you.'

Later I asked Pat, for the fifth time, if he was sure he hadn't left the hay knife in the rick.

'I can't understand how it got there, ma'am; I'm sartin' sure I put it away like I always do.'

I could not sleep that night. I left the lamp lighted and made myself sick with crying. The baby moved convulsively, disturbed by so much emotion. I saw in my mind's eyes the stiffening, bloodied body of my brother. I remembered my mother words on her deathbed. 'Look out for each other.' What had I brought him? How had I looked out for him? I heard again Tom's voice, 'Where is he; what kind of people are you?' Could Brian have come home and stayed there? Was he ill, injured? If he was alive why did he not contact me? And why would Harriet lie about him?

Father O'Dea called the following day. I was in the kitchen, sitting in the fireside chair, going over and over in my head the events which had led to Tom's death. Had it really been an accident? Tom had made a will before his marriage, 'made in contemplation of marriage' was the legal term, naming Harriet as his beneficiary. With Tom out of the way what need did she have for a guarantor? Everything he had was hers now.

'You're looking sick, Peg. You need a doctor!'

'I'm sick alright.' I told him what I had overheard Tom say to Harriet on that fateful afternoon. I told him that I was ill wondering what it meant. Tom had said there was no doubt but that Brian had come back; yet I have heard nothing from him.

The priest listened carefully.

'Peg, Peg, the RAF said he was lost in action. What more do you want? But sure, if it sets your mind at rest, maybe you should go back to Glenallen, for a visit. Tom was drunk, you said so yourself. I wouldn't take too much heed. And don't be so hard on your sister-in-law. She's a decent girl. She gave me quite a bit of money for the poor box.'

Thinking over this conversation later I had to concede that Father O'Dea was right. If the RAF said Brian had been lost in action that was what had happened. It wasn't the first time Tom had got himself into a state through drink. The cold light of reason did not admit of any possibility other than the obvious. And he would not have been the first person to have got a fright on the mountain.

On the following day I started to haemorrhage. For a moment I didn't know what was happening, this fountain pouring away with my life. I lay down on the kitchen floor, grabbing a towel to stem the bleeding. Luckily, Niamh was in the house at the time, ostensibly to borrow some of my father's books, but really to keep an eye on me. She rushed in from the parlour in response to my call, and Pat fetched the bluff and hearty Dr Tierney whom I had last seen kneeling in the bloodied hay on the evening of Tom's death.

'It's hospital for you, young woman.'

He took me in his car to the hospital in Galway. They gave me a transfusion; I was told I would have to stay in hospital - I had to rest. 'I want to go home' I said.

'If you go home you may start to bleed again and you will lose the baby and you will probably die,' the ward sister told me in a breezy matter of fact voice. 'The placenta is misplaced; always a big problem.'

'I can't afford to stay here.'

'You can't afford to die either!' she said, looking at me severely under her starched linen veil, as she took my pulse and regarded the watch pinned to her bosom. 'The graveyards are full of people who couldn't afford to stay in hospital. Have you no one to help you?'

Later that day I took pen to paper and wrote six words, addressing them to 4 Carlton Garden, London SW1.

'Dear Lucien,
I need you.
Peg.'

Dan was born on 29 January 1942 after a labour of twenty-four hours which left me torn and exhausted. The doctor gave me chloroform at the

410

end, just before the life which I had laboured to produce made its appearance, and I went into the darkness whirling in my head, wondering at the sense of suffocation from the red flannel pad placed over my nose and mouth. I woke in mid morning to find myself in bed, my back propped up with pillows, gloriously, luxuriously, comfortable. The curtains were drawn around my bed and through them I heard the sound of women's quiet voices and the rattle of trolleys and teacups. For a moment I did not know where I was.

The nurse carried my son in to me under her arm, wrapped up in a blue towel; I sat up and she placed him in my arms.

'Seven pounds. An heir on the first attempt!'

He moved jerkily, this little son of mine, his knees tucked under his chin, his head flopping unless supported, his fingers and toes like those of a doll, the cuticles perfect, the nails manicured. He had black hair, thin on the crown, longer at the back, very fine in texture and the fontanelle on the top of his skull throbbed gently with his life. He was so helpless, so tiny, so new. He had his father's mouth; there was no doubt about it, rose-bud and all as it was. I thought of the nights in London and Nottingham, in bed with his father, the passionate search for some kind of ultimate reality while there was still life in which to find it. 'Well Lucien, what would you say to this?'

Harriet came to see me that evening. She had visited several times with the O'Shaughnessys during my hospital stay and had put herself out to be charming, until I began to believe I had been mentally disturbed to have imagined her capable of anything ignoble. Her visits were always fun;

411

her spirits were high. She told me that the work was nearly finished at Glenallen.

'All that banging and thumping is about to stop, but the house is strange with dust covers and pink plaster and brand new ceilings upstairs.' She had no reason to be nice to me now, I thought, except genuine friendship and family ties. I was euphoric with the baby's birth, as though I could be free at last of the past.

I had spoken to her once more of what Tom had said to her on the day he died. 'I had never seen him violently drunk before. Harriet. Something must have happened to put him in that state.'

She had shrugged. 'Something probably did. Your brother was not the first person to get a fright on Knockshee.'

She arrived to see the baby, looking prosperous and radiant, staring into the crib.

'And who do we have here?' she asked in a bemused voice. She put a finger in his little clenched fist and he stirred and she said 'Oops! mustn't wake him.'

She turned to look at me, deposited the bunch of Christmas roses and kaffir lilies on the chair and peeled off her gloves. 'Lovely to see you, Peg, and to know that all is well. You're such a clever thing.'

A nurse came and took away the flowers and smiled back at the charming smile Harry gave her. Harriet opened her coat; she was wearing Aunt Rita's pearls and a warm wool dress with a soft belt. She peered at my son again. 'He's the image of his father,' and I looked at him, asleep in his crib beside me, hiding the expression I knew must be in my eyes. He breathed gently, almost inaudibly and twitched occasionally in his sleep.

412

There were wrinkles in his little clenched hands. He inspired in me a ferocity of protectiveness.

'What are you going to call him?'

'Daniel Lucien.'

She stared in surprise.

'Not Brian?'

'No,' I said flushing, 'I'm calling him after my father.'

Harriet seemed surprised. She shrugged. 'Well, he's your son!'

There was silence for a moment. 'When will you be able to come home?' she asked softly.

'I'm going home to Ballycloghan. I presume its still there?'

She shook her head at me. 'Oh Peg. Of course it's there. I'm your family now,' she added. 'You must come with the baby to live at Glenallen, at least until you have got yourself organised.'

'It's very kind of you, but I don't think so. Not now.' I was not able now for the questions concerning Glenallen. I could not bear to return there. Not yet. Not ever if I could help it.

Harriet left behind a bottle of orange and some sweets and I noted, without remarking it particularly, when a nurse poured me a glass of the orange drink, that it seemed to have been already opened. I saw tiny flecks floating in it, which I assumed to be orange peel. I drank some of it and offered the sweets to the nurses.

And some time later, maybe the next day because I lost the count of time, I had a visitor I did not expect and was glad to see him, forgetting that I should not have seen him. I told the night nurse later that my brother had called in and she said that was nice and then frowned and said she thought I had told her he was dead. Did I have two brothers? 'I must have been dreaming,' I said and went to sleep and dreamt of London and Lucien and Mary disappearing into the smoke of the blitz, red hair tangled out until it covered the city. And when I woke up Tom was there again, bloodied, frowning at me and the nurse came running with a doctor when they heard me screaming.

When the O'Shaughnessys came to see me a few days later I heard the ward sister tell them I was very strange in myself, whispering to them at some length. I knew she was informing them of my hallucination. Dr O'Shaughnessy glanced at me over his shoulder, a look of professional assessment which I feared and resented, especially coming from him. He said something about possible post natal syndrome. Then I heard the sister say, 'Her sister-in-law wants to look after her, but she wants to go back to that lonely farm where there isn't a soul,' and then Mrs O'Shaughnessy sat beside me in maternal fashion and asked me would I not go back to Glenallen with Harriet. 'She will look after you and the baby.'

I studied the flecks of powder on her face, the fine down on her upper lip and thought of Mrs Burton whom she did not in the least resemble.

'She cares so much for you and is dying to have the baby. And you must have someone look after you both for the moment.' She paused then and I sensed the unspoken comment about my mental state.

Then she asked what I was going to call him.

'Daniel,' I said, 'after my father, Daniel Lucien.'

She nodded, looking surprised.

'But why Lucien?'

I didn't answer, closing my eyes as though I hadn't heard.

'Harriet is coming,' my visitor said then. 'She came with us but wanted to do some shopping first. She'll be in later.' And then she told me about the lovely Fitzallen christening robe which Harriet had shown them the other day.

I stiffened. A Fitzallen christening robe, with lace and satin silk for my bastard son.

'I don't want her christening robe.'

Mrs Fitzallen studied me, half smiling, half frowning. 'Well it would be customary, Peg. In fact it will give offence if you refuse.'

Doctor O'Shaughnessy leaned over me, his waistcoat near my face; I could hear the ticking of the silver watch in his waistcoat pocket.

'Now what's all this, Peg? You've not been yourself since the baby.'

And then Harriet arrived. She appeared suddenly in the little ward, smiling at the four other new mothers, and the place was glamorous for her presence and alive because of her and the four tired young women perked up and smoothed their hair.

She was dressed in a tweed suit and exuded savoir faire and bonhomie and the faintest whiff of condescension. 'How is my favourite sister-in-law?' she demanded, leaning to peck my cheek. 'Where's my nephew?'

'He's in the nursery.

She turned to the O'Shaugnessys.

'Have you seen him? Isn't he adorable? You must be so proud, Peg. I'm simply dying to see him again. He's such a handsome fellow. And you're calling him after your father? Unusual for an Irishman to have a name like Daniel Lucien?'

I did not reply.

'Well, he's just divine,' Harry said. She sat on the edge of the bed and chatted with the O'Shaughnessys, a piece of local gossip about the cost of the new parish hall and then turned back to me and said how wonderful it would be when I came back to Glenallen. 'A family again. Like old times.'

The O'Shaughnessys smiled at her indulgently. I could sense how they approved of her, how they were flattered and charmed by her. She turned to them with total concentration, leaning forward with urbanity and wit and then, as they consulted each other on some point, I saw her eyes swivel sideways at me, a look so cold and calculating that I was sure I was imagining things. I was afraid now of my perceptions. I could no longer trust my eyes; others might think I was suffering from post natal chemical imbalance, but I knew better. I had seen something which had not been there when I saw Tom's 'ghost' and I was more frightened by this than I dared to pretend. Its possible implications were ones I could not bear to contemplate. I would do anything to ensure that it never happened again.

I got up to walk around because Dr O'Shaughnessy insisted I should.

'I feel so tired. My back is wobbling.'

'You'll feel better when we get you home. You need rest.'

'I want to go home to Ballycloghan.' I thought lovingly of the house and farm and the Garryogue and the old bridge and the great cloudy sky.

'Well,' Harriet said, 'please yourself. But the offer stands.'

As they were leaving I told Harriet I didn't have enough money to pay the hospital bill.

'I'll look after that, you silly girl. Were you worrying about that?'

I did not hear from Lucien. I was ashamed I had written. In December America had come into the war. I wondered had Paddy been called up.

Eilie arrived to see the baby before I left hospital. She bustled in, in warm winter coat and knitted scarf, bearing a small box of sweets. She was puffing from the hospital stairs and reminded me of the days she used to bring me my meals while I was laid up in Glenallen.

'I heard about the baby ma'am. Glory be to God,' and she examined him as he slept there in the mobile bassinet. 'He has a look of you, ma'am, but I don't see much of his father in him yet. Maybe in six months.'

She lingered over the cradle and when she looked up her eyes were wet with tears.

'It was terrible sad about his poor father, the poor, poor lamb.'

I took her hand. Even through the woollen mitts I could feel how cold it was. Her face was blotched with red broken veins.

'Sit down, Eilie, and tell me the news.'

She sank into the chair with a sigh. 'Me feet is killin' me.'

'It was very nice of you to come,' I said. 'How did you get here?'

'I have a new job. I'm housekeeper now to two priests, in the parish of Killbeg. I got the bus in. I wanted to see you, ma'am, and to congratulate you.'

'Why did you leave Glenallen?' I demanded in amazement.

'Miss Harriet said we had to go, Nora and I. She said she had no more money to pay us. Nora stayed on until she got the job in England. I would have stayed, but she wouldn't hear of it. I left just after the old man died. He was askin' for Master Brian on his deathbed. It was terrible sad, because they had parted on bad terms. And it was only a short while after his death that Miss Harry wrote to tell me the sad news that Master Brian was lost in action.'

She nodded her head up and down, the tears coming again.

'Where's Nora? What job did she get in England?'

'A factory job. She's making bombs or something. She came to see me before she left.' She looked around and lowered her voice. 'She gave me something she said she found in the cellar at Glenallen. She thought a ghost must have left it!'

'What thing?'

'It's a queer little thing to have found alright,' Eilie said softly., reaching into her pocket. 'I don't know what to make of it at all,' and she extracted something from the depths of the coat pocket and put a small, hard object into my hand. I looked at it curiously, recognising it with a start. I had seen ones like it before on a blue grey uniform. It was a gilt button with the RAF eagle, wings outstretched under the crown.

'How could this have been found in the cellar?'

Eilie made the sign of the cross.

'I don't know, ma'am,' she whispered. 'But I know what Murty would say!'

When the O'Shaughnessys next came to see me I asked them to tell Harry that I was taking her up on her offer.

Chapter 17

Harriet came with the O'Shaughnessys to take me to Glenallen.

The nurse carried the baby out to the car, let me get in and placed him in my arms. He was wearing a white flannel smock with three pixies on the bib and a blue matinee jacket with matching cap and bootees which Harriet had brought as a present. I waited in the car while she paid the bill, held my son in my arms, and both of us were solicitously wrapped in rugs by Mrs O'Shaughnessy.

Harriet came out and got in shivering. 'God, it's so cold,' she said, her teeth chattering. 'Are you sure he's warm enough?'

The baby opened his eyes and stared at her.

'Pet-ty, she said to him, bringing her face down near his, putting her index finger into the grasp of his tiny hand.

'Thanks for paying for me. I'll give it back to you as soon as I can.' I kept my voice low, embarrassed that I was reduced to these straits.

She frowned. 'Don't get exercised about that. There's plenty of time. What are families for?'

I met her eyes apologetically and she smiled back warmly.

Dan slept soundly for most of the journey. Harriet sat beside me, smiling down at the bundle in my arms from time to time, keeping up a running commentary for the first part of the drive and then lapsing into a brooding kind of silence.

Mrs O'Shaughnessy turned occasionally to look at the baby, eyes alight with concern.

'Are you comfortable there, Peg? Would you like Harriet or myself to hold him for a while?'

'No thanks. I'm fine.'

Harry took out cigarettes, Gold Flake and offered me one. I was gasping for a smoke and accepted it. The smell of the spent match and aroma of cigarette smoke filled the car. I inhaled greedily, thinking of Mary who also smoked Gold Flake, sitting back in Knightsbridge on the last day I had seen her.

'I love the smell of matches,' Mrs O'Shaughnessy said, declining a cigarette herself. 'I've never tried cigarettes, and Jim thinks they're probably bad for the lungs.'

'Oh, go on,' Harriet murmured. 'Nothing in the world compares with a ciggy when you need one. Peg will back me up on that.'

'Agreed,' I murmured.

'All the same,' our driver said, 'it can't be good drawing smoke into the lungs. You know the old rhyme about tobacco being the devil's weed. "It stains your fingers and burns your clothes and makes a chimney of your nose!"'

We laughed. From where I sat behind him I saw how he had aged, the skin puckering on his neck, the hair thin on the crown of his head. Occasionally I met his eyes on me in the rearview mirror; they were full of speculative concern.

Part of our drive was along by the Shannon and Dr O'Shaughnessy commented on the flooding. The river was swollen and many of the adjacent fields were under water. The leaden sky was reflected in these pools, fracturing when the wind shivered across the surface of the water. The vista

420

was lonely and bleak. The road was grey and empty. I was glad suddenly of human warmth and company and began to feel drowsy. Harriet opened the window a chink and threw out the cigarette butt, rolling back the glass against the blast of the icy outdoors. I finished my smoke and ground the butt into the ashtray.

'Why not have a snooze?' she said. 'I'll take the baby,' and she pulled down the dividing arm and I gave him to her, handing him over carefully, supporting his head. I saw that her eyes which were fixed on the baby were no longer smiling, but were hard and cold. I put my head back and shut my eyes, no longer drowsy, but aware of everything, peering under my lashes, watching my sleeping child in Harriet's arms. In my pocket was the gilt button with the eagle emblem. I had mentioned it to no one.

After a while Dr O'Shaughnessy said in a low voice. 'I think Peg's asleep. Are you asleep Peg?' adding when I didn't answer 'She'll need a lot of rest and building up. I gather she's been behaving very oddly and it's no wonder when you think of the year she has been through. It's important that she is free of stress; she's a dead ringer at the moment for a nervous breakdown.'

Harriet murmured assent. 'Poor old Peg. Don't worry; I'll look after her.' I rested. I listened to the car motor and occasionally looked through my lashes at the countryside. My mind was full of things I wanted answers to. Perhaps somewhere in Glenallen the answers were waiting.

We were almost there. Towering before us now was Knockshee, dark against the winter sky. I sat up, shivered, and Harry asked me solicitously was I cold. I shook my head. Then the gateway to

Glenallen came into sight, the bare trees along the avenue, the view of the house, with its shiny new slates and guttering, generating a sensation in my chest like as if a void had opened there, as though someone had reached in and plucked out my heart.

'Beautiful as ever,' I whispered.

'Yes,' Harriet agreed, so quietly that I hardly heard her, her voice low and full of passion.

Dr O'Shaughnessy drove the car to the stable yard near the back door and then I was helped alight and Harriet carried the baby into the house. There was a biting wind in the yard. I glanced at the loose boxes where I had so often seen Brian, sleeves rolled up, his rumpled hair curling at the nape of the neck, his face intent.

Where are you, my poor love? You said you were going home!

Murty appeared, his cap well jammed down on his forehead, his face full of smiles showing a few blackened teeth. He grasped my hand.

'Welcome back, ma'am.' He glanced at my son in Harriet's arms. 'I wish you joy,' he added awkwardly and then said with real candour, 'It was a terrible sad thing about poor Master Brian. Wasn't he the hero fighting that Hitler? His father was proud of him.'

I felt Harriet start; she was walking in front of me, carrying the baby.

'Thank you, Murty.

I expected to find Eilie and Nora in the kitchen, having forgotten for the moment that they were gone, but it was empty, warm because of the Aga, but devoid of the busy ambience which I had known.

'I had to let them go,' Harry explained. 'There's only Murty here now and two part timers. I will

422

hang on until the war is over and things pick up again. I've started breeding ponies to help us over the war; there's a good demand for fourteen or fifteen hand ponies.'

I nodded. I didn't tell her that Eilie had been to see me.

I took my baby back from Harriet and as the kitchen was deliciously warm I sat in the chair by the Aga rocking him.

Murty followed inside with my case and was told by his mistress to bring it upstairs.

'I've given you your old room. I'm next door so I'll be on hand if you need help with your man,' she said, indicating Dan.

'Your man' woke up, stared sleepily at her with round blank eyes, screwed his face into a grimace and started to howl. I rocked him against my shoulder.

'I'd better feed him.'

The O'Shaughnessys said they would leave us to it; that we must be tired. They refused offers of tea. I heard their departing footsteps, the shutting of the car doors, the sudden surge of the motor, the sound of the engine dying away. Then silence, except for the wind wailing in the yard and whistling at the back door.

I brought Dan upstairs for his feed, entering the room which had been Brian's bedroom, and mine, with nostalgia and fear that so much could have changed. The atmosphere in the house was different; it had become cold, unwelcoming, as though people had never lived or laughed in it. There were signs of the work which had been completed, pale pink plaster ceilings upstairs which were still waiting to be painted, small pockets of plaster dust in corners here and there.

The bed had been made up for me; there was the remains of a turf fire in the grate; beside the bed was a wonderful Victorian cradle, painted white with a patchwork quilt and a white canopy. But there was a sense of something else in the room, something very wrong, something tense and anguished. I tried to ignore it, attempting to resurrect the feeling of my first days in Glenallen. I was really an impostor now, but an apparently successful one and it gave me a respite, a chance to search for whatever it was Tom had been talking about, to find out, if I could, why an RAF button should have been found in the cellar. A chance to put Glenallen out of my mind and system forever.

I went to the window, saw the sweep of the lawn and the little lake, now empty of swans, surveyed the room again, the polished furniture, the vase of gleaming honesty on the table, Brian's gymkhana trophies, newly polished, which were set out on the mantelpiece. I picked up a small silver cup and looked at the inscription - 'Won by Brian Fitzallen on Trixie: 1934.' How nice of Harry, I thought. She has been to a lot of trouble. I threw a few sods on the fire and sat down on the bed to breast-feed my baby. He took the nipple fiercely, ecstatically clenching tiny fingers and toes.

I heard the door open and Harry came in. She sat in the armchair and watched for a while

'You don't mind, do you, Peg?' and then she murmured that of course it used not to be the done thing for people to breast-feed; only the tinkers did it, but she said it so genially that it would have been stupid to have taken offence. The baby began to fret, sucking in vigorous frustration.

'Silly,' I said. 'But I haven't got enough for him today, I think. I'll have to make him up some. I left the tin of Cow and Gate in the kitchen.'

I was hoping she would offer to make up the feed, but she said she would mind him while I was downstairs and I went down as quickly as I could, my back wobbling a little, being still weak, wondering why the milk had dried up on me.

In the kitchen I made up a feed, cooled it under the tap and then, as I was about to go back upstairs, Murty came in the back door with a creel of turf.

'Bitther cold today, ma'am.'

I assented, suddenly consumed with the desire to ask him what was burning into my brain.

'How are things, Murty?'

'Ah the place never really recovered from Master Brian goin' off,' he muttered. And then, glancing over his shoulder and lowering his voice, he added. 'But sure, he came back you know.'

I jumped. 'Where is he?'

'He's gone.' His face was screwed up in a frown, as though I had asked him something mad.

I stared at him, trying to see his eyes under the peak of his cap. 'For God's sake, Murty, explain what you're talking about.'

Murty coughed, rattling sputum in the back of his throat, then spoke in a husky whisper: 'I don't want to alarm you, ma'am, but I did see him, and I told no one else, so as not to be upsettin' them.'

'Where did you see him, Murty?'

'I saw him, at night, about the time they say he died, crossing the yard in the direction of the house. He was in a queer class of flying uniform and I heard his boots on the cobbles. 'Bout the

425

time he died.' He raised his thumb towards the mountain. 'The hill always calls them back!'

I leaned against the wall, feeling the shivers start from the middle of my backbone. 'He came down Knockshee. I saw him too in dreams.'

Murty nodded as though this came as no surprise to him.

Harriet's strident voice came from the landing.

'Peg! He's wet!'

I walked back up the kitchen stairs, heard my feet echo on the tiles in the hall, glancing into the dining-room and drawing-room en route. They were big and lifeless and cold and covered in dust sheets and for some reason I was terribly afraid.

Chapter 18

Harriet and I got along together, the sort of studied good relations which spring from deliberate diplomacy. She put herself out to be charming, refused initially to let me do anything except feed the baby and change him. 'I'll do that,' she would say, jumping up to prevent me going out for turf or sweeping the floor, or reaching for something on the shelves in the pantry. It was nice to be looked after like this; my back was like jelly for a few weeks.

When I suggested that in a month or two I should look out for myself she shook her head, pooh-poohing the suggestion. 'You can stay here. Why do you want the bother of a job? You're not well. You need to rest.'

'I'm perfectly well; only tired and that will go.'

She leaned back in the kitchen chair, long legs crossed, head thrown back, fair hair curving under at the shoulder, reminding me for a moment of Mary, except that she was wearing a jumper with several moth holes and an old pair of ski-pants that had seen better days. She did a lot of work on the farm herself and would come in with muddy boots and cheeks flayed from the cold. Later, having bathed, she would be elegant, manicured.

'You are very important to me, Peg,' she announced one day after lunch.' I don't have much left in the way of family. It can be lonely here, you know.'

I was touched and longed to trust her. But I dared not trust her, dared not allow myself to be drawn into the cosy camaraderie she offered. She was like a hypnotist offering a seductive delusion as substitute for reality, someone who sucked to herself one's sense of direction, one's will.

Behind her the heavy aluminium kettle was singing on the Aga, the coppers on the mantelpiece above were bright with the polishing I had given them the day before. I had in fact taken charge of the kitchen, despite Harry's protests, discovering culinary skills I did not know I possessed, my child near me in the pram which the O'Shaughnessys had brought over as a present. 'It used to be Cissie's,' Mrs O'Shaughnessy said, her eyes full of melancholy.

And the presence of the baby was the inducement which would have kept me anywhere just to be near him, as he slept and woke and smiled and gurgled and kicked. Sometimes he would look at me with a half smile when I talked to him, the smile Lucien would wear when pretending to be surprised at something I had said. I began to realise that I would never elude the memory of Lucien; I would have to consign it to the sector of the mind marked 'memorabilia' and leave it at that. It was not necessary to forget; it was necessary only that I should not reach out or yearn for him.

But why yearn for him and not for Brian? When had this change come about? It had emerged against my will; it had to do with the exhaustion associated with my relationship with the man I had married, the draining of my life force to sustain it. And it had to do with joy, the alchemy of the body and the spirit which Lucien had brought me, although it was not properly mine.

428

Despite Harriet's protestations I wrote a letter to Mother Mercy telling her that I had been widowed and now had a child and that I needed a job. Did she, by any chance, need a science teacher?

Were it not for the dreams, life would have been tolerable. But the dreams were worse; night after night I woke up sweating, hearing Brian calling me, hearing him scratch on the door. I saw him come down Knockshee in leather flying jacket and cap and his heavy tread sounded on the stairs. I told Harry about the dreams. 'I keep having those nightmares about Brian. Once I thought he might even have come back here. Murty said he saw his ghost.'

She started. 'Murty sees everyone's ghost,' she said and she shook her head and said I must still be very cut up about Brian. She never met my eyes when she spoke of him.

'In the dreams he tells me to go away!'

She did not react, except to narrow her eyes.

'You can't go away just because you were told to in a dream! This is the twentieth century, not Pharaoh's Egypt!'

I laughed. 'I know.' Then I added, 'Is there a tunnel or passage under this house?' It had been on my mind, prompted by the recollection of what Brian had told me on our first evening in Glenallen.

The question seemed to take her by surprise. She was silent, tense. Her voice, when she answered, was very soft, very conversational in tone. 'Why do you ask?'

'Brian told me once that there was one and that you had found it.'

429

'I see. He was right; there is a tunnel. We shall look at it sometime; it is difficult to open, but I will show it to you very soon!'

She put her cup down so suddenly that it overturned. I jumped to get a cloth from the sink. I mopped the table and then the floor, reminded of the day long ago when David had used the cat for this purpose and how Cissie and Mary and I had laughed.

And the longing for the sight of their faces was there with me, and the sense that time was a thing, a substance which caught and trapped the essence and reasons for one's life and hid them away forever.

'Do you think Mary McElligott is dead?' I asked her suddenly, squeezing out the rag in the chipped old sink, anxious that she shouldn't see how wet my face had become. I already had told her that Mary had disappeared in the London blitz.

'If she were dead Murty would have seen her on the mountain.'

After a short silence I asked quietly, something I had been longing to ask, 'What happened to her here, that day when she was hurt by the goat, when she was small?'

Harriet stood up, jerking her head to one side to fling back her hair. 'For God's sake, you don't want to know about that!'

'I do!'

'Well, if you must know, Peg. She was done in by a fellow we had working for us. The whole thing was hushed up, because it was more important that her reputation should be unblemished than that the man should be punished.' She paused, 'Usual bloody thing in this

430

country.' She spoke with cold anger, looking down at me.

'So he got off scot free?' I demanded. 'This man who destroyed her life?'

She gave a grim laugh.

'They generally do ... get off scot free. But not that one, not that one,' and she gave that same grim laugh again.

'What happened to him?'

I heard Murty clanking a bucket in the yard and prayed he wouldn't come in.

'He had made the mistake of trying the same thing on me.'

I watched the face before me and the faraway focus of her thought, the way her breathing quickened. 'What did you do?'

Harriet smiled to herself and made no answer.

Murty coughed, coming through the scraping back door, taking off his hat, washing his hands at the sink.

'There's stew in the pot, Murty.'

'Thank you, ma'am.'

That evening I went down to the cellar with a torch. It was cold and damp and full of a lonely, brooding atmosphere I could not endure. It contained various discarded household items, old brooms, bottles, washboards, a hand wringer, broken kitchen chairs, cracked basins and ewers. It was divided into rooms like the floor above, but the walls were bare granite, the chips of mica glinting in the torchlight, slick with damp. I crept around it quickly, full of fear because of the darkness, imagining all sorts of things in the shadows. I shone the torch over the flagged floor and over the walls, but found nothing remarkable. There was no sign of another strange

431

button or anything else which would require explanation. Did Nora really find the button in the cellar? Or had it been another instance of her proclivity for practical jokes. There had never been any proof that it had been Harriet and not Nora who had planted the necklace in my room the year before. Nora might have stage-managed the whole thing.

When I came up from the cellar I went through every room in the house, looking for anything which would indicate that Brian had come back. I found nothing. I began to feel foolish. Thousands of women lost their husbands in action; how many of them crept around old houses to find some kind of proof to the contrary. Should I confront Harry with the evidence? She would only laugh. Nora could have picked up that button anywhere. Plenty of Irishmen had joined the RAF.

The rooms were shrouded in dust sheets. I looked at myself in the drawing-room mirror and remembered the evening I had first stood in this room as a bride. The old relaxed atmosphere was gone, replaced by one that was tense and hostile. I put it down to the way the furniture was covered and the rooms unusable.

I caught sight of myself in some of the mirrors when I was not braced for it and registered shock at my figure, tummy still bulging. I needed exercise. I mentioned it to Harry later who told me I should do some riding - it would be just the thing to pull the tummy back. 'There's nothing as good for the insides of a person as the outsides of a horse.' So I went out to find Murty and tell him I would be riding the next day. I had been trying to pluck up enough courage to go to the top of Knockshee and now the time was ripe.

'I'll ride Joey.'

Murty was tidying the tack room and looked at me over his shoulder. 'Glory be to God - haven't you learnt yer lesson?'

I laughed. 'It's alright. It wasn't Joey's fault that time. It was mine! And he would have been very quiet if he hadn't been in a hunt.'

As I turned to leave I thought of what Harry had told me at lunch-time.

'Murty - can I ask you something?'

He looked back at me again from beneath his filthy peaked cap. 'Fire ahead.'

'I understand something awful happened here a number of years ago - a little girl was assaulted by the assistant stud groom. What happened to the man?'

Murty had gone back to saddle soaping some leathers with embarrassed gusto.

'Sure he was killed!

'How did he die, Murty?'

He shrugged. 'Didn't a stallion kill him. He was sacked anyway, but the stallion did for him, kicked his head in! Good enough for him too.'

'You're sure it was a stallion?'

'Of course I'm sure. Didn't I hear the animal going mad? Wasn't I in the yard. Though why the stallion should have taken on like that I don't know. '

'I don't suppose Miss Harry was around at the time?'

He turned to me, looking at me carefully.

'She was around, right enough. But don't be imagining she had anything to do with it. They were all warned to keep away from the stallions.'

'Of course I don't think that, Murty.'

433

I saw Dr and Mrs O'Shaughnessy at mass, two rows behind us. They smiled and Mrs O'Shaughnessy whispered, 'How's the baby?' and I whispered, 'Fine.'

After mass I went to the presbytery and talked to the curate about having Dan baptised and he suggested the following Saturday, noting in his small brown diary the names I wanted for my son - Daniel Lucien - with raised eyebrows. From the kitchen came a smell of cabbage and roast beef. The sitting room in the presbytery was spotlessly clean, turf fire smouldering, a photograph of the pope and a series of clerical photographs, men in long cassocks and black birettas. A tall bookcase with glass doors filled one corner, leather bound volumes behind the glass. There was a huge steel engraving in a black wooden frame, showing some sort of cataclysm, half naked people trying to shield themselves from mountains spitting fire and the earth opening under them. The legend on the picture read, 'The Opening of the Seventh Seal.'

As I left the Presbytery I saw Harriet waiting for me in the trap, staring across the fields towards Glenallen and the hill behind it. Knockshee looked olive green, with browny patches in the shifting light. I transposed it in my mind to the engraving in the sacristy, a mountain vomiting death. It looked very innocent in comparison.

Harriet's face looked into the wind and the fair strands of her hair blew under her hat. I approached the trap, aware that she did not know I was there, watching the thoughtful tension in the way she held her head. I was not prepared for the sudden surge of hatred, the memory of Tom's corpse in the haggard, of Brian's face in

Knightsbridge on the receipt of her letter, of the porcelain basin with the little body of my first baby under the bloodstained towel. I tried to freeze the emotion; maybe I was mad; I could not trust myself; afterall I had seen someone who had not been there; 'Maybe you're the jinx' she had said to me once.

Harriet turned, saw me, narrowed her eyes and her mouth smiled. 'Ah, there you are. Hurry up. We're dropping in on the O'Shaughnessys.'

I got into the trap, pulled up the step and shut the door.

'Your hands are shaking,' Harriet said after a moment. 'Did the priest say something to upset you?' She turned to look into my eyes, her own sharp and penetrating, as though she could read my soul. I clenched my hands to stop them trembling.

'No.'

She flicked the pony with the whip and we were off, swaying along, my driver waving at all the people who greeted her.

'Morning Pat! 'Morning Molly!'

'Miss Fitzallen. Grand day!'

Nobody addressed her as Mrs Donlon.

Here and there banks of daffodils had appeared; the trees were covered with small hard buds. Someone had a few cherry trees which were already in bloom. The lambs scampered about near their mothers, some with black faces, black legs.

I thought of my own small lamb, at Glenallen, being babysat by Peter, who had come home for the weekend and who had attended an earlier mass. I felt like an internee who has been let out for the day, but a turbulent one, struggling with violence.

435

'Well', Harriet demanded. 'Did you arrange the christening?' And I told her it would be on the following Saturday.

A few minutes later the gateway of Cissie's home came in view and I watched every nook and cranny along that road with greedy recollection. That first day was clear in my mind, with Des driving, Cissie laughing, the drizzle and the wet gravel spewing from the sudden braking, my introduction to this new world.

We turned into the short driveway, by the hedge which was yellow with forsythia and were met by our host at the door. Having a car, he was home well before us. He gave me his hand to help me down from the trap. I entered the front door of the house where I had known such contentment and the taste of being fourteen and happy came back into my mouth.

We were brought into the sitting-room, which was almost unchanged, except for the portraits of Cissie and Des as smiling teenagers, a photograph of Des in his airforce uniform, reminding me of Brian, and a recent one of the twins Barbie and David. I was struck with how the twins had matured; no longer the harum scarum pair of mischief makers. They were away at boarding school and the house felt empty. There was a cheerful turf fire and we stood around it for a moment chafing our hands.

Harry drank whiskey and water and I had a sherry and began to feel light-headed, finding in the glow of the alcohol some release from the pent up emotions of half an hour before. I answered questions about the baby with doting maternalism, while Harriet sat ostensibly patient, before saying that she would just love to see the garden.

'How are you getting on with your sister-in-law?' Dr O'Shaughnessy asked, when Harry and her hostess had gone into the garden to look at Mrs O'Shaughnessy's new herbaceous border where the daffs had put up their heads. He leant over to the brass log box and threw a couple of sods on to the fire. Some smoke escaped into the room filling it with aromatic pungency.

'Well. But I am damned with nightmares. I sleep with the light on and it does no good. Sometimes when I am dropping off I even hear Brian's voice.'

He studied me.

'What does he say?' he asked in a careful voice.

I reddened as I met his grey eyes, the whites untidy with red veins.

'He says, 'Leave us. Take the child and go.'

'Does this frighten you?'

'Terribly. But then I wake up and realise it's only been a dream.'

I looked away. The taste of my anger was still in my mouth, but its violence had dissipated and now seemed immoderate. The kindly atmosphere of the house enveloped me.

'I've been a bit peculiar for some time,' I said with as much lightness as I could summon. 'I'm getting worried. I was never like this.'

'Peculiar in what way?'

'I am full of secret violence.'

There was silence. Dr O'Shaughnessy looked at me carefully. I felt immediately that it had been dangerous to have made this avowal and laughed as though to indicate that I had been joking.

Dr O'Shaughnessy changed the subject.

'The baby is doing well?'

'Very well.'

'Good' he said. 'I'll drop by some day soon to look in on him. No feeding problems?'

'No. He's fond of his feed.'

'Well, I suppose you know it's important to follow the instructions for the formula, the exact amount of water?'

I looked at him sideways, certain that he was talking for the sake of talking, borrowing time while he made some kind of private assessment.

He laughed then.

'Sorry, Peg. I keep forgetting yesterday's children are the science graduates of the present. I am getting old! But I am concerned about these dreams of yours. You seem to have overheated your imagination. I hope things are easy for you in Glenallen. I hope you're not drinking tea before you go to bed. Warm milk's the thing, or cocoa, if you can get it.'

His voice was almost too gentle, but it had, at the same time, a careful professional ring to it.

Then he murmured, leaning towards me confidentially, 'I'm glad that you have settled down with Harriet. It's only natural that she should be concerned for your welfare - especially as your son is the heir.'

I coughed; sherry went down the wrong way.

'No!' I said, coughing and shaking my head. 'Of course he isn't.' And I was still coughing when Harry and Mrs O'Shaughnessy came back from the garden. We went out to the trap then and home along the blustery road in virtual silence, feeling the occasional bitter sting of the rain.

When we neared the house Harriet said suddenly, 'I'm going to have to sell Ballycloghan! But I'll get all your stuff out first.'

I turned to her. I wanted to knock her out of the trap. 'You can't. It's my home!'

She shrugged. 'Your home is here Peg. You belong here now.'

'I don't. I'll get a job; I'll buy it off you!'

She looked at me with a kindly expression. 'Don't get upset. No decision has been taken yet.'

Peter was in the kitchen, various papers spread out on the table, while he scribbled rapidly, one foot on a spring of the pram which he was gently rocking. He collected his papers when we came in and said he would retire to the library to finish his work. I glanced at the documents in his hand, bundles tied with pink ribbon, bearing headings like 'The High Court' and words like Plaintiff and Defendant, and one documents with the typed heading 'Case to Counsel to Advise and Settle Proceedings'. I saw how hard he worked, and was curious also at the nature of the work being done by this closed, cold man. I was afraid of him, afraid of his hauteur, afraid of the soul he carried within him which was capable of writing the kind of letter he had written to Cissie. I hated him because of it, but I was puzzled by him too.

Over lunch we discussed the forthcoming christening and Peter, to my surprise, said that he would come home for it.

'Mind you,' he said, indicating the baby in the pram who was waving fat fists in the air, 'he looks just the sort of chap who could sport a name like "Daniel Lucien".'

There were a few seconds of silence.

'I didn't call him Brian,' I said, 'because it is a name which causes me pain; the name was intended for the child I lost two years ago.'

439

'That's over,' Harry said, suddenly rubbing her hand over her eyes.

'Not to me!' There was silence. Everyone applied themselves to their food.

When Peter had come home for the weekend he had greeted me with his old aloofness. He was looking strained and a swatch of grey hair had made its appearance at one of his temples.

I wondered to what extent he, and not Harriet, had been the *eminence grise* in the events which had taken place at Glenallen and I avoided his presence while he was at home as much as possible. On a couple of occasions he had gone out of his way to talk with me privately. He had even mentioned Cissie. 'You remember Cissie, Peg. I don't think her family have got over her.' But I was not to be drawn. I had seen the sudden desperation in his eyes and put it down to a guilty conscience. He had cut short his stay and had gone back early to Dublin.

Now I wished I could talk to him, wished I could trust him. He was a lawyer; he could help put me straight about so much. But watching him and Harriet over lunch, the almost silent communion there seemed to exist between them, I knew that talking openly to him, asking for explanations, was out of the question. And yet I felt in him no animosity.

When lunch was finished I felt his eyes on me for a moment, caught in them a certain puzzled inquiry. Harriet went to bed with a migraine and I washed the dishes in the big old sink and stacked them methodically on the wooden draining board for Peter to dry. He applied the same careful attention to drying dishes that I had seen him give his legal papers.

'You're very efficient. I can't keep up with you.'

I scoured the pots and he took them from me, one by one, and dried and put them away and would have left the kitchen. 'Anything more I can do?' he asked.

'No!'

He was about to shut the door behind him when I said, 'Peter ...'

He turned back, waiting politely.

'You probably know that I'm having terrible problems with dreams about Brian. Harry's come into me several times during the night in the last couple of weeks because I was shouting in my sleep. You see, he left me a note to say he was going home. Murty says he saw his ghost. I suppose you don't know anything about him?'

I reddened, realising how foolish I must sound.

Peter's face closed, as Harry's had, at the mention of his brother's name, the old contempt at the ready.

'No. He didn't come back here. I'm sorry Peg, but you shouldn't listen to Murty, or any of the other bits and pieces of superstition you're likely to hear around here. You've been through a hard time. Listening to the likes of Murty only makes it worse.'

'Is there any truth in the suggestion Dr O'Shaughnessy made, that the baby is the heir,' I blurted then. I had been considering it over lunch and knew how bizarre such an assumption would be. The embarrassment of it was terrible.

Peter seemed to start. He looked into my eyes and said very slowly. 'I do not think so, Peg. I think you know so too. After all, we know who Brian was, but who is Lucien ?'

I paled, gasped.

441

'Don't mistake me,' he went on. 'I'm not condemning you. Brian had his chance and threw it away. Do you know if he actually made a will?'

'Not as far as I know,' I muttered. 'Sure he had nothing to bequeath.'

He looked at me with inscrutable eyes.

'Indeed!'

He would have left the room then, but I asked him one further question. 'Peter, do you know where the underground passage in the house is ?'

'It's a family legend,' he said after a moment or two, 'but that's all.'

'Harriet said there was a passage. She said she would show it to me. I thought it might be in the cellar, but when I was down there recently I saw no sign of anything that looked like an underground entrance.'

He shook his head. 'I think she's teasing you, Peg.'

When Dan was fast asleep I changed into slacks and took myself out to the stable yard. Murty saddled up my old friend Joey and helped me into the saddle. I could no longer jump up by putting my foot in the stirrup and grasping the saddle. 'I feel like an old woman.'

'It'll all come back ma'am. Don't worry. '

The two dogs came sniffing and yelping with delight, tails wagging, tongues lolling.

'You've got company.'

The dogs belted out of the stable yard ahead of me. Joey plodded along, which suited me exactly, breaking into a trot at one point, but I discouraged this.

It was a mild, damp day and the air was sweet. Here and there were crocuses, purple in the damp grass and the daffs had sent their slender green

442

spears up everywhere, ready to flower in all their glory in a week or two. I passed red fields of winter wheat, and fields of mangles, their battered fronds purpled by the frost. Joey stopped abruptly at one of the open clamps to bite at the sweet's roots, grinding and clanking them against the bit. Then he turned his head to each side and wiped the green froth on my legs.

I kicked him, urged him on, staying to the sides of the fields, and kept my eyes open for the grass harrow. I saw it eventually, rolled up and buried in the long grass by the gateway to the mare's paddock. I pressed on then with greater confidence to the Long Field and thought I would walk Joey down the length of it to the batty. Joey was skittish and it was difficult to get him to manoeuvre for gate closing. All the gates had iron drop loops at the top so I did not have to dismount.

The two red setters frisked ahead, chasing anything that moved, nosing into burrows, piddling and sniffing each other's behinds. A rabbit scampered suddenly into the field from the hedgerow, changed his mind and ran back and the dogs took off after it, returning defeated because their quarry had disappeared into a burrow with a flash of white scut. Higher up at the top of the field I saw at least two interrogative rabbity heads, with long twitching ears, sticking out of their warrens and inspecting us, before withdrawing to discuss matters underground. Sentinel rooks in the hawthorns and ash trees croaked a warning at my approach, but the flocks of rooks gleaning the fields ignored me because I carried no gun. The mountain was straight ahead of me, misty at the rise.

I let Joey graze at the top of the Long Field, stood in the stirrups to ease my back and looked over the hedge into the batty. The snipe bog was flooded and the High Field was full of mist. There was no point in going any further. But the dogs had other ideas and they wriggled through the hedge and tore across the higher fields in great delight, turning and wheeling. One of them returned with something in his jaws; I thought it was a piece of old wellington boot. My back was killing me so I turned Joey around and he trotted a bit, shaking me up. I had better be fit again at this rate, I thought, thinking longingly of a hot bath.

When we got back to the stable yard I took both feet out of the stirrups and slid off. My legs felt like jelly. I could hardly straighten them and leant against Joey for a moment. Murty came to take the horse.

'What's the dog got?' he asked, but Rex turned away from him and came towards me and I saw in his mouth the object that he had dropped several times on the journey home, but would not abandon. I took it, chewed and sodden with saliva, from his triumphant mouth, realising as I stared at it exactly what it was. I had seen them often enough in the cinema on the Pathe Newsreels covering the airforce, a pair of aviator's goggles. I heard the kitchen door open and pushed them into my pocket.

Chapter 19

Daniel changed; week by week he became bouncier, began to lose the deceptive fragility of the newborn; his eyes were now a confirmed brown; he had a goodly layer of fat and dimpled when he smiled. I used to examine his fists and wonder where the knuckles were, comparing them with my own. He was almost eight weeks old and Murty told me he would soon be 'self winding.'

I got a letter from Galway, St Catherine's. Mother Mercy wrote to say she was very sorry to hear about my having been widowed but that they had no teaching vacancies. The writing paper was stiff, watermarked, with the school crest - a coat of arms of sorts with a pierced heart of Mary radiating like the sun, ribbon-like embellishments drooping importantly underneath.

'I hope you will find a post elsewhere, and I hope that you will come to see us sometime and bring your little son.

Yours affectionately in JC .'

I remembered Brian's comment when Mother Mercy had written to congratulate me on my marriage. 'Why can't they leave the late JC out of it? '

I had accused him of blasphemy and he had laughed. 'Don't you see how handy a crime blasphemy is? It pre-empts questions. And if you can't question things, you are powerless.'

Harry saw me reading the letter at breakfast and asked me who it was from. I handed it to her and watched her face as she read.

'Surely you're not thinking of leaving, Peg. You can't. What will happen to poor little ducklet?'

She had taken to calling Dan 'ducklet' and it set my teeth on edge.

'You couldn't possibly look after him on your own ... you out working every day.'

'I don't know, Harry. I don't want to outstay my welcome here.' I was careful what I said; I had not told her what Rex had found in the batty. I felt sure that Peter must have shared with her his reservations about the baby's paternity which he had made so plain to me. But she showed no sign of this.

'Fiddle-sticks. But, of course, if you really want to go, you're welcome to leave Dan with me.'

Leave Dan with her! Leave his little fat fits and his clenched toes! 'Thanks, but I intend to keep him with me. And if I can't get a job in Ireland I'll just have to go back to England. Dan is old enough now for the journey.'

This was not true. The prospect of hauling a small baby to England was not one with filled me with any enthusiasm.

She leaned backwards towards the Aga, took the tea pot and poured herself another cup. 'That solicitor is coming tomorrow. With papers for me to sign. Maybe you'd let him in and put him in the drawing-room.'

'What papers are those?'

She raised her eyes to me, smiled and I saw, because of the way the light caught her, the almost imperceptible lines like thin ripples around her mouth, the wrinkles for some far future, when Time would have etched her story in her face.

'Have you forgotten? About Ballycloghan? You know it will have to be sold!'

I was stunned, filled with hatred for Tom; he was the one responsible for this state of affairs. And hatred for her. How could she do this? She had given me to understand that she had shelved the idea. The prospect of my old home not being there anymore was tantamount to a bereavement.

'Peg. I know how you must feel. But Ballycloghan was Tom's - not yours. You got your entitlement out of it, your education, and Tom got married. Is it so terrible that his widow should inherit it? Things never stay the same forever!'

She spoke gently. She was plausible; she spoke the truth, but I could not help the fury, or the pain.

'I'll get your things taken out, of course,' she added.

'I would like to go back before it's sold!'

She looked at me commiseratingly.

'There's no time! I'm signing the contracts tomorrow. Please try to understand!'

I was suddenly desperately homesick, resentful, blindly resentful although I knew I did not have the right to be. Harriet was Tom's widow. Ballcloghan belonged to her. What she had said was quite true. Tom would have married someday, if not her then someone else. I had my education. It was all I was entitled to.

But as I sat there, feeling the void inside me, the loss of Ballycloghan and all that it had stood for, something died inside me. Perhaps it was compassion, charity, or faith, or whatever was left of them. You had better look out for yourself now,

447

Harriet, I thought. You had better not turn your back.

She ate her breakfast with oblivious thoroughness, boiled egg, toast. It was raining outside, sudden squalls driving against the window. The yard was wet and the trees at the far side swayed in the wind. I saw poor old Murty out in it all, head down against the gale, a sack tied on his shoulders, a brown paper bag on his head. The old blue clock ticked on the dresser. Dan was awake in the pram, looking up at the coloured baubles hanging over his head. He was at peace, waving his hands, occasional small grunts escaping him. The kitchen was quiet, the kettle whispering at the back of the range.

'How are you feeling these days, Peg?'

'Grand,' I lied. I wanted the weather to change, so I could go back up to the mountain and search the batty and the hill itself. Now I was hit by the news of the sale of Ballycloghan. Everything, everything, that had been mine, was gone. And it was all explicable, all accident or coincidence, or the ravages of war; or so the fates which had decreed it would have me believe. Except that I did not believe in fate or accident or coincidence anymore.

She seemed to hesitate.

'In that case maybe you wouldn't mind helping Murty with the mucking out. He's hard pressed at the moment with the other two down with flu.'

I shrugged. I wanted to tell her to go to hell, but counselled patience. The show-down would come eventually. I would bide my tide.

'I'll do it when I've cleared the breakfast.'

'Thanks. I'll look after the lunch.' She stood up, straightening her back, bent over to look at Dan for a moment, smiling that cold smile of hers.

'Dar-ling,' she whispered. 'You won't leave your poor Aunty, will you?' and the baby gurgled and waved his little fists at her.

'Anyway, Peg' she added, lowering her voice, 'You'll never get a visa for both of you. The baby is hardly an essential immigrant.'

Dan began to cry, fretful peevish little wails gathering in intensity. He had already been fed so I picked him and rocked him, putting him against my shoulder and patting his back and he sighed with satisfaction. I put him back in the pram and he started howling again.

'Oh for God's sake, shut up,' I said crossly to him, thinking for a moment how he trapped me, how I was chained by him. I turned to find Harry at the door. She raised her eyebrows, saying she would mind him. Was he too much for me at the moment? Was it alright if she brought him upstairs?

Later, as I worked in the stables I thought again of what Peter had asserted - that Brian had not come back. I had acknowledged long since that this was true. Of course he had not come back; he had been lost in action over the Channel. So what was a pair of aviator goggles doing in the batty. How did a button with the insignia of the RAF get into the cellar?

I went into the kitchen during the course of the morning and found Harriet there. She was crushing something in a delph cup with the back of a dessert spoon, moving her arm when she saw me so that I couldn't see what was in the cup. There was a touch of white powder on the handle of the spoon.

'What's that?'

'Just something for one of the dogs.'

Harriet prepared lunch, Irish stew - which was her culinary forte. She took plates to the pot on the Aga and ladled it out. It was hot and good - plenty of carrots, onions and potatoes and tender pieces of lamb. But I thought I detected a slightly bitter aftertaste.

'Did you put some sort of spice into the stew?'

'Oh - just a hint of mace which I found in the pantry!'

As we finished lunch the garda sergeant, Tony Aherne, appeared. He was a tall big boned man with a prominent jaw. He came into the kitchen, filling the doorway, removed his peaked cap and sat by the table. I was giving the baby a bottle and he made some jocular comment about the child's appetite.

Harry offered him lunch - 'there's some stew left', but he declined.

He accepted a cup of tea, sugaring it plentifully. I saw Harry watching each spoon. He said then, in a very grave voice, that the dog licences had expired and that he would have no option but to prosecute.

'Oh God, I forgot. I have a hundred things to think of. I'll buy the licences tomorrow. Will that do?' She smiled at him, the old vivacious 'Don't be cross with poor me' smile and he nodded, melting. He turned to me.

'How are you feeling these days, Mrs Fitzallen?'

'I'm as good as I ever was. Why shouldn't I be?'

He glanced at Harry. 'No reason at all, ma'am,' he said uncomfortably, 'but I understand you've had a lot of trouble this past year.'

Harry made a face behind his back, copying his lugubrious expression, but when he turned to her she fixed her eyes gravely on the floor, and they bulged a little as they always did in contemplation.

Dan began to slobber. I wiped his mouth, burped him and he stared at the officer of the law, his lower lip wobbling, a trickle of saliva on his chin.

'What names have you chosen?' the Garda asked.

'Daniel Lucien.'

He frowned. 'Unusual. Lucien! It sounds foreign!'

I shrugged.

'Is there a Saint Lucien?'

'Of course there is.'

I remembered asking Lucien the same question in the summer twilight as he lay naked beside me. Now I suddenly, violently, wanted to laugh, remembering. 'He was a martyr. He died of starvation.'

I saw Harriet turn to look at me sharply.

'It was my father-in-law's name,' she murmured 'Daniel Lucien', glancing at me as she spoke. 'Isn't that right, Peg?'

I murmured non committally, busied myself with amusing the baby.

'Isn't it nice that we'll be using the old christening robe again?' she put in after a moment. 'So many Fitzallens have worn it.'

The guard nodded.

'It's nice to keep up old traditions.'

I felt the flush in my face.

'There's no need for that. '

Harry turned surprised eyes on me.

'Of course there's need for it ... Would you christen a Fitzallen in a flannel babyshirt?'

And abruptly there was silence, Harry waiting for response, the guard sipping his tea.

451

'You haven't even seen it,' she exclaimed, jumping up. 'It's really nice. I'll get it.' and she left the room and I heard the clip of her heels on the tiles in the hall, and her footsteps receding upstairs.

Sergeant Aherne smiled.

'Miss Fitzallen is a great young woman.'

'You mean Mrs Donlon,' I corrected him.

'Ah yes, of course. I heard she married and that there was a tragedy.'

I rocked Dan, turned to look at the range where the kettle had started spitting droplets on to the hot surface, saw the figure in the corner, the pale face staring before it disappeared. I cried out, gripped the baby, who screamed and in a moment I felt the sergeant's hand on my shoulder and Harry was back in the room, dropping the cardboard box she had been carrying, and taking Dan from me.

'You saw him,' I said to the guard; 'He was there!'

Harry became very still.

'Now, now, Mrs Fitzallen. You're overwrought.'

Sergeant Aherne looked at Harriet, whose own pallor was like that of the spectre I had seen by the range, Brian's face so white and the eyes so fearfully blank ; or had it been a trick of the light - that white face and eyes? But how could that have been a trick of the light.

Harriet put the baby carefully into the pram, turning her back.

'You should rest,' the sergeant told me uncomfortably and looked around for his cap, eager to be gone. He pushed his blue peaked cap down on his head with his long bony fingers and left, seeing himself out the back door.

I sat down in the rocking chair and wondered why the world seemed to have distanced itself; everything has assumed a dream-like quality, seductive because it offered escape. I saw Harriet rock the pram and stare at me and saw the speculation in her face. But she had receded into some dream. 'Are you alright, Peg?'

I heard her voice as though from a distance, heard Murty come in and look at me and I murmured yes, that I was fine. And I laughed a little, because I was comfortable in my dream world, where the colours were so bright, so rich; I could never have imagined such colours. I was comfortable so long as I did not venture out of the kitchen where I knew the monsters were waiting.

A whispered communication passed between Murty and Harry and he nodded and when he had washed his hands scooped the remains of the lamb stew on to a plate and pitched in. I heard his noisy chewing; it set up a kind of rhythm and I sang a little song to myself that I had heard long ago.

'Haste thee nymph and bring with thee,
Jest and youthful jollity.'

I was aware without caring particularly that Murty looked shiftily at Harriet as though this was in some way remarkable.

Doctor O'Shaughnessy came over later that afternoon; 'a fleeting visit' he said as he appeared in the kitchen; he was on his rounds and just wanted a quick word with Harry. He stared at me sharply, his eyes examining my face.

'Are you alright, Peg?'

'Why does everyone keep asking me that? I'm fine; I have a headache but otherwise I'm fine. Harry is upstairs with the baby.' I went out to the

453

hall to call her. I had dozed off in the chair and was now wide awake, but inwardly I was trembling, wishing I could escape from myself, from the weight which pressed on me and which I could not identify. My head was fuzzy; I remembered the dream I had after lunch with a sense of acute embarrassment and fear; fear for the ease with which I had parted company with sanity.

'Dr O'Shaughnessy is here,' I called up the well of the stairs and we heard her footsteps in the landing.

'Coming!' she called back.

The doctor went up the kitchen stairs to meet her. I went to the lower door, intending to go out to the stable yard for some fresh air, hoping it would clear my head. However, when I opened the door I found that it had begun to rain again, so I went back to the coat stand in the lower hall for a rain coat. I heard Harry and Doctor O'Shaughnessy talking in the hall above and then heard my name, and I waited, hidden by the stairs.

'Really quite frightening,' Harry was saying in a low voice, in which sadness was mingled with exasperation. 'And she's talking of taking that poor child when he has a home here. It's really very sad, but it's dangerous for the baby. She nearly dropped him.' It was difficult to make out the doctor's reply, but his voice sounded anxious.

'I thought she was recovering.'

'But do you think she should be sent somewhere ... for her own good and the baby's. For a while at least. She was shouting at him, just before she lost her marbles completely.'

Dr O'Shaughnessy cleared his throat.

'I don't think that's indicated. She's not dangerous - is she? Just keep an eye on her. She's been through so much. Of course if there's any sign of her becoming violent it will be another matter.'

I leaned back against the old wainscoting; my heart was thumping and the tears were smarting in my eyes. I heard her ask then for a new prescription for her migraine tablets.

'You can't have finished the last ones already. You know they're potentially dangerous - there's ergot in them - they must be taken only as directed. I've told you that.' He sounded alarmed.

'No, no - I just lost the bottle.'

I stumbled out into the rain, wandered into the tack room with its smells of saddle soap and leather and watched the back door.

When Dr O'Shaughnessy came out I ran to car as he started the engine. I half slipped on the cobbles, put up a hand to stop him from leaving.

He opened the passenger door and I sat in.

'I am not mad.'

He started. 'Of course you're not mad. Why do you say such a thing? But you are hallucinating, Peg. You had another turn today it seems.'

'What's the matter with me.'

'I don't know, my dear girl. I think you're of an excitable temperament and that you've had too much in the past year or so ... your husband's death, the birth of your son, the loss of your brother - these things can eventually become too much. I intend to prescribe sedatives and see how you get on. Plenty of rest, good food and no worries. You must forget your plan to go away; why not avail of Harriet's hospitality - she's really very fond of you and the baby.'

I looked out at the yard, at the kitchen window through which I could see Harriet looking out at us. 'She wants to put me away!'

He clicked his tongue, shaking his head.

'It's a pity you overhead that. It was idle speculation; she thinks you need a nursing home, but that would be expensive.'

'Dr O'Shaughnessy.'

'Yes Peg.'

'Could this be something I ate?'

He paused.

'Highly unlikely. There are hallucinogenic substances of course, as you know yourself, drugs and certain varieties of fungi for instance, but that's obviously out of the question here.'

He thought for a moment. 'You haven't been taking Harriet's migraine tablets?'

'No!'

He opened his black bag and took from one of the little drawers a packet of tablets. 'Take one of these when you go to bed. They're sedatives and will help you get a proper night's sleep.'

And then he handed me a small empty bottle.

'And just to be on the safe side Peg - I'd like a urine sample. I'll wait.'

Later, after supper, I put the dishes in the sink and put the butter and milk back into the pantry. And as I did so I noticed a covered butter dish, a dish with a yellow lid which usually belonged in the cupboard with the delph. I lifted the lid. It was full of dried grey mushroom pieces. I tore a piece of brown paper from the half full bag of sugar, wrapped them in it and put them into my pocket.

'Who did you think you saw today when you had that turn in the kitchen?' she demanded while I was setting the table for breakfast.

I felt the suspect fungi in my pocket. 'Brian. And I know you think I'm mad, but I'm not!'

The pupils of her eyes dilated at the mention of her brother's name.

'Oh, I don't think you're mad.'

James Regan, keen huntsman, owner of Conneely House, master of hounds, called that evening. I answered the imperious bell which rang in the kitchen, trudging all the way upstairs and down the hall to the front door. I looked up at this large, moustached man who held himself ramrod straight, all five foot eleven drawn up and looking down at me. I had not seen him for a long time and he obviously did not remember me.

'Is your mistress in?'

I showed him into the drawing-room, which was cold, and went down to the kitchen.

'Mr James Regan to see you, Madam!'

Harriet looked up from the paper, shot me a look of inquiry.

'He wanted to know if my mistress was in!'

She laughed, a genuine melodic tinkle of surprise. 'Poor little Peggie, little piqued Peggie,' and she rose leisurely and went upstairs to the drawing-room, returning about ten minutes later. I knew from her face that she was pleased with herself. She put the box of chocolates he had given her into the cupboard in the dresser. There were several such boxes, unopened, going stale in the darkness.

'He'll be back,' I said. 'He's besotted. '

Silence. 'Of course he is. If you were a man wouldn't you be mad about women?'

'I would be fascinated.'

She snorted, looked at me curiously.

'Are you going to marry him?' I asked after a moment. 'He seems kind ... all those chocolates.' I longed for a sweet, wished she would open a box. She neither ate them herself nor gave them to others.

She yawned noisily. 'Little batty Peggie. Did you do Macbeth when you were at school?'

'Yes. What's Macbeth got to do with anything?'

I was about to change rows on the matinee jacket I was knitting, but dropped the knitting needle and it clanged off the flags, reminding me of one summer's afternoon in Nottingham, long redbrick terraces, the smell of disinfectant and despair. I shivered, glancing at the pram where all that demanding life was sleeping.

'Do you remember the line - Win us with honest trifles, to betray us in deepest consequence?' Harriet went on.

I searched my memory.

'Wasn't that about the witches? What's that got to do with marriage?'

'Don't be obtuse.'

After a moment she said: 'Would you get out the whiskey.'

I opened the cupboard in the dresser to get the bottle, gazing at the boxes of confectionery as I did so.

'Get a couple of glasses. We are going to celebrate.'

I put the glasses on the table.

'What are we celebrating?'

'We are celebrating the fact that I am about to elude the clutches of James Regan Esquire.'

I glanced at her to see if she were joking, but her face was quite serious.

458

'Why do you want to elude him? He seems well set up and nice enough.'

'Well set up? My dear girl - Conneely House is as heavily in hock as this place was.'

'Before you married my brother,' I finished silently and bitterly.

I poured two measures of whiskey.

'Have you never loved anyone?' I demanded; 'Have you always been such a cynic. Did you love Tom?' I knew the answer. I was the cynic now. But I handed her the whiskey, met her eyes. She drank the whiskey neat, leaned her head back against the padded seat back of the rocker. 'I will not discuss Tom with you' she murmured, adding in a low tense voice, 'But this much I will tell you - there was one person I loved all my life.'

'Who was that?'

'My mother.'

I did not answer. I looked over at her covertly, saw that she had closed her eyes.

'But I think she must have died before I was born.'

I felt the fire of the whiskey in my stomach, felt it mount to my brain.

'An unlikely scenario. That would make you the child of the dead.'

I tried to stop the end of the sentence, but it bounced out, propelled by its own momentum. And then there was silence.

'You become reckless, little Peggie,' she murmured after a moment, so softly that I could hardly hear her. 'But perhaps you are right. My mother died at an early stage to everything except my father,' she went on after a moment. 'She came to life again when Brian was born, but it was a selective kind of living, as she only did it through

459

him. I used to follow her around, half blind with worship.'

She voice became so low again that I had to lean forward to catch the words: 'As blind with worship as she was blind to me.'

Her head was still back against the seat, eyes still closed, but from under her lashes I saw the tears escape, glistening as they fell backwards into her hair.

I finished the whiskey, picked up my sleeping baby, said goodnight.

Harriet did not respond. She was either asleep or incommunicado for reasons of her own. So I went upstairs, with Dan's head asleep against my shoulder, shivering as I always did when I entered my bedroom, because it was always so cold; even with a fire it was cold.

I felt the big house like a presence around me, the creaking of timbers somewhere, the dark corners, the brooding moonless night crowding against the window until I drew the curtains. The loneliness was vast, echoing with the spaces in my life that had once been filled. I thought of the pieces of dried mushroom which I had taken out of my pocket and left in a bedroom drawer. I had never really studied fungi and although I had examined the pieces of mushroom, and thought they looked unremarkable enough, I was not convinced that they were innocuous. If they were poisonous I had reason to question my 'instability'.

Dan started to whimper as I put him down. He was not due his feed for another hour, but I needed sleep; I needed deep, dreamless, sleep. And I had the little packet of sleeping tablets Dr

O'Shaughnessy had given me. I should feed him now and get some rest.

I had left his bottle, ready prepared, downstairs, as it would have to be warmed anyway in a jug of hot water. I went back to the kitchen wearily, down three flights of stairs, quietly in my stockinged feet so as not to arouse the echoes.

In the lower hall was a square wooden tool box containing saws and hammers and boxes of nails. It had been left there by the builder who had not as yet returned to retrieve it. Why did such a terrible compulsion seize me, the sudden urge to grasp the heavy hammer - the lump hammer - and bring it with me, to Harriet. It was like a voice in the bottom of my brain, telling me that I must take that heavy hammer and go to her. And, when I resisted, the voice said that all I had to do was to touch it, no need at all to pick it up, but that I must touch it. I stood looking at the box of tools, at the big blunt hammer and thought what harm could it be to touch it. If I only touched it I would be doing no harm and I would silence the awful driving suggestion which held me in a vice-like grip. I reached out my hand and touched the hammer and in a moment I had it in my hand. I stood bemused, staring at it, listening to the compulsive whisper which now told me just to find Harriet, that having a hammer in my hand was perfectly innocent, but that I must go with it to Harriet.

The kitchen door was open a chink, and as I approached I saw Harriet through this chink, head still thrown back, eyes closed, legs crossed, and I realised that she was rocking up and down, backwards and forward. And then, through the silence of the house came the noise of her sudden

461

bitter sobbing. The gasping sounds of grief echoed through the basement, breaking whatever bizarre enchantment had me standing there in the dead of night with a lump hammer in my hand. I dropped the thing back in its box as though it was red hot and ran upstairs, trembling at my own and Harriet's escape, sitting on the bed for a long time holding my head in my hands.

Dan went to sleep, sucking his thumb. I got the bottle for him later after I heard Harriet come up to bed.

Next morning, when I got Murty alone, I produced the little pieces of dried mushroom and showed them to him.

'What species of mushroom is that?'

He picked a piece up between finger and thumb. 'Sure they're just ordinary auld dried field mushrooms,' he said, looking at me in some perplexity. 'They're grand in a stew or boiled with a drop of milk'.

Chapter 20

Peter was down from Dublin for the christening.
The O'Shaughnessys collected us in their car. The
baby wore the camphor scented Fitzallen
christening robe of silk and lace. The white
woollen shawl, which Harriet had brought me
from Dublin, was wrapped around him. His
innocent round eyes stared up at me as I held him
on my knee in the car, focussing with fascination
on the sky where the clouds were constantly
changing shape. The three women sat with the
baby in the back, the two men in the front.

The sponsors were Harriet and Peter. Harriet
held my son as Father Moran, a lighted candle in
his hand, made the sign of the cross upon the
baby's forehead, put the salt of wisdom on his
tongue, exorcised the unclean spirit, poured water
from a cruet on to his head and anointed him
with chrism. Peter, on my child's behalf,
renounced the devil and all his works and pomps.
Dan roared gustily, filling the church with his
wails. They echoed back at us, sobs of fear and
outrage.

The air smelled of incense and burnt wax; long
tonguelets of fire spiralled from the guttering
candles before the statute of Our Lady, who stood
with feet pressing on the head of the serpent, her
eyes addressing Heaven. The stained glass
windows closed out the world, leaving us the
images of martyrdom.

When the christening was over Father Moran turned to me and said he would church me now. He said it as a matter of course, expecting compliance, indicating the back pew where I could kneel to him with lighted candle. I had forgotten about churching; had resented it when I had seen it done at home and had spoken to my mother of it. 'Musha isn't it only a prayer,' she had said. But I knew it was a bit more than that, having read it in her prayer-book - something to be performed at the entrance to the church, a purification ceremony, a readmission on one's knees to the male establishment after the godless female absence of parturition. I looked at the priest and his pious unquestioning certitude.

'No thanks.'

'But you have to be churched, Mrs Fitzallen; all women are after they have had a baby', he whispered.

I was silent. I wanted to say: 'Then all women are mad! Instead you should crown us with flowers and kiss our feet!'

The priest took the lighted candle from Peter and handed it to me. 'It is a blessing,' he said.

Why did it ring so untrue? Why could I not say - Who are you that you should presume to have power to bless me? What is your stole and your lighted candle and your words compared to the power of women?

I hesitated, caught Peter's eye, sensed in him some curious momentary empathy. Mrs O'Shaughnessy dropped her eyes. I read her mind. Was Peg really a bit touched? Surely she wasn't going to refuse. And I knew that women should endorse what betrayed them to avoid unpleasantness. And to avoid unpleasantness I knelt and held the end of the priest's stole as

464

directed and answered the prayers which claimed ascendancy over me and my biology.

We left the church in silence. Father Moran refused the invitation back to Glenallen. Mrs O'Shaughnessy seemed nervous; she whispered something to her husband and he shook his head brusquely. And something in the movement of his head, the quirk in his mouth, reminded me of someone.

Outside I handed my son to Mrs O'Shaughnessy. 'Please hold him for a moment' and I walked into the cemetery to Cissie's grave.

'Cissie' I said, 'I seem to be in trouble. I am trapped. I cannot find out what really happened to Brian. I may be going mad. If you can help me from wherever you are I hope you will. I love you as I always did; I miss you and nothing will ever make me forget you.'

As I returned to the little group by the church door I met Peter at the cemetery gate. 'Cissie's grave?' he asked in a low voice and I nodded.

The O'Shaughnessy left us back to Glenallen, had a drink, gave me a christening present of a silver mug, the name 'Daniel' inscribed on the front. They refused lunch and left to go back to Ballyharris. I brought Dan upstairs and watched the car disappear down the avenue, before divesting him of the Fitzallen christening robe. Did it matter so much afterall that he should have been dressed in this garment, this child who bore no Fitzallen blood? I put him into his cradle, noticing how much more of it he now occupied than he had on the day we had arrived back in Glenallen. I changed into old slacks and sat on the

465

edge of the bed, trying to sort out what I must do now.

I longed for Cissie, for her quiet presence, her unquestioning friendship, and for Mary's caustic good sense. I knew I would have to leave Glenallen as soon as possible. I knew this without understanding why; I had always been uneasy there, the more so of late because of the dreams and my increasingly unstable state which was now a source of immense anxiety to me. But now there was also a sort of subliminal panic which had grown since my visit to Cissie's grave that morning and which did not respond to logic. In my room was the tense atmosphere of despair which had gathered potency and which I had begun to recognise as something with its own reality, as though it were a living thing. I searched for the piece of paper on which Cissie had written that last note, which had so upset her mother, found it where I had left it in the old chocolate box which was home to various precious papers of mine, including some of my mother's and Brian's letters. I put it in my pocket as a sort of talisman.

As I was closing the box a folded letter fell out on the bed. I opened it out; it was Brian's letter - the one he had written to me of his plans to go to England. 'We were being destroyed in this mill of the spirit.' I saw his face as it had come to me in the kitchen recently, white, with blank eyes.

I would have to leave Glenallen, but I did not want to go before I had sorted out some kind of meaning from the confusing muddle that was my life.

Lunch was a quick affair. I excused myself after the main course, without waiting for a slice of the sponge cake Harry had made the day before from the dwindling supply of preserved eggs, 'to celebrate the baptism'.

She was in good form, very charming to Peter and myself and made a fuss of Dan who looked utterly angelic in his long white christening robe. She offered wine at lunch, a bottle which she had found in the cellar, but I refused. Instead, having fed and changed the baby and settled him down for his nap, I asked Harriet to keep an ear out for him, saddled Joey and rode over to Reilly's bank, driven by some need to establish by whatever means I could, a link with Cissie and the past. I needed to remember that the present I found myself in was not a closed circle, that there had been a past and that there would be a future.

It was what the country people called a 'soft day', the budding greenery and the mildness of the weather promising the return of summer. I slowed Joey to a walk, raising my face to the sky, grateful for the freshness of the air and the way it helped me slough off the sense of dread which dogged me.

When I was about a hundred yards from the ditch, I saw a figure on the near side, at what was more or less the exact spot where Cissie had lain with her dead hunter on top of her, her small hand thrust out for the help we were unable to give. It was Peter. He was standing there, his head bent, holding his horse by the reins. I waited indecisively, feeling that I was intruding. The ditch was full of water, as it had been that day, but the barbed wire fence on top of the ditch had been repaired long since.

He sensed my presence, turned, came towards me, studying my face.

'You mourn for her still' he said.

467

I nodded. I was about to urge Joey forward when Peter added suddenly, leaning forward and putting a restraining hand on my rein: 'Please ... there is something I must know...' His voice was suddenly hoarse; 'Why did she do it?'

I forgot in that moment the promise I had once made. 'Why do you think? She was young and desperately in love. And she was pregnant. And her child's father didn't give a curse about her, treated her as though she were some cheap little thrill.'

I saw him start, sensed the immediate imposition of control. 'But I didn't know,' he said. His voice very low; 'I would have done anything for her.'

'Well you had a great way of showing it! You wrote the horrible little letter which killed her.'

His looked up at me. His eyes burned; vulnerability had replaced arrogance.

'What letter? What letter did I write to her?'

'You know that better than I do; let go of my reins.'

But he held them, dragging Joey's head down as I tried to kick him into action. 'I didn't write her any letter. You'd better explain yourself.'

So I told him through angry tears about the letter which denied and insulted her, and took from my pocket the creased piece of paper with Cissie's handwriting, which Mrs O'Shaughnessy had shown myself and Mary on the day after her death, remembering the words without looking at them: 'You consume me, bind me and are only half aware of me. Do something finally ugly and irretrievable and let me go.'

I left the letter in his hands and turned my face to the mountain.

468

What had I to fear; it was only a hill, this Knockshee, fairy mountain, Balor's Eye, something thrown up by buckling of the earth's crust sometime in prehistory. Fairies did not exist; Balor was a myth. It was only a high place from where I could see the surrounding countryside, a good ride in the fresh air. I thought of Tom's words - 'Wasn't I up on the hill. - Didn't I see for myself?' Whatever he had seen for himself I was going to see also.

I crossed the fields. From far behind me I heard a man's cry, 'No. No. No!' and I turned and looked back. I saw Peter two fields away, still standing by the ditch, his head bowed, right arm raised in a repetitive, beating motion, while his horse flattened his ears in fright and jumped away from him. I could see in his raised fist the piece of paper I had given him.

Joey thought at first that he was going back to his stable and was disappointed and recalcitrant when I insisted on turning his head away from the house in the direction of Knockshee. The journey was pleasant to begin with, and I was glad that riding was no longer the onerous business it had been a few weeks ago. Joey lunged occasionally and abruptly for the grass in the ditch, rolling his eyes at me and showing his big yellow teeth as I pulled him away. I tore a stick from a branch, hurting my hand because the stick was strong and green and didn't want to let go, but Joey understand that now he would have to mind his manners and he found reserves of obedience he had not suspected.

I went up to the Long Field, into the batty, inspecting the ground carefully near where I had first seen Rex with the goggles. The batty led on to the high field and then into the common on the lower slopes of the mountain.

On the high land outside the perimeter of the farm the ground was covered in bracken and springy heather and the horse stumbled occasionally, nearly throwing me. There were wisps of dead grass among the heather and pale pink desiccated blooms.

I thought of the hunt and the fall and Lucien coming back to help me and Brian's cry carried back down the wind, 'Don't Cissie!' and Lucien's forehead streaming blood as he stood with Mary, impotent like the rest of us. Where was he now - in France with the Resistance? Was he alive, still thinking perhaps of his chateau with the white shutters, and Mary whom he had loved? Where was she? Even though I loved her I was jealous of her; I thought of Brian whom I had loved and who said he was going 'home', who had been cut away from me so abruptly and who might have left a pair of flying goggles behind him on the mountain, a button in the cellar. And very little else to show that he had lived.

I pressed on, looking back occasionally to find the house becoming smaller, the vista bigger. Over to the west was the O'Shaughnessy's, the hedge running by the road, the outbuildings behind, the lane winding down to the lake which shimmered in the distance. I saw people go by on the road, cycling or in traps. Gogarty's was being patronised - a couple of traps had stopped outside and there was movement around the door. The spire of the church rose through the trees, the cemetery hidden behind it, the new parish hall half built. A dog barked suddenly, his staccato bursts coming towards me, muted by distance.

I stood up in the stirrups to stretch and rest. The leathers creaked with the extra pressure. Joey lowered his head and scratched his foreleg with his chin. The mist was coming down. I was alone, barely visible to anyone scanning the mountain, even with binoculars. So why did I feel I was being watched, that my every step was known to something or someone. It was like the feeling I had in the dreams, the sense of being clearly visible to something I could not see myself, as though I lived behind one way glass. But I was not frightened as I had been in the dreams; I was here with a purpose; it was almost as though I belonged. I glanced into the distance where Brian had shown me the entrance to the souterrain and thought of the words inscribed on the Ogham Stone - *I know mine and mine know me.*

The terrain changed gradually, becoming marshy, brackish streamlets flowing here and there on black boggy ground. I found a path of sorts, followed it upwards.

The high bog on 'Balor's Eye' was almost flat - as Brian had told me once - a bog soggy with recent rains, too treacherous to ride or walk over at this time of year. The ground was lumpy, scarred by yesterday's toil, overgrown with heather.

The clouds were low; wisps blew here and there about my head. The mist shrouded me now, giving an extraordinary eerie sense of being dislocated from time and space and every accustomed thing, so that I began to feel like an elemental being without a human identity.

I picked my way around the edge of the bog, wondering had I been mad to have come up here. I could no longer see exactly where I was going and let the reins go slack, knowing that Joey

471

would find his way back home. It was very silent in the mist, except for the sucking noises of Joey's hooves, the hoarse rasp of his breathing and the rattle of the bit. Little beads of moisture clung to his mane. I rubbed my hand along his neck for the comfort of his warmth, smelt the pungent smell of him.

Joey stumbled; I pulled on the reins which were so slack that I had to straighten my legs and lean backward to pull up his head. He regained his footing and plodded on. I peered through the white fog around us without noticing anything out of the ordinary, scanned the ground within visibility and then, when I had more or less given up any expectancy of fulfilling the purpose of my journey, I thought I saw something materialising out of the mist over to my left, breaking the line of the bog by a con tour not natural to that environment. It was sticking out of the bog and was dirty green in colour. I stared at it for a long time, squinting to focus on it as best I could, cupping my hands around my eyes to cut out distractions and shield out the white light. I moved Joey forward as far as I dared until I was sure that my eyes were not deceiving me. With a sensation of both vindication and disbelief I recognised what I was looking at. It was the rounded fin of the tail of an aeroplane.

When I came back to the house I found Harry in my room playing with Dan. 'We're all fed and changed and happy.' She glanced at my face.

'Where have you been? Why are you shaking?'

I picked Dan up and he started to cry. She said something about him being a bit tetchy, and left the room. Dan opened his mouth wide, showing his little pink gums and his little pink tongue and

472

really howled. It was some time before I could quieten him. He wasn't to be fooled. He knew there was some sort of crisis.

On my way back down the mountain I had resolved to say nothing for the moment to Harry or Peter of what I had found. I was unsure of its implications, nervous, overwhelmed. It was possible that the pilot was still in the plane; it was possible that he was not and that my sister and brother-in-law knew more than were pretending. I would go to the police. I knew that Sergeant Aherne already thought I was mad, but there was no denying what I had found. He would not be able to doubt the evidence of his own two eyes.

Peter spoke clinically to his sister at supper, his voice unusually tight and measured like someone containing anger or hatred or some other powerful emotion. Harriet looked at him, puzzled, answered with jocularity.

'Is something wrong, Peter?'

'You know all about it.'

Later, their voices echoed through the house. Dan was asleep. I was going to cycle to the police station in Ballyharris to tell my story. I came to the top of the kitchen stairs and heard Peter's voice, raised, cutting, and Harriet's scornful replies.

As I approached the kitchen door I began to make sense of what Harriet was saying; her voice was unsteady.

'Why should she have it all - everything our family built during all those generations? This is my house. Daddy was going to leave it to me anyway - if Brian hadn't gone off and done the hero.'

473

'You can't change the facts,' Peter said. 'And you can't get rid of her, you know, because her existence is not altogether convenient.'

He paused. I peered through the crack between the door and the jamb. He raised his glass to his lips and put it down again. He was sipping his drink with unsteady movements.

'Perhaps we should explore what you have done so far?' he said in a dry, tight voice. You wrote a letter to Cissie O'Shaughnessy - don't try to deny it - a letter in response to one she had sent me. Did it occur to you for a moment what the result of that letter might be? Did you give a damn when you stood by her grave? Do you realise what I have gone through since? Does anyone else exist in the whole world except Harriet Fitzallen?'

He raised his hand. 'Let me finish. And what else have you done? Did you by any chance also leave the rat trap in the bran dip long ago? So that someone would find it and provide you with some light entertainment?' His voice was unnaturally calm. 'So that Brian would be blamed?' he added.

'No,' Harry said. 'I didn't plan it the way it happened. It was meant for Brian, but he was sent to bed. I was sorry Cissie found it. I would have taken it out myself except that Eilie was there and would have seen me. I was a child,' she added defensively, her voice trailing off.

'I see,' Peter resumed softly. 'You might have been caught. So you ruined Cissie's hand! I suppose you never noticed the way she spent her life trying to hide it? And you let Brian take the blame for seventeen years until attitudes had crystalised and family life for him was a mockery.'

474

'He doesn't count,' Harry said, with a laugh. 'Not now anyway! And he was always such a pig - Mummy running around after him and Daddy asking his opinion - as though no one else in the family knew anything about horses. You and I were invisible when he was around; even Eilie was crazy about him. And then he marries little Miss Muffat and we have all that nauseating newly wedded bliss, while Daddy gets ready to leave the farm to him. It made me sick.'

She was breathing deeply, tears streaming down her face.

'The farm was mortgaged. You were to get half of the capital in Mummy's marriage settlement. You knew that. And you got the money anyway when she died.'

Harriet snorted. 'Yes. It only paid off part of the mortgage. But I wanted the farm, not the money. Brian and Peg could have stayed. If I owned the place I wouldn't have cared: they could have had more children. I won't be thrown out of my home, made powerless, forced into marriage. It isn't fair.'

I pushed open the door and entered the room.

'Where is Brian?' I asked in a whisper.

I threw the gilt button and the aviator's goggles down on the table in front of Peter.

I heard the patter of rain against the window. There was a bottle of Jameson on the table. Peter's face was white and his hand tensed so hard on his glass that I thought it would shatter.

'His plane is sticking out of the high bog on Knockshee.' I added.

There was silence.

'Is that where you were?' Harriet asked.

Peter stared at the items on the table, examined the button, looked up at me.

'It's up there alright!' I said.

475

He turned to his sister, grabbed her hand and turned the wrist. 'The truth; or do I have to march you all the way to the high bog right now?'

Harriet looked from Peter to me and then back to her wrist. Her brother relaxed his grip.

'You think I had something to do with Brian's disappearance? You believe that of me?'

She wiped away tears with the back of her hand; her eyes were very red.

'Go on,' Peter said.

She pinched the bridge of her nose with thumb and index finger. 'I knew he brought his plane down on Knockshee. He told me where he had landed; it was June and the bog was dry.'

'So he was back here!' I whispered.

'He came back to see Dad, but he was too late.'

'Why didn't you tell me this? Why did you deny it.'

'Because you would believe I had something to do with his disappearance. There is nothing you think me incapable of!'

She turned to Peter. 'It was the week after Dad's death. You had gone back to Dublin and I was here alone; Nora had gone to visit Eilie and say goodbye because she was going to a factory job in England. It was a fine night, just dark. I was in my room and I heard something move downstairs. Then I heard the dogs going mad and then quieten. I thought then it might be you, Peter.

'He gave me a terrible fright - to see him in the kitchen in his flying outfit, boots, leather jacket, - like something out of a newsreel.'

'How's Dad? he wanted to know. So I told him that he was dead. He was very upset. He said that Daddy had written to him to come back to see him.'

'Where did he go?'

She looked up at me.

'How do I know?. He left; he said he was going to be in trouble. He took two cans to get petrol from the tank. Then he left.'

'And that's it?' Peter inquired after a moment's silence.

She gestured. 'That's it. He went back up Knockshee - at least I thought he did! Afterall we have only Peg's story that the plane is still up there!'

'Did he ask you about Daddy's will?' Peter demanded.

'No. He didn't stay very long!'

Peter put his head in his hands. 'So he's still out there somewhere?'

'I don't know. He could have gone off anywhere.'

She glanced at both our faces, her expression candid, the tears wet on her face again. 'Why do you think me capable of the most awful things - What did you think I would do to him? And, for the record Peter, I didn't write to Cissie O'Shaughnessy. I don't know what you're talking about! Show me the letter I'm supposed to have written! Or is this another figment of Peg's imagination?'

I saw the doubt in Peter's eyes.

'I did one bad thing in my life' Harry went on; 'I put the rat trap in the bran dip. I was seven. And you're treating me as though I was the Wicked Witch of the West! I'm sorry that it turned out so badly; I was a child, just a little child! I didn't know what I was doing.'

She burst into passionate sobbing, put a hand over her eyes. 'I'm going to bed. I have a headache.'

477

As she stood up Peter asked, 'Where is this passage under the house that you were going to show to Peg?'

She started. 'What passage. For God's sake. I was joking.' She walked past me to the door and I caught the long sideways glance she threw me before she averted her head. And I saw that her eyes were full of sadness.

When she was gone I turned back to Peter.

'Do you believe her?'

'No! I have spent years watching people lie.'

'Maybe she did tell the truth. There's no proof of anything, except that the plane is on Knockshee.'

'The guards can check that out tomorrow.'

And then I asked, 'What was she talking about before I came in?'

Peter didn't answer. He went into the hall, returned with a huge bunch of keys, the keys Harriet kept in the cupboard by the back door. He handed them to me.

'These belong to you. Surely you must have realised that you are the owner of Glenallen. Brian made a will in England.

'Harry made enquiries from the RAF and they sent it to you. It was forwarded from Nottingham to Ballycloghan. She kept it from you. I didn't know about it until today.'

'How does that make me the owner of Glenallen?'

'Quite simple. My father left Glenallen to Brian. He intended to anyway, and he was impressed that he had joined the RAF; he also thought that he could save Glenallen. And Brian, in his turn, left his entire estate to you.'

I dropped the keys on the floor.

478

'I don't want Glenallen. I only ever wanted to be accepted. I only ever wanted that and to have Brian. Why was that so difficult? You can have it. I'll sign it back to you!'

He shrugged, white faced.

'You may not want Glenallen, but I can assure you that neither do I.'

'Harry does,' I said.

He was silent for a moment, gazing at the rain spattered window, the focus of his eyes far away, his mouth pinched.

'Are you going to give it to her?'

I thought of the past, Cissie dead, Brian gone, Tom stiffening on bloodied hay. I thought of the future, all the years ahead, days and hours interminable. What would they be like for Harriet if she did not possess the only thing, the only place, which made sense of her existence, made life tolerable for her? The place possessed her; it had made her incapable of other love. What would life be like for her if she was excluded from it forever?

I turned to Peter and shook my head.

He looked at me casually as though he had expected nothing else, as though the answer pleased him. 'You have not escaped it either,' he said.

479

Chapter 21

It rained all night. I lay awake listening to the downpour gushing down the eaveshoots, hissing steadily outside the window. I tried to trace in my mind Brian's steps after he had left the house, the long walk to the top of Knockshee. He would have been found by the men if anything had happened to him within the confines of the farm. The only place the men did not frequent were the environs of the souterrain entrance and the mountain. He must be still on the mountain I thought; his body was there. But then I thought - if it were there the ravens would have flocked and someone would have investigated.

The events of the past few months had almost made me forget him as a person, so avid had I been to unravel the possible mystery of his death. Now, since last night, I felt his presence, saw the sudden, teasing quirk of his smile, the crinkling of his eyes. Again, in my mind, he chased me down the avenue and bundled me on to the grass, tickling me, laughing. I remembered Lettergesh, the taste of his breath and his skin and his innocence.

Next morning it was still raining. I put on a raincoat and hat and cycled with Peter to the barracks, splashing through pools on the road, speaking in monosyllables. I told Sergeant Aherne my story, while he looked at me with pity and at Peter with perplexity.

'I see. You saw an aeroplane ma'am? On Knockshee?'

'Yes. Brian came home. Harriet will corroborate this. His body must be somewhere on the mountain. Will you arrange a search ?'

He glanced at Peter, as though to commiserate on my infirm state. How easy was the destruction of credibility. He was quite convinced that he was dealing with someone of infirm mind. No matter what I might say now, it would be met with the same compassionate dismissal. I took the aviator goggles and the RAF button from my pocket and put them down in front of him.

'These were found in Glenallen.'

He examined them with non-committal surprise. 'With all due respect to you, ma'am, this does not mean there's an aeroplane on the top of Knockshee!'

'Please conduct a search,' Peter said, using the courtroom voice I had heard him use the night before to his sister. The sergeant wrinkled up his forehead, gave me the statement to sign and said he would see what he could do. He nodded his head as he spoke, his eyes considering us. There was only himself and Garda McGrath. Tomorrow maybe. When the rain had stopped.

Sergeant Ahearne came to see Harriet that evening, but she had gone to Dublin without warning, leaving only a note to say she was going to stay with Claire de Lacy. The sergeant seemed disinclined to trouble himself further, but Peter insisted the search must be made. 'You can ask some members of the Local Defence Force to help, if you want.'

'Sure you wouldn't want that! Think of the embarrassment if there's nothing up there!' He spoke in a half whisper, turning his head so that I might not hear.

481

So next day we set off on horseback, the sergeant, Peter and myself, for the high bog on Knockshee. It was a cold fresh day, the ground very soft after the rain, the sky clear except towards the west where a grey cloud-bank was massing.

We reached the high bog without incident, stopping at intervals to inspect the terrain around us. Peter had binoculars and used them constantly to scan the sides of the hill. The ground squelched and sucked at the horses' hooves. It was not possible to walk across the bog and I could not remember where exactly I had seen the tail fin of the plane; the mist had shrouded any physical features which would have been a landmark. I had seen it purely by accident, having given Joey his head, being lost myself. It had come out of the mist, a green tail fin, sticking up at a forty-five degree angle, so bizarre in that environment that I could not possibly have been mistaken.

I explained all this when the sergeant asked where exactly I had seen 'the object in question'. He listened without comment, but as we scanned the ground before us, walking around the perimeter of the bog, it was clear there was nothing to be seen that was in any way unusual. The bog was a quagmire after the rain, broken with square holes in which the brackish water shivered.

'It's probably sunk; there was only the tail visible,' I said, desperate for vindication. 'But it was here. I saw it with my own eyes.'

The sergeant was uncomfortable in the saddle. 'An aeroplane wouldn't sink that fast,' he muttered. His face was a study of pained exasperation and he looked at Peter as though reassessing him. I imagined his perspective. The strange Fitzallens, an old inbred family, with no luck in the new blood either. Hunting for an aeroplane on Knockshee!

Peter, having intently scanned the area, now seemed sunk in his own thoughts, his chin on his collarbone. Joey rattled the bit. The wind stung my eyes and shivered among the reeds and the heather.

'We'd better go back. There's nothing here, ma'am.'

They turned their horses and I trailed behind, Joey picking his way carefully on the soft ground. Everywhere I looked was the same, reeds and heather and black scars from old toil, bog holes full of water, and the wind whistling. I would never find him now. Below us stretched the townland; to the left at the foot of the mountain was the mound with the entrance to the souterrain and the Ogham Stone with its ancient boast.

When we dismounted in the stable yard I overheard the sergeant advise Peter that Mrs Fitzallen ought to be seen by a doctor. 'It's a mistake to believe everything you're told by people in a nervous and excitable state.' He dropped his voice. 'They're not right for a year after they've had a babby.'

Peter thanked him brusquely for his trouble.

'Yeh have thim all in a state, ma'am,' was Murty's whispered communiqué when he came to take Joey. 'There's no use looking for anything above on Knockshee. It hides what it wants to hide. And bides its time.'

Indoors, Peter made tea and I fed Dan who had been left in Murty's charge.

483

We were silent, avoiding each other's eyes.

'Perhaps you don't believe me either?' I said after a while. 'I sometimes wonder myself whether it's me or circumstances. I can't understand how it could have been there two days ago.'

'I believe you saw what you say you did. Whether it's there or not now is another matter. Or indeed whether it was some trick of the light! You know yourself that when they cut turf they mark the plot with a wooden cross so that they can re-locate the place. You could have seen something like that!'

'It was not a trick of the light! It was not a wooden cross.'

The room seemed tense with oppression, the atmosphere which had begun to permeate the house. I had noticed it most in my bedroom; now it was everywhere, in the echoing hall, the shrouded rooms, the kitchen.

Peter reached into the cupboard by the Aga for two bicycle lamps, handed me one.

'Shall we examine the cellar then?' he said. I put Dan into the pram and followed Peter into the lower hall and down the stone steps. The house seemed to gather around us, close in over us. The thick smell of must and damp met us. And through it came the taste of despair. I could go no further. I sat on the stairs and waited while Peter searched the cellar with his lamp. He went out of sight behind the internal support walls of the house, his steps echoing on the flags, his torchlight stabbing the dark, till I saw only a glimmer of his light and was then left in darkness. I shone my own lamp around on the unremarkable domestic paraphernalia below. I heard sounds from deeper into the cellar where I could not see because of the walls, as though Peter were stamping his feet on the floor. Then I heard him calling his brothers name - 'Brian, Brian'. The sounds welled and gathered echoes and reverberated back, rolling upwards through the empty house until it seemed as though the whole place moaned to itself, crying his name.

Then there was a heavy expectant hush. The sorrow of the place was suffocating. I sat on the stairs transfixed by it. The footsteps came back, the lamplight returned, the spell was broken.

I fled back up to the kitchen, wondering at the noise of my heart. Dan had woken and begun to wail. I picked him up and rocked him against my shoulder. I turned to Peter who came in behind me. 'Did you find anything?'

He sat down heavily, pushing the lamp away from him across the table.

I repeated the question, alarmed by his face.

'Only this!'

He took out his handkerchief and spread it out before me. Part of it was covered with a slimy brown stain.

'What's that?' I whispered, blocking for a moment the objective assessment of my mind.

'I am not one hundred percent sure, of course,' he answered without looking at me. 'But wouldn't you say that this was blood?'

The silence surged around us. I wanted to pick up the handkerchief and examine it in detail, but could not bear to touch it. All I knew was the refrain in my brain: 'Let me get away from here, dear God. Let me get away.'

'There is absolutely nothing to indicate the entrance to anything underground,' he added. 'And the blood could be animal or human.'

485

'It mightn't be blood at all,' I said. 'Some unicellular algae grow on weeping stone and if it's wet enough it looks like blood. We should get the guards, have it analysed.'

He looked at me pityingly.

'For what? What will we tell them this time? Whatever happened it is too late now. One thing is certain - Brian is not here.'

'I'm going away,' I said. 'I want to leave at once.'

Peter did not seem surprised. 'Where will you go? What will you do with Glenallen?'

'You can have it.'

'No. I need to be away from it.'

'I'll stay with the O'Shaughnessys for a little while. I don't know what I'll do with Glenallen. But I will not give it to your sister. She's had too much of mine already.'

He was silent for a moment.

'I've done with everything here,' I added.

He sighed. 'That may be so. But what makes you think Glenallen has done with you?'

The O'Shaughnessys were welcoming. Peter brought me over in the trap and explained that he had to return to Dublin and that Harriet was away for the time being.

'Of course you can't stay alone in that big old house with a small baby, Peg,' Dr O'Shaughnessy said. 'And why didn't you tell me the truth about taking Harriet's medicine? No wonder you had hallucinations. Don't you realise that stuff is based on ergot? I'm surprised at you. If you have headaches, take aspirin.'

'What makes you think I was taking Harry's medicine?'

He sighed. 'It was in the urine, in sufficient concentration to do you a lot of damage.'

I did not stay long with the O'Shaughnessys. I went to Dublin, bringing the baby despite my hosts' protestations.

'I have my living to earn. I can't stay here. I have to get on with my life. I have to find a purchaser for Glenallen!'

'You're going to sell?'

'Certainly!'

Mrs O'Shaughnessy's face registered dismayed astonishment.

'And what about Harriet? This will kill her.'

The capital was gloomy without Mary. Food was in short supply compared to the country. There were plenty of children with rickets, pinched faces, women in black shawls, beggars, cinema queues. Traffic was sparse, a lot of it horsedrawn; people got around on bicycles.

I found a bedsitter on the north side in a little house near the Tolka river, a small room with kitchenette, and the use of the bathroom and the yard. Peter had given me money to tide me over. I was alone, except for an occasional visit by the glimmerman.

I had my mind made up now as to my course of action. Glenallen must be sold. But it must be sold to someone who would keep it and not sell it back to Harriet. It must be put out of her reach forever.

I visited the Land Commission Officers at Merrion Square. Glenallen would be sold for land bonds. Peter could have the land bonds. And I could reclaim my life.

I saw a solicitor. He wrote to Harriet who had returned home and told her, on my behalf, to vacate Glenallen in readiness for sale. Harriet wrote to me through the solicitor, begging me not to sell, to rent it to her or sell her the place. She had enough money to give me a price for it, she said.

I did not reply.

'Glenallen is my life, Peg,' she had written.' Don't do this to me. I will never forgive you if you do.'

The solicitor was an elderly man with bushy white hair and a Dickensian office in Middle Abbey Street where the dust clung to the windows and to the pyramids of old brown files holding up the walls. His secretary clacked away at a typewriter in the outer room beside shelves of leather-backed ledgers and bundles of deeds tied up with coarse pink ribbon.

He made no secret that he found my disposal of Glenallen very strange.

'Well child, why wouldn't you ask for a decent price at least. If you're going to sell why not get the best price you can? Why not get real money for it instead of land bonds. Your sister-in-law seems to have cash at her disposal and her money is as good as anyone's.'

And, knowing whose money it was, I shook my head. 'I will not sell Glenallen to Harriet. I want her out of there. It's the only thing I want from Glenallen.'

In my mind I saw Harriet's face when she got the letter. Where would she go now? What would she do? Would she marry James Regan and enter into the powerless status of wife which she so dreaded? I felt the satisfaction of my revenge, to have taken from her the only thing she cared for. Without Glenallen she was nothing. This was her assessment, not mine.

'What has this lady done to you?' the solicitor inquired, raising his eyebrows, his voice becoming squeaky with surprise. 'It is her family home after all; she wants it, which is understandable; your attitude is not christian, if you will forgive me for saying so.'

'You are quite right. It isn't christian. Now will you do the conveyance or will I instruct someone else? '

I found a job at last as a substitute teacher in a national school, a stand-in for a member of staff who had been taken ill and hospitalised. The school was run by the Holy Faith nuns. It was temporary, badly paid work, but a stop gap while I applied for jobs in England for the following September, when Dan would be eight months old and able for the journey. Mrs O'Leary, my landlady who lived upstairs, looked after the baby for an extra weekly payment.

The summer came back, the summer of 1942. My income dried up when school closed down at the end of July. It was back to foot slogging it, trying to find some job, any job at all to keep body and soul together. I found one eventually as a waitress in Dawson Street's Royal Hibernian Hotel. The hours were long and I had less time to spend with Dan. He would wail when I set out for work in the mornings and I deafened myself to his cries. 'There's no help for it. How do you think we are going to survive?' I asked him, but he was not to be pacified. In the evenings the wailing would recommence as soon as I put my nose in the door.

'He's been an angel all day,' my landlady said. 'He only cries when he sees you!'

He looked more like Lucien every day, the same eyes, the same mouth, the same certainty that the world was his. I thought of him all day and of the future I would make for us, as I scurried between dining-room and kitchen, or washed dishes. The skin on my hands became red and tender. My nails split. My feet ached. I had no money for clothes; my hair grew out of any recognisable style and I cut it myself with a nail scissors. There were holes in the soles of my shoes and I put in some cardboard insoles, relieved that it was summer. I put away four shillings weekly towards the expenses I would face in going to England. After paying my rent and baby-sitting extras, I had little left to live on. I didn't care. The world would yield to me eventually, little by little. I would build a career and a life and be free.

After I had sent Peter the land bonds I lost touch with him. I had not given my address to him. I did not want charity from him, or censure either. But I was happy. I was free, at last, of Glenallen.

It was a Saturday. I was due to go to England for interviews the following week and would have to buy some clothes. I wondered how much I could afford to spend.

The dining-room was filling up. I was responsible for five tables, one of them a table for two. I took the orders, my mind with Dan, wondering whether Mrs O'Leary had taken him out to the park.

The room was aromatic with dinner scents; there was the quiet buzz of voices, the clink of cutlery. The head waiter seated someone at the small table and I turned to take his order.

'Black and white is most becoming on you, Madame,' the foreign voice said at the same moment as I registered the face. 'But you look more than a little tired. Perhaps you could take time off to be my guest for lunch?'

I looked into Lucien's eyes.

He was dressed impeccably as always, leaning back, enjoying my surprise. He conjured up another world, one I had left behind me, one I had no wish to look back on or revisit. I had closed the door on it. I had only the future and it was unmarked and pristine. He belonged in the sector marked 'memorabilia.' I had it all worked out.

'I thought you were in France,' I said, flushing scarlet and wishing I was anywhere except serving tables in a waitress's uniform. He understood this at once, for his face was gentle, but his eyes were sharp with inquiry.

He shook his head. 'Did you think I would disappear? Did you think I would not come in response to your letter?'

I thought of the awful note, 'I need you.' I wished I could go back and cancel it. And yet, in terms of the unconscious response, the way my body reacted, the surge in my mind, the leap of surprised joy, it was as though no time had elapsed at all. But I knew I had changed. Not just through the struggle to keep going, to find some niche where I could live in peace. It was my capacity for belief which had changed, belief in love, belief in him.

He asked me then to take the day off.

'I can't. I need the money.'

'I could give you the money.'

I laughed. 'I don't think so, Lucien.'

'I will take you out when your day is over.'

'I have to go home.'

But he was not to be dissuaded; the more I found excuses, while I desperately tried to decide what I would tell him, the more calmly persistent he became. 'Very well, I will escort you home.'

In the taxi that evening he said, taking one of my hands and looking at the broken nails, 'You sent me a letter. I did not get it until four weeks ago and have been trying to find you since. Why did you need me? Why have you changed so much? What has happened? Why do you look thin and tired and not the indomitable Peg I used to know?'

His gallantry annoyed me. It seemed out of place and mocking. Peg was not indomitable. She was sick at heart and tired to death, and all the other clichés which describe an empty spirit clinging only to survival. She had no more room in her for being used, for romantic belief, for realities which shifted like quicksand and drained her soul.

'I sorted the particular problem out,' I said.

He seemed taken aback at my tone.

'I see. So I should take myself off? Not trouble you further?' he asked softly. 'Is that what you want?'

I did not answer. He would go. I saw the future as bleak and cold. Without him, compared to him, it would be devoid of life, of meaning. I wanted to shout at him: 'Why did you have to come back? I have nothing more to give you. I am empty. The enchantment you carry around with you has already betrayed me. I could have managed fine if you had never come back! Now I will have to work on it all over again!' And then I thought - What will Dan say to me someday if I let you go without the truth?

He got out of the car to see me to the door. At the gate I turned to him. 'Will you come in? There is someone you might care to meet.'

492

My little room seemed to shrink around him, become claustrophobic, a place where the daily struggle for existence was writ large and clear. He was the foil against which the ordinary seemed weary, pointless, and toilsome. I resented this. In the corner was the cot where Dan was fast asleep, his hands thrown above his head, his little face flushed, small beads of perspiration and damp curls on his forehead.

'His name,' I said, 'is Daniel Lucien.'

It was the first and only time I ever saw Lucien stuck for words. His face registered shock, disbelief, sudden calculation, wonder, joy. He stood beside the cot looking down for some time and then he slowly touched the baby's hand with his finger.

He turned to me. 'He is a fine boy!'

'He is.'

He had a strange look on his face, reminding me of Peter Fitzallen the day he watched Cissie win the gymkhana on Banner.

He sat down on the bed. The room was close and I opened the window on to the yard and let in the cool night air. He looked from the baby to me, shaking his head, murmuring something to himself in French.

'Why didn't you tell me in your letter? I had a right to know!'

'The reason I didn't tell you,' I said, 'has to do with a little deadly sin called Pride, and the desire to forge my own existence on my own terms.'

'After what was between us?'

I didn't answer. I was thinking of Mary's diary.

He went out and sent the taxi away.

Mrs O'Leary came downstairs and saw Lucien coming back into the hall.

'No gentlemen callers,' she hissed in my ear, her face filled with surprise and condemnation.

'I am a relation,' Lucien assured her, at his most charming. 'I will be gone soon. There are pressing family matters I must discuss with Mrs Fitzallen. I have been trying to find her for several days. But I am glad to find her well and happy in your charming house.'

'Oh, well, just for a while then,' she muttered, and went back upstairs.

Lucien sat on my narrow bed while I made some tea. 'You touch me, little Peg. You live in this tiny place and you work until your hands are ruined and you are thin and tired. Tell me everything that has happened. Come here and tell me.'

I poured two cups and we sat and drank. I told him briefly that I had inherited Glenallen and sold it to the Land Commission. I told him that Harriet wanted it and would have bought it from me.

'Why didn't you let her have it?'

'There were reasons,' I said.

I sat on the chair. He patted the bed.

'No. You are dangerous to me, Lucien, and I have a life to live.'

I expected false contrition, but his face was serious as I had never seen it. The baby stirred in the cot, the sound of his shallow breathing gentle in the room. Mrs O'Leary moved around upstairs. Lucien leaned back against the wall, studying me, interlocking his hands, staring from time to time at the baby, his demeanour very subdued. I saw the hair on his wrists, his well kept nails, the sallowness of his skin. Smelt the faint scent of his cologne.

'It seems to me that it is you who are the dangerous one,' he said after a moment. 'You have been entirely ruthless with Harriet's life, and with your own. And you were quite prepared to be equally ruthless with our son's.'

'You don't understand, Lucien.'

He would think of the lost financial opportunity, be shocked by its waste, be shocked by the breach of family loyalty. What could he know of Glenallen, of Knockshee, of Balor watching from his half sleep, of being caught in a dimension where the parameters constantly shifted, where family membership was a recipe for destruction, where what made sense one moment was meaningless the next? He came from the real world with its immediate pragmatic problems, its wide-ranging perspectives. What could he know of the spiritual inbreeding, the subtle, dreaming, cruel soul of Ireland?

'Did you find Mary?' I asked, changing the subject.

He didn't answer for a moment.

'Yes and no.'

'What do you mean?'

He watched Dan sleep, his expression careful, as though he were trying to find expression for some new certainty.

'A young red headed woman was lost in the blitz that night of the 10 May when you and I were in Knightsbridge. She had been involved in auxiliary nursing services for those injured in the bombing, stretcher bearer, that kind of thing. She was killed when a building collapsed on her.'

'That couldn't have been Mary,' I said, checking the tears.' She was never caught at anything. It must have been someone else. Didn't they have a name for her?'

'No. It may have been someone else. But I have a few of her possessions, little things, a pen I have never seen before, a perfectly nondescript comb and a small curio. I brought them with me in case you might recognise them.'

He took an envelope out of his pocket, extracted a brown fountain pen, a brown tortoise-shell comb and a twisted paper packet.

'I don't recognise these things,' I said.

I picked up the small paper packet, unscrewed it and removed its contents. It was a little cardboard figure wound round with plaited hair, red hair, dark hair and fair-to-mousey hair interwoven together, the waist tied in with crimson thread, the head made of a chewed lump of paper wound around with hair to make a chignon. It was about three inches long.

'This was in her pocket with the other items.'

I held it in my hand, stroking the silken mix of hair. 'There were three of them,' I said after a while. 'I spent half the day making them for three young friends who thought they were invincible.'

We sat together then for a long time in silence. And after a long time I reached out for Lucien's hand.

496

Epilogue

Years later Lucien asked me 'Will you go back?' He looked up at me from the letter in his hand, the light from the tall sitting-room windows catching the bald crown of his head. Outside the cypress trees threw shade along the veranda and over the lawn. I saw the white sundial in the middle of the centre gravel walk and the forest beyond, dense and dreaming, and above it the clear French sky. The room was cool, the windows open to the veranda, the curtains stirring in the current between it and the open door. I could see our two children, playing on the grass.

'She died young,' he said.

I felt his censure, gentle as it always was. The humanitarian in him, the civilised man, had baulked long since. I had that morning received a letter from Peter with whom I had re-established contact, and had shown it to Lucien.

'Harriet is becoming a cause of concern. She wanders over from Conneely and spends the day beside Glenallen, looking at the house over the gate, walking up Knockshee or through the fields there. James is worried sick. She talks sometimes about the cellar in Glenallen and keeps saying 'It was an accident.' Nobody knows what she's talking about, but if things go on as they are she will have to be hospitalised for her own protection.'

And now she was dead, her body recovered from Saleen lake. I had spent years imagining her haunt Glenallen, until she haunted me. Now it was all over, or would have been but for Lucien's quiet remonstrance, 'Ma chère, you have no proof of all these things you say she did!'

My certitude had deserted me. The further I got from Glenallen, the more the years bore me away, the more I doubted myself. 'I did one wrong thing in my life,' she had said. But it was far too late to make amends. The Land Commision had divided the land between neighbouring farmers and the house itself, along with fifty acres, had been bought by an order of nuns. And Harriet had married her despised James Regan, been forced into wifehood, compelled into motherhood of one withdrawn child, a girl.

'I won't go to her funeral,' I told Lucien.

He looked at me carefully. You were right, Harriet, I thought, avoiding his eyes, thinking of what she had said to me once. 'Do you think it is that simple? Do you think you can escape Glenallen?'

I never heard from Paddy again. He joined the See Bees and was killed in the Battle of the Pacific. After the war I was contacted by an attorney in Chicago who said there was a specific provision in the will of Mr Patrick Stapleton that uncut diamonds to the value of thirty thousand dollars were to be purchased for me out of his estate, 'in fulfillment of an old promise' was how the will had put it. I remembered in my astonishment the happy summer day by the Garryogue, shifting patterns of sun and shade across the fields and Paddy lying on the bank, long bare legs sticking out of short patched trousers. 'Someday I will give you diamonds as big as thrushes' eggs.'

In a rush of enthusiasm I suggested to Lucien that I might buy back Glenallen now. 'I could let her have it, live in it; I cannot bear it that she is going mad. I could lay the whole thing to rest if I could forget her.'

He had shrugged. 'If she is mad it is already too late.'

Then the letter had come with the news of her death. I wrote Peter a short letter of condolence but did not attend her funeral.

And life went on. I buried the past so deep that I thought nothing could resurrect it. I destroyed all my memorabilia of Glenallen. Peter died from a stroke not long after his sister so I had nothing to remind me of the past. But the dreams could not be stifled, the planchette glass shivering in fragments, Brian on the mountain in a shroud, the faces of my brother and friends unclear in the night. Harriet smiling with a hay knife; Harriet wandering around Glenallen.

My children grew up, but the dreams went on.

The nuns wrote to me a few weeks ago to tell me that during renovation works in Glenallen the remains of a young man had been found in what was a tunnel under the floor of the cellar, 'an old tunnel connected to the souterrain built in early times'. And then I got a letter from the guards in Ballyharris asking me to help identify the remains. I did not want to go back, but Dan, now middle-aged and very curious, said he would like to see this mysterious house of which I would never speak. I thought that seeing it with him would lay it and all its memories. And I desperately needed to know the identity of the bones beneath the cellar floor. It had to do with vindication.

'Go back only if you must,' Lucien warned.

He is frail now and does not like to leave the house and the garden.

I visited the morgue where the bones had been taken and gazed, for a moment, at the skeletal remains. Where was all that life now, that introversion, that boyish charm? And what were they to me, these poor rat-gnawed bones? They were not even identifiable. There were the half decayed remains of some sort of leather flying jacket dating from the second world war. I cried bitterly. How long had Brian been there, before the rats got him? How had she managed to entice him into the cellar? How did she live those years with the knowledge of what she had done?

I told the police who I believed the remains belonged to and arranged a funeral. I asked them if they had found a wedding ring, my father's ring which I had given Brian. 'He always wore it. It would be proof positive of his identity.' But they said there had been no jewellery. 'No rings or anything of that kind, ma'am! Just what you see.'

The Coroner brought in an open verdict. There was the funeral then for the remains and I put flowers on the grave. We laid him to rest not far from the gravestone erected to the memory of 'Harriet Regan nee Fitzallen, beloved wife of James Regan.' I looked around for Peter's grave before remembering he had been buried in Deansgrange cemetery in Dublin by explicit instructions in his will. Above the cemetery I saw Knockshee watching us, the recent afforestation hiding the mound at the souterrain, with its Ogham Stone - '*I know mind and mine know me*'.

'I am the only one to have escaped Glenallen!' I told Brian's coffin almost defensively. But even as I thought it I knew the truth.

Afterwards, pressed by the nuns, I went back to the house.

Why did I go back? A passion of nostalgi. perhaps, the hunger which had been aroused ir me to rewrite the past, impossible though that was. And we sat in the drawing-room, Dan and I, and sipped tea and little Michael was brought off by one of the sisters to see the aquarium in the community-room. I looked around the drawing-room, now changed, smelling and feeling like a convent, full of religious pictures, but with most of the old furniture, the sofa table, the Chippendale cabinet. I imagined for a moment that a young Peg and Brian would come in the door and the house would be full of laughter and Harry would have been everything she seemed, and Cissie and Mary would come down the drive to visit, and Tom would be safe at home in Ballycloghan with his horses. Would all of that have made the future different, an eternal Arcadia of peace?

'They tell us in the hotel that you have a ghost,' Dan said to the Sister Superior.

'Oh. we've had a few strange occurrences alright, but we pray for the eternal rest of the poor soul.'

'The hotel receptionist said it's Harriet Fitzallen!'

The nun looked at me. 'Mrs Regan? I knew the poor thing,' she said, her voice low. 'But she haunted the place more when she was alive. We

501

would see her at the gate, or she might turn up in the yard at the back, or on the mound of stones where there was once an entrance to a souterrain. She was very strange in herself, let herself go. But we pray for her, that she may have rest. This is a lovely place and we are very happy here.'

And it was true. It felt happy, this house; other lives, cheerful lives of goodwill, had marked it.

I could see that Dan was glad to leave. He has a meeting in Paris tomorrow and I too want to get back and talk to Lucien, bask in normality. Young Michael was restive. We said goodbye, and went back to the car. My grandson had lost interest in his red fire engine and sat very still staring out the window. I asked Dan to drive slowly past the ivy covered house that had belonged to the O'Shaughnessys.

'Stop the car for a minute.'

Dan stopped at the gate and I got out and approached the house. A young woman opened the door.

'Is Mr Des O'Shaughnessy living here still?' I asked.

'No one of that name has lived here for a long time.'

Young Michael was very quiet in the back seat.

'Did you see the nun's fish?' his father asked him. 'Were they nice?'

'Yes. there was a striped fish and a funny fish with a long tail and a black one. Then I got lost and I went to the toilet.'

Dan laughed. 'All in the one breath?'

Michael didn't answer and lapsed back into silence, bending his head over something in his hand.

'What have you got there?' I asked him, turning around to see what he was holding in his fist. It was a ring and he was pushing it up and down on his thumb.

'Where did you get that? Let me see it.'

He dropped it into my hand and I held it up to the light. It was a plain gold wedding ring. On the inside was the legend 'Daniel & Maura 16.6.1914.

'Where did you get this?' I demanded again, my voice hoarse. Dan looked at me, sensing something was awry, then pulled the car in to the side of the road and stopped. He examined the ring and we both turned to the little boy in the back seat who was staring back at us, brown eyes dark in his pale face.

He turned up the palms of his hands, knit his forehead, tears starting in his eyes because of the tension around him.

'I don't know,' he answered. 'Someone, I can't remember, gave it to me in that house.'

THE END

MARY RYAN was born in County Roscommon and now lives in Dublin with her family. She is the author of the best-selling novel *Whispers in the Wind*. Mary is currently working on her third novel.